JUST LIKE HEAVEN

Julia Quinn

WINDSOR
PARAGON

First published 2011
by Piatkus
This Large Print edition published 2013
by AudioGO Ltd
by arrangement with
Little, Brown Book Group

Hardcover   ISBN: 978 1 4713 1833 7
Softcover   ISBN: 978 1 4713 1834 4

British Library Cataloguing in Publication Data available

Printed and bound in Great Britain by
MPG Books Group Limited

For Pam Spengler-Jaffee.
You are a goddess in every way.

And also for Paul,
even though when I went to him
for medical advice to save my ailing hero,
he replied, 'He has to die.'

Prologue

Marcus Holroyd was always alone.

His mother died when he was four, but this had surprisingly little effect on his life. The Countess of Chatteris mothered her son the way *her* mother had mothered her children—from afar. She was not irresponsible; she took great care and pride in finding the very best baby nurse for her husband's new heir. Miss Pimm was on the darker side of fifty and had already cared for two ducal heirs and a viscount. Lady Chatteris placed her baby into Pimm's arms, reminded the nurse that the earl could not tolerate strawberries and thus it was likely that the baby could not either, and then left to enjoy the London season.

At the time of her death, Marcus had seen his mother on precisely seven occasions.

Lord Chatteris was more fond of country life than his wife and was more frequently in residence at Fensmore, the great big rambling Tudor house in northern Cambridgeshire that had been home to the Holroyds for generations. But he fathered his son the way *his* father had fathered him. Which was to say that other than making sure the child was put atop a horse at the age of three, he didn't see any reason to bother with him until the boy was old enough to conduct a reasonably intelligent conversation.

The earl did not wish to remarry, even though he was warned that he ought to get himself a spare to go along with his heir. He looked at Marcus and saw a boy of good intelligence, excellent

1

athleticism, and passable looks. Most importantly, he was as healthy as a horse. With no cause to suppose that Marcus might kick up and die, the earl saw no reason to subject himself to another round of wife-hunting, or even worse, another wife. He chose instead to invest in his son.

Marcus had the best tutors. He was schooled in every possible corner of a gentleman's education. He could name all the local fauna and flora. He could ride like he'd been born to a saddle, and if his fencing and shooting weren't going to win any competitions, he was still well above average. He could do lengthy products and sums without even a drop of wasted ink. He could read Latin and Greek.

By the age of twelve.

Which was, perhaps coincidentally, about the age his father decided he might be able to carry on a decent conversation.

It was also the age at which his father decided that Marcus must take the next step in his education, which was to leave Fensmore and attend Eton College, where all Holroyd boys began their formal educations. This turned out to be the most fortuitous and happy circumstance of the young boy's life. Because what Marcus Holroyd, heir to the Earldom of Chatteris, did *not* have was friends.

Not a one.

There were no appropriate boys in northern Cambridgeshire with whom Marcus might play. The closest noble family were the Crowlands, and they had only girls. The next best family was landed gentry, which would have been acceptable under the circumstances, but their sons were of entirely the wrong age. Lord Chatteris wasn't about to have his son consorting with peasants, so he simply hired more tutors. A busy boy couldn't be a lonely boy, and besides, no son of his could possibly want to run wild across the fields with the baker's rowdy brood.

If the earl had asked Marcus his opinion, he might have got a different answer. But the earl saw his son once per day, just prior to the evening meal. Their interview lasted about ten minutes, then Marcus went up to the nursery and the earl to his formal dining room, and that was that.

In retrospect, it was nothing short of remarkable that Marcus was not utterly miserable at Eton. He certainly had no idea how to interact with his peers. On the first day, when all the other boys were running about like (in the words of his father's valet, who had dropped him off) a pack of savages, Marcus stood to the side, trying not to stare, trying to look as if he *meant* to stand at the side, looking off in the other direction.

He did not know how to act. He did not know what to say.

But Daniel Smythe-Smith did.

Daniel Smythe-Smith, besides being the heir to the Earldom of Winstead, had five siblings and thirty-two first cousins. If ever there was a boy who knew how to get on with other children, it was he. Within hours, he was the undisputed king among the youngest boys at Eton. He had a way about him—an easy smile, a happy confidence, an utter lack of shyness. He was a born leader—able to make decisions just as quickly as he made jokes.

And he was assigned to the bed directly next to Marcus's.

They became the best of friends, and when Daniel invited Marcus home for their first holiday, he went. Daniel's family lived at Whipple Hill, which wasn't very far from Windsor, so it was easy for him to make frequent trips home. Marcus, on the other hand . . . Well, it wasn't as if he lived all the way in Scotland, but it did take more than a day to get back to the northern reaches of Cambridgeshire. Plus, his father had never gone home for the minor holidays and saw no reason why his son should do so, either.

So when the second holiday came up, and Daniel invited Marcus again, he went.

And then again.

And again.

And again until Marcus was spending more time with the Smythe-Smiths than he did with his own family. Of course, his family consisted of exactly one person, but still, if Marcus stopped to think about it (and he did, quite frequently) he spent more time with each individual member of the Smythe-Smith family than he did with his father.

Even Honoria.

Honoria was Daniel's youngest sister. Unlike the rest of the Smythe-Smiths, she had no siblings close to her own age. She hung off the end of the family by a good five years, a presumably happy accident to cap off Lady Winstead's marvelous procreative career.

But five years was a large gulf, especially if one was but six years old, which was Honoria's age when Marcus first met her. Her three oldest sisters were already married or engaged to be, and Charlotte, who was eleven, wanted nothing to do with her. Neither did Daniel, but absence must have made Honoria's heart grow ridiculously fond, because when he was home from school, she followed him

4

around like a puppy.

'Don't make eye contact,' Daniel once told Marcus as they were trying to avoid her on a hike down to the lake. 'If you acknowledge her, it's all over.'

They walked purposefully, heads forward. They were going fishing, and the last time Honoria had joined them she had dumped out all the worms.

'Daniel!' she yelled.

'Ignore her,' Daniel muttered.

'Daniel!!!!!!!!!!!!' She went from yell right to shriek.

Daniel flinched. 'Faster,' he said. 'If we make it to the woods she won't find us.'

'She knows where the lake is,' Marcus felt compelled to point out.

'Yes, but—'

'*Daniel!!!!!!!!!!!!*'

'—she knows Mother will have her head if she goes into the woods alone. Even she's not foolish enough to press Mother on that.'

'Dan—' But she cut herself off. And then, in a voice so pathetic one could not help but turn, she said, 'Marcus?'

He turned.

'Noooooooooooooooo!' Daniel moaned.

'Marcus!' Honoria called out happily. She skipped forward, coming to a bounce and a stop in front of them. 'What are you doing?'

'We're going fishing,' Daniel growled, 'and you're not coming.'

'But I like to fish.'

'So do I. Without you.'

Her face screwed up.

'Don't cry,' Marcus said quickly.

5

Daniel was unimpressed. 'She's faking.'

'I'm not faking!'

'Just don't cry,' Marcus repeated, because truly, that had to be the most important thing.

'I won't,' she said, batting her lashes, 'if you let me go with you.'

How did a six-year-old know how to bat her lashes? Or maybe she didn't, because a moment later she was squirming and rubbing her eye.

'Now what's wrong?' Daniel asked.

'I got something in my eye.'

'Maybe it was a fly,' Daniel said slyly.

Honoria screamed.

'That might not have been the best thing to say,' Marcus pointed out.

'Get it out! Get it out!' she shrieked.

'Oh, settle down,' Daniel said. 'You're perfectly fine.'

But she kept screaming, batting at her face with her hands. Finally Marcus grabbed her hands in his and held her head utterly still, her hands at her temples, his hands over hers. 'Honoria,' he said firmly, 'Honoria!'

She blinked, gasped, and finally stilled.

'There is no fly,' he said to her.

'But—'

'It was probably an eyelash.'

Her mouth formed a little O.

'Can I let go of you now?'

She nodded.

'You won't start screaming?'

She shook her head.

Slowly, Marcus released her and took a step back.

'Can I come with you?' she asked.

'No!' Daniel practically howled.

And the truth was, Marcus didn't really want her company, either. She was *six*. And a girl. 'We're going to be very busy,' he said, but he lacked Daniel's indignation.

'Please?'

Marcus groaned. She looked so forlorn, standing there with tear-stained cheeks. Her light-brown hair, parted on the side and pulled back with some kind of clip, hung rather straight and limp, ending in straggle just below her shoulders. And her eyes—almost the exact shade of Daniel's, an arrestingly unique shade of light purplish-blue; they were huge, and wet, and—

'I told you not to make eye contact,' Daniel said.

Marcus groaned. 'Maybe just this once.'

'Oh, goody!' She leapt straight up into the air, bringing to mind a surprised cat, then gave Marcus an impulsive (but thankfully quick) hug. 'Oh, thank you, Marcus! Thank you! You are the absolute best! The best of the best!' She narrowed her eyes and shot a look over at Daniel that was frighteningly adult. 'Unlike *you*.'

His expression was equally malevolent. 'I take *pride* in being the absolute worst.'

'I don't care,' she announced. She grabbed Marcus's hand. 'Shall we go?'

He looked down at her hand in his. It was an utterly foreign sensation, and a strange and somewhat unpleasant feeling began to flutter in his chest that he belatedly realized was panic. He couldn't remember the last time anyone had held his hand. His nurse, maybe? No, she had liked to grab his wrist. She got a better grip that way, he once heard her tell the housekeeper.

7

Had his father? His mother, sometime before she had died?

His heart pounded, and he felt Honoria's little hand grow slick in his. He must be sweating, or she was, although he was fairly certain it was he.

He looked down at her. She was beaming up at him.

He dropped her hand. 'Er, we have to go now,' he said awkwardly, 'while the light is good.'

Both Smythe-Smiths looked at him curiously. 'It's barely noon,' Daniel said. 'How long did you want to go fishing?'

'I don't know,' Marcus said defensively. 'It might take a while.'

Daniel shook his head. 'Father just stocked the lake. You could probably swing a boot through the water and catch a fish.'

Honoria gasped with glee.

Daniel turned on her in an instant. 'Don't even think about it.'

'But—'

'If my boots end up anywhere near the water I swear I will have you drawn and quartered.'

She pouted and looked down, muttering, 'I was thinking about *my* boots.'

Marcus felt a little laugh bubble over his lips. Honoria immediately looked back up, regarding him with an expression of utter betrayal.

'It would have to be a very small fish,' he said quickly.

This did not seem to satisfy her.

'You can't eat them when they're that small,' he tried. 'They're mostly bones.'

'Let's go,' Daniel muttered. And they did, tramping off through the woods, Honoria's little

8

legs pumping at double speed, just to keep up.

'I'm not fond of fish, actually,' she said, keeping up a steady stream of chatter. 'They smell horrid. And they taste fishy . . .'

And then, on the way back—

'. . . I still think that pink one looked big enough to eat. If you liked fish, which I don't. But if you *did* like fish . . .'

'Do not ever invite her to come with us again,' Daniel said to Marcus.

'. . . which I don't. But I think Mother likes fish. And I am sure she would like a *pink* fish . . .'

'I won't,' Marcus assured him. It seemed the height of rudeness to criticize a little girl, but she was exhausting.

'. . . although Charlotte wouldn't. Charlotte hates pink. She won't wear it. She says it makes her look gaunt. I don't know what gaunt means, but it sounds unpleasant. I like lavender, myself.'

The two boys let out identical sighs and would have kept walking except that Honoria jumped in front of them and grinned. 'It matches my eyes,' she said.

'The fish?' Marcus asked, glancing down at the bucket in his hand. There were three nice-sized trout bumping up against the sides. There would have been more, except that Honoria had accidentally kicked the bucket, sending Marcus's first two prizes back into the lake.

'No. Haven't you been *listening*?'

Marcus would always remember that moment. It was to be the first time he would ever be faced with that most vexing of female quirks: the question that had nothing but wrong answers.

'*Lavender* matches my eyes,' Honoria said with

9

great authority. 'My father told me so.'

'Then it must be true,' Marcus said with relief.

She twirled her hair around her finger, but the curl immediately fell out when she let go. 'Brown matches my hair, but I prefer lavender.'

Marcus finally set the bucket down. It was growing heavy, and the handle was digging into his palm.

'Oh, no,' Daniel said, grabbing Marcus's bucket with his free hand and giving it back to Marcus. 'We are going home.' He glared at Honoria. 'Out of our way.'

'Why are you nice to everyone but me?' she asked.

'Because you are a pest!' he fairly yelled.

It was true, but Marcus still felt sorry for her. Some of the time. She was practically an only child, and he knew precisely how that felt. All she wanted was to be a part of things, to be included in games and parties and all those activities her family was constantly telling her she was too young for.

Honoria took the verbal blow without flinching. She stood still, staring venomously at her brother. Then she sucked in one long, loud breath through her nose.

Marcus wished he had a handkerchief.

'Marcus,' she said. She turned to face him, although it really wasn't so much that as it was turning her back on her brother. 'Would you like to have a tea party with me?'

Daniel snickered.

'I will bring my best dolls,' she said with complete gravity.

Dear God, anything but this.

'And there will be cakes,' she added, in a prim

little voice that scared him to death.

Marcus shot a panicked look at Daniel, but he was no help whatsoever.

'Well?' Honoria demanded.

'No,' Marcus blurted out.

'No?' She gave him an owlish stare.

'I can't. I'm busy.'

'Doing what?'

Marcus cleared his throat. Twice. 'Things.'

'What kinds of things?'

'*Things*.' And then he felt terrible, because he hadn't meant to be so adamant. 'Daniel and I have plans.'

She looked stricken. Her lower lip began to tremble, and for once Marcus did not think she was faking.

'I'm sorry,' he added, because he hadn't wanted to hurt her feelings. But for heaven's sake, it was a *tea party*! There wasn't a twelve-year-old boy alive who wanted to attend a tea party.

With dolls.

Marcus shuddered.

Honoria's face grew red with rage as she swung around to face her brother. 'You made him say that.'

'I didn't say a word,' Daniel replied.

'I hate you,' she said in a low voice. 'I hate you both.' And then she yelled it. 'I hate you! Especially you, Marcus! I really hate you!'

And then she ran to the house as fast as her skinny little legs could carry her, which wasn't very fast at all. Marcus and Daniel just stood there, silently watching her go.

When she was nearly to the house, Daniel nodded and said, 'She hates you. You are officially a member of the family.'

And he was. From that moment on, he was.

Until the spring of 1821, when Daniel went and ruined it all.

Chapter One

Lady Honoria Smythe-Smith was desperate.

Desperate for a sunny day, desperate for a husband, desperate—she thought with an exhausted sigh as she looked down at her ruined blue slippers—for a new pair of shoes.

She sat down heavily on the stone bench outside Mr. Hilleford's Tobacco Shoppe for Discerning Gentlemen and pressed herself up against the wall behind her, desperately (there was that awful word again) trying to wedge her entire body under the awning. It was pouring. *Pouring.* Not drizzling, not merely raining, but pouring proverbial cats, dogs, sheep, and horses.

At this rate, she wouldn't have been surprised if an elephant tumbled down from the sky.

And it stank. Honoria had thought that cheroots produced her least favorite smell, but no, mold was worse, and Mr. Hilleford's Tobacco Shoppe for Gentlemen who Did Not Mind if Their Teeth Turned Yellow had a suspicious black substance creeping along its outer wall that smelled like death.

Really, could she possibly be in a worse situation?

Why, yes. Yes, she could. Because she was (of course) quite alone, the rain having taken thirty seconds to go from drip to downpour. The rest of her shopping party was across the street, happily

13

browsing in the warm and cozy Miss Pilaster's Fancy Emporium of Ribbons and Trinkets, which, in addition to having all sorts of fun and frilly merchandise, smelled a great deal better than Mr. Hilleford's establishment.

Miss Pilaster sold perfume. Miss Pilaster sold dried rose petals and little candles that smelled like vanilla.

Mr. Hilleford grew mold.

Honoria sighed. Such was her life.

She had lingered too long at the window of a bookshop, assuring her friends that she would meet them at Miss Pilaster's in a minute or two. Two minutes had turned to five, and then, just as she'd been preparing to make her way across the street, the heavens had opened and Honoria had had no choice but to take refuge under the only open awning on the south side of the Cambridge High Street.

She stared mournfully at the rain, watching it pummel the street. The drops were pelting the cobblestones with tremendous force, splashing and spraying back into the air like tiny little explosions. The sky was darkening by the second, and if Honoria was any judge of English weather, the wind was going to pick up at any moment, rendering her pathetic spot under Mr. Hilleford's awning completely useless.

Her mouth slipped into a dejected frown, and she squinted up at the sky.

Her feet were wet.

She was cold.

And she'd never once, not in her entire life, left the boundaries of England, which meant that she *was* a rather good judge of English weather, and in

14

about three minutes she was going to be even more miserable than she was right now.

Which she really hadn't thought possible.

'Honoria?'

She blinked, bringing her gaze down from the sky to the carriage that had just rolled into place in front of her.

'Honoria?'

She knew that voice. *'Marcus?'*

Oh, good heavens, her misery only needed *this*. Marcus Holroyd, the Earl of Chatteris, happy and dry in his plush carriage. Honoria felt her jaw go slack, although really, she didn't know why she should be surprised. Marcus lived in Cambridgeshire, not too far from the city. More to the point, if anyone were to see her while she was looking like a wet, bedraggled creature of the rodential variety, it would be he.

'Good God, Honoria,' he said, scowling down at her in that supercilious way of his, 'you must be freezing.'

She managed the barest of shrugs. 'It is a bit brisk.'

'What are you doing here?'

'Ruining shoes.'

'What?'

'Shopping,' she said, motioning across the street, 'with friends. And cousins.' Not that her cousins weren't also friends. But she had so many cousins they almost seemed a category unto themselves.

The door opened wider. 'Get in,' he said. Not *Will you please get in* or *Please, you must dry yourself off.* Just: *'Get in.'*

Another girl might have tossed her hair and said, *You can't order me about!* Another, slightly less

15

prideful girl might have thought it, even if she'd lacked the courage to say it aloud. But Honoria was cold, and she valued her comfort more than her pride, and more to the point, this was Marcus Holroyd, and she'd known him since she was in pinafores.

Since the age of six, to be precise.

That was also probably the last time she'd managed to show herself to advantage, she thought with a grimace. At seven she'd made such a pest of herself that he and her brother Daniel had taken to calling her Mosquito. When she'd claimed to be complimented, that she'd loved how exotic and dangerous it had sounded, they'd smirked and changed it to Bug.

Bug she'd been, ever since.

He'd seen her wetter than this, too. He'd seen her completely soaked, back when she was eight and she'd thought she'd been completely hidden in the boughs of the old oak tree at Whipple Hill. Marcus and Daniel had built a fort at its base, no girls allowed. They had pelted her with pebbles until she'd lost her grip and tumbled down.

In retrospect, she really shouldn't have chosen the branch that hung over the lake.

Marcus had fished her out of the dunk, though, which was more than she could say for her own brother.

Marcus Holroyd, she thought ruefully. He'd been in her life almost as long as she could remember. Since before he was Lord Chatteris, since before Daniel was Lord Winstead. Since before Charlotte, her closest-in-age sister, had married and left home.

Since before Daniel, too, had left.

'*Honoria.*'

16

She looked up. Marcus's voice was impatient, but his face held a hint of concern. 'Get in,' he repeated.

She nodded and did as he said, taking his large hand in hers and accepting his help into his carriage. 'Marcus,' she said, trying to settle herself into her seat with all the grace and nonchalance she might exhibit in a fine drawing room, never mind the puddles at her feet. 'What a lovely surprise to see you.'

He just stared at her, his dark brows coming ever-so-slightly together. He was trying to decide the most effective way to scold her, she was sure.

'I am staying here in town. With the Royles,' she told him, even though he hadn't yet asked. 'We are here for five days—Cecily Royle, my cousins Sarah and Iris, and I.' She waited for a moment, for some sort of flash of recognition in his eyes, then said, 'You don't remember who they are, do you?'

'You have a great many cousins,' he pointed out.

'Sarah is the one with the thick, dark hair and eyes.'

'Thick eyes?' he murmured, cracking a tiny smile.

'*Marcus*.'

He chuckled. 'Very well. Thick hair. Dark eyes.'

'Iris is very pale. Strawberry blond hair?' she prompted. 'You still don't recall.'

'She comes from that family of flowers.'

Honoria winced. It *was* true that her uncle William and aunt Maria had chosen to name their daughters Rose, Marigold, Lavender, Iris, and Daisy, but still.

'I know who Miss Royle is,' Marcus said.

'She's your neighbor. You have to know who she is.'

17

He just shrugged.

'At any rate, we are here in Cambridge because Cecily's mother thought we could all use a bit of improving.'

His mouth tipped into a vaguely mocking smile. 'Improving?'

Honoria wondered why females always needed improving, while males got to go to school. 'She bribed two professors into allowing us to listen to their lectures.'

'Really?' He sounded curious. And dubious.

'The life and times of Queen Elizabeth,' Honoria recited dutifully. 'And after that, something in Greek.'

'Do you speak Greek?'

'Not a one of us,' she admitted. 'But the professor was the only other one who was willing to speak to females.' She rolled her eyes. 'He intends to deliver the lecture twice in a row. We must wait in an office until the students leave the lecture hall, lest they see us and lose all sense of reason.'

Marcus nodded thoughtfully. 'It is nearly impossible for a gentleman to keep his mind upon his studies in the presence of such overwhelming female loveliness.'

Honoria thought he was serious for about two seconds. She managed one sideways glance in his direction before she burst out with a snort of laughter. 'Oh, please,' she said, giving him a light punch in the arm. Such familiarities were unheard of in London, but here, with Marcus . . .

He was practically her brother, after all.

'How fares your mother?' he asked.

'She is well,' Honoria replied, even though she wasn't. Not really. Lady Winstead had never quite

18

recovered from the scandal of Daniel being forced to leave the country. She alternated between fussing over supposed slights and pretending her only son had never existed.

It was . . . difficult.

'She hopes to retire to Bath,' Honoria added. 'Her sister lives there, and I think the two of them would get on well together. She doesn't really like London.'

'Your mother?' Marcus asked, with some surprise.

'Not as she used to,' Honoria clarified. 'Not since Daniel . . . Well. You know.'

Marcus's lips tightened at the corners. He knew.

'She thinks people are still talking about it,' Honoria said.

'Are they?'

Honoria shrugged helplessly. 'I have no idea. I don't think so. No one has given me the cut direct. Besides, it was nearly three years ago. Wouldn't you think everyone has something else to talk about?'

'I would have thought that everyone would have had something else to talk about when it happened,' he said darkly.

Honoria lifted a brow as she regarded his scowl. There was a reason he scared off so many debutantes. Her friends were terrified of him.

Well, that wasn't entirely true. They were only scared while in his presence. The rest of the time they sat at their escritoires, writing their names entwined with his—all in ridiculous loopy script, adorned with hearts and cherubs.

He was quite the matrimonial catch, Marcus Holroyd.

It wasn't that he was handsome, because he

wasn't, not exactly. His hair was a nice dark color; his eyes, too, but there was something about his face that Honoria found harsh. His brow was too heavy, too straight, his eyes set a bit too deeply.

But still, there was something about him that caught the eye. An aloofness, a tinge of disdain, as if he simply did not have the patience for nonsense.

It made the girls mad for him, even though most were nonsense personified.

They whispered about him as if he were some dark storybook hero, or if not that, then the villain, all gothic and mysterious, needing only to be redeemed.

Whereas to Honoria he was simply Marcus, which wasn't anything simple at all. She hated the way he patronized her, watching her with that disapproving stare. He made her feel as she'd been years ago, as an annoying child, or gawky adolescent.

And yet at the same time, there was something so comforting in having him about. Their paths did not cross as often as they used to—everything was different now that Daniel was gone—but when she walked into a room, and he was there . . .

She knew it.

And oddly enough, that was a good thing.

'Do you plan to come down to London for the season?' she asked politely.

'For some of it,' he replied, his face inscrutable. 'I have matters to attend to here.'

'Of course.'

'And you?' he asked.

She blinked.

'Do you plan to go down to London for the season?'

20

Her lips parted. Surely he could not be serious. Where else would she possibly go, given her unmarried state? It wasn't as if—

'Are you laughing?' she asked suspiciously.

'Of course not.' But he was smiling.

'It's not funny,' she told him. 'It's not as if I have a choice. I have to go for the season. I'm desperate.'

'Desperate,' he repeated, and he looked dubious. It was a frequent expression on his face.

'I *have* to find a husband this year.' She felt her head shaking back and forth, even though she wasn't sure what she might be objecting to. Her situation was not so very different from most of her friends'. She wasn't the only young lady hoping for marriage. But she wasn't looking for a husband so that she could admire the ring on her finger or bask in the glory of her status as a dashing young matron. She wanted a house of her own. A family—a large, noisy one that didn't always mind their manners.

She was just so sick of the silence that had taken over her home. She hated the sound of her footsteps clacking across the floor, hated that it was so frequently the only noise she heard all afternoon.

She needed a husband. It was the only way.

'Oh, come now, Honoria,' Marcus said, and she didn't need to see his face to know his expression precisely—patronizing and skeptical, with just a touch of ennui. 'Your life cannot possibly be so dire.'

She grit her teeth together. She despised that tone. 'Forget I said anything,' she muttered, because really, it wasn't worth it, trying to explain it to him.

He let out a breath, and even that managed to be

21

condescending. 'You're not likely to find a husband here,' he said.

She pressed her lips together, regretting that she'd brought up the subject.

'The students here are too young,' he remarked.

'They are the same age as I am,' she said, falling neatly into his trap.

But Marcus did not gloat; he wasn't the sort. 'That is why you're here in Cambridge, isn't it? To visit with the students who have not yet gone down to London?'

She looked determinedly straight ahead as she said, 'I told you, we're here to listen to lectures.'

He nodded. 'In Greek.'

'*Marcus.*'

He grinned at that. Except it wasn't really a grin. Marcus was always so serious, so stiff, that a grin for him would be a dry half-smile on anyone else. Honoria wondered how often he smiled without anyone realizing it. He was lucky she knew him so well. Anyone else would think him completely without humor.

'What was that about?' he asked.

She started and looked over at him. 'What was what about?'

'You rolled your eyes.'

'Did I?' Honestly, she had no idea if she had or not. But more to the point, why was he watching her so closely? This was *Marcus,* for heaven's sake. She looked out the window. 'Do you think the rain has let up?'

'No,' he replied, not turning his head even an inch. Honoria supposed he didn't need to. It had been a stupid question, meant for nothing but changing the subject. The rain was still beating down on the carriage mercilessly.

'Shall I convey you to the Royles'?' he asked politely.

'No, thank you.' Honoria craned her neck a bit, trying to see through the glass and the storm and the next bit of glass into Miss Pilaster's. She couldn't see a thing, but it was a good excuse not to look at him, so she made a good show of it. 'I'll join my friends in a moment.'

'Are you hungry?' he inquired. 'I stopped at Flindle's earlier and have a few cakes wrapped to take home.'

Her eyes lit up. 'Cakes?'

She didn't say the word as much as she sighed it. Or maybe moaned it. But she didn't care. He knew that sweets were her weakness; he was the same way. Daniel had never been particularly fond of dessert, and more than once, she and Marcus had found themselves together as children, huddled over a plate of cakes and biscuits.

Daniel had said they looked like a pack of savages, which had made Marcus laugh uproariously. Honoria never did understand why.

He reached down and drew something out of a box at his feet. 'Are you still partial to chocolate?'

'Always.' She felt herself smile in kinship. And perhaps in anticipation, as well.

He started to laugh. 'Do you remember that torte Cook made—'

'The one the dog got into?'

'I almost cried.'

She grimaced. 'I think I did cry.'

'I got one bite.'

'I got none,' she said longingly. 'But it smelled divine.'

'Oh, it was.' He looked as if the memory of it might send him into a rapture. 'It was.'

'You know, I always thought Daniel might have had something to do with Buttercup getting into the house.'

'I'm sure he did,' Marcus agreed. 'The look on his face . . .'

'I hope you thrashed him.'

'To within an inch of his life,' he assured her.

She grinned, then asked, 'But not really?'

He smiled in return. 'Not really.' He chuckled at the memory and held out a small rectangle of chocolate cake, lovely and brown atop a crisp piece of white paper. It smelled just like heaven. Honoria took a deep, happy breath and smiled.

Then she looked over at Marcus and smiled anew. Because for a moment she'd felt like herself again, like the girl she'd been just a few years ago, when the world lay before her, a bright shiny ball that glittered with promise. It had been a feeling she hadn't even realized she'd been missing—of belonging, of place, of being with someone who knew you utterly and completely and still thought you were worth laughing with.

Strange that it should be Marcus who should make her feel that way.

And in so many ways, not strange at all.

She took the cake from his hand and looked down at it questioningly.

'I'm afraid I haven't any sort of utensil,' he said apologetically.

'It might make a terrible mess,' she said, hoping that he realized that what she was really saying was *Please tell me that you don't mind if I spread crumbs all over your carriage*.

24

'I shall have one, too,' he told her. 'So that you don't feel alone.'

She tried not to smile. 'That is most generous of you.'

'I am quite certain it is my gentlemanly duty.'

'To eat cake?'

'It is one of the more appealing of my gentlemanly duties,' he allowed.

Honoria giggled, then took a bite. 'Oh, my.'

'Good?'

'Heavenly.' She took another bite. 'And by that I mean *beyond* heavenly.'

He grinned and ate some of his own, devouring half in one bite. Then, while Honoria watched with some surprise, he popped the other half into his mouth and finished it.

The piece hadn't been very large, but still. She took a nibble of her own, trying to make it last longer.

'You always did that,' he said.

She looked up. 'What?'

'Ate your dessert slowly, just to torture the rest of us.'

'I like to make it last.' She gave him an arch look, accompanied by a one-shouldered shrug. 'If you feel tortured by that, that must be your own problem.'

'Heartless,' he murmured.

'With you, always.'

He chuckled again, and Honoria was struck by how different he was in private. It was almost as if she had the old Marcus back, the one who had practically lived at Whipple Hill. He had truly become a member of the family, even joining their dreadful pantomimes. He had played a tree every

25

time; for some reason that had always amused her.

She liked that Marcus. She had *adored* that Marcus.

But he'd been gone these past few years, replaced by the silent, scowling man known to the rest of the world as Lord Chatteris. It was sad, really. For her, but probably most of all, for him.

She finished her cake, trying to ignore his amused expression, then accepted his handkerchief to wipe the crumbs from her hands. 'Thank you,' she said, handing it back.

He nodded his welcome, then said, 'When are you—'

But he was cut off by a sharp rap at the window.

Honoria peered past him to see who was knocking.

'Beg your pardon, sir,' said a footman in familiar livery. 'Is that Lady Honoria?'

'It is.'

Honoria leaned forward. 'That's . . . er . . .' Very well, she had no idea of his name, but he had accompanied the group of girls on their shopping expedition. 'He's from the Royles.' She gave Marcus a quick, awkward smile before standing, then crouching so that she might exit the carriage. 'I must go. My friends will be waiting for me.'

'I shall call upon you tomorrow.'

'*What*?' She froze, bent over like a crone.

One of his brows rose in mocking salute. 'Surely your hostess won't mind.'

Mrs. Royle, mind that an unmarried earl not yet thirty planned to pay a call upon her home? It would be all Honoria could do to stop her from organizing a parade.

'I'm sure that would be lovely,' she managed to

26

say.

'Good.' He cleared his throat. 'It has been too long.'

She looked at him in surprise. Surely he didn't give her a thought when they were not both in London, swanning about for the season.

'I am glad you are well,' he said abruptly.

Why such a statement was so startling, Honoria couldn't have begun to say. But it was.

It really was.

* * *

Marcus watched as the Royles' footman escorted Honoria into the shop across the street. Then, once Marcus was assured of her safety, he rapped three times on the wall, signaling to the coachman to continue.

He had been surprised to see her in Cambridge. He did not keep close tabs on Honoria when he was not in London, but still, he somehow thought he'd have known if she was going to be spending time so close to his home.

He supposed he ought to start making plans to go down to town for the season. He had not been lying when he'd told her he had business to attend to here, although it probably would have been more accurate to say that he simply preferred to remain in the country. There was nothing that required his presence in Cambridgeshire, just quite a lot that would be made easier by it.

Not to mention that he hated the season. Hated it. But if Honoria was hell-bent on acquiring herself a husband, then he would go to London to make sure she made no disastrous mistakes.

27

He had made a vow, after all.

Daniel Smythe-Smith had been his closest friend. No, his only friend, his only *true* friend.

A thousand acquaintances and one true friend.

Such was his life.

But Daniel was gone, somewhere in Italy if the latest missive was still current. And he wasn't likely to return, not while the Marquess of Ramsgate still lived, hell-bent on revenge.

What a bloody cock-up the whole thing had been. Marcus had told Daniel not to play cards with Hugh Prentice. But no, Daniel had just laughed, determined to try his hand. Prentice always won. Always. He was bloody brilliant, everyone knew it. Maths, physics, history—he'd ended up teaching the dons at university. Hugh Prentice didn't cheat at cards, he simply won all the time because he had a freakishly sharp memory and a mind that saw the world in patterns and equations.

Or so he'd told Marcus when they'd been students together at Eton. Truth was, Marcus still didn't quite understand what he'd been talking about. And he'd been the second best student at maths. But next to Hugh . . . Well, there could be no comparison.

No one in their right mind played cards with Hugh Prentice, but Daniel hadn't been in his right mind. He'd been a little bit drunk, and a little bit giddy over some girl he'd just bedded, and so he'd sat down across from Hugh and played.

And won.

Even Marcus hadn't been able to believe it.

Not that he'd thought Daniel was a cheat. No one thought Daniel was a cheat. Everyone liked him. Everyone trusted him. But then again, no one ever beat Hugh Prentice.

But Hugh had been drinking. And Daniel had been drinking. And they'd all been drinking, and when Hugh knocked over the table and accused Daniel of cheating, the room went to hell.

To this day Marcus wasn't sure exactly what was said, but within minutes it had been settled—Daniel Smythe-Smith would be meeting Hugh Prentice at dawn. With pistols.

And with any luck, they'd be sober enough by then to realize their own idiocy.

Hugh had shot first, his bullet grazing Daniel's left shoulder. And while everyone was gasping about that—the polite thing would have been to shoot in the air—Daniel raised his arm and fired back.

And Daniel—bloody hell but Daniel had always had bad aim—Daniel had caught Hugh at the top of his thigh. There had been so much blood Marcus still felt queasy just thinking about it. The surgeon had screamed. The bullet had hit an artery; nothing else could have produced such a torrent of blood. For three days all the worry had been whether Hugh would live or die; no one gave much thought to the leg, with its shattered femur.

Hugh lived, but he didn't walk, not without a cane. And his father—the extremely powerful and extremely angry Marquess of Ramsgate—vowed that Daniel would be brought to justice.

Hence Daniel's flight to Italy.

Hence Daniel's breathless, last-minute, promise-me-now-because-we're-standing-at-the-docks-and-the-ship-is-about-to-leave request:

'Watch over Honoria, will you? See that she doesn't marry an idiot.'

29

Of course Marcus had said yes. What else could he have said? But he'd never told Honoria of his promise to her brother. Good God, that would have been disaster. It was difficult enough keeping up with her without her knowledge. If she'd known he was acting *in loco parentis,* she'd have been furious. The last thing he needed was her trying to thwart him.

Which she would do. He was sure of it.

It wasn't that she was deliberately willful. She was, for the most part, a perfectly reasonable girl. But even the most reasonable of females took umbrage when they thought they were being bossed about.

So he watched from afar, and he quietly scared off a suitor or two.

Or three.

Or maybe four.

He'd promised Daniel.

And Marcus Holroyd did not break his promises.

Chapter Two

'When will he be here?'

'I don't know,' Honoria replied, for what must have been the seventh time. She smiled politely at the other young ladies in the Royles' green and gray drawing room. Marcus's appearance the day before had been discussed, dissected, analyzed, and—by Lady Sarah Pleinsworth, Honoria's cousin and one of her closest friends—rendered into poetry.

'He came in the rain,' Sarah intoned. 'The day had been plain.'

Honoria nearly spit out her tea.

'It was muddy, this lane—'

Cecily Royle smiled slyly over her teacup. 'Have you considered free verse?'

'—our heroine, in pain—'

'I *was* cold,' Honoria put in.

Iris Smythe-Smith, another of Honoria's cousins, looked up with her signature dry expression. '*I* am in pain,' she stated. 'Specifically, my ears.'

Honoria shot Iris a look that said clearly, *Be polite*. Iris just shrugged.

'—her distress, she did feign—'

'Not true!' Honoria protested.

'You can't interfere with genius,' Iris said sweetly.

'—her schemes, not in vain—'

'This poem is devolving rapidly,' Honoria stated.

'I am beginning to enjoy it,' said Cecily.

'—her existence, a bane . . .'

Honoria let out a snort. 'Oh, come now!'

'I think she's doing an admirable job,' Iris said, 'given the limitations of the rhyming structure.' She looked over at Sarah, who had gone quite suddenly silent. Iris cocked her head to the side; so did Honoria and Sarah.

Sarah's lips were parted, and her left hand was still outstretched with great drama, but she appeared to have run out of words.

'Cane?' Cecily suggested. 'Main?'

'Insane?' offered Iris.

'Any moment now,' Honoria said tartly, 'if I'm trapped here much longer with you lot.'

Sarah laughed and flopped down on the sofa. 'The Earl of Chatteris,' she said with a sigh. 'I shall never forgive you for not introducing us last year,' she said to Honoria.

'I did introduce you!'

'Well, then you should have done so twice,' Sarah added impishly, 'to make it stick. I don't think he said more than two words to me the whole season.'

'He barely said more than two words to me,' Honoria replied.

Sarah tilted her head, her brows arching as if to say, *Oh, really?*

'He's not terribly social,' Honoria said.

'I think he's handsome,' Cecily said.

'Do you?' Sarah asked. 'I find him rather brooding.'

'Brooding *is* handsome,' Cecily said firmly, before Honoria could offer an opinion.

'I am trapped in a bad novel,' Iris announced, to no one in particular.

'You didn't answer my question,' Sarah said to Honoria. 'When will he be here?'

'I do not know,' Honoria replied, for what was surely the eighth time. 'He did not say.'

'Impolite,' Cecily said, reaching for a biscuit.

'It's his way,' Honoria said with a light shrug.

'This is what I find so interesting,' Cecily murmured, 'that you know "his way."'

'They have known each other for decades,' Sarah said. 'Centuries.'

'*Sarah* . . .' Honoria adored her cousin, she really did. Most of the time.

Sarah smiled slyly, her dark eyes alight with mischief. 'He used to call her Bug.'

'Sarah!' Honoria glared at her. She did not need it put about that she had once been likened to an insect by an earl of the realm. 'It was a long time

32

ago,' she said with all the dignity she could muster. 'I was seven.'

'How old was he?' Iris asked.

Honoria thought for a moment. 'Thirteen, most likely.'

'Well, that explains it,' Cecily said with a wave of her hand. 'Boys are beasts.'

Honoria nodded politely. Cecily had seven younger brothers. She ought to know.

'Still,' Cecily said, all drama, 'how coincidental that he should come across you on the street.'

'Fortuitous,' Sarah agreed.

'Almost as if he were following you,' Cecily added, leaning forward with widened eyes.

'Now that is just silly,' Honoria said.

'Well, of course,' Cecily replied, her tone going right back to brisk and businesslike. 'That would never happen. I was merely saying that it *seemed* as if he had.'

'He lives nearby,' Honoria said, waving her hand in the direction of nothing in particular. She had a terrible sense of direction; she couldn't have said which way was north if her life depended on it. And anyway, she had no idea which way one had to travel out of Cambridge to get to Fensmore in the first place.

'His estate adjoins ours,' Cecily said.

'It does?' This, from Sarah. With great interest.

'Or perhaps I should say it surrounds us,' Cecily said with a little laugh. 'The man owns half of northern Cambridgeshire. I do believe his property touches Bricstan on the north, south, and west.'

'And on the east?' Iris wondered. To Honoria she added, 'It's the logical next question.'

33

Cecily blinked, considering this. 'That would probably send you onto his land, as well. You can make your way out through a little section to the southeast. But then you would end up at the vicarage, so really, what would be the point?'

'Is it far?' Sarah asked.

'Bricstan?'

'No,' Sarah retorted, with no small measure of impatience. 'Fensmore.'

'Oh. No, not really. We're twenty miles away, so he would be only a little farther.' Cecily paused for a moment, thinking. 'He might keep a town home here as well. I'm not sure.'

The Royles were firm East Anglians, keeping a town home in Cambridge and a country home just a bit to the north. When they went to London, they rented.

'We should go,' Sarah said suddenly. 'This weekend.'

'Go?' Iris asked. 'Where?'

'To the country?' Cecily replied.

'Yes,' Sarah said, her voice rising with excitement. 'It would extend our visit by only a few days, so surely our families could make no objection.' She turned slightly, sending her words directly toward Cecily. 'Your mother can host a small house party. We can invite some of the university students. Surely they will be grateful for a respite from school life.'

'I've heard the food there is very bad,' Iris said.

'It's an interesting idea,' Cecily mused.

'It's a spectacular idea,' Sarah said firmly. 'Go ask your mother. Now, before Lord Chatteris arrives.'

Honoria gasped. 'Surely you don't mean to invite

him?' It had been lovely to see him the day before, but the last thing she wanted was to spend an entire house party in his company. If he attended, she could bid any hopes of attracting the attention of a young gentleman good-bye. Marcus had a way of glowering when he disapproved of her behavior. And his glowers had a way of scaring off every human being in the vicinity.

That he might not disapprove of her behavior never once crossed her mind.

'Of course not,' Sarah replied, turning to Honoria with a most impatient expression. 'Why would he attend, when he can sleep in his own bed just down the road? But he will wish to visit, won't he? Perhaps come to supper, or for shooting.'

It was Honoria's opinion that if Marcus was trapped for an afternoon with this gaggle of females he'd likely start shooting at *them*.

'It's perfect,' Sarah insisted. 'The younger gentlemen will be so much more likely to accept our invitation if they know Lord Chatteris will be there. They'll want to make a good impression. He's very influential, you know.'

'I thought you weren't going to invite him,' Honoria said.

'I'm not. I mean—' Sarah motioned toward Cecily, who was, after all, the daughter of the one who would be doing the inviting. '*We're* not. But we can put it about that he is likely to call.'

'He'll appreciate that, I'm sure,' Honoria said dryly, not that anyone was listening.

'Who shall we invite?' Sarah asked, ignoring Honoria's statement entirely. 'It should be four gentlemen.'

'Our numbers will be uneven when Lord

35

Chatteris is about,' Cecily pointed out.

'The better for us,' Sarah said firmly. 'And we can't very well invite only three and then have too many ladies when he is not here.'

Honoria sighed. Her cousin was the definition of tenacious. There was no arguing with Sarah when she had her heart set on something.

'I had better talk to my mother,' Cecily said, standing up. 'We'll need to get to work immediately.' She left the room in a dramatic swish of pink muslin.

Honoria looked over at Iris, who surely recognized the madness that was about to ensue. But Iris just shrugged her shoulders and said, 'It's a good idea, actually.'

'It's why we came to Cambridge,' Sarah reminded them. 'To meet gentlemen.'

It was true. Mrs. Royle liked to talk about exposing young ladies to culture and education, but they all knew the truth: They had come to Cambridge for reasons that were purely social. When Mrs. Royle had broached the idea to Honoria's mother, she'd lamented that so many young gentlemen were still at Oxford or Cambridge at the beginning of the season and thus not in London where they should be, courting young ladies. Mrs. Royle had a supper planned for the next evening, but a house party away from town would be even more effective.

Nothing like trapping the gentlemen where they couldn't get away.

Honoria supposed she was going to need to pen a letter to her mother, informing her that she would be in Cambridge a few extra days. She had a bad feeling about using Marcus as a lure to get

36

other gentlemen to accept, but she knew she could not afford to dismiss such an opportunity. The university students were young—almost the same age as the four young ladies—but Honoria did not mind. Even if none were ready for marriage, surely some had older brothers? Or cousins. Or friends.

She sighed. She hated how calculated it all sounded, but what else was she to do?

'Gregory Bridgerton,' Sarah announced, her eyes positively aglow with triumph. 'He would be perfect. Brilliantly well-connected. One of his sisters married a duke, and another an earl. *And* he's in his final year, so perhaps he will be ready to marry soon.'

Honoria looked up. She'd met Mr. Bridgerton several times, usually when he'd been dragged by his mother to one of the infamous Smythe-Smith musicales.

Honoria tried not to wince. The family's annual musicale was never a good time to make the acquaintance of a gentleman, unless he was deaf. There was some argument within the family about who, precisely, had begun the tradition, but in 1807, four Smythe-Smith cousins had taken to the stage and butchered a perfectly innocent piece of music. Why they (or rather, their mothers) had thought it a good idea to repeat the massacre the following year Honoria would never know, but they had, and then the year after that, and the year after that.

It was understood that all Smythe-Smith daughters must take up a musical instrument and, when it was their turn, join the quartet. Once in, she was stuck there until she found a husband. It was, Honoria had more than once reflected, as good an argument as any for an early marriage.

The strange thing was, most of her family didn't seem to realize how *awful* they were. Her cousin Viola had performed in the quartet for six years and still spoke longingly of her days as a member. Honoria had half-expected her to leave her groom at the altar when she had married six months earlier, just so she could continue in her position as primary violinist.

The mind boggled.

Honoria and Sarah had been forced to assume their spots the year before, Honoria on the violin and Sarah on the piano. Poor Sarah was still traumatized by the experience. She was actually somewhat musical and had played her part accurately. Or so Honoria was told; it was difficult to hear anything above the violins. Or the people gasping in the audience.

Sarah had sworn that she would never play with her cousins again. Honoria had just shrugged; she didn't really mind the musicale—not terribly, at least. She actually thought the whole thing was a bit amusing. And besides, there was nothing she could do about it. It was family tradition, and there was nothing that mattered more to Honoria than family, nothing.

But now she had to get serious about her husband hunting, which meant she was going to have to find a gentleman with a tin ear. Or a very good sense of humor.

Gregory Bridgerton seemed to be an excellent candidate. Honoria had no idea if he could carry a tune, but they had crossed paths two days earlier, when the four young ladies were out for tea in town, and she had been instantly struck by what a lovely smile he had.

She liked him. He was amazingly friendly and outgoing, and something about him reminded her of her own family, the way they used to be, gathered together at Whipple Hill, loud and boisterous and always laughing.

It was probably because he, too, was from a large family—the second youngest of eight. Honoria was the youngest of six, so surely they would have a great deal in common.

Gregory Bridgerton. Hmmm. She didn't know why she hadn't thought of him before.

Honoria Bridgerton.

Winifred Bridgerton. (She'd always wanted to name a child Winifred, so it seemed prudent to test this one out on the tongue as well.)

Mr. Gregory and Lady Honor—

'Honoria? Honoria!'

She blinked. Sarah was staring at her with visible irritation. 'Gregory Bridgerton?' she said. 'Your opinion?'

'Er, I think he would be a very nice choice,' Honoria answered, in the most unassuming manner possible.

'Who else?' Sarah said, rising to her feet. 'Perhaps I should make a list.'

'For four names?' Honoria could not help but ask.

'You're terribly determined,' Iris murmured.

'I have to be,' Sarah retorted, her dark eyes flashing.

'Do you really think you're going to find a man and then marry him in the next two weeks?' Honoria asked.

39

'I don't know what you're talking about,' Sarah replied in a clipped voice.

Honoria glanced toward the open door to make sure that no one was approaching. 'It's just the three of us right now, Sarah.'

'Does one have to play at the musicale if one is engaged?' Iris asked.

'Yes,' Honoria answered.

'No,' Sarah said firmly.

'Oh, yes, you do,' Honoria said.

Iris sighed.

'Don't you complain,' Sarah said, turning on her with narrowed eyes. 'You didn't have to play last year.'

'For which I am eternally grateful,' Iris told her. She was due to join the quartet this year on cello.

'You want to find a husband just as badly as I do,' Sarah said to Honoria.

'Not in the next two weeks! And not,' she added, with a bit more decorum, 'merely to get out of playing in the musicale.'

'I am not saying that I would marry someone awful,' Sarah said with a sniff. 'But if Lord Chatteris just happened to fall desperately in love with me . . .'

'He's not going to,' Honoria said baldly. Then, realizing how unkind that sounded, she added, 'He's not going to fall in love with anyone. Trust me.'

'Love works in mysterious ways,' Sarah said. But she sounded more hopeful than certain.

'Even if Marcus did fall in love with you, which isn't going to happen, not that it has anything to do with you, he's just not the sort to fall in love with someone quickly.' Honoria paused, trying to remember where she had started her sentence because she was fairly certain she had not completed it.

Sarah crossed her arms. 'Was there a point in there, hidden amid the insults?'

Honoria rolled her eyes. 'Just that even if Marcus did fall in love with someone, he would do it in the most ordinary, regular manner.'

'Is love ever ordinary?' Iris asked.

The statement was just philosophical enough to silence the room. But only for a moment.

'He would never rush a wedding,' Honoria continued, turning back to Sarah. 'He hates drawing attention to himself. Hates it,' she repeated, because frankly, it bore repeating. 'He'll not get you out of the musicale, that is for certain.'

For a few seconds Sarah stood still and straight, and then she sighed, her shoulders falling into a slump. 'Maybe Gregory Bridgerton,' she said dejectedly. 'He seems like he might be a romantic.'

'Enough to elope?' Iris asked.

'No one is eloping!' Honoria exclaimed. 'And you are all playing in the musicale next month.'

Sarah and Iris stared at her with identical expressions—two parts surprise and one part indignation. With a healthy dash of dread.

'Well, you are,' Honoria muttered. 'We all are. It's our duty.'

'Our duty,' Sarah repeated. 'To play terrible music?'

Honoria stared at her. 'Yes.'

Iris burst out laughing.

'It's not funny,' Sarah said.

Iris wiped her eyes. 'But it is.'

'It won't be,' Sarah warned, 'once you have to

play.'

'Which is why I shall take my laughter now,' Iris replied.

'I still think we should have a house party,' Sarah said.

To which Honoria replied, 'I agree.'

Sarah looked at her suspiciously.

'I just think that it would be ambitious to think of it as a means to getting out of playing at the musicale.' Foolish more than ambitious, but Honoria wasn't about to say *that*.

Sarah sat at a nearby writing desk and picked up a pen. 'We agree on Mr. Bridgerton, then?'

Honoria looked over at Iris. They both nodded.

'Who else?' Sarah asked.

'Don't you think we should wait for Cecily?' Iris asked.

'Neville Berbrooke!' Sarah said firmly. 'He and Mr. Bridgerton are related.'

'They are?' Honoria asked. She knew quite a lot about the Bridgerton family—everyone did—but she didn't think they'd ever married any Berbrookes.

'Mr. Bridgerton's brother's wife's sister is married to Mr. Berbrooke's brother.'

It was just the sort of statement that begged for a sarcastic comment, but Honoria was too dumbfounded by the speed at which Sarah had rattled it off to do anything but blink.

Iris, however, was not as impressed. 'And this makes them . . . casual acquaintances?'

'Cousins,' Sarah said, shooting Iris a peevish glance. 'Brothers. In-law.'

'Thrice removed?' Iris murmured.

Sarah looked over at Honoria. 'Make her stop.'

Honoria burst out laughing. Iris did, too, and then finally Sarah succumbed to her own giggles. Honoria rose and gave Sarah an impulsive hug. 'Everything will be all right, you'll see.'

Sarah smiled sheepishly in return. She started to say something, but just then Cecily sailed back into the room, her mother at her heels. 'She loves the idea!' Cecily announced.

'I do,' Mrs. Royle affirmed. She strode across the room to the writing table, sliding into the chair as Sarah quickly hopped out.

Honoria watched her with interest. Mrs. Royle was such a *medium* woman—medium height, medium build, medium brown hair and medium brown eyes. Even her dress was of a medium shade of purple, with a medium-sized ruffle circling the bottom.

But there was nothing medium about her expression at that moment. She looked ready to command an army, and it was clear that she would take no prisoners.

'It's brilliant,' Mrs. Royle said, frowning slightly as she looked for something on her desk. 'I don't know why I didn't think of it earlier. We will have to work quickly, of course. We shall send someone down to London this afternoon to notify your parents that you will be detained.' She turned to Honoria. 'Cecily says that you can ensure that Lord Chatteris makes an appearance?'

'*No,*' Honoria answered with alarm. 'I can try, of course, but—'

'Try hard,' Mrs. Royle said briskly. 'That will be your job while the rest of us plan the party. When *is* he coming, by the way?'

'I have no idea,' Honoria replied, for what had

to be—oh, bother it all, it did not matter how many times she had answered that question. 'He did not say.'

'You don't think he's forgotten?'

'He is not the sort to forget,' Honoria told her.

'No, he doesn't seem as if he would,' Mrs. Royle murmured. 'Still, one can never count upon a man to be as devoted to the mechanics of courtship as a female.'

The alarm that had been percolating inside Honoria exploded into full-form panic. Dear heavens, if Mrs. Royle was thinking to pair her up with *Marcus* . . .

'He's not courting me,' she said quickly.

Mrs. Royle gave her a calculating look.

'He's not, I promise you.'

Mrs. Royle turned her gaze to Sarah, who immediately straightened in her seat.

'It does seem unlikely,' Sarah said, since it was clear that Mrs. Royle wished for her to chime in. 'They are rather like brother and sister.'

'It's true,' Honoria confirmed. 'He and my brother were the closest of friends.'

The room went silent at the mention of Daniel. Honoria wasn't sure if this was out of respect, awkwardness, or regret that a perfectly eligible gentleman was lost to the current crop of debutantes.

'Well,' Mrs. Royle said briskly. 'Do your best. It is all we can ask of you.'

'Oh!' Cecily yelped, stepping back from the window. 'I think he's here!'

Sarah jumped to her feet and began smoothing her perfectly unwrinkled skirts. 'Are you certain?'

'Oh, yes.' Cecily practically sighed with delight.

'Oh, my, but that's a gorgeous carriage.'

They all stood still, awaiting their guest. Honoria thought Mrs. Royle might actually be holding her breath.

'Won't we feel foolish,' Iris whispered in her ear, 'if it is not even he?'

Honoria bit back a laugh, shoving her cousin with her foot.

Iris only grinned.

In the silence it was easy to hear the knock at the door, followed by the slight creak as the butler opened it.

'Stand straight,' Mrs. Royle hissed at Cecily. And then, as an afterthought: 'The rest of you, too.'

But when the butler appeared in the doorway, he was alone. 'Lord Chatteris has sent his regrets,' he announced.

Everyone slumped. Even Mrs. Royle. It was as if they'd each been pricked by a pin, the air squeezed right out of them.

'He sent a letter,' the butler said.

Mrs. Royle held out her hand, but the butler said, 'It is addressed to Lady Honoria.'

Honoria straightened and, aware that every eye was now trained on her, worked a little harder to suppress the relief that she was sure showed on her face. 'Er, thank you,' she said, taking the folded sheet of parchment from the butler.

'What does it say?' Sarah asked, before Honoria could even break the seal.

'Just one moment,' Honoria murmured, taking a few steps toward the window so that she might read Marcus's letter in relative privacy. 'It's nothing, really,' she said, once she'd finished the three short sentences. 'There was an emergency at his home, and he is unable to visit this afternoon.'

'That's all he said?' Mrs. Royle demanded.

'He's not one for lengthy explanations,' Honoria said.

'Powerful men do not explain their actions,' Cecily announced dramatically.

There was a moment of silence while everyone digested *that*, and then Honoria said, in a purposefully cheerful voice, 'He wishes all well.'

'Not well enough to grace us with his presence,' Mrs. Royle muttered.

The obvious question of the house party hung in the air, with the young ladies glancing back and forth between them, silently wondering who would step forward to ask it. Finally, all eyes settled on Cecily. It had to be her. It would have been rude coming from anyone else.

'What shall we do about the party at Bricstan?' Cecily asked. But her mother was lost in thought, eyes narrowed and lips pursed. Cecily cleared her throat and then said, a bit louder, 'Mother?'

'It's still a good idea,' Mrs. Royle said suddenly. Her voice was loud with determination, and Honoria almost felt the syllables echo off her ears.

'Then we shall still invite the students?' Cecily said.

'I had thought of Gregory Bridgerton,' Sarah put in helpfully, 'and Neville Berbrooke.'

'Good choices,' Mrs. Royle said, marching across the room to her desk. 'Good family, the both of them.' She pulled out several sheets of cream-colored paper, then flipped through the corners, counting them out. 'I shall write the invitations immediately,' she said, once she had the

46

correct number of sheets. She turned to Honoria, arm outstretched. 'Except this one.'

'I beg your pardon?' Honoria said, even though she knew exactly what Mrs. Royle meant. She just didn't want to accept it.

'Invite Lord Chatteris. Just as we planned. Not for the entire party, just for an afternoon. Saturday or Sunday, whichever he prefers.'

'Are you sure the invitation should not come from you?' Cecily asked her mother.

'No, it is better from Lady Honoria,' Mrs. Royle stated. 'He will find it more difficult to decline, coming from such a close family friend.' She took another step forward, until there was no way Honoria could avoid taking the paper from her hand. 'We are good neighbors, of course,' Mrs. Royle added. 'Do not think we are not.'

'Of course,' Honoria murmured. There was nothing else she could have said. And, she thought as she looked down at the paper in her hand, nothing else she could do. But then her luck turned. Mrs. Royle sat at the desk, which meant Honoria had no choice but to retire to her room to pen the invitation.

Which meant that no one besides Honoria—and Marcus, of course—knew that what it actually said was:

Marcus—

Mrs. Royle has asked me to extend an invitation to Bricstan this weekend. She plans a small house party, with the four ladies I mentioned, along with four young gentlemen from the university. I beg of you, do not accept. You shall

47

be miserable, and then I shall be miserable, fretting over your misery.

With affection, et cetera & et cetera,
Honoria

A different sort of gentleman would take such an 'invitation' as a dare and accept immediately. But not Marcus. Honoria was certain of that. He might be supercilious, he might be disapproving, but one thing he was *not* was spiteful. And he wasn't going to make himself miserable just to make her miserable.

He was occasionally the bane of her existence, but he was, at heart, a good person. Reasonable, too. He would realize that Mrs. Royle's gathering was exactly the sort of event that made him want to gouge his eyes out. She'd long wondered why he ever went to London for the season; he always looked so bored.

Honoria sealed the letter herself and brought it downstairs, handing it to a footman to deliver to Marcus. When Marcus's reply arrived several hours later, it was addressed to Mrs. Royle.

'What does it say?' Cecily asked breathlessly, rushing to her mother's side as she opened it. Iris, too, crowded in, trying to peer over Cecily's shoulder.

Honoria hung back and waited. She knew what it would say.

Mrs. Royle broke the seal and unfolded the missive, her eyes moving quickly across the writing as she read. 'He sends his regrets,' she said flatly.

Cecily and Sarah let out wails of despair. Mrs.

Royle looked over at Honoria, who hoped she was doing a good job at looking shocked as she said, 'I did ask. It's just not his sort of entertainment, I think. He's really not terribly sociable.'

'Well, that much is true,' Mrs. Royle grumbled. 'I can't remember more than three balls last season at which I saw him dancing. And with so many young ladies without partners. It was downright rude.'

'He's a good dancer, though,' Cecily said.

All eyes turned to her.

'He is,' she insisted, looking a bit surprised that her statement had garnered so much attention. 'He danced with me at the Mottram Ball.' She turned to the other girls, as if to offer an explanation. 'We are neighbors, after all. It was only polite.'

Honoria nodded. Marcus was a good dancer. Better than she was, that was for certain. She never could understand the intricacies of rhythm. Sarah had tried endlessly to explain the difference between a waltz and common time, but Honoria had never been able to grasp it.

'We shall persevere,' Mrs. Royle said loudly, placing a hand over her heart. 'Two of the other four gentlemen have already accepted, and I am certain that we will hear from the others in the morning.'

But later that night, as Honoria was heading upstairs to bed, Mrs. Royle took her aside and quietly asked, 'Do you think there is any chance Lord Chatteris will change his mind?'

Honoria swallowed uncomfortably. 'I'm afraid not, ma'am.'

Mrs. Royle shook her head and made a little clucking sound. 'Such a pity. He really would have

49

been the feather in my cap. Well, good night, dear. Pleasant dreams.'

*   *   *

Twenty miles away, Marcus was sitting alone in his study with a hot cup of cider, mulling over his recent missive from Honoria. He had burst out laughing upon reading it, which he imagined had been her intention. Perhaps not her primary intention—that had certainly been to stop him from attending Mrs. Royle's party—but she would have known that her words would amuse him to no end.

He looked down at the paper again, smiling as he reread it. Only Honoria would write him such a note, begging him to decline the invitation that she had put forth but two sentences prior.

It had been rather nice, seeing her again. It had been an age. He did not count the numerous times their paths had crossed in London. Such meetings could never be like the carefree times he had spent with her family at Whipple Hill. In London he was either dodging the ambitious mamas who were absolutely certain their daughters were born to be the next Lady Chatteris, or he was trying to keep an eye on Honoria. Or both.

In retrospect, it was remarkable that no one thought he was interested in her himself. He'd certainly spent enough time discreetly meddling in her business. He'd scared off four gentlemen the previous year—two of them fortune hunters, one with a cruel streak, and the last an aging, pompous ass. He was fairly certain that Honoria would have had the sense to refuse the last, but the one with the cruel streak hid it well, and the fortune hunters were, he was told, charming.

Which he supposed was a prerequisite for the position.

She was probably interested in one of the gentlemen who would be attending Mrs. Royle's party and didn't want him there to ruin things for her. He didn't particularly want to be there, either, so in that they were in agreement.

But he needed to know on whom she had set her sights. If it wasn't someone with whom he was familiar, inquiries would have to be made. It wouldn't be too difficult to obtain the guest list; the servants always knew how to get hold of things like that.

And maybe if the weather was fine, he would go for a ride. Or a walk. There was a path in the woods that wandered back and forth across the property line between Fensmore and Bricstan. He couldn't recall the last time he'd walked it. It was irresponsible of him, really. A landowner ought to know his property in intimate detail.

A walk it would be, then. And if he happened along Honoria and her friends, he could converse with them just long enough to get the information he needed. He could avoid the party and find out who she planned to set her cap for.

Marcus finished off his cider and smiled. He couldn't imagine a more pleasing outcome.

Chapter Three

By Sunday afternoon, Honoria was convinced she had made the right choice. Gregory Bridgerton would make an ideal husband. They had been seated next to each other at the supper at the Royles' town home a few days earlier, and he had been utterly charming. True, he had shown no signs of being particularly smitten with her, but neither had he seemed taken with anyone else. He was kind, courteous, and had a sense of humor to match her own.

More to the point, Honoria thought that if she made the effort, she had more than a passing chance at capturing his interest. He was a younger—no, a *youngest* son—which meant that ladies hoping to snag a title would consider him beneath their notice. And he would probably need money. His family was passably wealthy and would likely provide him with an income, but younger sons were notoriously in need of dowries.

Which Honoria had. Nothing staggering, but Daniel had revealed the amount to her before he'd left the country, and it was more than respectable. She would not enter into a marriage empty-handed.

All that was left was to make Mr. Bridgerton see that they were perfectly matched. And Honoria had a plan.

It had come to her in church that morning. (The ladies went; the gentlemen somehow managed to get out of it.) It wasn't terribly complicated; she needed only a sunny day, a halfway acceptable sense of direction, and a shovel.

The first was easy, and indeed already a given. The sun had been shining brightly when she'd entered the small parish church, which was probably what had given her the idea in the first place. More to the point, it was still shining when she left, which, given the vagaries of English weather, was not something one could always count upon.

The second would be trickier. But they had taken a walk through the woods the day before, and Honoria was fairly sure that she could find her way again. She might not be able to tell north from south, but she could follow a well-tended path.

As for the shovel, she was going to have to figure that one out later.

When the ladies returned to Bricstan after church, they were informed that the gentlemen had gone shooting and would return for a late lunch. 'They will be extremely hungry,' Mrs. Royle announced. 'We must adjust our preparations accordingly.'

Honoria was apparently the only one who did not realize that this meant she required an assistant. Cecily and Sarah immediately rushed upstairs to choose their afternoon dresses, and Iris spouted some nonsense about a stomachache and fled. Honoria was immediately drafted to serve on Mrs. Royle's committee of two.

'I had planned to serve meat pies,' Mrs. Royle said. 'They are so easy to handle out of doors, but I think we shall need another meat. Do you think the gentlemen will enjoy chilled, roasted beef?'

'Of course,' Honoria replied, following her to the kitchen. Didn't everyone?

'With mustard?'

Honoria opened her mouth to reply, but Mrs. Royle must not have been expecting an answer, because she kept right on talking: 'We shall serve three kinds. And a compote.'

Honoria waited for a moment and then, when it became apparent that this time Mrs. Royle *did* expect her to comment, she said, 'I'm sure that would be lovely.'

It was not the most vibrant example of her conversational skills, but given the subject matter, it was the best she could do.

'Oh!' Mrs. Royle stopped and whirled around so suddenly that Honoria nearly crashed into her. 'I forgot to tell Cecily!'

'Tell her what?' Honoria asked, but Mrs. Royle was already six steps down the hall, summoning a maid. When she returned, she said, 'It is very important that she wear blue this afternoon. I have heard that it is the favorite color of two of our guests.'

How she had determined that Honoria could not begin to guess.

'And it complements her eyes,' Mrs. Royle added.

'Cecily has lovely eyes,' Honoria agreed.

Mrs. Royle looked at her with a queer expression, then said, 'You should consider wearing blue more often, too. It will make your eyes look less uncommon.'

'I'm fond of my eyes,' Honoria said with a smile.

Mrs. Royle's lips pressed together. 'The color is very unusual.'

'It's a family trait. My brother's are the same.'

'Ah, yes, your brother.' Mrs. Royle sighed. 'Such a pity.'

54

Honoria nodded. Three years ago she would have taken offense at the comment, but she was less impetuous now, more pragmatic. And besides, it was true. It *was* a pity. 'We hope he may return someday.'

Mrs. Royle snorted. 'Not until Ramsgate dies. I have known him since he was in leading strings, and he's as stubborn as an ass.'

Honoria blinked at that. Such plain speaking from Mrs. Royle was unexpected.

'Well,' Mrs. Royle said with a sigh, 'there is nothing I can do about it, more's the pity. Now then, Cook is making individual trifles for dessert, with strawberries and vanilla cream.'

'That is a wonderful idea,' Honoria said, having by now figured out that her job was to agree with Mrs. Royle whenever possible.

'Perhaps she should bake biscuits, too,' Mrs. Royle said with a frown. 'She does quite a good job with them, and the gentlemen will be very hungry. Shooting is quite strenuous.'

Honoria had long thought that the sport of shooting was far more strenuous for the birds than the humans, but this she kept to herself. Still, she could not help saying, 'Isn't it interesting they went shooting this morning instead of to church?'

'It is not my place to tell young gentlemen how to conduct their lives,' Mrs. Royle said primly. 'Unless they are my sons, in which case, they must do as I say at all times.'

Honoria tried to detect irony in the statement but could find none, so she simply nodded. She had a feeling that Cecily's future husband would be included in the 'must do as I say' group.

She hoped the poor man—whoever he might

55

turn out to be—knew what he was getting into. Daniel had once told her that the best advice he'd ever received on the subject of marriage had come (unsolicited, of course) from Lady Danbury, a terrifying old dowager who seemed to enjoy giving advice to anyone who would listen.

And quite a few who didn't listen, either.

But apparently Daniel had taken her words to heart, or at the very least committed them to memory. And that was that a man should understand that when he married, he was marrying his mother-in-law just as much as he was marrying his bride.

Well, almost as much. Daniel had laughed slyly as he'd added his own postscript. Honoria had just looked at him blankly, which had made him laugh all the more.

He really was a wretch sometimes. Still, she missed him.

But in truth, Mrs. Royle wasn't that bad. She was simply determined, and Honoria knew from experience that determined mothers were a fearsome lot. Her own mother had once been determined. Her sisters still told stories of their days as young unmarried ladies, when their mother had been as ambitious a parent as the *ton* had ever seen. Margaret, Henrietta, Lydia, and Charlotte Smythe-Smith had been outfitted in the very best of clothing, had always been seen in the right places at the right times, and they had all married well. Not brilliantly, but well. And they'd all managed to do it in two seasons or less.

Honoria, on the other hand, saw season three looming ahead, and her mother's interest in seeing her well-settled was tepid at best. It wasn't that she *didn't* want Honoria to marry; rather, she just couldn't bring herself to care overmuch.

She hadn't cared overmuch about anything after Daniel had left the country.

So if Mrs. Royle ran about cooking extra sweets and forcing her daughter to change gowns based upon something she might have overheard about someone's favorite color, she was doing it out of love, and Honoria could never fault her for that.

'You're a dear to help me with the preparations,' Mrs. Royle said, giving Honoria a pat on the arm. 'All tasks are made easier with an extra pair of hands, that is what my mother always told me.'

Honoria rather thought she was providing an extra set of ears, not hands, but she murmured her thanks nonetheless and followed Mrs. Royle to the garden, where she wished to supervise the picnic arrangements.

'I think Mr. Bridgerton has been looking rather keenly at my Cecily,' Mrs. Royle said, stepping out into the not-quite-sunshine. 'Don't you?'

'I had not noticed,' Honoria said. She *hadn't* noticed, but drat it all, *had* he?

'Oh, yes,' Mrs. Royle said, quite definitively, 'at supper last night. He was smiling most broadly.'

Honoria cleared her throat. 'He's a rather smiling sort of gentleman.'

'Yes, but he was smiling *differently*.'

'I suppose.' Honoria squinted up at the sky. Clouds were rolling in. It didn't quite look like rain, though.

'Yes, I know,' Mrs. Royle said, following Honoria's gaze and misinterpreting the reason for it. 'It is not quite as sunny as it was this morning. I do hope the weather holds for the picnic.'

And for at least two hours thereafter, Honoria hoped. She had plans. Plans which—she looked about; they *were* in the garden, after all—required a shovel.

'It will be such a tragedy if we have to move indoors,' Mrs. Royle continued. 'One could hardly call it a picnic in such a case.'

Honoria nodded absently, still analyzing the clouds. There was one that was a bit more gray than the rest, but was it drifting toward or away?

'Well, I suppose there is nothing I can do but wait and see,' Mrs. Royle said. 'And no true harm done. A gentleman is just as likely to fall in love indoors as out, and if Mr. Bridgerton does have his eye on Cecily, at least she will be able to impress him at the pianoforte.'

'Sarah is quite accomplished as well,' Honoria remarked.

Mrs. Royle actually stopped and turned. 'She is?'

Honoria wasn't surprised that Mrs. Royle sounded surprised. She knew for a fact that she had attended last year's musicale.

'We probably won't be inside, anyway,' Mrs. Royle went on before Honoria could comment further. 'The sky doesn't look so terribly ominous. Hmmph. I suppose I must admit that I had been hoping Mr. Bridgerton might take an interest in Cecily—oh, I do hope that maid catches her in time to get out the blue dress; she'll be cross if she has to change—but of course Lord Chatteris would be even more exciting.'

Alarmed, Honoria spun back around to face her. 'But he's not coming.'

'No, of course not, but he *is* our neighbor. And as Cecily said the other day, this means that he will dance with her in London, and one must seize one's opportunities where one can.'

'Yes, of course, but—'

'He does not bestow his favor on many young ladies,' Mrs. Royle said proudly. 'You, I suppose, due to your prior connection, and maybe one or two others. It will make it easier for her to capture his attention. This way, Lady Honoria,' she said, motioning toward a row of flower arrangements on a nearby table. 'And besides,' she added, 'our property is like a little bite out of his. Surely, he'll want it.'

Honoria cleared her throat, not at all certain how to respond.

'Not that we could give it all to him,' Mrs. Royle continued. 'None of it is entailed, but I couldn't possibly slight Georgie that way.'

'Georgie?'

'My eldest son.' She turned to Honoria with an assessing eye, then waved her hand through the air. 'No, you're too old for him. Pity.'

Honoria decided there could not possibly be an appropriate reply to that.

'We could add a few acres to Cecily's dowry, though,' Mrs. Royle said. 'It would be worth it, to have a countess in the family.'

'I'm not sure he's looking for a wife just yet,' Honoria ventured.

'Nonsense. Every unmarried man is looking for a wife. They just don't always know it.'

Honoria managed a small smile. 'I shall be sure to remember that.'

Mrs. Royle turned and gave Honoria a close look. 'You should,' she finally said, apparently having decided that Honoria was not mocking her.

59

'Ah, here we are. What do you think of these flower arrangements? Are they a bit too heavy on the crocuses?'

'I think they're beautiful,' Honoria said, admiring the lavender ones in particular. 'Besides, it is still so early in the spring. Crocuses are what is in bloom.'

Mrs. Royle let out a heavy sigh. 'I suppose. But I find them rather common myself.'

Honoria smiled dreamily and trailed her fingers across the petals. Something about the crocuses made her feel utterly content. 'I prefer to think of them as pastoral.'

Mrs. Royle cocked her head to the side, considered Honoria's comment, and then must have decided it required no response, because she straightened and said, 'I think I *will* ask Cook to make biscuits.'

'Would it be acceptable if I remained here?' Honoria asked quickly. 'I rather enjoy arranging flowers.'

Mrs. Royle looked at the flowers, which were already expertly arranged, and then back at Honoria.

'Just to fluff them out,' Honoria explained.

Mrs. Royle waved her hand through the air. 'If you wish. But don't forget to change before the gentlemen return. Nothing blue, though. I want Cecily to stand out.'

'I don't believe I even brought a blue dress,' Honoria said diplomatically.

'Well, that will make it easy,' Mrs. Royle said briskly. 'Have fun . . . er . . . fluffing.'

Honoria smiled and waited until her hostess disappeared back into the house. Then she waited a bit more, because there were several maids dashing about, fussing with forks and spoons and the like. Honoria poked at the flowers, gazing this way and that until she saw the flash of something silver over by a rosebush. With a glance to make sure the maids were occupied, she took off across the lawn to investigate.

It was a small spade, apparently forgotten by the gardeners. 'Thank you,' she mouthed. It wasn't a shovel, but it would do. Besides, she hadn't exactly figured out how one might use the words 'shovel' and 'inconspicuous' in the same sentence.

The spade was still going to take some planning. None of her frocks had pockets, and even if they did, she somehow did not think she'd be able to conceal a piece of metal half the size of her forearm. But she could stash it somewhere and pick it up later, when the time was right.

In fact, she decided, that was exactly what she would do.

Chapter Four

What was she *doing*?

Marcus hadn't been trying to keep himself hidden, but when he came across Honoria digging in the dirt, he couldn't help himself. He had to step back and watch.

She was working with a little spade, and whatever type of hole she was digging, it couldn't have been very big, because after barely a minute she stood up, inspected her handiwork first with her eyes, then with her foot, and then—here was where Marcus ducked more carefully behind a tree—

looked about until she found a pile of dead leaves under which she could hide her small shovel.

At that point he almost made his presence known. But then she returned to her hole, stared down on it with furrowed brow, and went back to the pile of leaves to retrieve her spade.

Tiny shovel in hand, she squatted down and made adjustments to her handiwork. She was blocking his view, though, so it wasn't until she went back to the dead leaves to dispose of what was clearly now a piece of evidence that he realized that she had piled up loose dirt in a ring around the hole she'd dug.

She'd dug a mole hole.

He wondered if she realized that most mole holes did not exist in isolation. If there was one, there was usually another, quite visibly nearby. But perhaps this didn't matter. Her intention—judging by the number of times she tested the hole with her foot—was to feign a fall. Or perhaps to cause someone else to trip and fall. Either way, it was doubtful that anyone would be looking for a companion mole hole in the aftermath of a twisted ankle.

He watched for several minutes. One would have thought it a dull enterprise, staring at a lady who was doing nothing but standing over a homemade mole hole, but he found it surprisingly entertaining. Probably because Honoria was working so hard to keep herself from getting bored. First she appeared to be quietly reciting something, except judging by the scrunch of her nose, she couldn't remember how it ended. Then she danced a little jig. Then she waltzed, arms outstretched for her invisible partner.

She was surprisingly graceful, out there in the

62

woods. She waltzed considerably better without music than she ever had with it. In her pale green dress she looked a bit like a sprite. He could almost see her in a dress sewn of leaves, hopping about in the wood.

She had always been a country girl. She'd run wild at Whipple Hill, clambering up trees and rolling down hills. She'd usually tried to tag along with him and Daniel, but even when they refused her company, she'd always found ways to entertain herself, usually out-of-doors. Once, he recalled, she had walked around the house fifty times in one afternoon, just to see if it could be done.

It was a large house, too. She'd been sore the next day. Even Daniel had believed her complaints.

He pictured Fensmore, his own manse. It was monstrously huge. No one in her right mind would walk around it ten times in one day, much less fifty. He thought for a moment—had Honoria ever visited? He couldn't imagine when she would have done; he'd certainly never invited anyone when he was a child. His father had never been known for his hospitality, and the last thing Marcus would have wanted was to invite his friends into his silent mausoleum of a childhood.

After about ten minutes, however, Honoria grew bored. And then Marcus grew bored, because all she was doing was sitting at the base of a tree, her elbows propped on her knees, her chin propped in her hands.

But then he heard someone coming. She heard it, too, because she jumped to her feet, dashed over to her mole hole, and jammed her foot into it. Then, with an awkward squatting motion, she lowered herself to the ground, where she arranged herself into as graceful a position as one might think possible with one's foot in a mole hole.

She waited for a moment, clearly on alert, and then, when whoever it was in the woods was as close as he was likely to get, she let out a rather convincing shriek.

All those family pantomimes had served her well. If Marcus hadn't just seen her orchestrate her own downfall, he would have been convinced she'd injured herself.

He waited to see who would show up.

And he waited.

And waited.

She waited, too, but apparently for too long before letting out her second cry of 'pain.' Because no one showed up to rescue her.

She let out one last cry, but her heart clearly wasn't into it. 'Blast it!' she bit off, yanking her foot out of the hole.

Marcus started to laugh.

She gasped. 'Who's there?'

Damn, he hadn't meant to be so loud. He stepped forward. He didn't want to scare her.

'Marcus?'

He raised a hand in salute. He would have said something, but she was still on the ground, and her slipper was covered with dirt. And her face . . . Oh, he had never seen anything so amusing. She was outraged and mortified and couldn't quite seem to decide which was the stronger emotion.

'Stop laughing!'

'Sorry,' he said, not sorry at all.

Her brows came together in a hilariously ferocious scowl. 'What are you doing here?'

'I live here.' He stepped forward and offered her

64

his hand. It seemed the gentlemanly thing to do.

Her eyes narrowed. She didn't believe him for one second, that much was clear.

'Well, I live close by,' he amended. 'This path ambles back and forth across the property line.'

She took his hand and allowed him to help her up, brushing the dirt from her skirts as she rose. But the ground had been damp, and bits of earth clung to the fabric, eliciting grumbles and sighs from Honoria. Finally, she gave up, then looked up, asking, 'How long have you been here?'

He grinned. 'Longer than you'd wish.'

She let out an exhausted groan, then said, 'I don't suppose you'd keep this to yourself.'

'I shan't breathe a word,' he promised, 'but who, exactly, were you attempting to attract?'

She scoffed at that. 'Oh, please. You are the last person I would tell.'

He quirked a brow. 'Really. The last.'

She gave him an impatient look.

'Past the queen, past the prime minister . . .'

'Stop.' But she was hiding a smile as she said it. And then she deflated again. 'Do you mind if I sit back down?'

'Not at all.'

'My dress is already filthy,' she said, finding a spot at the base of the tree. 'A few more minutes in the dirt won't make a difference.' She sat and looked up at him with a wry expression. 'This is where you are supposed to tell me I look as fresh as a daisy.'

'It depends on the daisy, I think.'

At that, she gave him a look of the utmost disbelief, the expression so familiar it was almost comical. How many years had she now been rolling her eyes at him? Fourteen? Fifteen? It hadn't really occurred to him until this moment, but she was almost certainly the only woman of his acquaintance who spoke frankly with him, healthy doses of sarcasm included.

This was why he hated going down to London for the season. The women simpered and preened and told him what they thought he wanted to hear.

The men, too.

The irony was, they were almost always wrong. He'd never wanted to be surrounded by sycophants. He hated having his every word hung upon. He didn't want his perfectly ordinary, identical-to-everyone-else's waistcoat being complimented upon for its remarkable cut and fit.

With Daniel gone, there was no one left who truly knew him. No family unless one was willing to go back four generations to find a common ancestor. He was the only child of an only child. The Holroyds were not known for their procreative prowess.

He leaned against a nearby tree and watched Honoria, looking all tired and miserable on the ground. 'The party was not the success you envisioned, then?'

She glanced up, her eyes questioning.

'You made it sound so appealing in your letter,' he remarked.

'Well, I knew *you* would hate it.'

'I might have found it amusing,' he said, even though they both knew that wasn't true.

She gave him another one of those looks. 'It would have been four unmarried young ladies, four young gentlemen from the university, Mr. and Mrs. Royle, and you.' And while she waited for that to sink in she added, 'And possibly a dog.'

He gave her a dry smile. 'I like dogs.'

That earned him a chuckle. She picked up a twig that lay near her hip and began to draw circles in the dirt. She looked utterly forlorn, bits of her hair falling poker-straight from its chignon. Her eyes looked tired, too. Tired and . . . something else. Something he didn't like.

She looked defeated.

That was just wrong. Honoria Smythe-Smith should never look like that.

'Honoria,' he began.

But she looked up sharply at the sound of his voice. 'I'm twenty-one, Marcus.'

He paused, trying to calculate. 'That can't be possible.'

Her lips pressed together peevishly. 'I assure you, it is. There were a few gentlemen last year I thought might be interested, but none came up to scratch.' She shrugged. 'I don't know why.'

Marcus cleared his throat, then found he needed to adjust his cravat.

'I suppose it was all for the best,' she went on. 'I didn't adore any of them. And one of them was— well, I once saw him kick a dog.' She frowned. 'So I couldn't possibly consider—well, you know.'

He nodded.

She straightened and smiled, looking quite resolutely cheerful. Perhaps too resolutely cheerful. 'But this year I am determined to do better.'

'I am sure you will,' he said.

She looked up at him suspiciously.

'What did I say?'

'Nothing. But you needn't be so condescending.'

What the devil was she talking about? 'I wasn't.'

67

'Oh, please, Marcus. You are *always* condescending.'

'Explain yourself,' he said sharply.

She looked at him as if she couldn't believe he didn't see it. 'Oh, you know what I mean.'

'No, I *don't* know what you mean.'

She let out a snort as she clambered to her feet again. 'You are always looking at people like this.' And then she made a face, one he couldn't possibly begin to describe.

'If I ever look like *that*,' he said dryly, '*precisely* like that, to be more precise, I give you leave to shoot me.'

'There,' she said triumphantly. 'Like that.'

He began to wonder if they were speaking the same language. 'Like what?'

'*That!* What you just said.'

He crossed his arms. It seemed the only acceptable reply. If she couldn't speak in complete sentences, he saw no reason why he had to speak at all.

'You spent all of last season glowering at me. Every time I saw you, you looked so disapproving.'

'I assure you that was not my intention.' At least not about *her*. He disapproved of the men who courted her favor, but never Honoria.

She folded her arms and stared at him with a cross expression. He had the distinct impression she was trying to decide whether to take his words as an apology. Never mind that they hadn't actually *been* an apology.

'Is there anything with which I may help you?' he asked, choosing his words—and his tone—with great care.

'No,' she said succinctly. And then: 'Thank you.'

68

He sighed wearily, thinking it might be time to change his approach. 'Honoria, you have no father, your brother is somewhere in Italy—we think—and your mother wants to retire to Bath.'

'What is your point?' she bit off.

'You are alone in this world,' he replied, almost as snappishly. He couldn't recall the last time anyone had spoken to him in such a tone. 'Or you might as well be.'

'I have sisters,' she protested.

'Has any of them offered to take you in?'

'Of course not. They know I live with Mother.'

'Who wants to retire to Bath,' he reminded her.

'I am not alone,' she said hotly, and he was horrified to hear a choke in her voice. But if she was near to tears, she pushed them back, because she was all anger and indignation when she said, 'I have scads of cousins. Scads. And four sisters who would take me into their homes in a heartbeat if they thought it was necessary.'

'Honoria . . .'

'And I have a brother, too, even if we don't know where he is. I don't need—' She broke off, and she blinked, as if surprised by the words on her tongue.

But she said it anyway. 'I don't need you.'

There was a horrible silence. Marcus did not think about all the times he'd sat at her supper table. Or the family pantomimes in which he'd always played a tree. They'd been dreadful, every last one of them, but he'd loved every branchy, leafy moment. He'd never wanted the lead roles— he was thrilled never to have to speak at all—but he'd loved taking part. He'd loved being there. With them. As a family.

But he didn't think about any of this. He was

69

quite sure he wasn't thinking about any of this as he stood there staring at the girl who was telling him she didn't need him.

And maybe she didn't.

And maybe she was no longer a girl, either.

Bloody hell.

He let out a pent-up breath and reminded himself that it didn't matter what she thought she felt about him. Daniel had asked him to watch over her, and watch over her he would.

'You need . . .' He sighed, trying to think of some way to say it that wouldn't make her irate. There was none, he concluded, so he just said it. 'You need help.'

She drew back. 'Are you offering yourself as my guardian?'

'No,' he said vehemently. 'No. Believe me, that's the last thing I'd want.'

She crossed her arms. 'Because I'm such a trial.'

'*No.*' Good God, how had the conversation deteriorated so quickly? 'I am merely trying to help.'

'I don't need another brother,' she said sharply.

'I don't want to *be* your brother,' he shot back. And then he saw her again, rather, saw her *differently* again. Maybe it was her eyes, or her skin, high with color. Or the way she was breathing. Or the curve of her cheek. Or the little spot where her—

'You have dirt on your cheek,' he said, handing her his handkerchief. She didn't, but he needed something with which to change the subject.

Now.

She dabbed at her face with the handkerchief, then looked down at the still snowy-white cloth,

70

frowned, and dabbed again.

'It's gone,' he said.

She returned his handkerchief, then just stood there, giving him a sullen, stony stare. She looked twelve again, or at least was wearing the expression of a twelve-year-old, which was just fine with him.

'Honoria,' he said carefully, 'as Daniel's friend—'

'Don't.' Nothing more. Just *don't*.

He took a breath, using the time to choose his words. 'Why is it so difficult to accept assistance?'

'Do you?' she countered.

He stared at her.

'Do *you* like to accept assistance?' she clarified.

'It depends upon who is offering it.'

'Me.' She crossed her arms, looking somewhat satisfied with her reply, although for the life of him, he had no idea why. 'Just imagine it. Imagine the tables were turned.'

'Assuming it was a topic about which you had some expertise, then yes, I would be happy to accept assistance from you.' He crossed his arms, too, rather pleased with himself. It was a perfect sentence, placating and agreeable, and saying nothing at all.

He waited for her reply, but after a few moments she just gave her head a little shake and said, 'I have to get back.'

'They'll be missing you?'

'They should have already been missing me,' she muttered.

'The twisted ankle,' he murmured. With a sympathetic nod.

She returned that with a scowl and marched off. In the wrong direction.

'Honoria!'

71

She turned around.

He took great care not to smile as he pointed her in the correct direction. 'Bricstan is that way.'

Her jaw tensed, but she just said, 'Thank you,' and turned about. But she spun too fast and lost her footing. She let out a shriek as she tried to regain her balance, and Marcus did what any gentleman would instinctively do. He rushed forward to steady her.

Except he stepped in that damned mole hole.

The next cry of surprise was his, and somewhat profane, he was ashamed to admit. They both went down when he lost his balance, and they landed on the damp earth with a thud, Honoria on her back, and Marcus right on top of her.

He immediately rose to his elbows, trying to take some of his weight off her as he looked down. He told himself it was to see if she was all right. He was going to ask her this once he caught his breath. But when he looked at her, she was trying to catch her own breath. Her lips were parted, and her eyes were dazed, and he did what any man would instinctively do. He lowered his head to kiss her.

Chapter Five

One moment Honoria was upright—oh, very well, she hadn't been upright, not completely. She'd wanted so desperately just to get away from Marcus that she'd turned too quickly, slid on the damp earth and lost her balance.

But she'd almost been upright, and in fact *would* have been upright in mere moments if Marcus hadn't come (quite literally) hurtling through the air at her.

This would have been disorienting enough, except that his shoulder caught her directly in her midsection. Her breath flew from her lungs, and they both tumbled to the ground, Marcus landing squarely on top of her.

That was when Honoria quite possibly stopped thinking altogether.

She'd never felt a male body against hers—dear heavens, when would she have done? She'd waltzed, occasionally more closely than was proper, but that had been nothing like this. The weight of him, the heat. It felt oddly primitive, and even stranger, there was something almost pleasant about it.

She moved her lips to speak, but as she lay there, staring up at him, she couldn't seem to find words. He looked different to her. She'd known this man for nearly as long as she could remember—how was it possible that she had never quite noticed the shape of his mouth? Or his eyes. She'd known they were brown, but it was astounding how richly colored they were, with flecks of amber near the edges of the iris. And even now, they seemed to change as he moved closer . . .

Closer?

Oh, dear God. Was he going to *kiss* her? Marcus?

Her breath caught. And her lips parted. And something within her clenched with anticipation, and all she could think was—

Nothing. Or at least that was all she should be thinking about, because Marcus was most definitely not planning to kiss her. He bit off a string of curses the likes of which she had not heard since Daniel had left the country, and then he wrenched himself up and off her, taking a step back, and then—

'Bloody hell!'

There was a frenetic flurry of movement, followed by a thud and a grunt, and another string of blasphemy that Honoria was far too sensible to take offense at. With a horrified gasp, she pushed herself up on her elbows. Marcus was back on the ground, and from the expression on his face, this time he'd actually been hurt.

'Are you all right?' she asked frantically, even though it was clear he was not.

'It was the hole,' he bit off, gritting his teeth against the pain. And then, as if it might possibly require clarification, he added, 'Again.'

'I'm sorry,' she said quickly, scrambling to her feet. And then, because the situation clearly called for a more substantial apology, she said it again. 'I'm very, very sorry.'

He did not speak.

'You must know it wasn't my intention to . . .' She didn't finish. A stream of babble wasn't going to help her cause, and indeed, he appeared very much *not* to want to hear her voice.

She swallowed nervously, taking the tiniest step in his direction. He was still on the ground, not quite on his back and not quite on his side. There was mud on his boots and on his breeches. And on his coat.

Honoria winced. He wasn't going to like that. Marcus had never been overly fastidious, but it was a very nice coat.

'Marcus?' she asked hesitantly.

He scowled. Not specifically at her, but still, it

74

was enough to confirm her decision not to tell him about the dead leaves in his hair.

He rolled slightly to one side until he was more squarely on his back, then he closed his eyes.

Her lips parted, and she almost spoke, but then she waited. He took a breath, then another, then a third, and when he opened his eyes, his expression had changed. He was calmer now.

Thank God.

Honoria leaned a little forward. She still thought it prudent to tread carefully around him, but she did think he might have calmed enough for her to venture, 'May I help you up?'

'In a moment,' he grunted. He scooted himself into an almost-sitting position, then grabbed his calf with his hands, lifting his injured leg up and out of the mole hole.

Which, Honoria noticed, was significantly bigger now that he'd stepped in it twice.

She watched as he gingerly rotated his ankle. He flexed his foot forward and back, then side to side. It was the latter that seemed to cause him the most pain.

'Do you think it's broken?' she asked.

'No.'

'Twisted?'

He grunted his assent.

'Do you—'

He speared her with such a ferocious glare that she shut her mouth immediately. But after about fifteen seconds of wincing at his pain, she couldn't help herself. 'Marcus?'

He hadn't been facing her when she said his name, and he didn't turn around when he heard it. He did, however, stop moving.

75

'Do you think you should take off your boot?'

He didn't reply.

'In case your ankle is swollen.'

'I *know*'—he stopped, let out a breath, then continued in a slightly more controlled tone of voice— 'why to do it. I was just thinking.'

She nodded even though he still had his back to her. 'Of course. Just let me know, ehrm . . .'

He stopped moving again.

She actually took a step back. 'Never mind.'

He reached forward to touch his injured ankle through his boot, presumably to test the swelling. Honoria scooted around so that she could see his face. She tried to discern the extent of his pain by his expression, but it was difficult. He looked so at the edge of his temper that one really couldn't tell much beyond that.

Men were so ridiculous that way. She realized that it was her fault that he'd twisted his ankle, and she understood that he was going to be at least a little bit irritated with her, but still, it was obvious he was going to need her help. He didn't look able to come to his feet on his own, much less walk all the way back to Fensmore. If he were thinking sensibly, he would realize this and allow her to come to his aid sooner rather than later. But no, he needed to snap about like a wounded tiger, as if that might make him feel he was in charge of the situation.

'Ehrm . . .' She cleared her throat. 'Just so I'm sure I'm doing the right thing . . . Can I help you in any way, or would it just be best for me not to make a sound?'

There was an agonizingly long pause, and then he said, 'Will you please help me remove my boot?'

'Of course!' She rushed over. 'Here, let me, er . . .' She'd done this long ago, when she was a little girl aiding her father, but not since, and certainly not with a man who had just been lying on top of her two minutes earlier.

She felt her face burn. Where on earth had that thought just come from? It had been an *accident*. And this was Marcus. She needed to remember this. Marcus. This was only Marcus.

She sat opposite him, on the far end of his outstretched leg, and grasped the boot with one hand at the back of the ankle and the other on the sole. 'Are you ready?'

He nodded grimly.

She pulled with the ankle hand and pushed with the other, but Marcus let out such a cry of pain that she dropped his foot immediately.

'Are you all right?' She almost did not recognize her own voice. She sounded terrified.

'Just try again,' he said gruffly.

'Are you certain? Because—'

'Just do it,' he ground out.

'Very well.' She took up his foot again, grit her teeth, and pulled. Hard. Marcus did not cry out this time, but he was making an awful noise, the sort an animal made before it was put down. Finally, when it was more than Honoria could bear, she let up. 'I don't think this is working.' She looked back at him. 'And by that I mean I will *never* get it off.'

'Try again,' he said. 'These boots are always difficult to remove.'

'Like this?' she asked, in complete disbelief. And people said that ladies' garments were impractical.

'*Honoria.*'

'All right.' She tried again, with the same results.

77

'I'm sorry, but I think you're going to have to cut it off when you get home.'

A flicker of pain crossed his face.

'It's only a boot,' she murmured sympathetically.

'It's not that,' he snapped. 'It hurts like the devil.'

'Oh.' She cleared her throat. 'Sorry.'

He let out a long, shaky exhale. 'You're going to have to help me to my feet.'

She nodded and rose to her own. 'Here, let me take your hand.' She took his hand in hers and yanked up, but he couldn't get his balance right. After a moment he let go.

Honoria looked down at her hand. It looked empty. And felt cold.

'You're going to have to grab me under my arms,' he said.

This might have shocked her before, but after trying to take off his boot for him, she couldn't see how this could possibly be any more improper.

She nodded again and bent down, sliding her arms around him. 'Here we are,' she said, letting out a little grunt of exertion as she tried to get him up to his feet. It was strange to be holding him, and terribly awkward. Ironic, too. If it hadn't been for his stepping in the mole hole and crashing into her, this would have been the closest she had ever been to him.

Of course, if he hadn't stepped in the mole hole *again,* they wouldn't be in this position.

With a bit of maneuvering and one more half--uttered curse on Marcus's part, they got him onto his feet. Honoria stepped back, putting a more proper distance between them, although she did put his hand on her shoulder to steady him. 'Can you put any weight on it?' she asked.

'I don't know,' he said, testing it out. He made a complete step, but his face twisted with pain as he did it.

'Marcus?' she asked hesitantly.

'I'll be fine.'

He looked awful to her. 'Are you sure?' she asked, 'because I really think—'

'I said I'm fi—ow!' He stumbled, clutching onto her shoulder to prevent himself from going down.

Honoria waited patiently while he collected himself, offering her other hand for extra balance. He took it in his firm grasp, and once again she was struck by what a nice hand it was, large and warm. And safe, too, although she wasn't sure that made any sense.

'I might need help,' he said, clearly loath to admit it.

'Of course. I'll just . . . ah . . .' She moved toward him, then a bit away, then readjusted.

'Stand next to me,' he said. 'I'm going to have to lean on you.'

She nodded and let him drape his arm over her shoulder. It felt heavy. And nice. 'Here we are,' she said, sliding her arm around his waist. 'Now which way is it to Fensmore?'

He motioned with his head. 'Over there.'

She turned them so they were facing the right direction, then said, 'Actually, I think the more pertinent question might be, how *far* is it to Fensmore?'

'Three miles.'

'*Thr*—' She caught herself, bringing her volume down from a shriek to something almost normal. 'I'm sorry, did you say three miles?'

'Approximately.'

79

Was he insane? 'Marcus, there is no way I can prop you up for three miles. We're going to have to go to the Royles'.'

'Oh no,' he said, deadly serious. 'I am not showing up on their doorstep in this condition.'

Privately, Honoria agreed with him. An injured, unmarried earl, completely dependent on her mercy? Mrs. Royle would see it as a gift from heaven. He'd probably find himself ushered to a sickroom before he could protest. With Cecily Royle as his nurse.

'You won't have to help me the whole way, anyway,' he said. 'It will improve as I walk on it.'

She looked at him. 'That makes no sense.'

'Just help me home, will you?' He sounded exhausted. Maybe exasperated. Probably both.

'I'll try,' she agreed, but only because she knew it would not work. She gave it five minutes at most before he admitted defeat.

They hobbled a few yards, then Marcus said, 'A mole hole would have been much smaller.'

'I know. But I needed to be able to fit my foot in it.'

He took another step, then half-hopped the next one. 'What did you think was going to happen?'

She let out a sigh. She'd long since passed the point of embarrassment. There seemed no point in pretending she had any remaining pride. 'I don't know,' she said wearily. 'I suppose I thought my prince charming was going to come and save me. Perhaps help me home in precisely the manner I'm helping you.'

He glanced over at her. 'And Prince Charming is . . .'

She looked at him as if he'd gone mad. Surely he

80

didn't think she was going to give him a name.

'Honoria . . . ,' he prodded.

'It's none of your business.'

He actually chuckled. 'What do you think I will do with the information?'

'I just don't want—'

'You crippled me, Honoria.'

It was a low blow, but an effective one.

'Oh, very well,' she said, giving up the fight. 'If you must know, it was Gregory Bridgerton.'

Marcus stopped walking and looked at her with a touch of surprise. 'Greg—'

'The youngest one,' she interrupted. 'The youngest son, I mean. The one who is unmarried.'

'I know who he is.'

'Very well, then. What is wrong with him?' At that she cocked her head to the side and waited expectantly.

He thought for a moment. 'Nothing.'

'You—wait.' She blinked. 'Nothing?'

He shook his head, then shifted his weight a little; his good foot was beginning to fall asleep. 'Nothing comes immediately to mind.' It was true. She could do a good deal worse than Gregory Bridgerton.

'Really?' she asked suspiciously. 'You find nothing at all objectionable about him.'

Marcus pretended to think about this a bit longer. Clearly he was supposed to be playing a role here, probably that of the villain. Or if not that, then the grumpy old man. 'I suppose he's a bit young,' he said. He motioned to a fallen tree about five yards away. 'Help me over there, would you? I need to sit down.'

Together they hobbled over to the long, thick

log. Carefully, Honoria unwrapped his arm from her shoulder and eased him down. 'He's not so young,' she said.

Marcus looked down at his foot. It looked so normal inside the boot, and yet it felt like someone had wrapped manacles around it. And then shoved the whole thing in the boot. 'He's still at university,' he said.

'He's older than I am.'

He looked back up at her. 'Has he kicked any dogs lately?'

'Not that I know of.'

'Well, there.' He gestured with his free hand in an uncharacteristically expansive motion. 'You have my blessing.'

Her eyes narrowed. 'Why do I need your blessing?'

Good Lord, she was difficult. 'You don't. But would it be so very painful to receive it, anyway?'

'No,' she said slowly, 'but . . .'

He waited. And then finally, 'But what?'

'I don't know.' She bit off each word with remarkable enunciation, her eyes never leaving his.

He stifled a laugh. 'Why are you so suspicious of my motives?'

'Oh, I don't know,' she replied, all sarcasm. 'Perhaps because you spent all of last season glowering at me.'

'I did not.'

She snorted. 'Oh, you did.'

'I might have glowered at one or two of your suitors'—damn it, he hadn't meant to say that— 'but not at you.'

'Then you *were* spying on me,' she said triumphantly.

'Of course not,' he lied. 'But I couldn't very well *miss* you.'

She gasped in horror. 'What does that mean?'

Bloody hell, he was in for it now. 'It doesn't mean a thing. You were in London. I was in London.' When she didn't respond, he added, 'I saw every other lady, too.' And then, before he realized it was the worst thing he could have said, he added, 'You're just the only one I remember.'

She went utterly still, staring at him with that haunting, owlish expression of hers. He hated when she did that. It meant that she was thinking too hard, or seeing too much, and he felt exposed. Even when she was a child, she'd seemed to see him more deeply than the rest of the family. It hadn't made sense; most of the time she was happy, jolly Honoria, but then she'd look at him that way, with those amazing lavender eyes of hers, and he'd realize what her family never did, that she understood people.

She understood him.

He shook his head, trying to shake away the memories. He didn't want to think about her family, about how he'd felt sitting at their table, being a part of their world. And he didn't want to think about her, either. He didn't want to look at her face and think that her eyes were the exact color of the grape hyacinths that had just begun to pop up all over the landscape. They came each year at this time, and he always thought—just for a moment before he pushed it away—that they were *her* flower. But not the petals; they were too dark. Honoria's eyes matched the younger part at the base of the flower, where the color hadn't quite turned blue.

His chest had grown tight; he tried to breathe. He really didn't want to think about the fact that he knew that, that he could look at a flower and pinpoint the exact spot on the petal that matched her eyes.

He wished she'd say something, but of course she didn't. Not now, not when he would have actually welcomed her babble.

And then finally, softly, she said, 'I could introduce you.'

'What?' He had no idea what she was talking about.

'I could introduce you,' she said again, 'to some of the young ladies. The ones you said you didn't know.'

Oh, for God's sake, was *that* what she thought the problem was? He'd met every lady in London; he just didn't *know* any of them.

'I would be happy to do it,' she said kindly.

Kindly?

Pityingly?

'Unnecessary,' he said in a brusque voice.

'No, of course, you've been introduced—'

'I just don't like—'

'You find us silly—'

'They talk about nothing—'

'Even I would grow bored—'

'The truth is,' he announced, eager to be done with this conversation, 'I hate London.'

His voice came out much louder than he'd intended, and he felt like a fool. A fool who was probably going to have to take a knife to his second-best pair of boots. 'This isn't going to work,' he said.

She looked confused.

'We'll never make it back to Fensmore like this.' He could see her struggling to contain an *I-told-you-so* and decided to save them both the indignity by saying, 'You'll need to go back to Bricstan. It's closer, and you know the way.' Then he remembered who he was talking to. 'You do know the way, don't you?'

To her credit, she did not take offense. 'I just need to stay on the path until I get to the small pond. Then it's up the hill, and I'm almost there.'

He nodded. 'You'll have to send someone to get me. Not from Bricstan. Send instructions over to Fensmore. To Jimmy.'

'Jimmy?'

'My head groom. Just tell him I'm on the Bricstan path, about three miles from home. He'll know what to do.'

'You'll be all right here on your own?'

'As long as it doesn't rain,' he quipped. They both looked up. A thick blanket of gray stretched ominously across the sky. 'Damn,' he said.

'I'll run,' she said.

'Don't.' She was liable to step in a real mole hole, and then where would they be? 'We don't need you tripping and falling as well.'

She turned to leave, then stopped and said, 'You'll send word when you're safely at home?'

'Of course.' He couldn't remember the last time he'd had to send word about his well-being to anyone. There was something rather disconcerting about it. But nice, too.

He watched her go, listening until the sounds of her footsteps disappeared. How long would it take before help arrived? She needed to get back to Bricstan, which was a bit more than a mile,

85

assuming she did not lose her way. Then she had to write a letter and send someone off to deliver it to Fensmore. Then Jimmy had to saddle two horses and make his way through the woods on a path that was much better suited for walking.

An hour? No, ninety minutes. Probably longer.

He slid to the ground so that he could lean against the fallen log. Lord, he was tired. His ankle hurt far too much for him to sleep, but he closed his eyes, anyway.

That was when he felt the first raindrop.

Chapter Six

By the time Honoria reached Bricstan, she was drenched to the bone. The rain had started barely five minutes after she left Marcus at the fallen tree. It had been light at first—just a few fat drops here and there. Enough to annoy, not enough to do damage.

But as soon as she'd reached the end of the path it had started coming down in a fury. She'd raced across the lawn as quickly as she was able, but it had made no difference. Ten seconds in the downpour and she was soaked through.

She didn't even want to think about Marcus, stranded in the woods for at least another hour. She tried to recall the topography where she'd left him. Would the trees shelter him from the rain? It was still spring, and the branches were not yet thick with leaves.

She first tried to enter Bricstan through a side door, but it was locked and she had to skirt the building to the front. The door opened before she could even knock, and she tumbled in.

'Honoria!' Sarah exclaimed, rushing forward to steady her. 'I was watching for you through the window. Where have you been? I have been frantic. We were just about to send out a party to search for you. You said you were going off to collect flowers, but then you never returned.'

Honoria tried to interrupt between each of Sarah's sentences, but she only managed to catch enough of her breath to say, 'Stop.' She looked down; pools of water had formed at her feet. One rivulet had broken free of the circle and was slowly rolling toward the wall.

'We need to dry you off,' Sarah said. She took Honoria's hands. 'You're freezing.'

'Sarah, stop.' Honoria pulled Sarah's hands free and grabbed hold of her cousin's shoulder. 'Please. I need some paper. I must write a letter.'

Sarah looked at her as if she'd gone mad.

'*Now*. I have to—'

'Lady Honoria!' Mrs. Royle hurried into the hall. 'You had us all so worried! Where on earth did you go off to?'

'I was just looking for flowers,' Honoria lied, 'but please, I need to write a letter.'

Mrs. Royle felt her forehead. 'You don't feel feverish.'

'She's shivering,' Sarah said. She looked at Mrs. Royle. 'She must have got lost. She's terrible that way.'

'Yes, yes,' Honoria said, willing to agree with any insult if it would only mean the end of this conversation. 'But please, just listen to me for a moment. I must act quickly. Lord Chatteris is stranded in the woods, and I told him I would—'

'What?' Mrs. Royle screeched. 'What are you talking about?'

Briefly, Honoria related the story she'd concocted while hurrying home. She'd wandered off from the group and lost her way. Lord Chatteris had been walking in the woods. He had told her that the path went back and forth between the two properties. Then he'd twisted his ankle.

It was mostly true.

'We will bring him back here,' Mrs. Royle said. 'I will send someone at once.'

'No,' Honoria said, still a bit out of breath. 'He wants to go home. He asked me to send word to the head of his stables. He told me exactly what to say.'

'No,' Mrs. Royle said firmly. 'I think he should come here.'

'Mrs. Royle, *please*. Every moment we're arguing, he is stranded out there in the rain.'

Mrs. Royle was clearly conflicted, but finally she gave a nod and said, 'Follow me.' There was a writing desk in an alcove down the hall. She took out paper, pen, and ink and stepped aside so that Honoria could sit down. But Honoria's fingers were numb; she could barely grip the pen. And her hair would surely drip all over the paper.

Sarah stepped forward. 'Would you like me to do it for you?'

Honoria nodded gratefully and told Sarah exactly what to write, all the while trying to ignore Mrs. Royle, who was hovering behind her, interrupting every so often with what she thought were helpful comments.

Sarah finished the letter, signed Honoria's name, and then, at Honoria's nod, handed it to Mrs.

Royle.

'Please send it with your swiftest rider,' Honoria begged.

Mrs. Royle took it and hurried off. Sarah immediately stood and took her cousin by the hand. 'You need to get warm,' she said in a voice that brooked no protest. 'You're coming with me right now. I already told a maid to heat water for a bath.'

Honoria nodded. She had done what she needed to do. Now she could finally collapse.

*　　　*　　　*

The following morning dawned mockingly clear. Honoria had slept for twelve hours straight, bundled under quilts, with a hot brick at her feet. Sarah had crept into her room at some point to tell her that they'd received word from Fensmore; Marcus had arrived safely at home and was probably in his own bed, with his own hot brick at his feet.

But as Honoria got dressed, she was still worried. She had been utterly frozen by the time she'd reached Bricstan, and he had been out in the rain for far longer than she had. It had been windy, too; she'd heard the trees rustling and creaking through her window when she'd been taking her bath. Marcus would almost certainly have caught a chill. And what if his ankle was not merely twisted but broken? Would they have sent for a surgeon already to set it? Would they have known to do so?

And who were 'they,' anyway? Marcus had no family that she knew of. Who would care for him if he took ill? Was there anyone at Fensmore besides the servants?

She was going to have to check on his welfare. She wouldn't be able to live with herself otherwise.

Down at breakfast, the other guests were surprised to see her. The gentlemen had all returned to Cambridge, but the young ladies were gathered around the table, eating their coddled eggs and toast.

'Honoria!' Sarah exclaimed. 'What on earth are you doing out of bed?'

'I'm perfectly well,' Honoria assured her. 'I haven't even a sniffle.'

'Her fingers were like icicles last night,' Sarah said to Cecily and Iris. 'She could not even grip a pen.'

'It was nothing that a hot bath and a good night's sleep could not cure,' Honoria said. 'But I would like to travel to Fensmore this morning. It was my fault that Lord Chatteris twisted his ankle, and I really do feel I must check on him.'

'How was it your fault?' Iris asked.

Honoria nearly bit her lip. She'd forgotten that that was one of the missing elements of her tale. 'It was nothing, really,' she improvised. 'I tripped over a tree root and he stepped forward to steady me. He must have stepped in a mole hole.'

'Oh, I hate moles,' Iris said.

'I find them rather sweet,' Cecily put in.

'I must find your mother,' Honoria said. 'I need to arrange for a carriage. Or I suppose I could ride over. It's not raining any longer.'

'You should eat breakfast first,' Sarah said.

'She'll never let you go alone,' Cecily replied. 'Fensmore is a bachelor household.'

'He's hardly by himself,' Iris said. 'He must have loads of servants.'

'At least a hundred, I should think,' Cecily said. 'Have you seen the house? It's enormous. But that doesn't signify.' She turned back to Honoria. 'He still lives alone. There is no one to act as a proper chaperone.'

'I'll take someone with me,' Honoria said impatiently. 'I really don't care. I just want to get going.'

'Take someone with you where?' Mrs. Royle asked, entering the breakfast room.

Honoria repeated her request to Mrs. Royle, who immediately agreed. 'Absolutely, we must see to the earl's welfare. It would be positively unchristian of us if we did not.'

Honoria blinked. She had not expected this to be so easy.

'I will go with you,' Mrs. Royle said.

A teacup slammed down against its saucer. When Honoria looked over at the table, Cecily wore a tight smile, but her fingers were practically biting through her teacup.

'Mother,' Cecily said, 'if you go, then I should, too.'

Mrs. Royle paused to consider this, but before she could reply, Sarah said, 'If Cecily goes, I should go, too.'

'Why?' Cecily asked.

'I am fairly certain,' Iris said dryly, 'that under no circumstances should I go.'

'I really don't care who accompanies me,' Honoria said, trying not to sound as snappish as she felt. 'I would just like to depart as soon as possible.'

'Cecily will go with you,' Mrs. Royle announced. 'I will stay here with Iris and Sarah.'

Sarah was visibly put out at this turn of events,

but she did not argue. Cecily, on the other hand, jumped to her feet with a wide smile on her face.

'Cecily, do go upstairs and have Peggy redress your hair,' Mrs. Royle said. 'We can't have—'

'Please,' Honoria interrupted. 'I would really rather leave immediately.'

Mrs. Royle looked conflicted, but even she could not bring herself to argue that her daughter's coiffure was more important than the welfare of the Earl of Chatteris. 'Very well,' she said briskly. 'Off with the two of you, then. But I want to be clear. If he is terribly ill, you must insist upon moving him here to recuperate.'

Honoria was quite sure that was not going to happen, but she didn't say anything as she strode toward the front door, Cecily and Mrs. Royle right at her heels.

'And make sure he knows that we do not plan to return to Cambridge for several weeks,' Mrs. Royle continued.

'We don't?' Cecily asked.

'No, and as you are completely free of obligations, you may go over each day to oversee his care.' Mrs. Royle paused. 'Er, if that is what Lord Chatteris wishes.'

'Of course, Mother,' Cecily said, but she looked embarrassed.

'And do give him my regards,' Mrs. Royle continued.

Honoria hurried down the steps to wait for the carriage to be brought around.

'And tell him that Mr. Royle and I pray for his speedy recovery.'

'He might not be sick, Mother,' Cecily said.

Mrs. Royle scowled at her. 'But if he is . . .'

92

'I shall relate your good wishes,' Cecily finished for her.

'Here comes the carriage,' Honoria said, nearly desperate to escape.

'Remember!' Mrs. Royle called out as Honoria and Cecily were helped up by a footman. 'If he's sick, bring him—'

But they were already rolling away.

*   *   *

Marcus was still in bed when his butler quietly entered his room and informed him that Lady Honoria Smythe-Smith and Miss Royle had arrived and were waiting in the yellow drawing room.

'Shall I tell them you are not available to receive guests?' the butler inquired.

For a moment Marcus was tempted to say yes. He felt awful, and he was sure he looked worse. By the time Jimmy had found him the previous evening, he had been shivering so hard he was amazed he hadn't knocked out his own teeth. Then when he got home they had to cut the boot from him. Which would have been bad enough—he rather liked those boots—but his valet had been a bit more aggressive than necessary, and Marcus now sported a four-inch gash on his left leg.

But if their situations had been reversed, he would have insisted upon ascertaining Honoria's welfare with his own eyes, so it seemed that he would have to allow her to do the same with him. As for the other girl—Miss Royle, he thought the butler had said—he just hoped she was not a female of delicate sensibilities.

Because the last time he'd looked in the mirror,

93

he could have sworn his skin had been green.

With help from his valet—both in dressing and making it downstairs to the drawing room—Marcus thought he looked moderately presentable when he greeted the two ladies.

'Good God, Marcus,' Honoria exclaimed as she came to her feet. 'You look like death.'

Apparently, he was wrong. 'Lovely to see you, too, Honoria.' He motioned to a nearby sofa. 'Do you mind if I sit?'

'No, please, go ahead. Your eyes are terribly sunken in.' She grimaced as she watched him attempt to maneuver his way around a table. 'Shall I help you?'

'No, no, I'm quite all right.' He hopped twice to get to the edge of the cushions and then practically fell backward onto the sofa. Dignity, it seemed, had no place in a sickroom.

'Miss Royle,' he said, giving a nod to the other lady. He'd met her once or twice over the years, he was fairly certain.

'Lord Chatteris,' she said politely. 'My parents send their regards and wish you a speedy recovery.'

'Thank you,' he said, giving her a weak nod. He felt overpoweringly tired all of a sudden. The trip from his bedroom downstairs must have been more difficult than he'd anticipated. He hadn't slept well the night before, either. He'd started coughing the moment his head had touched his pillow, and he hadn't stopped since.

'Excuse me,' he said to the two ladies as he placed a cushion on the table in front of him, then propped his foot on it. 'I'm told I'm meant to elevate it.'

'Marcus,' Honoria said, immediately dispensing

with any pretense of polite conversation, 'you should not be out of bed.'

'It's where I was,' he said dryly, 'until I was informed that I had visitors.'

This earned him a look of such reproach that it brought to mind Miss Pimm, his nurse from oh-so-many years ago. 'You should have told your butler you were not receiving,' she said.

'Really?' he murmured. 'I'm sure you would have accepted that meekly and gone home assured of my welfare.' He looked over at the other lady with an ironic tilt to his head. 'What do you think, Miss Royle? Would Lady Honoria have left without comment?'

'No, my lord,' Miss Royle said, her lips twitching with amusement. 'She was most firm in her wish to see you for herself.'

'Cecily!' Honoria said indignantly. Marcus decided to ignore her.

'Is that so, Miss Royle?' he said, twisting even more in her direction. 'My heart warms at her concern.'

'Marcus,' Honoria said, 'stop this right now.'

'She is a dogged little thing,' he said.

'Marcus Holroyd,' Honoria said sternly, 'if you do not stop poking fun at me this instant, I shall inform Mrs. Royle that indeed you do wish to be moved to Bricstan for the remainder of your convalescence.'

Marcus froze, trying not to laugh. He looked at Miss Royle, who was also trying not to laugh. They both lost the battle.

'Mrs. Royle is most eager to show off her nursing skills,' Honoria added with a devilishly placid smile.

'You win, Honoria,' Marcus said, sitting back

against the sofa cushions. But his laughter gave way to a fit of coughing, and it took him nearly a minute before he felt himself again.

'How long were you in the rain last night?' Honoria demanded. She rose to her feet and touched his forehead, causing Miss Royle's eyes to widen at the intimacy.

'Have I a fever?' he murmured.

'I don't think so.' But she was frowning as she spoke. 'You might be a little warm. Perhaps I should get you a blanket.'

Marcus started to tell her that that would not be necessary, but then he realized that a blanket sounded rather nice, actually. And he was strangely grateful that she had suggested it. So he nodded.

'I'll get it,' Miss Royle said, hopping to her feet. 'I saw a maid in the hall.'

As she left, Honoria sat back down, looking over at him with concern in her eyes. 'I'm so sorry,' she said once they were alone. 'I feel terrible about what happened to you.'

He waved away her apology. 'I'll be fine.'

'You never told me how long you were out in the rain,' she reminded him.

'An hour?' he guessed. 'Probably two.'

She let out a miserable sigh. 'I'm so sorry.'

He quirked a small smile. 'You said that already.'

'Well, I *am*.'

He tried to smile at her again, because really, it was a ridiculous conversation, but he was overtaken by another fit of coughing.

She frowned with concern. 'Maybe you *should* come to Bricstan.'

He couldn't yet speak, but he speared her with a glare nonetheless.

'I worry about you here all alone.'

'Honoria,' he managed, coughing two more times before saying, 'you'll be going back to London soon. Mrs. Royle is the kindest of neighbors, I'm sure, but I would much prefer to recuperate in my own home.'

'Yes,' Honoria answered, shaking her head, 'not to mention that she'd probably have you married off to Cecily before the end of the month.'

'Did someone say my name?' Cecily asked brightly, returning to the room with a dark blue blanket.

Marcus was overcome with another fit of coughing, this one only slightly feigned.

'Here you are,' Cecily said. She walked over with the blanket, then appeared not to know what to do with it herself. 'Perhaps you should help him,' she said to Honoria.

Honoria took the blanket from her and walked over, unfolding it as she approached. 'Here you are,' she said softly, leaning over to spread the soft wool over him. She smiled gently as she tucked the corners in. 'Is that too tight?'

He shook his head. It was strange, being cared for.

When she was done with her task, she straightened, taking a deep breath before announcing that he needed tea.

'Oh, yes,' Miss Royle agreed. 'That would be just the thing.'

Marcus didn't even try to protest this time. He was sure he looked pathetic, all wrapped in a blanket with his foot stuck up on the table, and he couldn't even imagine what they thought every time he started coughing. But he was finding it rather comforting to be fussed over, and if Honoria wanted to insist that he needed tea, he would be glad to make her happy by drinking it.

He told her where to find the pull to ring for tea, and she did so, settling back in her spot across from him after a maid came in and took their order.

'Has a surgeon been by to look at your ankle?' she asked.

'It's not necessary,' he told her. 'It's not broken.'

'Are you certain? It's not the sort of thing one wants to take chances with.'

'I'm certain.'

'I would feel better if—'

'Honoria, hush. It's not broken.'

'And your boot?'

'His boot?' Miss Royle asked. She looked perplexed.

'That, I'm afraid, *is* broken,' he answered.

'Oh, dear,' Honoria said. 'I thought they might have to cut it off.'

'They had to cut off your boot?' Miss Royle echoed. 'Oh, but that's *terrible*.'

'His ankle was horribly swollen,' Honoria told her. 'It was the only way.'

'But a *boot*,' Miss Royle persisted.

'It wasn't one of my favorite boots,' Marcus said, trying to cheer poor Miss Royle up. She looked as if someone had decapitated a puppy.

'I wonder if one could have a single boot made,' Honoria mused. 'To match the other. Then it wouldn't be a complete waste.'

'Oh, no, that would never work,' Miss Royle said, apparently an expert on such topics. 'The leather would never quite match.'

Marcus was saved from a lengthy discussion

98

of footwear by the arrival of Mrs. Wetherby, his longtime housekeeper. 'I had already started on the tea before you asked for it,' she announced, bustling in with a tray.

He smiled, unsurprised. She was always doing things like that. He introduced her to Honoria and Miss Royle, and when she greeted Honoria her eyes lit up.

'Oh, you must be Master Daniel's sister!' Mrs. Wetherby exclaimed, setting down the tea service.

'I am,' Honoria replied, beaming. 'Do you know him, then?'

'I do. He visited a few times, usually when the previous earl was out of town. And of course he has come by once or twice since Master Marcus became the earl.'

Marcus felt himself blush at her use of his childhood honorific. But he would never correct her. Mrs. Wetherby had been like a mother to him growing up, often the only warm smile or encouraging word in all of Fensmore.

'It is lovely to meet you,' Mrs. Wetherby continued. 'I have heard so much about you.'

Honoria blinked with surprise. 'You have?'

Marcus also blinked with surprise. He couldn't recall ever having mentioned Honoria to anyone, much less his housekeeper.

'Oh, yes,' Mrs. Wetherby said. 'When they were children, of course. I must confess, I still quite thought of you as a young child. But you are quite grown up now, aren't you?'

Honoria smiled and nodded.

'Now, how do you take your tea?' the housekeeper asked, splashing milk into all three cups after Honoria and Miss Royle gave her their preferences.

'It has been much too long since I have seen Master Daniel,' she continued, lifting the pot to pour. 'He is a bit of a rascal, but I do like him. Is he well?'

There was an awkward silence, and Honoria looked to Marcus for aid. He immediately cleared his throat and said, 'I must not have told you, Mrs. Wetherby. Lord Winstead has been out of the country for several years.' He would tell her the rest of the story later, but not in front of Honoria and her friend.

'I see,' she said, correctly interpreting the silence as a cue not to pursue the subject. She cleared her throat a few times, then handed the first cup and saucer to Honoria. 'And one for you, too,' she murmured, handing the second set to Miss Royle.

They both thanked her, and she stood to hand Marcus his cup. But then she turned to Honoria. 'You will make sure he drinks all of it, won't you?'

Honoria grinned. 'Absolutely.'

Mrs. Wetherby leaned down and loudly whispered, 'Gentlemen make terrible patients.'

'I heard that,' Marcus remarked.

His housekeeper gave him a sly look. 'You were meant to.' And with that she curtsied and left the room.

The rest of the visit passed without incident. They drank their tea (two cups for Marcus, at Honoria's insistence), ate their biscuits, and chatted about various niceties until Marcus started coughing again, this time with such duration that Honoria insisted that he go back to bed.

'It is time we left anyway,' she said, standing with Miss Royle. 'I am sure Mrs. Royle will be eager for

100

our return.'

Marcus nodded and smiled his thanks when they insisted he did not stand on their account. He really was feeling dreadful, and he suspected that he might have to swallow his pride and ask to be carried back up to his room.

After the two ladies left, of course.

He stifled a groan. He hated being sick.

*   *   *

Once in the carriage, Honoria allowed herself to sit back and relax. Marcus looked ill, but it was nothing that a week of rest and broth would not cure. But her moment of peace was brought abruptly short when Cecily announced, 'One month.'

Honoria looked up. 'I beg your pardon?'

'That is my prediction.' Cecily held up her index finger, twirled it in a little circle, then snapped it straight. 'One month before Lord Chatteris proposes.'

'To whom?' Honoria asked, trying to hide her shock. Marcus had not shown any marked preference for Cecily, and more to the point, it was unlike her to be so boastful.

'To you, you ninny.'

Honoria nearly choked on her own tongue. *'Oh,'* she said, with great feeling. 'Oh. Oh. Oh. Oh, no.'

Cecily smirked.

'No, no.' Honoria might have been rendered a monosyllabic idiot, but she was a vocal monosyllabic idiot. 'No,' she said again. 'Oh, no.'

'I'd even be willing to make a wager,' Cecily said archly. 'You will be married by the end of the season.'

'I hope so,' Honoria said, finally finding her vocabulary, 'but it won't be to Lord Chatteris.'

'Oh, so it's Lord Chatteris now, is it? Don't think I didn't notice that you called him by his given name the entire time we were there.'

'That's how he is known to me,' Honoria protested. 'I've known him since I was six.'

'Be that as it may, the two of you were . . . Oh, how do I say it?' Cecily pursed her lips and glanced up toward the roof of the carriage. 'Acting like you were already married, perhaps?'

'Don't be ridiculous.'

'I speak the truth,' Cecily said, looking extremely pleased with herself. She chuckled. 'Wait until I tell the others.'

Honoria very nearly leapt across the carriage. 'Don't you dare!'

'Methinks the lady doth protest too much.'

'Please, Cecily, I assure you, there is no love between Lord Chatteris and me, and I promise you, we will never be wed. Spreading rumors will do nothing but make my life miserable.'

Cecily cocked her head to the side. '*No* love?'

'Now you're twisting my words. Of course I *care* for him. He was like a brother to me.'

'Very well,' Cecily acceded. 'I won't say anything.'

'Th—'

'*Until* you are betrothed. And then I shall shout it to anyone who will listen: I predicted this!'

Honoria didn't even bother to respond. There would be no betrothal, and thus no shouting of anything. But what she did not realize until later was that for the first time she had said that Marcus *was* like a brother to her.

102

Past tense.

And if he wasn't a brother to her any longer, what was he?

Chapter Seven

Honoria returned to London the next day. The season would not begin for over a month, but there was much to be done in preparation. According to her recently married cousin Marigold, who came by to visit the first afternoon Honoria was back, pink was now all the rage, although if one visited the modiste, one had to take care to call it primrose, poppy, or ruby. Furthermore, one simply *had* to have a collection of bracelets. No one could do without them, Marigold assured her.

As that was only the beginning of Marigold's fashion advice, Honoria made plans to visit the modiste later that week. But before she could do more than select her favorite shade of pink (primrose, just to keep things simple), a letter arrived for her from Fensmore.

Honoria assumed it must be from Marcus, and she opened it eagerly, surprised that he would have taken the time to write to her. But when she unfolded the single sheet of foolscap, the writing was far too feminine to have ever come from his hand.

Her brow knit with concern, she sat down to read the letter.

My dear Lady Honoria,

Forgive my forwardness in writing to you, but I do not know to whom else I may turn. Lord Chatteris is not well. He has been feverish for three days and last night was quite insensible. The doctor has called each afternoon, but he has no advice other than to wait and observe.

As you know, the earl has no family. But I feel I must notify someone, and he has always spoken so highly of your family.

Yrs.
Mrs. Wetherby
Housekeeper to the Earl of Chatteris

'Oh, no,' Honoria murmured, staring down at the letter until her eyes crossed. How could this be possible? When she had left Fensmore, Marcus had had a terrible cough, yes, but he hadn't shown any signs of fever. There had been nothing in his aspect to indicate that he might take such a sharp turn for the worse.

And what did Mrs. Wetherby mean by sending her a letter? Was she simply informing her of Marcus's condition, or was she tacitly asking her to come to Fensmore? And if it was the latter, did that mean Marcus's condition was grim?

'Mother!' Honoria called out. She rose to her feet without thinking and starting walking through the house. Her heart began to race, and she started moving faster. Her voice, too, grew louder. 'Mother!'

'Honoria?' Lady Winstead appeared at the top

of the stairs, waving at herself with her favorite Chinese silk fan. 'Whatever can be the matter? Was there any problem at the modiste? I thought you were planning to go with Marigold.'

'No, no, it's not that,' Honoria said, hurrying up the stairs. 'It's Marcus.'

'Marcus Holroyd?'

'Yes. I received a letter from his housekeeper.'

'From his housekeeper? Whyever would she—'

'I saw him in Cambridge, do you recall? I told you about—'

'Oh, yes, yes.' Her mother smiled. 'What a lovely coincidence to have run into him. Mrs. Royle wrote me a note about it. I think she is hoping that he might form a *tendre* for her daughter.'

'Mother, here, please read this.' Honoria held out the letter from Mrs. Wetherby. 'He is very ill.'

Lady Winstead quickly read the short note, her mouth pressing into a worried frown. 'Oh, dear. This is very bad news indeed.'

Honoria placed a heavy hand on her mother's arm, trying to impress upon her the gravity of the situation. 'We must leave for Fensmore. At once.'

Lady Winstead looked up in surprise. 'Us?'

'He has no one else.'

'Well, that can't be true.'

'It is,' Honoria insisted. 'Don't you remember how often he came to stay with us when he and Daniel were at Eton? It was because he had nowhere else to go. I don't think he and his father got on very well.'

'I don't know, it seems very presumptuous.' Her mother frowned. 'We are not family.'

'He doesn't *have* family!'

Lady Winstead caught her lower lip between her

105

teeth. 'He was such a nice boy, but I just don't think . . .'

Honoria planted her hands on her hips. 'If you do not come with me, I will go alone.'

'Honoria!' Lady Winstead drew back with shock, and for the first time in the conversation, a spark flared in her pale eyes. 'You will do no such thing. Your reputation will be in tatters.'

'He might be *dying.*'

'I'm sure it's not as serious as that.'

Honoria clutched her hands together. They had begun to shake, and her fingers felt terribly cold. 'I hardly think his housekeeper would have written to me if it weren't.'

'Oh, all right,' Lady Winstead said with a little sigh. 'We will leave tomorrow.'

Honoria shook her head. 'Today.'

'Today? Honoria, you know such trips take planning. I couldn't possibly—'

'Today, Mother. There is no time to lose.' Honoria hurried back down the stairs, calling over her shoulder, 'I will see to having the carriage prepared. Be ready within the hour!'

But Lady Winstead, showing some of the fire she'd possessed before her only son had been banished from the country, did even better than that. She was ready in forty-five minutes, bags packed, accompanied by her maid, and waiting for Honoria in the front drawing room.

Five minutes later they were on their way.

*　　　*　　　*

The journey to northern Cambridgeshire could be made in one (long) day, and so it was near to

106

midnight by the time the Winstead carriage pulled up in front of Fensmore. Lady Winstead had fallen asleep a bit north of Saffron Walden, but Honoria was wide awake. From the moment they had turned onto the long drive that led to Fensmore, her posture had become tense and alert, and it was all she could do to keep herself from gripping the handle to the door. As it was, when they finally came to a stop, she did not wait for anyone to come to her aid. Within seconds she had pushed open the door, hopped down, and was hurrying up the front steps.

The house was quiet, and Honoria spent at least five minutes banging the knocker up and down before she finally saw a flicker of candlelight in a window and heard footsteps hurriedly approaching.

The butler opened the door—Honoria could not remember his name—and before he could utter a word, she said, 'Mrs. Wetherby wrote to me about the earl's condition. I must see him at once.'

The butler drew back slightly, his manner every bit as proud and aristocratic as his employer's. 'I'm afraid that's impossible.'

Honoria had to grab hold of the door frame for support. 'What do you mean?' she whispered. Surely Marcus could not have succumbed to his fever in the short time since Mrs. Wetherby had written to her.

'The earl is asleep,' the butler replied testily. 'I will not wake him at this time of night.'

Relief rushed through Honoria like blood to a sleeping limb. 'Oh, thank you,' she said fervently, reaching out and taking his hand. 'Now, please, I must see him. I promise I will not disturb him.'

The butler looked vaguely alarmed by her hand

on his. 'I cannot permit you to see him at this time. May I remind you that you have not even seen fit to give me your name.'

Honoria blinked. Were visitors so common at Fensmore that he could not recall her visit less than a week prior? Then she realized that he was squinting in the darkness. Good heavens, he probably could not see her clearly. 'Please accept my apologies,' she said in her most placating voice. 'I am Lady Honoria Smythe-Smith, and my mother, the Countess of Winstead, is waiting in the carriage with her maid. Perhaps someone might help her.'

An enormous change came over the butler's wrinkled face. 'Lady Honoria!' he exclaimed. 'I beg your pardon. I did not recognize you in the darkness. Please, please, come in.'

He took her by the arm and led her inside. Honoria allowed him to steer her along, slowing the pace ever-so-slightly to turn around and look back at the carriage. 'My mother . . .'

'I shall have a footman attend to her with all possible haste,' the butler assured her. 'But we must get you to a room immediately. We do not have one prepared, but there are several that can be made ready at short notice.' He paused at a doorway, leaned in, and pulled several times on a cord. 'The maids will be up and about at once.'

'Please do not rouse them on my accord,' Honoria said, although from the vigor with which he had yanked on the bellpull, she suspected it was too late for that. 'Might I confer with Mrs. Wetherby? I hate to wake her, but it is of the utmost importance.'

'Of course, of course,' the butler assured her, still ushering her deeper into the house.

'And my mother . . .' Honoria said with a nervous backward glance. After her original protests, Lady Winstead had been a marvelously good sport all day. Honoria did *not* want to leave her sleeping in a carriage. The driver and grooms would never leave her unattended, and of course her maid sat on the opposite cushion, also fast asleep, but still, it did not seem right.

'I will greet her just as soon as I convey you to Mrs. Wetherby,' the butler said.

'Thank you, er . . .' It did feel awkward, not knowing his name.

'Springpeace, my lady.' He took her hand in both of his and squeezed. His hands were rheumy, and his grip unsteady, but there was an urgency in his grasp. Gratitude, too. He looked up, his dark eyes meeting hers. 'May I say, my lady, that I am very glad that you are here.'

* * *

Ten minutes later, Mrs. Wetherby was standing with Honoria outside the door to Marcus's room. 'I don't know that the earl would like your seeing him in such a state,' the housekeeper said, 'but seeing as you've come so far to see him . . .'

'I won't disturb him,' Honoria assured her. 'I just need to see for myself that he is well.'

Mrs. Wetherby swallowed and gave her a frank look. 'He is not well, miss. You should be prepared for that.'

'I-I didn't mean "well,"' Honoria said haltingly. 'I meant, oh I don't know what I meant, just that—'

The housekeeper laid a gentle hand on her arm. 'I understand. He is a bit better than he was yesterday, when I wrote to you.'

Honoria nodded, but the motion felt tight and awkward. She *thought* that the housekeeper was telling her that Marcus was not at death's door, but this did little to reassure her, because it meant that he had *been* at death's door. And if that was true, there was no reason to think he would not be there again.

Mrs. Wetherby put her forefinger to her lips, signaling to Honoria to be quiet as they entered the room. She turned the doorknob slowly, and the door pushed open on soundless hinges.

'He's sleeping,' Mrs. Wetherby whispered.

Honoria nodded and stepped forward, blinking in the dim light. It was very warm inside, and the air was thick and dense. 'Isn't he hot?' she whispered to Mrs. Wetherby. She could barely breathe in the stuffy room, and Marcus appeared to be buried under a mound of blankets and quilts.

'It is what the doctor said to do,' Mrs. Wetherby replied. 'Under no circumstances were we to allow him to become chilled.'

Honoria tugged at the neck of her day dress, wishing there were some way to loosen the collar. And good heavens, if she was uncomfortable, Marcus must be in agony. She couldn't imagine it was healthy to be cocooned in such heat.

But if he was overheated, at least he was sleeping. His breathing sounded normal, or at least what Honoria thought was normal. She had no idea what one might listen for at a sickbed; she supposed anything out of the ordinary. She moved a little closer, bending down. He looked terribly sweaty. She could only see one side of his face, but his skin glistened unnaturally, and the air held the stale scent of human exertion.

'I really don't think he should be under so many blankets,' Honoria whispered.

Mrs. Wetherby gave a helpless little shrug. 'The doctor was most explicit.'

Honoria stepped even closer, until her legs touched the side of his bed. 'It doesn't look comfortable.'

'I know,' Mrs. Wetherby agreed.

Honoria reached a tentative hand out to see if she might be able to pull his covers back, even if just for an inch or two. She caught hold of the edge of the topmost quilt, gave the tiniest of tugs, and then—

'Aaaaaach!'

Honoria shrieked and jumped back, grabbing onto Mrs. Wetherby's arm. Marcus had practically thrown himself into a sitting position and was looking wildly around the room.

And he did not appear to be wearing any clothing. At least not from the waist up, which was what she could see.

'It's all right, it's all right,' she said, but her voice lacked confidence. It didn't seem all right to her, and she didn't know how to sound as if she thought otherwise.

He was breathing hard, and he was terribly agitated, but his eyes did not seem to focus on her. Indeed, she wasn't sure if he realized she was there. His head snapped back and forth, as if he were looking for something, and then it seemed to speed up into a strange shake. 'No,' he said, although not forcefully. He didn't sound angry, just upset. 'No.'

'He's not awake,' Mrs. Wetherby said softly.

Honoria nodded slowly, and the enormity of

111

what she had undertaken finally settled upon her. She didn't know anything about sickness, and she certainly didn't know how to care for someone with a fever.

Was that why she had come? To care for him? She had been so frantic with worry after reading Mrs. Wetherby's message that all she'd been able to think about was seeing him for herself. She hadn't thought ahead to anything past that.

What an idiot she had been. What had she thought she was going to do once she saw him? Turn around and go home?

She was going to have to care for him. She was here now, and to do anything else would be unthinkable. But the prospect terrified her. What if she did something wrong? What if she made him worse?

But what else could she do? He needed her. Marcus had no one, and Honoria was startled—and a little bit ashamed—that she had not realized this until now.

'I'll sit with him,' she told Mrs. Wetherby.

'Oh, no, miss, you couldn't. It wouldn't be—'

'Someone should be with him,' Honoria said firmly. 'He should not be alone.' She took the housekeeper's arm and led her to the far side of the room. It was impossible to conduct a conversation so close to Marcus. He had lain back down, but he was tossing and turning with such violence that Honoria flinched every time she looked at him.

'I will stay,' Mrs. Wetherby said. But she didn't sound as if she truly wanted to.

'I suspect you have spent many hours at his side already,' Honoria said. 'I will take a turn. You need to rest.'

112

Mrs. Wetherby nodded gratefully, and as she reached the door to the corridor, she said, 'No one will say anything. About your being in his room. I promise you, not a soul at Fensmore would say a word.'

Honoria gave her what she hoped was a reassuring smile. 'My mother is here. Perhaps not here in the room, but she is here at Fensmore. That ought to be enough to keep the gossip away.'

With a nod, Mrs. Wetherby slipped out of the room, and Honoria listened to the sound of her footsteps until they retreated into silence.

'Oh, Marcus,' she said softly, moving slowly back to his side. 'What happened to you?' She reached out to touch him, then thought, *No, better not*. It wouldn't be proper, and besides, she didn't want to disturb him any more than she already had.

He threw an arm out from under the covers, rolling about until he settled into position on his side, his free arm lying atop the quilt. She hadn't realized he was so muscular. Of course she knew he was strong. It was obvious. He was— She stopped for a moment, thinking. Actually, it wasn't obvious. She couldn't remember the last time she'd seen him lift anything. But he seemed strong. He just had that look about him. Capable. Not all men had it. In fact, most didn't, at least most of Honoria's acquaintance.

Still, she hadn't realized that the muscles of a man's arm would be so well defined.

Interesting.

She leaned forward a little more, tilting her head to the side, then moving the candle a bit forward. What was that muscle on the shoulder called? His was really quite nice.

113

She gasped, horrified by the inappropriate direction of her thoughts, and took a step back. She wasn't here to ogle the poor man, she was here to take care of him. And furthermore, if she was going to ogle someone, it absolutely shouldn't be Marcus Holroyd.

There was a chair just a few feet away, so she took it and pulled it forward, close enough to his bed that she could jump up and be with him in an instant, but not so close that he could strike her in his flailings.

He looked thinner. She wasn't sure how she could tell this amidst all the quilts and coverlets, but he had definitely lost weight. His face was gaunt, and even in the dim light of her candle, she could see unfamiliar shadows beneath his eyes.

She sat very still for several minutes, feeling rather foolish, actually. It seemed as if she should be *doing* something. She supposed watching him was something, but it didn't feel like much, especially since she was trying so hard *not* to watch certain parts of him. He seemed to have calmed down; every now and then he would shift restlessly beneath his covers, but for the most part, he slept.

But, Lord, it was hot. Honoria was still in her day dress, a pretty little frock that buttoned up the back. It was one of those ridiculous pieces of feminine attire that she could not possibly get into (or out of) on her own.

She smiled. Rather like Marcus's boots. It was nice to know that men could be as impractically devoted to fashion as women.

Still, the frock was the absolute wrong thing to be wearing in a sickroom. She managed to undo a few of the top buttons, practically gasping for breath

114

when she got them loose.

'This cannot be healthy,' she said aloud, holding onto her collar with two fingers and moving it back and forth in an attempt to fan her sweaty neck.

She looked over at Marcus. He did not seem to have been disturbed by her voice.

She kicked off her shoes, and then, because really, she was already undressed enough to ruin her reputation should anyone come upon her, she reached down and peeled off her stockings.

'Ew.' She looked down at her legs in dismay. The stockings were almost soaked through.

With a sigh of resignation she laid them out over the back of a chair, then thought the better of it. Probably best not to have them on such display. So she crumpled them into a ball and shoved them into her shoes. And while she was standing, she grasped her skirt in her hands and swished it back and forth, trying to cool off her legs.

This was intolerable. She didn't care what the doctor had said. She could not believe that this was healthy. She walked back over to his bed to peer down at him again, keeping a safe distance in case he lashed out.

Carefully, gingerly, she reached out a hand. She didn't touch him, but she came close. The air near his shoulder was at least ten degrees warmer than the rest of the room.

Allowing for slight exaggeration, which she thought she was entitled to, given her overheated state. But still.

She looked around the room for something with which she might fan him. Drat, she should have nicked one of her mother's Chinese silk fans. Mama was *always* fanning herself these days. She

115

never went anywhere without at least three packed in her trunk. Which was really for the best, since she tended to leave them all over town.

But there was nothing suitable for fanning, so Honoria leaned over and blew gently at Marcus. He didn't stir, which she took as a good sign. Emboldened by her success (if indeed that was what it was; she really had no idea) she tried it again, with a little more force. This time he gave a little shiver.

She frowned, unsure if that was a good thing or not. If he was as sweaty as he looked, she risked overchilling him, which was precisely what the doctor had warned against.

She sat down again, then stood, then sat, tapping her hand restlessly against her thigh. It got so bad that she had to practically slam her other hand down on top of it, just to keep it still.

This was ridiculous. She jumped to her feet and walked back over to him. He was moving about again, thrashing under his covers, although not with enough force to actually throw them off.

She should touch him. She really should. It was the only way to determine just how hot his skin was. What she was going to do with that information she wasn't sure, but that didn't matter. If she was his nurse—and it appeared she was—she needed to be more observant about his condition.

She reached forward and lightly touched her fingers to his shoulder. He didn't feel quite as warm as she'd expected, but that might have been due to the fact that she, too, was roasting. He was sweaty, though, and this close up she could see that his sheets were soaked.

Should she try to remove them? He'd still have

all the other blankets. She reached out and gave the sheet a tug, holding the top quilt with her other hand to keep it in place. It didn't work, though; the whole set came sliding toward her, revealing one long, slightly bent leg.

Honoria's lips parted. He was rather muscular there, too.

No, no, no, no, no, no, no. She was not looking at Marcus. She was not. Not at him. Definitely not at him. And furthermore, she had to get a blanket back into place before he rolled over and revealed himself entirely, because she had no idea if he was wearing any undergarments. He had nothing on his arms, and nothing on his legs, so it stood to reason . . .

She looked down at his midsection. She couldn't not. He was still covered, of course, but if she accidentally bumped into the bed . . .

She grabbed a piece of the quilt and shoved, trying to get him covered back up. Someone else was going to have to change his sheets. Good Lord, she was hot. How on earth could it have grown warmer in here? Maybe she could go outside for a moment. Or go open the window a crack and stand near it.

She fanned the air near her face with her hand. She should sit back down. There was a perfectly good chair, and she could sit there with her hands demurely in her lap until morning. She'd just take one more peek at him, just to be sure he was all right.

She picked up the candle and held it up over his face.

His eyes were open.

She took a careful step back. He'd opened his

117

eyes before. This didn't mean he was awake.

'Honoria? What are you doing here?'

That, however, did.

Chapter Eight

Marcus felt like hell.

No, he felt like he'd been to hell. And come back. And perhaps gone again, just because it hadn't been hot enough the first time.

He had no idea how long he'd been sick. A day, maybe? Two? The fever had started . . . Tuesday? Yes, Tuesday, although that didn't really signify, as he had no idea what day it was now.

Or night. He thought it might be night. It seemed dark, and—God damn, it was hot. Truly, it was difficult to think of anything other than the overwhelming heat.

Maybe he'd been to hell and then brought the whole damned place back with him. Or maybe he still was in hell, although if so, the beds were certainly comfortable.

Which did seem to contradict everything he'd learned in church.

He yawned, stretching his neck to the left and the right before settling his head back into his pillow. He knew this pillow. It was soft, and goosedown, and just the right thickness. He was in his own bed, in his own bedchamber. And it was definitely night. It was dark. He could tell that even though he couldn't quite muster the energy to open his eyelids.

He could hear Mrs. Wetherby shuffling about

the room. He supposed she'd been at his bedside throughout his illness. This didn't surprise him, but still, he was grateful for her care. She had brought him broth when he had first begun to feel sick, and he vaguely recalled her consulting with a doctor. The couple of times he'd broken through his feverish haze, she'd been in the room, watching over him.

She touched his shoulder, her fingers soft and light. It wasn't enough to rouse him from his stupor, though. He couldn't move. He was so tired. He couldn't remember ever being so tired. His whole body ached, and his leg *really* hurt. He just wanted to go back to sleep. But it was so hot. Why would anyone keep a room so hot?

As if eavesdropping on his thoughts, Mrs. Wetherby tugged at his quilt, and Marcus happily rolled to his side, throwing his good leg out from under the covers. Air! Dear God, it felt good. Maybe he could shove off his covers entirely. Would she be completely scandalized if he just lay there almost naked? Probably, but if it was for the sake of medicine . . .

But then she started shoving the blankets back on top of him, which was almost enough to make him want to cry. Summoning every last reserve of energy, he opened his eyes, and—

It wasn't Mrs. Wetherby.

'Honoria?' he croaked. 'What are you doing here?'

She jumped back about a foot, letting out an odd chirping sound that hurt his ears. He closed his eyes again. He didn't have the energy to talk to her, although her presence was quite curious.

'Marcus?' she said, her voice strangely urgent.

'Can you say something? Are you awake?'

He gave a very small nod.

'Marcus?' She was closer now, and he could feel her breath on his neck. It was awful. Too hot, and too close.

'Why are you here?' he asked again, his words slurring on his tongue like hot syrup. 'You should be . . .' Where *should* she be? London, he thought. Wasn't that right?

'Oh, thank heavens.' She touched his forehead with her hand. Her skin felt hot, but then again, everything felt hot.

'Hon— Honor—' He couldn't quite manage the rest of her name. He tried; he moved his lips, and he took a few more breaths. But it was all too much effort, especially since she wouldn't seem to answer his question. Why was she here?

'You've been very ill,' she said.

He nodded. Or he might have done. He thought about nodding, at least.

'Mrs. Wetherby wrote to me in London.'

Ah, so that was it. Still, very odd.

She took his hand in hers, patting it in a nervous, fluttery gesture. 'I came up just as soon as I could. My mother is here, as well.'

Lady Winstead? He tried to smile. He liked Lady Winstead.

'I think you still have a fever,' Honoria said, sounding unsure of herself. 'Your forehead is quite warm. Although I must say, it is bursting hot in this room. I don't know that I can tell how much of the heat is you, and how much is simply the air.'

'Please,' he groaned, lurching one arm forward to bat against hers. He opened his eyes, blinking in the dim light. 'The window.'

She shook her head. 'I'm sorry. I wish I could. Mrs. Wetherby said the doctor said—'

'*Please.*' He was begging—hell, he almost sounded as if he might cry. But he didn't care. He just wanted her to open the damned window.

'Marcus, I can't . . .' But she looked torn.

'I can't breathe,' he told her. And honestly, he did not think he was exaggerating.

'Oh, all right,' she said, bustling over to the window. 'But don't tell anyone.'

'Promise,' he mumbled. He couldn't rouse himself to turn his head to watch, but he could hear her every movement in the thick silence of the night.

'Mrs. Wetherby was quite firm,' she said, pulling back the curtain. 'The room was to remain hot.'

Marcus grunted and tried to lift a hand in a dismissive wave.

'I don't know anything about caring for invalids'—ah, now there was the sound of the window being shoved open—'but I can't imagine it's healthy to bake in such heat when one has a fever.'

Marcus felt the first stirrings of cooler air touch his skin, and he almost cried with happiness.

'I've never had a fever,' Honoria said, coming back to his side. 'Or at least not that I can remember. Isn't that odd?'

He could hear the smile in her voice. He even knew exactly what sort of smile it was—a little bit sheepish, with just a touch of wonderment. She often smiled like that. And every time, the right side of her mouth tipped ever-so-slightly higher than the left.

And now he could hear it. It was lovely. And

strange. How odd that he knew her so well. He *knew* her, of course, better than almost anyone. But that wasn't the same as knowing someone's smiles.

Or was it?

She pulled a chair closer to his bed and sat. 'It never even occurred to me until I came here to care for you. That I'd never had a fever, I mean. My mother says they're dreadful.'

She came for him? He didn't know why he found this so remarkable. There was no one else at Fensmore she would have come for, and she was here, in his sickroom, but still, somehow it seemed ... Well, not odd. Not surprising, either. Just ...

Unexpected.

He tried to nudge his tired mind. Could something be not surprising *and* unexpected? Because that's what it was. He would never have expected Honoria to drop everything and come to Fensmore to care for him. And yet now that she was here, it wasn't surprising at all.

It felt almost normal.

'Thank you for opening the window,' he said softly.

'You're welcome.' She tried to smile, but she could not hide the worry on her face. 'I'm sure it didn't take much to convince me. I don't think I've ever been so hot in my life.'

'Nor I,' he tried to joke.

She smiled then, and it was a real one. 'Oh, Marcus,' she said, reaching forward to smooth his hair from his forehead. She shook her head, but she didn't look as if she knew why she was doing so. Her own hair was falling in her face, poker-straight as always. She blew at it, trying to move it away from her mouth, but it flopped right back down.

122

Finally, she batted it away with her fingers, shoving it behind her ear.

It fell back onto her face.

'You look tired,' he said, his voice hoarse.

'Said the man who cannot keep his eyes open.'

'Touché,' he said, somehow managing to punctuate the statement with a little flick of his forefinger.

She was silent for a moment, then gave a little start. 'Would you like something to drink?'

He nodded.

'I'm so sorry. I should have asked the moment you woke up. You must be terribly thirsty.'

'Just a bit,' he lied.

'Mrs. Wetherby left a pitcher of water,' she said, reaching for something on the table behind her. 'It's not cold, but I think it will still be refreshing.'

He nodded again. Anything short of boiling would be refreshing.

She held out a glass, then realized that he wasn't going to be able to use it in his current, supine pose. 'Here, let me help you up,' she said, setting the glass back down on the table. She reached around him and, with more determination than strength, helped him into a sitting position. 'Here you are,' she said, sounding as efficient as a governess. 'Just, ehrm, we should tuck in that blanket, and have some water.'

He blinked a few times, each motion so slow that he was never quite sure if he'd get his eyes open again. He wasn't wearing a shirt. Funny how he was only just realizing it. Funnier still that he couldn't seem to summon any concern for her maidenly sensibilities.

She might be blushing. He couldn't tell. It was

123

too dark to see. But it didn't matter. This was Honoria. She was a good egg. A sensible egg. She wouldn't be scarred forever by the sight of his chest.

He took a gulp of water, and then another, barely noticing when some of it dribbled down his chin. Dear Lord, it felt good in his mouth. His tongue had been thick and dry.

Honoria made a little murmuring sound, then reached forward and wiped the moisture from his skin with her hand. 'I'm sorry,' she said. 'I don't have a handkerchief.'

He nodded slowly, something within him memorizing the way her fingers felt against his cheek. 'You were here before,' he said.

She looked at him in question.

'You touched me. My shoulder.'

A faint smile tilted at her lips. 'That was only a few minutes ago.'

'It was?' He thought about that. 'Oh.'

'I've been here for several hours,' she said.

His chin bobbed a fraction of an inch. 'Thank you.' Was that his voice? Damn, he sounded weak.

'I can't tell you how relieved I am to see you up. I mean, you look terrible, but you look so much better than you did before. You're speaking. And you're making sense.' Her hands came up and she clasped them together, the gesture nervous and maybe even a little bit frantic. 'Which is more than I can say for myself right now.'

'Don't be silly,' he said.

She shook her head quickly, then looked away. But he saw her wipe a quick hand at her eyes.

He'd made her cry. He felt his head droop a little to one side. Just the thought of it was exhausting. Heartbreaking. He'd never wanted to make

Honoria cry.

She . . . She shouldn't be . . . He swallowed. He didn't want her to cry. He was so tired. He didn't feel like he knew much, but he knew that.

'You scared me,' she said. 'I'd wager you didn't think you could do that.' She sounded as if she was trying to joke with him, but he could tell she was faking it. He appreciated the effort, though.

'Where is Mrs. Wetherby?' he asked.

'I sent her to bed. She was exhausted.'

'Good.'

'She has been caring for you quite diligently.'

He nodded again, that tiny little motion he hoped she could see. His housekeeper had cared for him the last time he'd had a fever, back when he was eleven. His father had not entered the room once, but Mrs. Wetherby had not left his side. He wanted to tell Honoria about that, or maybe about the time his father had left home before Christmas and she had taken it upon herself to put up so much holly that Fensmore had smelled like a forest for weeks. It had been the best Christmas ever, until the year he'd been invited to spend it with the Smythe-Smiths.

That had been the best. That would always be the best.

'Do you want more water?' Honoria asked.

He did, but he wasn't sure he had the energy to swallow it properly.

'I'll help you,' she said, placing the glass to his lips.

He took a tiny sip, then let out a tired sigh. 'My leg hurts.'

'It's probably still sprained,' she said with a nod.

He yawned. 'Feels . . . little fiery. Little poker.'

125

Her eyes widened. He couldn't blame her. He had no idea what he meant either.

She leaned forward, her brow knit with concern, and she once again touched her hand to his forehead. 'You're starting to feel warm again.'

He tried to smile. He thought he might have managed it on at least one side of his mouth. 'Was I ever not?'

'No,' she said frankly. 'But you feel warmer now.'

'It comes and goes.'

'The fever?'

He nodded.

Her lips tightened, and she looked older than he'd ever seen her before. Not old; she couldn't possibly look old. But she looked worried. Her hair looked the same, pulled back in her usual loose bun. And she moved the same way, with that bright little gait that was so singularly hers.

But her eyes were different. Darker, somehow. Pulled into her face with worry. He didn't like it.

'May I have some more water?' he asked. He couldn't remember ever being so thirsty.

'Of course,' she said quickly, then poured more water from the pitcher to the cup.

He gulped it down, once again too quickly, but this time he wiped the excess water away with the back of his hand. 'It will probably come back,' he warned her.

'The fever.' This time, when she said it, it wasn't a question.

He nodded. 'I thought you should know.'

'I don't understand,' she said, taking the glass from his trembling hand. 'You were perfectly well when I saw you last.'

He tried to raise a brow. He wasn't sure if he was

successful.

'Oh, very well,' she amended. 'Not perfectly well, but you were clearly mending.'

'There was that cough,' he reminded her.

'I know. But I just don't think . . .' She let out a self-deprecating snort and shook her head. 'What am I saying? I don't know anything about illness. I don't even know why I thought I might be able to take care of you. I didn't think, actually.'

He had no idea what she was talking about, but for some inexplicable reason, it was making him happy.

She sat in the chair next to him. 'I just came. I got the letter from Mrs. Wetherby, and I didn't even stop to think about the fact that there was nothing I could do to help you. I just came.'

'You're helping,' he whispered. And she was.

He was feeling better already.

Chapter Nine

Honoria woke the following morning in pain. Her neck was stiff, her back ached, and her left foot had fallen completely asleep. *And* she was hot and sweaty, which, in addition to making her uncomfortable, made her feel remarkably unattractive. And possibly fragrant. And by fragrant, she meant—

Oh, bother, she knew what she meant, and so would anyone else who came within five feet of her.

She'd closed the window after Marcus had dozed off. It had nearly killed her to do so; it went against all common sense. But she was not confident enough to defy the doctor's instructions and leave it open.

She shook out her foot, wincing as tiny needles of pain shot through her. Blast it all, she hated when her foot fell asleep. She reached down to squeeze it, trying to restore her circulation, but this just made her entire lower leg feel as if she'd set it on fire.

With a yawn and a groan, she pushed herself to her feet, trying to ignore the ominous creaking in her joints. There was a reason human beings didn't sleep in chairs, she decided. If she was still here the next night, she was taking to the floor.

Half walking and half hobbling, she made her way over to the window, eager to pull back the curtains and allow at least a little sunshine in. Marcus was sleeping, so she didn't want to make it too bright, but she was feeling a rather urgent need to *see* him. The color of his skin, the circles under his eyes. She wasn't sure what she'd do with this information, but then again, she hadn't been sure of anything since she'd entered his room the night before.

And she needed a reason to get out of the bloody chair.

She pulled back one side of the curtains, blinking in the flood of early morning light. It couldn't be too much past dawn; the sky was still hung with wisps of pink and peach, and the morning mist was flowing softly across the lawn.

It looked lovely out there, gentle and fresh, and Honoria cracked the window open again, even pressing her face up to the small opening, just to breathe in the cool moisture.

But she had a job to do. So she took a step back

128

and turned around, with every intention of laying a gentle hand on Marcus's forehead to check if his fever had returned. But before she'd taken more than two steps, he rolled over in his sleep and—

Good God, had his face been so red the night before?

She hurried to his side, stumbling over her still tingling left foot. He looked awful—red and puffy, and when she touched him his skin was dry and parched.

And hot. Terrifyingly hot.

Quickly, Honoria ran to the pitcher of water. She didn't see any towels or handkerchiefs, so she just dunked her hands in, then laid them on his cheeks, trying to cool him down. But it was clear that this was not going to be a tenable solution, so she dashed over to a set of drawers, yanking them open in turn until she found what she thought were handkerchiefs. It was only when she shook one out to dunk it in the pitcher of water that she realized it was something else altogether.

Oh, dear Lord. She was about to put his unmentionables on his face.

She felt her own face go red as she squeezed out the excess water and hurried back to his side. She mumbled an apology—not that he was sensible enough to understand it, or the offense she was about to commit—and pressed the wet linen against his forehead.

He immediately began to toss and turn, making strange, worrisome sounds—grunts and half-words, sentences with no beginnings or ends. She heard 'Stop,' and 'No,' but she also thought she might have heard 'Facilitate,' 'Monkfish,' and 'Footbridge.'

129

She definitely heard him say, 'Daniel.'

Blinking back tears, she left his side for a moment to bring the pitcher of water closer. He'd knocked the cooling cloth from his face by the time she returned, and when she tried to reapply it, he pushed her away.

'Marcus,' she said sternly, even though she knew he wouldn't hear her, 'you have to let me help you.'

But he struggled against her, thrashing this way and that until she was practically sitting on him just to keep him down. 'Stop it,' she snapped when he pushed up against her. 'You. Will. Not. Win. And by that'—she jammed down hard on one of his shoulders with her forearm—'I mean that if I win, you win.'

He jerked up suddenly and their heads knocked. Honoria let out a grunt of pain, but she didn't let go. 'Oh, no, you don't,' she ground out. 'And by *that* I mean'—she put her face close to his—'you will not die.'

Using all her weight to keep him down, she jabbed one arm out toward the pitcher of water, trying to resoak the linen. 'You're going to hate me tomorrow when you realize what I put on your face,' she told him, slapping it back down on his forehead. She hadn't meant to be so rough, but he wasn't really offering her any opportunities for gentle movement.

'Calm down,' she said slowly, moving the cloth to his neck. 'I promise you, if you are calm, you will feel much better.' She dunked the cloth again. 'Which really pales in comparison to how much better *I* will feel.'

The next time she managed to get the wet cloth on his chest, which she'd long since ceased to notice was bare. But he didn't seem to like that; he pushed back against her, hard, and she went tumbling off the far side of the bed, landing on the carpet with a jarring thud.

'Oh, no, you don't,' she muttered, ready to come back with all she had. But before she could scoot around the bed to the water pitcher, he thrust one leg out from under the covers, catching her in her belly.

She stumbled, flailing her arms forward in a desperate attempt to catch her balance before she hit the floor again. Without thinking, she grabbed the first object with which her hand connected.

Marcus screamed.

Honoria's heart slammed into triple speed, and she let go of what she now realized was his leg. Without anything to hold her up, she fell back to the floor, landing hard on her right elbow.

'Owwwww!' she cried, letting out her own shriek of pain as electric spasms shot down to her fingertips. But somehow she pushed herself to her feet, clutching her elbow to her side. The noise Marcus had made . . .

It had been inhuman.

He was still whimpering when she reached the side of the bed, and he was breathing hard, too— the kind of short, shallow breaths people made to ward off pain.

'What happened?' Honoria whispered. This wasn't the fever. This was something far more acute.

His leg. She had grabbed his leg.

That was when she realized her hand was sticky.

Still clutching her elbow, she turned her free hand over, twisting until her palm faced up.

131

Blood.

'Oh, my God.'

With an unsettled feeling in her stomach, she stepped toward him. She didn't want to startle him; he'd already knocked her down twice. But the blood . . . It wasn't her blood.

He'd pulled his leg back under the covers, so she carefully lifted the blanket, pushing it back until his leg was bare to the knee.

'Oh, my God.'

A long, angry gash split the side of his calf, oozing blood and something else she didn't even want to consider. The leg was terribly swollen and discolored, the skin near the wound red and glistening with a horrible sheen. It looked awful, like something rotting, and with horror Honoria wondered if *he* was rotting.

She dropped the blanket and lurched back, barely able to keep down the contents of her stomach.

'Oh, my God,' she said again, unable to say anything else, barely able to *think* anything else. This had to be the cause of the fever. It had nothing to do with the chill and his cough.

Her mind spun. He had an infected wound. It must have been when he'd cut off his boot. But he hadn't said that he'd been cut. Why hadn't he mentioned that? He should have told someone. He should have told *her*.

A light knock sounded at the door, and Mrs. Wetherby poked her head in. 'Is everything all right? I heard a tremendous crashing.'

'No,' Honoria answered, her voice shrill and panicked. She tried to quell the rising terror within her. She needed to be rational. She was no help to

132

anyone like this. 'His leg. Did you know about his leg?'

'What are you talking about?' Mrs. Wetherby asked, coming quickly to her side.

'His leg. It's terribly infected. I'm sure it's the cause of the fever. It has to be.'

'The doctor said it was the cough. He—oh!' Mrs. Wetherby flinched when Honoria lifted the blanket to show her Marcus's leg. 'Oh, my dear heavens.' She took a step back, covering her hand with her mouth. She looked as if she might be sick. 'I had no idea. None of us did. How could we not have seen it?'

Honoria was wondering the very same thing, but this wasn't the time to point fingers. Marcus needed them to work together to help him, not to argue over who was to blame. 'We need to summon the doctor,' she said to Mrs. Wetherby. 'It needs to be cleaned, I would imagine.'

The housekeeper gave a quick nod. 'I'll send for him.'

'How long will it take for him to get here?'

'It depends on whether he is out seeing other patients. If he's at home, the footman can be back with him in less than two hours.'

'Two hours!' Honoria bit her lip in a belated attempt to muffle her shriek. She'd never seen anything like this, but she'd heard stories. This was the kind of infection that killed a man. Quickly. 'We can't wait two hours. He needs medical attention now.'

Mrs. Wetherby turned to her with frightened eyes. 'Do you know how to clean a wound?'

'Of course not. Do you?'

'Nothing like that,' Mrs. Wetherby answered,

133

eyeing Marcus's leg with a queasy expression.

'Well, how would you take care of one that is smaller?' Honoria demanded. 'A wound, I mean.'

Mrs. Wetherby wrung her hands together, panicked eyes darting from Honoria to Marcus. 'I don't know,' she sputtered. 'A compress, I imagine. Something to draw out the poison.'

'The poison?' Honoria echoed. Good God, it sounded positively medieval. 'Summon the doctor,' she said, trying to sound more confident than she felt. 'Now. And then come right back. With hot water. And towels. And anything else you can think of.'

'Shall I bring your mother?'

'My mother?' Honoria gaped at her, not because there was anything particularly wrong with having her mother in the sickroom. Rather, why was Mrs. Wetherby thinking of it now? 'I don't know. Whatever you think is best. But hurry.'

Mrs. Wetherby nodded and ran from the room.

Honoria looked back at Marcus. His leg was still exposed to the air, the furious gash facing her like a seething frown. 'Oh, Marcus,' she whispered. 'How could this have happened?' She took his hand, and for once he didn't pull away. He seemed to have calmed down a bit; his breathing was more even than it had been just a few minutes earlier, and was it possible that his skin wasn't quite so red?

Or was she so desperate for any sign of improvement that she was seeing things that weren't there?

'Maybe,' she said aloud, 'but I will take any sign of hope.' She forced herself to look at his leg more closely. Her stomach roiled dangerously, but she pushed down her distaste. She needed to start cleaning the wound. Heaven only knew how long it would take the doctor to return, and although a compress would be better with hot water, there didn't seem any good reason not to start with what she had.

Marcus had flung the wet linen she'd been using to cool him across the room, so she went to his bureau and retrieved another pair of his unmentionables, trying not to notice anything about them other than the fact that they were made of reasonably soft linen.

She wound them into a loose cylindrical shape and dunked one end in the water. 'I'm so sorry, Marcus,' she whispered, then touched the wet cloth ever-so-gently against the wound.

He didn't flinch.

She let out the breath she'd been holding and looked at the cloth. It was red in spots from his blood, and yellowish, too, with the infection that was oozing from the wound.

Feeling slightly more confident of her nursing abilities, she adjusted the cloth to a clean area and again pressed it against the wound, applying a tiny bit more pressure than the first time. It didn't seem to bother him overmuch, so she repeated the procedure, and then again, until there was very little clean cloth remaining.

She glanced worriedly at the door. Where was Mrs. Wetherby? Honoria was making progress, but she was sure she could do a better job with hot water. Still, she wasn't about to stop, not while Marcus remained relatively calm.

She went to the bureau and got another pair of Marcus's unmentionables. 'I don't know what you're going to wear when I'm through with you,' she said to him, hands on hips.

'Back in the water,' she said to herself, dunking the cloth. 'And back on you.' She pressed, harder this time. One was supposed to press on cuts and scrapes to stop the bleeding, this much she knew. He wasn't exactly bleeding now, but surely the pressure couldn't hurt.

'And by that I mean hurt you in a permanent manner,' she said to Marcus, who remained blessedly unconscious. 'I'm quite certain it will hurt you right now.'

She dunked the cloth again, finding a nice clean patch of linen, then she moved to the part of the wound she knew she'd been avoiding. There was a spot near the top that was uglier than the rest— quite a bit more yellow, definitely more swollen.

She dabbed lightly, trying not to hurt him, and then, when he did nothing but mutter in his sleep, pressed a little harder. 'One step at a time,' she whispered, forcing herself to take a calming breath. 'Just one.'

She could do this. She could help him. No, she could *fix* him. It was as if everything in her life had led to this moment. 'This is why I didn't get married last year,' she said to him. 'I wouldn't be here to nurse you.' She thought about that for a moment. 'Of course, one could make the argument that you wouldn't be in this situation if not for me. But we're not going to dwell upon that.'

She kept up her work, carefully cleaning his wound, then paused to stretch her neck from side to side. She looked down at the cloth in her hands. It was still disgusting, but she wasn't bothered by it any longer.

'There, you see,' she said to him. 'It must mean I

am getting better at this.'

She thought she was doing better, too. She was trying to be so very matter-of-fact and practical, but then, out of nowhere, right after she so jauntily declared that she was getting better at 'this,' a huge choking sound burst from her throat. It was part gasp, part hideous wheeze, and it surprised her completely.

Marcus could *die*. The reality of this slammed into her with smothering force. He could die, and then she would be truly alone. It wasn't even as if they'd seen much of each other in recent years, except for the past few weeks, of course.

But she'd always known he was there. The world was simply a better place, knowing that he was in it.

And now he might die. She'd be lost without him. How had she not realized that?

'Honoria!'

Honoria turned. It was her mother, bursting through the door.

'I came as quickly as I could,' Lady Winstead said, hurrying across the room. Then she saw Marcus's leg. 'Oh, my God.'

Honoria felt another one of those gaspy, wheezing noises blowing up within her. There was something about seeing her mother, about her mother seeing Marcus. It was like the time when she was twelve, and she'd fallen off her horse. She'd thought she was fine; she'd walked all the way home, bruised and achy, her face bleeding where she'd scratched it against a rock.

And then she'd seen her mother, and her mother's expression, and she'd started to bawl.

It was the same thing. She wanted to bawl. Dear God, all she wanted to do was push back and turn

137

away and cry and cry and cry.

But she couldn't. Marcus needed her. He needed her to be calm. And capable. 'Mrs. Wetherby is getting hot water,' she told her mother. 'She should be back soon.'

'Good. We'll need lots of it. And brandy. And a knife.'

Honoria looked at her mother with surprise. She sounded as if she knew what she was doing. Her mother.

'The doctor is going to want to take off the leg,' Lady Winstead said grimly.

'*What*?' Honoria hadn't even considered that.

'And he may be right.'

Honoria's heart stopped beating. Until her mother said, 'But not yet.'

Honoria stared at her mother in shock. She could not remember the last time she'd heard her speak with such decisiveness. When Daniel had fled the country, he'd taken a piece of their mother with him. She'd been utterly lost, unable to commit herself to anything or anyone, even her daughter. It was almost as if she could not bring herself to make any decisions, because to do so would mean that she accepted her life as it now was, with her only son gone, possibly forever.

But maybe all she had needed was a reason to wake up. A critical moment.

Maybe she'd needed to be needed.

'Stand back,' Lady Winstead said, pushing up her sleeves.

Honoria stepped aside, trying to ignore the tiny pang of jealousy that flared to life within her. Hadn't *she* needed her mother?

'Honoria?'

She looked at her mother, who was watching her with an expectant expression. 'Sorry,' Honoria mumbled, holding out the cloth in her hand. 'Do you want this?'

'A clean one, please.'

'Of course.' Honoria rushed to do her mother's bidding, further depleting Marcus's supply of under-things.

Her mother took the cloth, then looked at it with a confused expression. 'What is . . .'

'It was all I could find,' Honoria explained. 'And I thought time was of the essence.'

'It is,' her mother confirmed. She looked up, her eyes meeting Honoria's with grave directness. 'I have seen this before,' she said, her shaky breath the only sign of nerves. 'Your father. On his shoulder. It was before you were born.'

'What happened?'

Her mother looked back at Marcus's leg, narrowing her eyes as she examined the wound. 'See if you can shed more light on this.' And then, while Honoria went to the windows to pull the curtains fully open, she said, 'I don't even know how he cut himself. Just that it became horribly infected.' Very softly, she added, 'Almost as bad as this.'

'But he was fine,' Honoria said, returning to her mother's side. This was a story to which she knew the ending. Her father had had two perfectly strong arms until the day he died.

Her mother gave a nod. 'We were very lucky. The first doctor wanted to amputate. And I—' Her voice broke, and it was a moment before she continued. 'I would have let him do it. I was so concerned for your father's life.' She used the clean cloth to dab at Marcus's leg, trying to get a better look. When she spoke again, her voice was very soft. 'I would have done anything they told me to.'

'Why didn't they take his arm?' Honoria asked quietly.

Her mother let out a short puff of a breath, as if expelling a bad memory. 'Your father demanded to see another doctor. He told me that if the second agreed with the first, he would do as they asked. But he was not cutting off his arm because one man told him to.'

'The second one said they didn't have to?'

Her mother let out a grim chuckle. 'No, he said he almost certainly would have to cut it off. But he told your father they could try cleaning the wound first. *Really* cleaning it.'

'That's what I've been doing,' Honoria said in a rush. 'I've got quite a bit of the infection out, I think.'

'It's a good start,' her mother said. 'But . . .' She swallowed.

'But what?'

Her mother kept her attention firmly on Marcus's wound, pressing it lightly with the cloth as she examined. She did not look at Honoria when she said in a very low voice, 'The doctor said that if your father wasn't screaming, we weren't cleaning it well enough.'

'Do you remember what he did?' Honoria whispered.

Lady Winstead nodded. 'Everything,' she said softly.

Honoria waited for more. And then she wished she hadn't.

Her mother finally looked up. 'We're going to have to tie him down.'

Chapter Ten

It took less than ten minutes to turn Marcus's bedroom into a makeshift operating theater. Mrs. Wetherby returned with hot water and a supply of clean cloths. Two footmen were instructed to tie Marcus tightly to the bed, which they did, despite the horror that showed clearly on their faces.

Her mother asked for scissors. The sharpest, smallest pair they had. 'I need to cut away the dead skin,' she told Honoria, tiny lines of determination forming at the corners of her mouth. 'I watched the doctor do it with your father.'

'But did *you* do it?' Honoria asked.

Her mother looked her in the eye, then turned away. 'No.'

'Oh.' Honoria swallowed. There didn't seem to be anything else that could possibly serve as a reply.

'It's not difficult as long as one can control one's nerves,' her mother said. 'One doesn't need to be terribly precise.'

Honoria looked at Marcus, then back at her mother, mouth agape. 'Not precise? What do you mean? It's his leg!'

'I realize that,' her mother replied. 'But I promise you, it won't hurt him if I cut away too much.'

'Not *hurt*—'

'Well, of course it will hurt.' Lady Winstead looked down at Marcus with an expression of

141

regret. 'That's why we had to tie him down. But it will do no permanent damage. It's better to cut away too much than too little. It is absolutely essential that we eliminate all of the infection.'

Honoria nodded. It made sense. It was gruesome, but it made sense.

'I'm going to get started now,' her mother told her. 'There is much I can do even without the scissors.'

'Of course.' Honoria watched as Lady Winstead sat at Marcus's side and dipped a cloth in the steaming water. 'Is there anything I can do to help?' Honoria asked, feeling rather ineffectual at the foot of the bed.

'Sit on the other side,' her mother answered. 'Near his head. Talk to him. He might find comfort in it.'

Honoria wasn't so sure that Marcus found comfort in anything she did, but she knew *she* would find comfort in it. Anything would be better than standing around like an idiot, doing absolutely nothing.

'Hello, Marcus,' she said, pulling the chair close to the bed.

She didn't expect him to answer, and indeed, he did not.

'You're quite sick, you know,' she continued, trying to keep her voice bright and happy, even if her words were not. She swallowed, then continued in the brightest voice she could manage, 'But it turns out that my mother is a bit of an expert at this sort of thing. Isn't that remarkable?' She looked over at her mother with a swelling sense of pride. 'I must confess, I had no idea she knew such things.' She leaned down and murmured in his ear, 'I rather

142

thought she was the sort who would faint at the sight of blood.'

'I heard that,' her mother said.

Honoria gave her an apologetic smile. 'Sorry. But—'

'There is no need to apologize.' Her mother glanced over at her with a wry smile before resuming her work. When she spoke, however, she did not look up. 'I have not always been as . . .'

There was a hint of a pause, just enough for Honoria to realize that her mother was not quite sure what to say.

'As resolute as you may have needed me to be,' Lady Winstead finally finished.

Honoria sat very still, sucking in her upper lip as she let her mother's words settle upon her. It was an apology, just as much as if her mother had actually said the words *I'm sorry.*

But it was also a request. Her mother did not want to discuss it any further. It had been difficult enough just to say what she did. And so Honoria accepted the apology in exactly the manner her mother hoped she would. She turned back to Marcus and said—

'Anyway, I don't think anyone thought to look at your leg. The cough, you know. The doctor thought that was the cause of the fever.'

Marcus let out a little cry of pain. Honoria glanced quickly down toward her mother, who was now working with the scissors Mrs. Wetherby had brought. She'd opened them fully and was pointing one end toward Marcus's leg like a scalpel. With one fluid motion, her mother made a long cut, right down the middle of the wound.

'He didn't even flinch,' Honoria said with

surprise.

Her mother didn't look up. 'That's not the painful part.'

'Oh,' Honoria said, turning back to Marcus. 'Well. See, that wasn't so bad.'

He screamed.

Honoria's head snapped back up just in time to see her mother handing a bottle of brandy back to a footman.

'Very well, *that* was bad,' she said to Marcus. 'But the good news is it's unlikely to get much worse.'

He screamed again.

Honoria swallowed. Her mother had adjusted the scissors and was now actually trimming away bits of tissue.

'Very well,' she said again, giving his shoulder a little pat. 'It might not get better, either. The truth is, I have no idea. But I shall be here with you the whole time. I promise.'

'This is worse than I thought,' her mother said, mostly to herself.

'Can you fix it?' Honoria asked.

'I don't know. I can try. It's just . . .' Lady Winstead paused, letting out a long, low breath through pursed lips. 'Can someone wipe my brow?'

Honoria started to rise, but Mrs. Wetherby leapt into action, dabbing Lady Winstead's face with a cool cloth.

'It's so hot in here,' Lady Winstead said.

'We were told to keep the windows shut,' Mrs. Wetherby explained. 'The doctor insisted.'

'The same doctor who did not notice this massive injury to his leg?' Lady Winstead asked sharply.

Mrs. Wetherby did not reply. But she did move to the window to open it partway.

144

Honoria watched her mother intently, barely able to recognize this focused, determined woman. 'Thank you, Mama,' she whispered.

Her mother looked up. 'I am not going to let this boy die.'

He wasn't a boy any longer, but Honoria was not surprised that her mother still thought of him as such.

Lady Winstead returned to her work and said, in a very low voice, 'I owe it to Daniel.'

Honoria went absolutely still. It was the first time she had heard her mother utter his name since he'd left the country in disgrace. 'Daniel?' she echoed, her voice even and careful.

Her mother did not look up. 'I've lost one son already' was all she said.

Honoria stared at her mother in shock, then down at Marcus, and then back up. She had not realized her mother had thought of him that way. And she wondered if Marcus knew, because . . .

She looked down at him again, trying to choke back her tears as quietly as possible. He'd spent his whole life longing for a family. Had he even realized that he'd had one in hers?

'Do you need to take a break?' her mother asked.

'No,' Honoria answered, shaking her head even though her mother was not looking at her. 'No. I'm quite all right.' She took a moment to compose herself, then bent to whisper in Marcus's ear. 'Did you hear that? Mama is quite determined. So don't disappoint her.' She stroked his hair, pushing a thick, dark lock off his forehead. 'Or me.'

'Aaaargh!'

Honoria flinched, thrown back by his cry. Every

now and then her mother would do something that hurt him more than usual, and his entire body bucked against the strips of cloth they'd used to tie him down. It was awful to see, and even worse to feel. It was as if his pain shot through her.

Except it didn't hurt. It just made her feel sick. Sick to her stomach. Sick with herself. It was her fault he'd stepped in that stupid fake mole hole, her fault that he'd twisted his ankle. It was her fault they'd had to cut off his boot, and her fault he was so sick because of it.

And if he died, it would be her fault, too.

She swallowed, trying to quell the choking lump that was forming in her throat, and she leaned a little closer to say, 'I'm so sorry. I could never even begin to tell you how sorry I am.'

Marcus went quite still, and for a breathless moment Honoria thought he had heard her. But then she realized it was only because her mother had paused in her work. It was her mother who had heard her words, not Marcus. But if her mother was curious, she did not pursue it. She did not ask for the meaning of Honoria's apology, just gave a little nod and went back to work.

'I am thinking that when you are better you should come to London,' Honoria went on, fixing her voice back into a facsimile of good cheer. 'If nothing else, you will need a new pair of boots. Maybe something of a looser fit. It's not the style, I know, but perhaps you can set a new trend.'

He flinched.

'Or we could remain in the country. Skip the season. I know I told you I was desperate to marry this year, but—' She cast a surreptitious glance at her mother, then leaned closer to his ear and

146

whispered, 'My mother seems suddenly quite different. I think I can manage another year in her company. And twenty-two is not so very old for marriage.'

'You're twenty-one,' her mother said, not looking up.

Honoria froze. 'How much of what I said did you hear?'

'Just the last bit.'

Honoria had no idea if her mother was telling the truth. But they seemed to have a tacit agreement not to ask questions, so Honoria decided to respond by saying, 'I meant that if I don't marry until next year, when I am twenty-two, I shall not mind.'

'It will mean another year with the family quartet,' her mother said with a smile. And not a devious smile. A completely sincere, completely encouraging smile.

Honoria wondered, not for the first time, if her mother might be just a little bit deaf.

'I'm sure your cousins will be glad to have you for another year,' Lady Winstead continued. 'When you leave, Harriet will have to take your place, and she's really still a bit young. I don't think she's even sixteen yet.'

'Not until September,' Honoria confirmed. Her cousin Harriet—Sarah's younger sister—was quite possibly the worst musician in the Smythe-Smith family. And that was really saying quite a lot.

'I think she might need a little more practice,' Lady Winstead said with a grimace. 'Poor girl. She just can't seem to get the hang of it. It must be difficult for her, with such a musical family.'

Honoria tried not to gape at her. 'Well,' she

said, perhaps a little desperately, 'she does seem to prefer pantomimes.'

'It's hard to believe there is no one to play the violin between you and Harriet,' Lady Winstead remarked. She frowned, squinting down at Marcus's leg, then set back to work.

'Just Daisy,' Honoria replied, referring to yet another cousin, this one from a different branch of the family, 'but she's already been drafted into service now that Viola has married.'

'Drafted?' her mother echoed with a tinkle of laughter. 'You make it sound as if it's a chore.'

Honoria paused for just a moment, trying not to let her mouth fall open. Or laugh. Or perhaps cry. 'Of course not,' she finally managed to say. 'I adore the quartets.'

That much was true. She loved practicing with her cousins, even if she had to stuff her ears with wads of cotton ahead of time. It was just the performances that were awful.

Or, as Sarah was wont to put it, horrific.

Ghastly.

Apocalyptic.

(Sarah always did have a bit of a tendency toward hyperbole.)

But for some reason Honoria never did take the embarrassment personally, and she was able to keep a smile on her face the entire time. And when she touched her bow to her instrument, she did so with gusto. Her family was watching, after all, and it meant so much to them.

'Well, anyway,' she said, trying to bring the conversation back to the previous topic, which was now so 'previous' that it took her a moment to remember what it was, 'I'm sure I won't skip the season. I was just talking. Making conversation.' She swallowed. 'Babbling, really.'

'It is better to marry a good man than to rush into a disaster,' her mother said, sounding terribly sage. 'Your sisters all found good husbands.'

Honoria agreed, even if her brothers-in-law were not generally the sort of men to whom she might find herself attracted. But they treated their wives with respect, every last one of them.

'They did not all marry in their first season, either,' Lady Winstead added, not looking up from her work.

'True, but I believe they all did by the end of their second.'

'Is that so?' Her mother looked up and blinked. 'I suppose you're right. Even Henrietta . . . ? Well, yes, I suppose she did, right at the end.' She turned back to her task. 'You'll find someone. I'm not worried.'

Honoria let out a little snort. 'I'm glad *you're* not.'

'I'm not sure what happened last year. I truly thought Travers would propose. Or if not him, then Lord Fotheringham.'

Honoria shook her head. 'I have no idea. I thought they would, too. Lord Bailey in particular seemed quite keen. But then, all of a sudden . . . nothing. It was as if they lost interest overnight.' She shrugged and looked back down at Marcus. 'Maybe it's for the best. What do you think, Marcus? You didn't much like any of them, I think.' She sighed. 'Not that that has anything to do with it, but I suppose I value your opinion.' She let out a tiny snort of laughter. 'Can you believe I just said that?'

149

He turned his head.

'Marcus?' Was he awake? She peered down at him more closely, searching his face for some sign of . . . anything.

'What is it?' her mother asked.

'I'm not certain. He moved his head. I mean, of course he's done that before, but this was different.' She squeezed his shoulder, praying that he could feel her through the haze of his fever. 'Marcus? Can you hear me?'

His lips, dry and cracked, moved the tiniest bit. 'Hon— Hon—'

Oh, thank God.

'Don't speak,' she said. 'It's all right.'

'Hurts,' he gasped. 'Like the . . . devil.'

'I know. I know. I'm so sorry.'

'Is he conscious?' her mother asked.

'Barely.' Honoria stretched her arm down along the bed so that she could take Marcus's hand. She laced her fingers through his and held tight. 'You have a terrible cut on your leg. We're trying to clean it. It's going to hurt. Rather badly, I'm afraid, but it must be done.'

He gave a small nod.

Honoria looked over at Mrs. Wetherby. 'Do we have any laudanum? Perhaps we should give him some while he is able to swallow.'

'I believe so,' the housekeeper said. She had not stopped wringing her hands since she'd come back with the hot water and towels, and she looked relieved to have something to do. 'I can go look right now. There is only one place it would be.'

'Good idea,' Lady Winstead said. Then she stood and moved toward the head of the bed. 'Can you hear me, Marcus?'

His chin moved. Not much, but a bit.

'You're very ill,' she said.

He actually smiled.

'Yes, yes,' Lady Winstead said, smiling in return, 'stating the obvious, I know. But you're going to be perfectly fine, I assure you. It's just going to be a little painful at first.'

'Little?'

Honoria felt a wobbly smile touch upon her lips. She couldn't believe that he could joke at such a moment. She was so proud of him. 'We'll get you through this, Marcus,' she said, and then, before she had a clue what she was about, she leaned down and kissed his brow.

He turned again to face her, his eyes now almost fully open. His breathing was labored, and his skin was still so terribly heated. But when she looked in his eyes, she saw him there, through the fever, under the pain.

He was still Marcus, and she would not let anything happen to him.

*   *   *

Thirty minutes later, Marcus's eyes were closed again, his sleep aided considerably by a dose of laudanum. Honoria had adjusted his position so that she could hold his hand, and she had kept up a steady stream of conversation. It didn't seem to matter what she said, but she was not the only one who noticed that the sound of her voice soothed him.

Or at least she hoped it did, because if it didn't, then she was utterly useless. And that was more than she could bear.

151

'I think we're almost finished,' she told him. She cast a wary glance at her mother, who was still working diligently at his leg. 'I think we'd have to be. I can't imagine what there is left to clean.'

But her mother let out a frustrated breath and sat back, pausing to wipe her brow.

'Is there a problem?' Honoria asked.

Her mother shook her head and resumed her work, but after only a moment she pulled away. 'I can't see.'

'What? No, that's impossible.' Honoria took a breath, trying to keep calm. 'Just put your head closer.'

Lady Winstead shook her head. 'That's not the problem. It's just like when I read. I have to hold the book away from my eyes. I just— I can't—' She let out a resigned, impatient sigh. 'I just can't see it well enough. Not the small bits.'

'I'll do it,' Honoria said, her voice far more certain than the rest of her.

Her mother looked at her, but not with surprise. 'It's not easy.'

'I know.'

'He might scream.'

'He already has done,' Honoria said. But her throat felt close, and her heart was pounding.

'It is harder to hear when you are the one with the scissors,' her mother said softly.

Honoria wanted to say something elegant, something heroic about how much harder it would be if he died and she hadn't done everything she could to save him. But she didn't. She couldn't. She had only so much left within her, and words were no longer the best use of her energy.

'I can do it,' was all she said.

She looked at Marcus, still bound tightly to the bed. Sometime in the past hour he'd gone from burning red to deathly pale. Was that a good sign? She'd asked her mother, but she didn't know, either.

'I can do it,' Honoria said again, even though her mother had already handed her the scissors. Lady Winstead rose from her chair, and Honoria sat down, taking a deep breath.

'One step at a time,' she said to herself, looking closely at the wound before proceeding. Her mother had shown her how to identify which tissue needed to be cut away. All she needed to do was look at one piece and trim it. And then when that was done, she'd find another.

'Cut as close to the healthy tissue as you can,' her mother said.

Honoria nodded, moving her scissors further up the wound. Gritting her teeth, she cut.

Marcus let out a moan, but he didn't wake up.

'Well done,' Lady Winstead said softly.

Honoria nodded, blinking back tears. How could such small words make her feel so emotional?

'There was a bit at the bottom I didn't get to,' her mother said. 'I couldn't see the edges well enough.'

'I see it,' Honoria said grimly. She trimmed some of the dead skin, but the area still felt swollen. Taking the tip of the scissors as she'd seen her mother do, she angled them against him and punctured the tissue, allowing the yellow ooze of the infection to escape. Marcus strained against his bonds, and she whispered an apology, but she did not stop. She took a cloth and pressed hard.

'Water, please.'

Someone handed her a cup of water, and she

poured it on the wound, trying so very hard not to hear Marcus moaning with pain. The water was hot, very hot, but her mother swore that it was what had saved her father all those years ago. The heat drew out the infection.

Honoria prayed she was right.

She pressed a cloth against him, soaking up the excess water. Marcus made a strange noise again, although not as wrenching as before. But then he began to shake.

'Oh, my God,' she yelped, yanking the cloth away. 'What did I do to him?'

Her mother peered down with a puzzled expression. 'He almost looks as if he's laughing.'

'Can we give him more laudanum?' Mrs. Wetherby asked.

'I don't think we should,' Honoria said. 'I've heard of people not waking up when they've been given too much.'

'I really think he looks as if he's laughing,' her mother said again.

'He's not laughing,' Honoria said flatly. Good heavens, what on earth could he have to laugh about at such a time? She gave her mother a little nudge to back away, and she poured more hot water on Marcus's leg, working until she was satisfied that she'd cleaned the wound to the best of her ability.

'I think that's all of it,' Honoria said, sitting back. She took a deep breath. She felt hopelessly tense, every muscle in her body pulled tight. She set down the scissors and tried to stretch out her hands, but they felt like claws.

'What if we poured laudanum directly on the wound?' Mrs. Wetherby asked.

Lady Winstead blinked. 'I have no idea.'

'It couldn't hurt, could it?' Honoria asked. 'It's not likely to irritate his skin if it's something that can be swallowed. And if it can do something to dull the pain . . .'

'I have it right here,' Mrs. Wetherby said, holding up the small brown bottle.

Honoria took it and pulled out the cork. 'Mother?'

'Just a little,' Lady Winstead replied, not looking at all sure of her decision.

Honoria splashed a little laudanum on Marcus's leg, and he instantly howled with pain.

'Oh, dear,' Mrs. Wetherby moaned. 'I'm so sorry. It was my idea.'

'No, no,' Honoria said. 'That's the sherry. It's how they make it.' Why she knew this she had no idea, but she was fairly certain that the ominously labeled bottle (it said POISON in much bigger letters than LAUDANUM) also contained cinnamon and saffron. She dabbed her finger in and took a little taste.

'Honoria!' her mother exclaimed.

'Oh, my God, it's hideous,' Honoria said, rubbing her tongue against the roof of her mouth in a fruitless attempt to rid herself of the taste. 'But there is definitely sherry in it.'

'I can't believe you took some of that,' Lady Winstead said. 'It's dangerous.'

'I was just curious. He made such a face when we gave it to him. And it was clearly painful when we poured it on. Besides, it was only a drop.'

Her mother sighed, looking very much aggrieved. 'I wish the doctor would arrive.'

'It will still be some time,' Mrs. Wetherby said.

'At least an hour, I should think. And that is if he is at home to receive the summons. If he's out . . .' Her words trailed off.

For several moments no one spoke. The only sound was Marcus's breathing, strangely shallow and labored. Finally, Honoria was unable to take the silence any longer, and she asked, 'What do we do now?' She looked down at Marcus's leg. It looked raw and open, still bleeding slightly in places. 'Should we put a bandage on it?'

'I don't think so,' her mother said. 'We'll only have to take it off when the doctor arrives.'

'Are you hungry?' Mrs. Wetherby asked.

'No,' Honoria said, except she was. Ravenous. She just didn't think she could eat.

'Lady Winstead?' Mrs. Wetherby said quietly.

'Perhaps something small,' she murmured, not taking her worried eyes off Marcus.

'A sandwich, perhaps?' Mrs. Wetherby suggested, 'or my goodness, breakfast. Neither one of you has had breakfast. I could ask Cook to prepare eggs and bacon.'

'Whatever is easiest,' Lady Winstead replied. 'And please, something for Honoria, too.' She looked at her daughter. 'You should try to eat.'

'I know. I just . . .' She didn't finish. She was sure her mother knew exactly what she was feeling.

A hand settled gently on her shoulder. 'You should sit, too.'

Honoria sat.

And waited.

It was the hardest thing she'd ever done.

Chapter Eleven

Laudanum was an excellent thing.

Marcus normally eschewed the drug, and indeed he had a feeling he had looked down upon those who used it, but now he was wondering if perhaps he owed them all an apology. Maybe an apology to the entire world. Because clearly he had never been in real pain before. Not like this.

It wasn't so much the poking and snipping. One would think it would be painful to have bits of one's body hacked away like a woodpecker jabbing at a tree trunk, but that actually wasn't so bad. It hurt, but it wasn't anything he couldn't bear.

No, what killed him (or at least felt like it) was when Lady Winstead took out the brandy. Every so often she would dump what had to have been a gallon of the stuff over his open, gaping wound. She could have set him on fire and it wouldn't have hurt so much.

He was never drinking brandy again. Not unless it was the really good stuff. And even then, he would only do so on principle. Because it was the really good stuff.

Which needed to be drunk.

He thought about that for a moment. It had made sense when he'd first considered it. No, it still made sense. Didn't it?

Whatever the case, sometime after Lady Winstead had poured what he dearly hoped was not the good brandy on his leg, they'd got a dose of laudanum down his throat, and really, he had to say—it was lovely. His leg still felt as if it were being slow-roasted on a spit, which most people would consider unpleasant, but after enduring Lady Winstead's 'care' without any anesthesia, he was finding it positively pleasant to be stabbed with a knife under the influence of an opiate.

Almost relaxing.

And beyond that, he felt rather unaccountably happy.

He smiled up at Honoria, or rather he smiled up at where he thought she might be; his eyelids had clearly been weighted down with rocks.

Actually, he only *thought* he smiled; his mouth felt rather heavy, too.

But he wanted to smile. He would have done, if he'd been able. Surely that had to be the most important thing.

The jabbing at his leg stopped for a bit, then started up again. Then there was a lovely, short pause, and then—

Damn, that hurt.

But not enough to cry out. Although he might have moaned. He wasn't sure. They'd poured hot water on him. Lots of it. He wondered if they were trying to poach his leg.

Boiled meat. How terribly British of them.

He chuckled. He was funny. Who knew he was so funny?

'Oh, my God!' he heard Honoria yell. 'What did I do to him?'

He laughed some more. Because she sounded ridiculous. Almost as if she were speaking through a foghorn. *Oooorrrrrhhhh myyy Grrrrrrrrrd.*

He wondered if she could hear it, too.

Wait a moment . . . *Honoria* was asking what she'd done to him? Did that mean *she* was wielding

158

the scissors now? He wasn't sure how he ought to feel about this.

On the other hand . . . boiled meat!

He laughed again, deciding he didn't care. God, he was funny. How was it possible no one had ever told him he was funny before?

'Should we give him more laudanum?' Mrs. Wetherby said.

Oh, yes, please.

But they didn't. Instead they tried to boil him again, with a bit more of the poking and stabbing for good measure. But after only a few more minutes, they were done.

The ladies started talking about laudanum again, which turned out to be incredibly cruel of them, because no one got out a glass or a spoon to feed him. Instead they poured the stuff right on his leg, which—

'Aaaargh!'

—hurt more than the brandy, apparently.

But the ladies must have finally decided they were through torturing him, because after some discussion, they untied his bindings and moved him to the other side of his bed, which wasn't wet from all the hot water they'd been using to boil him.

And then, well . . . He might have slept for a bit. He rather hoped he was sleeping, because he was quite certain he'd seen a six-foot rabbit hopping through his bedchamber, and if that wasn't a dream, they were all in very big trouble.

Although really, it wasn't the rabbit that was so dangerous as much as the giant carrot he was swinging about like a mace.

That carrot would feed an entire village.

He liked carrots. Although orange had never

159

really been one of his favorite colors. He'd always found it a little jarring. It seemed to pop up when he didn't expect it, and he preferred his life without surprises.

Blue. Now, there was a proper color. Lovely and soothing. Light blue. Like the sky. On a sunny day.

Or Honoria's eyes. She called them lavender— she had since she was a child—but they weren't, not in his opinion. First of all, they were far too luminous to be lavender. Lavender was a flat color. Almost as gray as it was purple. And far too fussy. It made him think of old ladies in mourning. With turbans on their heads. He'd never understood why lavender was considered the appropriate step up from black in the mourning calendar. Wouldn't brown have been more appropriate? Something more medium-toned?

And why *did* old ladies wear turbans?

This was really very interesting. He didn't think he'd ever thought so hard about color before. Maybe he should have paid more attention when his father had made him take those painting classes so many years ago. But really, what ten-year-old boy wants to spend four months on a bowl of fruit?

He thought about Honoria's eyes again. They really were a bit more blue than lavender. Although they did have that purplish touch to them that made them so uncommon. It was true—no one had eyes quite like hers. Even Daniel's weren't precisely the same. His were darker. Not by much, but Marcus could tell the difference.

Honoria wouldn't agree, though. When she was a child she had frequently gone on about how she and Daniel had the same eyes. Marcus had always thought she was looking for a bond between them,

160

something that connected them in a special way.

She'd just wanted to be a part of things. That was all she'd ever wanted. No wonder she was so eager to be married and out of her silent, empty home. She needed noise. Laughter.

She needed not to be lonely. She needed never to be lonely.

Was she even in the room? It was rather quiet. He tried again to open his eyes. No luck.

He rolled onto his side, happy to be free of those damned bindings. He'd always been a side-sleeper.

Someone touched his shoulder, then pulled up his blankets to cover him. He tried to make a little murmuring sound to show his appreciation, and he guessed he must have been successful because he heard Honoria say, 'Are you awake?'

He made the same sound again. It seemed to be the only one he could make work.

'Well, maybe a little bit awake,' she said. 'That's better than nothing, I suppose.'

He yawned.

'We're still waiting for the doctor,' she said. 'I'd hoped he would be here by now.' She was quiet for a few moments, then added in a bright voice, 'Your leg looks quite improved. Or at least that's what my mother says. I'll be honest—it still looks dreadful to me. But definitely not as dreadful as it did this morning.'

This morning? Did that mean it was afternoon? He wished he could get his eyes to open.

'She went to her room. My mother, I mean. She said she needed respite from the heat.' Another pause, and then: 'It *is* quite hot in here. We opened the window, but only a very little bit. Mrs. Wetherby was afraid you would catch a chill. I know, it's hard

161

to imagine you could get a chill when it's this hot, but she assures me that it's possible.

'I like to sleep in a cold room with a heavy blanket,' she added. 'Not that I imagine you care.'

He did care. Well, not so much what she said. He just liked listening to her voice.

'And Mama is always hot lately. It drives me batty. She's hot, then she's cold, then she's hot again, and I swear there is no rhyme or reason to it. But she does seem to be hot more often than cold. Should you ever wish to buy her a gift, I recommend a fan. She is *always* in need of one.'

She touched his shoulder again, then his brow, lightly brushing his hair from his forehead. It felt nice. Soft, and gentle, and caring in a way that was utterly unfamiliar to him. It was a bit like when she'd come over and forced him to drink tea.

He liked being fussed over. Imagine that.

He let out a little sigh. It sounded like a happy one to his ears. He hoped she thought so, too.

'You've been sleeping for quite some time,' Honoria said. 'But I think your fever is down. Not all the way, but you seem peaceful. Although did you know you talk in your sleep?'

Really?

'Really,' she said. 'Earlier today I could have sworn you said something about a monkfish. And then just a little while ago I think you said something about onions.'

Onions? Not carrots?

'What are you thinking about, I wonder? Food? Monkfish with onions? It wouldn't be what I would want while sick, but to each his own.' She stroked his hair again, and then, to his complete surprise and delight, she lightly kissed his cheek. 'You're not

162

so terrible, you know,' she said with a smile.

He couldn't see the smile, but he knew it was there.

'You like to pretend that you are terribly standoffish and brooding, but you're not. Although you do scowl quite a bit.'

Did he? He didn't mean to. Not at her.

'You almost had me fooled, you know. I was really starting to not like you in London. But it was just that I'd forgotten you. Who you used to be, I mean. Who you probably still are.'

He had no idea what she was talking about.

'You don't like to let people see who you really are.'

She was quiet again, and he thought he heard her moving, maybe adjusting her position in her chair. And when she spoke, he heard her smiling again. 'I think you're shy.'

Well, for God's sake, he could have told her *that*. He hated making conversation with people he did not know. He always had.

'It's strange to think that of you,' she continued. 'One never thinks of a *man* as being shy.'

He couldn't imagine why not.

'You're tall,' she said in a thoughtful voice, 'and athletic, and intelligent, and all those things men are supposed to be.'

He did notice she didn't call him handsome.

'Not to mention ridiculously wealthy, oh, and of course, there's that title, too. If you were of a mind to get married, I'm quite certain you could choose anyone you wish.'

Did she think he was ugly?

She poked his shoulder with her finger. 'You can't imagine how many people would love to be in

163

your shoes.'

Not right now, they wouldn't.

'But you're shy,' she said, almost wonderingly. He could feel that she'd moved closer; her breath was landing lightly on his cheek. 'I think I like that you're shy.'

Really? Because he'd always hated it. All those years in school, watching Daniel talk to everyone and anyone without even a moment's hesitation. Always needing a little bit longer to figure out just how he might fit in. It was why he'd loved spending so much time with the Smythe-Smiths. Their home had always been so chaotic and crazed; he'd slipped almost unnoticed into their life of un-routine and become one of the family.

It was the only family he'd ever known.

She touched his face again, running a finger down the bridge of his nose. 'You would be too perfect if you weren't shy,' she said. 'Too much of a storybook hero. I'm sure you never read novels, but I've always thought my friends saw you as a character in one of Mrs. Gorely's gothics.'

He knew there was a reason he'd never liked her friends.

'I was never quite sure if you were the hero or the villain, though.'

He decided not to find insult in that statement. He could tell she was smiling slyly as she said it.

'You need to get better,' she whispered. 'I don't know where I'll be if you don't.' And then, so softly that he barely heard her: 'I think you might be my touchstone.'

He tried to move his lips, tried to say something, because that wasn't the sort of thing one let go without a reply. But his face still felt thick and heavy, and all he could manage were a few gasping noises.

'Marcus? Do you want some water?'

He did, actually.

'Are you even awake?'

Sort of.

'Here,' she said. 'Try this.'

He felt something cold touch his lips. A spoon, dribbling lukewarm water into his mouth. It was hard to swallow, though, and she only let him have a few drops.

'I don't think you're awake,' she said. He heard her settle back down in her chair. She sighed. She sounded tired. He hated that.

But he was glad she was here. He had a feeling she might be his touchstone, too.

Chapter Twelve

'Doctor!' Honoria jumped to her feet about twenty minutes later as a surprisingly young man entered the room. She didn't think she'd ever met a doctor who didn't have gray hair. 'It's his leg,' she said. 'I don't think you saw it when—'

'I didn't see him before,' the doctor said brusquely. 'My father did.'

'Oh.' Honoria took a respectful step back as the doctor bent over Marcus's leg. Her mother, who had come in just behind him, walked over to Honoria's side.

And then took her hand. Honoria squeezed it as if it were a lifeline, grateful for the connection.

The young man looked at Marcus's leg for not

nearly as long as Honoria would have thought necessary, then bent and put his ear to his chest. 'How much laudanum did you give him?'

Honoria looked at her mother. She had been the one to dose him.

'A spoonful,' Lady Winstead said. 'Perhaps two.'

The doctor's mouth tightened as he straightened and faced them. 'Was it one, or was it two?'

'It's difficult to say,' Lady Winstead answered. 'He didn't swallow it all.'

'I had to wipe his face,' Honoria put in.

The doctor did not comment. He put his ear back on Marcus's chest, and his lips moved, almost as if he were counting to himself. Honoria waited for as long as she could stand, then said, 'Doctor, er . . .'

'Winters,' her mother supplied.

'Yes, er, Dr. Winters, please tell us, did we give him too much?'

'I don't think so,' Dr. Winters answered, but he still kept his ear to Marcus's chest. 'The opium suppresses the lungs. That is why his breathing is so shallow.'

Honoria put her hand to her mouth in horror. She hadn't even realized his breathing was shallow. In fact, she'd thought he sounded better. More peaceful.

The doctor straightened and turned his attention to Marcus's leg. 'It is critical that I have all of the pertinent information,' he said brusquely. 'I would be much more worried if I did not know that he'd been given laudanum.'

'You're not worried?' Honoria asked in disbelief.

Dr. Winters looked at her sharply. 'I didn't say I wasn't worried.' He returned to Marcus's leg,

166

examining it closely. 'Just that I'd be more worried if he hadn't had it. If his breathing was this shallow without laudanum, it would indicate a serious infection indeed.'

'This isn't serious?'

The doctor gave her another annoyed look. He did not appreciate her questions, that much was clear. 'Kindly hold your comments until I finish examining him.'

Honoria felt her entire face clench in irritation, but she stepped back. She would be polite to Dr. Winters if it killed her; if anyone had a chance at saving Marcus's life, it would be he.

'Explain to me exactly what you did to clean the wound,' the doctor demanded, glancing up briefly from his examination of Marcus's leg. 'And I also want to know what it looked like before you started.'

Honoria and her mother took turns telling him what they'd done. He seemed to approve, or at the very least, he didn't disapprove. When they were done, he turned back to Marcus's leg, looked at it one more time, and let out a long breath.

Honoria waited for a moment. He looked like he was taking time to think. But bloody hell, he was taking a *long* time to think. Finally she couldn't stand it. 'What is your opinion?' she blurted out.

Dr. Winters spoke slowly, almost as if he were thinking out loud. 'He might keep the leg.'

'Might?' Honoria echoed.

'It's too soon to tell for sure. But if he does keep it'—he looked at both Honoria and her mother—'it will have been due to your good work.'

Honoria blinked in surprise; she had not expected a commendation. Then she asked the question she dreaded: 'But will he live?'

The doctor's eyes met Honoria's with frank steadiness. 'He will certainly live if we amputate his leg.'

Honoria's lips trembled. 'What do you mean?' she whispered. But she knew exactly what he meant; she just needed to hear him say it.

'I am confident that if I remove his leg at this moment he will live.' He looked back over at Marcus, as if another glance might offer one last clue. 'If I do not remove his leg, he may very well recover completely. Or he may die. I cannot predict how the infection will progress.'

Honoria went still. Only her eyes moved, from Dr. Winters's face, to Marcus's leg, and then back. 'How will we know?' she asked quietly.

Dr. Winters tilted his head to the side in question.

'How will we know when to make the decision?' she clarified, her voice rising in volume.

'There are signs to look for,' the doctor replied. 'If you begin to see streaks of red moving up or down his leg, for example, we will know we must amputate.'

'And if that does not happen, does that mean he is healing?'

'Not necessarily,' the doctor admitted, 'but at this point, if there is no change in the wound's appearance, I shall take that as a good sign.'

Honoria nodded slowly, trying to take it all in. 'Will you remain here at Fensmore?'

'I cannot,' he told her, turning to pack up his bag. 'I must see to another patient, but I will be back this evening. I do not think we will need to make any decision before then.'

168

'You do not *think*?' Honoria asked sharply. 'Then you are not certain?'

Dr. Winters sighed, and for the first time since he'd entered the room, he looked tired. 'One is never certain in medicine, my lady. I would that were not the case.' He looked over at the window, whose curtains were pulled back to reveal the endless green of Fensmore's south lawn. 'Perhaps someday that will change. But not in our lifetime, I fear. Until then, my job remains as much of an art as a science.'

It was not what Honoria had wanted to hear, but she recognized it as the truth, and so she gave him a nod, thanking him for his attentions.

Dr. Winters returned the courtesy with a bow, then gave Honoria and her mother instructions and left, promising that he would return later that night. Lady Winstead escorted him out, leaving Honoria once again alone with Marcus, who lay terrifyingly still on his bed.

For several minutes, she stood motionless in the center of the room, feeling strangely limp and lost. There really wasn't anything to do. She had been just as scared that morning, but at least then she had been able to concentrate on treating his leg. Now all she could do was wait, and her mind, denied of a specific task, had nothing but fear to fill it.

What a choice. His life or his leg. And *she* might have to be the one to make it.

She didn't want the responsibility. Dear God, she didn't want it.

'Oh, Marcus,' she sighed, finally walking over to the chair at his bedside. 'How did this happen? *Why* did it happen? It's not fair.' She sat and leaned

169

down against the mattress, folding her arms and resting her head in the crook of one elbow.

She would, of course, sacrifice his leg to save his life. That was what Marcus would choose if he were sensible enough to speak for himself. He was a proud man, but not so much so that he would prefer death over handicap. She knew this about him. They had never talked about it, of course— who talked about such things? No one sat at the dining table talking about whether to amputate or die.

But she knew what he would want. She had known him for fifteen years. She did not need to have asked him the question to know his choice.

He would be angry, though. Not at her. Not even at the doctor. At life. Maybe at God. But he would persevere. She would make sure of it. She would not leave his side until he . . . Until he . . .

Oh, dear God. She couldn't even imagine it.

She took a breath, trying to steady herself. Part of her wanted to run out of the room and beg Dr. Winters to remove his leg right now. If that was what it would take to guarantee his survival, then she would hold the damn saw. Or at least hand it over to the doctor.

She couldn't face the thought of a world without him. Even if he wasn't *in* her life, if he stayed here in Cambridgeshire and she went and married someone who lived in Yorkshire or Wales or the Orkney Islands and she never saw him again, she would still know that he was alive and well, riding a horse, or reading a book, or perhaps sitting in a chair by a fire.

It wasn't time to make that decision yet, though, no matter how much she hated the uncertainty. She could not be selfish. She needed to keep him whole as long as possible. But what if, in doing so, she waited too long?

She closed her eyes tight even though her head was buried in her arms. She could feel her tears burning against her eyelids, threatening to burst forth with all the terror and frustration building within her.

'Please don't die,' she whispered. She rubbed her face against her forearm, trying to wipe away her tears, then settled back down in the cradle of her arms. Maybe she should be pleading with his leg, not with him. Or maybe with God, or the devil, or Zeus, or Thor. She'd plead with the man who milked the cows if she thought it would make a difference.

'Marcus,' she said again, because saying his name seemed to bring her solace. 'Marcus.'

''Noria.'

She froze, then sat up. 'Marcus?'

His eyes did not open, but she could see movement beneath the lids, and his chin bobbed ever so slightly up and down.

'Oh, Marcus,' she sobbed. The tears poured forth. 'Oh, I'm sorry. I shouldn't be crying.' She looked helplessly for a handkerchief and then finally just wiped her eyes on his bedsheet. 'I'm just so happy to hear your voice. Even though you don't sound at all like you.'

'W-w-wa—'

'Do you want water?' she asked, jumping on his broken words.

Again, his chin moved.

'Here, let me sit you up just a bit. It will make it easier.' She reached under his arms and managed

171

to straighten him a few inches. It wasn't much, but it was something. A glass of water sat on the bedside table, the spoon still in it from the last time she'd tried to give him a drink. 'I'm just going to give you a few drops,' she told him. 'Just a little at a time. I'm afraid you'll choke if I give you too much.'

He did much better this time, though, and she got the better part of eight spoonfuls into him before he signaled that he'd had enough and slumped back down to horizontal.

'How do you feel?' she asked, trying to fluff his pillow. 'Other than terrible, I mean.'

He moved his head slightly to the side. It seemed to be a sickly interpretation of a shrug.

'Of course you're feeling terrible,' she clarified, 'but is there any change? More terrible? Less terrible?'

He made no response.

'The same amount of terrible?' She laughed. She actually laughed. Amazing. 'I sound ridiculous.'

He nodded. It was a small movement, but bigger than he'd managed so far.

'You heard me,' she said, unable to contain the huge, trembling smile on her face. 'You mocked me, but you heard me.'

He nodded again.

'That's good. You can feel free. When you're better, and you will be better, you're not allowed to do that, and by that I mean mock me, but for now, you may go right ahead. Oh!' She jumped to her feet, suddenly bursting with nervous energy. 'I should check your leg. It hasn't been long since Dr. Winters left, I know, but there's no point in not looking.'

It took only two steps and one second to see

172

that his leg was unchanged. The wound was still an angry, glistening red, but it was no longer tinged with that sickly yellow, and more importantly, she saw no red streaks sneaking up the limb.

'The same,' she told him. 'Not that I thought there would be a change, but as I said, there's no point in not . . . well, you know.' She smiled sheepishly. 'I already said it.'

She held silent for a moment, content just to gaze at him. His eyes were closed, and indeed, he didn't look any different than he had when Dr. Winters had been examining him, but Honoria had heard his voice, and she'd given him water, and that was enough to bring hope to her heart.

'Your fever!' she suddenly exclaimed. 'I should check that.' She touched his forehead. 'You feel the same to me. Which is to say, warmer than you should. But better than you were. You are definitely better than you were.' She paused, wondering if she was speaking into the proverbial mist. 'Can you still hear me?'

He moved his head.

'Oh, good, because I know I sound foolish, and there is no point sounding foolish for no one.'

His mouth moved. She thought he might be smiling. Somewhere in his mind, he was smiling.

'I am happy to be foolish for you,' she announced.

He nodded.

She put one hand to her mouth, letting her elbow rest on the opposite arm, which was banded across her waist. 'I wish I knew what you were thinking.'

He gave a tiny shrug.

'Are you trying to tell me you're not thinking of much of anything?' She pointed a finger at him.

173

'Because that I will not believe. I know you far too well.' She waited for another response, no matter how small. She didn't get one, so she kept on talking.

'You're probably figuring out how best to maximize your corn harvest for the year,' she said. 'Or maybe wondering if your rents are too low.' She thought about that for a moment. 'No, you'd be wondering if your rents are too high. I'm quite certain you're a softhearted landlord. You wouldn't want anyone to struggle.'

He shook his head. Just enough so that she could tell what he meant.

'No, you don't want anyone to struggle, or no, that's not what you're thinking about?'

'You,' he rasped.

'You're thinking about me?' she whispered.

'Thank you.' His voice was soft, barely even audible, but she heard him. And it took every last ounce of her strength not to cry.

'I won't leave you,' she said, taking his hand in hers. 'Not until you're well.'

'Th-th—'

'It's all right,' she told him. 'You don't need to say it again. You didn't need to say it the first time.'

But she was glad that he did. And she wasn't certain which of his statements had touched her more—his two words of thanks, or the first, his simple, solitary *You.*

He was thinking about her. While he was lying there, possibly near death, even more possibly at the brink of an amputation, he was thinking about her.

For the first time since she had arrived at Fensmore, she wasn't terrified.

174

Chapter Thirteen

The next time Marcus woke up, he could tell that something had changed. First of all, his leg hurt like the devil again. But somehow he suspected that wasn't such a bad thing. Secondly, he was hungry. Famished, in fact, as if he had not eaten in days.

Which was probably true. He had no idea how much time had passed since he'd fallen ill.

Lastly, he could open his eyes. *That* was excellent.

He wasn't sure what time it was. It was dark, but it could just as easily have been four in the morning as ten at night. It was bloody disorienting, being sick.

He swallowed, trying to moisten his throat. Some more water would be nice. He turned his head toward the bedside table. His eyes still had not adjusted to the dark, but he could see that someone had fallen asleep in a chair by his bed. Honoria? Probably. He had a feeling she had not left his room throughout the ordeal.

He blinked, trying to remember how she had even come to be at Fensmore. Oh, yes, Mrs. Wetherby had written to her. He could not imagine why his housekeeper had thought to do so, but he would be eternally grateful that she had.

He rather suspected that he would be dead if not for the agony Honoria and her mother had inflicted upon his leg.

But that wasn't the whole of it. He knew that he had been in and out of consciousness, and he knew that there would always be huge gaps in his memory of this terrible time. But even so, he had known that Honoria was there, in his room. She had held his hand, and she had talked to him, her soft voice reaching his soul even when he hadn't been able to make out the words.

And knowing she was there . . . It had just been easier. He hadn't been alone. For the first time in his life, he hadn't been alone.

He let out a little snort. He was being overly dramatic. It wasn't as if he walked about with some invisible shield, keeping all other people at bay. He could have had more people in his life. He could have had many more people. He was an earl, for the love of God. He could have snapped his fingers and filled his house.

But he'd never wanted company for the sake of idle chatter. And for everything in his life that had meant anything, he had been alone.

It was what he'd wanted.

It was what he'd thought he wanted.

He blinked a few more times, and his room began to come into focus. The curtains had not been pulled shut, and the moon shed enough light for him to make out the barest gradations of color. Or maybe it was just that he knew that his walls were burgundy and the giant landscape hanging above the fireplace was mostly green. People saw what they expected to see. It was one of the most basic truisms of life.

He turned his head again, peering at the person in the chair. It was definitely Honoria, and not just because she was the person he expected to see. Her hair had come partly undone, and it was clearly light brown, not nearly dark enough to be Lady Winstead's.

176

He wondered how long she'd been sitting there. She couldn't possibly be comfortable.

But he shouldn't bother her. She surely needed her sleep.

He tried to push himself up into a sitting position but found he was too weak to manage more than a few inches. Still, he could see a little better, maybe even reach across Honoria to the glass of water on the table.

Or maybe not. He lifted his arm about half a foot before it fell back to his side. Damn, he was tired. And thirsty. His mouth felt as if it had been packed in sawdust.

That glass of water looked like heaven. Heaven, just out of reach.

Damn it.

He sighed, then wished he hadn't, because it made his ribs hurt. His entire body ached. How was it possible that a body could ache absolutely everywhere? Except for his leg, which burned.

But he thought that maybe he didn't have a fever any longer. Or at least not much of one. It was hard to tell. He certainly felt more lucid than he had in some time.

He watched Honoria for a minute or so. She didn't move at all in her sleep. Her head was cocked to the side at an unnatural angle, and he could only think that she was going to wake up with a terrible crick in her neck.

Maybe he should wake her up. It would be the kind thing to do.

'Honoria,' he croaked.

She didn't move.

'Honoria.' He tried to say it louder, but it came out the same—raspy and hoarse, like an insect

177

hurling itself against the window. Not to mention that the effort was exhausting.

He tried reaching out to her again. His arm felt like a dead weight, but somehow he got it off the bed. He meant to just poke her, but instead his hand landed heavily on her outstretched leg.

'Aaaaah!' She came awake with a shriek, her head snapping up so fast she hit the back of it on the bedpost. 'Ow,' she moaned, bringing her hand up to rub the sore spot.

'Honoria,' he said again, trying to get her attention.

She mumbled something and let out a huge yawn as she rubbed her cheek with the heel of her hand. And then: 'Marcus?'

She sounded sleepy. She sounded wonderful.

'May I have some water, please?' he asked her. Maybe he should have said something more profound; he had, after all, practically come back from the dead. But he was thirsty. Wandering the desert thirsty. And asking for water was about as profound as one got in his condition.

'Of course.' Her hands fumbled about in the darkness until they landed on the glass. 'Oh, blast,' he heard her say. 'One moment.'

He watched as she got to her feet and made her way to another table, where she picked up a pitcher. 'There isn't much left,' she said groggily. 'But it should be enough.' She poured some into the glass, then picked up the spoon.

'I can do it,' he told her.

She looked at him with surprise. 'Really?'

'Can you help me sit up?'

She nodded and wrapped her arms around him, almost like an embrace. 'Here we are,' she

178

murmured, pulling him up. Her words landed softly in the crook of his neck, almost like a kiss. He sighed and went still, allowing himself a moment to savor the warmth of her breath against his skin.

'Are you all right?' she asked, pulling back.

'Yes, yes, of course,' he said, snapping out of his reverie with as much speed as a man in his condition could manage. 'Sorry.'

Together, they got him into a sitting position, and Marcus took the glass and drank without assistance. It was remarkable how much that felt like a triumph.

'You look so much better,' Honoria said, blinking sleep from her eyes. 'I— I—' She blinked again, but this time he thought it might be to keep from crying. 'It's so nice to see you again.'

He nodded and held out the glass. 'More, please.'

'Of course.' She poured another and handed it to him. He drank it greedily, exhaling only when he had finished the whole thing.

'Thank you,' he said, handing it back.

She took it, set it down, then set herself back down in the chair. 'I was so worried about you,' she said.

'What happened?' he asked. He remembered some of it—her mother and the scissors, the giant rabbit. And she'd called him her touchstone. He would always remember that.

'The doctor has been by to see you twice,' she told him. 'Dr. Winters. The younger Dr. Winters. His father— Well, I'm not sure what happened to his father, but honestly, I don't care to know. He never even looked at your leg. He had no idea you'd an infected wound. If he'd seen it before it got so

179

bad, well, I suppose it all may have turned out the same.' Her lips pressed together in frustration. 'But maybe not.'

'What did Dr. Winters say?' Marcus asked, then clarified, 'The younger one.'

She smiled. 'He thinks you're going to keep your leg.'

'What?' He shook his head, trying to understand.

'We were afraid we might have to amputate it.'

'Oh, my God.' He felt himself sinking down into the pillows. 'Oh, my God.'

'It's probably for the best that you didn't know it was a possibility,' she said gently.

'Oh, my God.' He couldn't imagine life without a leg. He supposed no one could, until they had to.

She took his hand in hers. 'It's going to be all right.'

'My leg,' he whispered. He had an irrational urge to sit up and look at it, just to make sure it was still there. He forced himself to lie still; she'd surely think him beyond foolish for wanting to see it for himself. But it hurt. It hurt a lot, and he was grateful for the pain. At least he knew it was still where it was supposed to be.

Honoria pulled her hand free to stifle an enormous yawn. 'Oh, excuse me,' she said when she was done. 'I'm afraid I haven't slept very much.'

His fault, he realized. Yet another reason he owed her his gratitude. 'That chair can't possibly be comfortable,' he told her. 'You should take the other side of the bed.'

'Oh, I couldn't.'

'It couldn't possibly be any more improper than anything else that's happened today.'

'No,' she said, looking as if she might laugh if

she weren't so tired, 'I mean really, I couldn't. The mattress is still wet from when we cleaned your leg.'

'Oh.' And then he did laugh. Because it was funny. And because it felt so good to smile.

She squirmed a little, trying to get comfortable in the chair. 'Maybe I could lie on top of the blanket,' she said, craning her neck to look over him to the empty spot.

'Whatever you wish.'

She let out an exhausted sigh. 'My feet might get wet. But I don't think I care.'

A moment later she was up on the bed, lying on the blanket. He was, too, actually, although most of him was under a second quilt; he supposed they'd wanted to leave his leg open to the air.

She yawned again.

'Honoria,' he whispered.

'Mmmm?'

'Thank you.'

'Mmm-hmm.'

A moment went by, and then he said, because he had to, 'I'm glad you were here.'

'Me, too,' she said sleepily. 'Me, too.'

Her breathing slowly evened out, and then so did his. And they slept.

*   *   *

Honoria woke the next morning delightfully snuggly and warm. Her eyes still closed, she pointed her toes, then flexed her feet, rolling her ankles one way and then the other. It was her morning ritual, stretching in bed. Her hands were always next. Out they went like little starfishes and then back into claws. Then her neck, back and forth and around in

181

a circle.

She yawned, balling her hands into fists as she stretched her arms forward and—

Crashed into someone.

She froze. Opened her eyes. It all came back to her.

Dear heavens, she was in bed with Marcus. *No.* That was not the right way to phrase it. She was in Marcus's bed.

But she wasn't *with* him.

Improper, yes, but surely there was a special dispensation given to young ladies who find themselves in bed with a gentleman who is clearly too ill to compromise them.

Slowly, she tried to inch away. No need to wake him. He probably had no idea she was even there. And by *there* she meant right next to him, side to side, feet touching his. Certainly not on the far end of the bed, where she'd started the night before.

Bending her knees, she planted the soles of her feet on the mattress for traction. First she lifted her hips, moving them an inch to the right. Then her shoulders. Then her hips again, and then her feet to catch up. Time for the shoulders, and then—

Whomp!

One of Marcus's arms came down heavily across her.

Honoria froze again. Good heavens, what was she supposed to do now? Maybe if she waited a minute or two, he'd roll back to his previous position.

She waited. And she waited. And he moved.

Toward her.

Honoria swallowed nervously. She had no idea what time it was—sometime after dawn, but other than that, she had not a clue—and she really did not want Mrs. Wetherby coming in to find her pressed up against Marcus in bed. Or worse, her mother.

Surely no one would think badly of her, especially not after all that had transpired the day before. But she was unmarried, and so was he, and it was a bed, and he was wearing very little clothing, and—

That was it. She was getting out. If he woke up, he woke up. At least he wouldn't wake up with a proverbial gun at his back, pointing him toward marriage.

She wrenched herself up and out of the bed, trying to ignore the rather pleasantly sleepy sounds he made as he rolled over and nestled beneath his quilt. Once she had her feet firmly on the carpet, she took a quick peek at his leg. It seemed to be healing properly, with no sign of those ominous red streaks Dr. Winters had warned about.

'Thank you,' she whispered, sending up a quick prayer for his continued recovery.

'You're welcome,' Marcus murmured.

Honoria let out a little shriek of surprise, jumping back nearly a foot.

'Sorry,' he said, but he was laughing.

It was quite the loveliest sound Honoria had ever heard.

'I wasn't thanking you,' she said pertly.

'I know.' He smiled.

She tried to smooth down her skirts, which were horribly wrinkled. She was wearing the same blue dress she'd donned in London, which had been— oh, dear heavens—two days earlier. She couldn't even imagine what a fright she must look.

'How are you feeling?' she asked.

'Much better,' he said, sitting up. She noticed he pulled the blankets along with him. Which was surely the only reason her blush was pink instead of deep red. It was funny—almost. She'd seen his bare chest a hundred times the day before, had poked and jabbed at his naked leg, and even—not that she would ever tell him about it—caught a glimpse of one of his buttocks when he'd been tossing about. But now, when they were both fully awake and he was no longer at death's door, she could not even bring her eyes to meet his.

'Is it still very painful?' she asked, motioning to his leg, which stuck out from under the covers.

'More of a dull ache.'

'You will have a terrible scar.'

He smiled wryly. 'I shall wear it with pride and mendacity.'

'Mendacity?' she echoed, unable to contain her amusement.

He cocked his head to the side as he regarded the huge wound on his leg. 'I was thinking I might set it about that I'd wrestled with a tiger.'

'A tiger. In Cambridgeshire.'

He shrugged. 'It's more likely than a shark.'

'Wild boar,' she decided.

'Now that's just undignified.'

She pressed her lips together, then let out a little bubble of laughter. He did, too, and it was only then that she allowed herself to believe it: He was going to get better. It was a miracle. She could think of no other word to describe it. The color had returned to his face, and if perhaps he looked a little too thin, that was nothing compared to the clarity in his eyes.

He was going to be all right.

'Honoria?'

She looked up in question.

'You swayed,' he said. 'I would help you, but . . .'

'I do feel a little unsteady,' she said, making her way to the chair by his bed. 'I think . . .'

'Have you eaten?'

'Yes,' she said. 'No. Well, some. I probably should do. I think I'm just . . . relieved.' And then, to her utmost horror, she began to sob. It came on suddenly, hitting her like a tall ocean wave. Every bit of her had been wound so tightly. She had pulled herself as long and as far as she could go, and now that she knew he would be well, she fell apart.

She was like a violin string, pulled taut, and then snapped in two.

'I'm sorry,' she said, gasping for breath between the sobs. 'I don't know . . . I didn't mean . . . I'm just so happy . . .'

'Shhhh,' he crooned, taking her hand. 'It's all right. Everything is going to be all right.'

'I know,' she sobbed. 'I know. That's why I'm crying.'

'That's why I'm crying, too,' he said softly.

She turned. There were no tears rolling down his face, but his eyes were wet. She had never seen him show such emotion, never even thought it possible. With a trembling hand, she reached out and touched his cheek, then the corner of his eye, drawing her fingers back when one of his tears slid onto her skin. And then she did something so unexpected that it took both of them by surprise.

She threw her arms around him, burying her face in the crook of his neck, and held tight. 'I was so scared,' she whispered. 'I don't think I even knew how scared I was.'

His arms came around her, hesitantly at first, but then, as if he needed only that little push, he relaxed into the embrace, holding her softly against him, stroking her hair.

'I just didn't know,' she said. 'I didn't realize.' But these were only words now, with meanings even she did not understand. She had no idea what she was talking about—what it was she didn't know or didn't realize. She just . . . She just . . .

She looked up. She just needed to see his face.

'Honoria,' he whispered, looking down at her as if he'd never seen her before. His eyes were warm, chocolaty brown and rich with emotion. Something flared in their depths, something she didn't quite recognize, and slowly, ever so slowly, his lips dipped to meet hers.

*   *   *

Marcus could never have explained why he kissed Honoria. He didn't *know* why he'd done it. He was holding her while she cried, and it had seemed the most natural, innocent thing to do. There had been no inclination to kiss her, though, no urge to take it further.

But then she looked at him. Her eyes—oh, those amazing eyes—glistening with tears, and her lips, full and trembling. He stopped breathing. He stopped thinking. Something else took over, something deep within him that felt the woman in his arms, and he was lost.

He was changed.

He had to kiss her. He had to. It was as basic and elemental as his breath, his blood, his very soul.

And when he did . . .

The earth stopped spinning.

The birds stopped singing.

Everything in the world came to a halt, everything but him and her and the feather-light kiss that connected them.

Something stirred to life within him, a passion, a desire. And he realized that if he hadn't been so weak, so debilitated, he would have taken it further. He would not have been able to stop himself. He would have pressed her body against his, glorying in her softness, her scent.

He would have kissed her deeply, and he would have touched her. Everywhere.

He would have begged her. He would have begged her to stay, begged her to welcome his passion, begged her to take him within her.

He wanted her. And nothing could have terrified him more.

This was Honoria. He had sworn to protect her. And instead . . .

He lifted his lips from hers, but he couldn't quite pull himself away. Resting his forehead against hers, savoring one last touch, he whispered, 'Forgive me.'

She left then. She could not exit the room fast enough. He watched her go, saw her hands shaking, her lips trembling.

He was a beast. She had saved his life, and this was what he had done in return?

'Honoria,' he whispered. He touched his fingers to his lips, as if he might somehow feel her there.

And he did. It was the damnedest thing.

He still felt her kiss, still tingled with the light touch of her lips under his.

187

She was with him still.

And he had the strangest feeling she always would be.

Chapter Fourteen

Mercifully, Honoria didn't have to spend the next day of her life agonizing over her brief kiss with Marcus.

Instead, she slept.

It was a short walk from Marcus's bedchamber to her own, so she set her mind to the task at hand—namely, putting one foot in front of the other and remaining upright long enough to reach her bedchamber. And once she did that, she lay on her bed and did not rise again for twenty-four hours.

If she dreamed, she remembered nothing.

It was morning when she finally awakened, and she was still in the same frock she'd been wearing since she'd got dressed—how many days ago was it?— in London. A bath seemed in order, and a fresh change of clothing, and then breakfast, of course, where she quite happily insisted that Mrs. Wetherby join her at the table and talk about all sorts of things that had nothing to do with Marcus.

The eggs were extremely interesting, as was the bacon, and the hydrangeas outside the window were absolutely fascinating.

Hydrangeas. Who would have imagined?

All in all, she avoided not just Marcus but all thoughts of Marcus quite well until Mrs. Wetherby asked, 'Have you been by to see his lordship yet this morning?'

Honoria paused, her muffin suspended halfway to her mouth. 'Er, not yet,' she said. The butter from her muffin was dripping onto her hand. She set it back down and wiped her fingers.

And then Mrs. Wetherby said, 'I'm sure he would love to see you.'

Which meant that Honoria had to go. After all the time and effort she'd put into caring for him when he'd been in the depths of his fever, it would have looked very odd if she'd simply waved her hand and said, 'Oh, I'm sure he's fine.'

The walk from the breakfast room to Marcus's bedchamber took approximately three minutes, which was three minutes longer than she wanted to spend thinking about a three-second kiss.

She had kissed her brother's best friend. She had kissed *Marcus* . . . who, she supposed, had become one of her own best friends, too.

And that stopped her almost as short as the kiss had done. How had that happened? Marcus had always been Daniel's friend, not hers. Or rather, Daniel's friend first, and hers second. Which wasn't to say—

She stopped. She was making herself dizzy.

Oh, bother. He probably hadn't even thought of it once. Maybe he'd even still been a little bit delirious. Maybe he wouldn't even remember.

And could it even really be called a kiss? It had been very, very short. And did it mean anything if the kisser (him) had been feeling terribly grateful to the kissee (her) and possibly even indebted, in the most elemental of ways?

She'd saved his life, after all. A kiss was not entirely out of order.

Plus, he had said, 'Forgive me.' Did it count as a

kiss if the kisser had asked for forgiveness?

Honoria thought not.

Still, the last thing she wanted was to talk with him about it, so when Mrs. Wetherby told her that he had still been sleeping when she'd gone to check on him, Honoria decided to make her visit posthaste in order to catch him before he awakened.

His door had been left slightly ajar, so she placed her palm against the dark wood and pushed very slowly. It was unfathomable that a house as well run as Fensmore might have creaky hinges on its doors, but one could never be too careful. Once she'd made a head-sized opening, she poked in, turned her neck so that she could see him, and—

He turned and looked at her.

'Oh, you're awake!' The words popped out of her mouth like the chirp of a small, stunned bird.

Drat it all.

Marcus was sitting up in bed, his blankets tucked neatly around his waist. Honoria noticed with relief that he had finally donned a nightshirt.

He held up a book. 'I've been trying to read.'

'Oh, then I won't bother you,' she said quickly, even though the tone of his voice had been clearly of the *I've-been-trying-to-read-but-I-just-can't-get-into-it* variety.

Then she curtsied.

Curtsied!

Why on earth had she curtsied? She'd never curtsied to Marcus in her life. She'd nodded her head, and she'd even done a little bob at the knees, but good heavens, he would have collapsed laughing if she'd curtsied to him. In fact, he was quite possibly laughing right at that moment. But she would never know, because she fled before he could make a sound.

Still, when she came across her mother and Mrs. Wetherby in the drawing room later that day, she could say with utmost honesty that she had been to visit Marcus and she had found him to be quite improved.

'He's even reading,' she said, sounding gorgeously casual. 'That must be a good sign.'

'What was he reading?' her mother asked politely, reaching forward to pour her a cup of tea.

'Ehrm . . .' Honoria blinked, recalling nothing beyond the dark red leather of the book cover. 'I didn't notice, actually.'

'We should probably bring him some more books from which to choose,' Lady Winstead said, handing Honoria her tea. 'It's hot,' she warned. Then she continued, 'It is dreadfully dull to be confined to bed. I speak from experience. I was confined for four months while I was carrying you, and three with Charlotte.'

'I didn't know.'

Lady Winstead waved it off. 'There was nothing to be done about it. It's not as if I had a choice. But I can tell you that books positively saved my sanity. One can either read or embroider, and I don't see Marcus picking up a needle and thread.'

'No,' Honoria agreed, smiling at the thought.

Her mother took another sip of her tea. 'You should investigate his library and see what you can find for him. And he can have my novel when we leave.' She set down her cup. 'I brought that one by Sarah Gorely. I'm almost done with it. It is marvelous thus far.'

'*Miss Butterworth and the Mad Baron*?' Honoria

191

asked dubiously. She'd read it, too, and had found it to be highly diverting, but it was almost farcically melodramatic, and she could not imagine Marcus enjoying it. If Honoria recalled correctly, there was quite a lot of hanging from cliffs. And from trees. And window ledges. 'Don't you think he would prefer something more serious?'

'I'm sure he *thinks* he would prefer something more serious. But that boy is far too serious already. He needs more levity in his life.'

'He's hardly a boy any longer.'

'He will always be a boy to me.' Lady Winstead turned to Mrs. Wetherby, who had remained silent during the entire exchange. 'Don't you agree?'

'Oh, indeed,' Mrs. Wetherby agreed. 'But of course I have known him since he was in nappies.'

Honoria was *certain* Marcus would not approve of this conversation.

'Perhaps you can choose some books for him, Honoria,' her mother said. 'I am sure you know his taste better than I.'

'I'm not sure that I do, actually,' Honoria said, looking down at her tea. For some reason that bothered her.

'We have a comprehensive library here at Fensmore,' Mrs. Wetherby said with pride.

'I'm sure I'll find something,' Honoria said, pasting a bright smile on her face.

'You shall have to,' her mother said, 'unless you wish to teach him to embroider.'

Honoria shot her a panicked look, then saw the laughter in her eyes. 'Oh, can you imagine?' Lady Winstead said with a chuckle. 'I know that men make marvelous tailors, but I am sure they have teams of needlewomen hiding in their back rooms.'

'Their fingers are too big,' Mrs. Wetherby agreed. 'They can't hold the needles properly.'

'Well, he couldn't be any worse than Margaret.' Lady Winstead turned to Mrs. Wetherby and explained, 'My eldest daughter. I have never seen anyone less skilled with a needle.'

Honoria looked over at her mother with interest. She had never realized that Margaret was so dismal at needlework. But then again, Margaret was seventeen years older than she was. She had been married and out of the Smythe-Smith household before Honoria had even been old enough to form memories.

'It's a good thing she had such talent for the violin,' Lady Winstead continued.

Honoria looked up sharply at that. She'd heard Margaret play. 'Talent' was not a word she'd have used to describe it.

'All my daughters play the violin,' Lady Winstead said proudly.

'Even you, Lady Honoria?' Mrs. Wetherby asked.

Honoria nodded. 'Even me.'

'I wish you had brought your instrument. I should have loved to have heard you play.'

'I'm not as capable as my sister Margaret,' Honoria said. Which, tragically, was true.

'Oh, don't be silly,' her mother said, giving her a playful pat on the arm. 'I thought you were magnificent last year. You need only to practice a bit more.' She turned back to Mrs. Wetherby. 'Our family hosts a musicale every year. It is one of the most sought-after invitations in town.'

'Such a treasure to come from such a musical family.'

'Oh,' Honoria said, because she wasn't sure she'd be able to manage much of anything else. 'Yes.'

'I do hope your cousins are rehearsing in your absence,' her mother said with a worried expression.

'I'm not sure how they could,' Honoria said. 'It's a quartet. One can't really rehearse with one of the violins missing.'

'Yes, I suppose so. It's just that Daisy is so green.'

'Daisy?' Mrs. Wetherby asked.

'My niece,' Lady Winstead explained. 'She is quite young and'—her voice dropped to a whisper, although for the life of her, Honoria couldn't figure out why—'she's not very talented.'

'Oh, dear,' Mrs. Wetherby gasped, one of her hands rising to her chest. 'Whatever will you do? Your musicale will be ruined.'

'I am quite certain Daisy will keep up with the rest of us,' Honoria said with a weak smile. Truthfully, Daisy *was* bad. But it was difficult to imagine her actually making the quartet *worse*. And she would bring some badly needed enthusiasm to the group. Sarah was still claiming that she'd rather have her teeth pulled than perform with the quartet again.

'Has Lord Chatteris ever been to the musicale?' Mrs. Wetherby asked.

'Oh, he comes every year,' Lady Winstead replied. 'And sits in the front row.'

He was a saint, Honoria thought. At least for one night a year.

'He does love music,' Mrs. Wetherby said.

A saint. A martyr, even.

'I suppose he will have to miss it this year,' Lady

Winstead said with a sad sigh. 'Perhaps we can arrange for the girls to come here for a special concert.'

'No!' Honoria exclaimed, loudly enough that both the other women turned to look at her. 'I mean, he wouldn't like that, I'm sure. He doesn't like people going out of their way for him.' She could see from her mother's expression that she was not finding this to be a strong argument, so she added, 'And Iris doesn't travel well.'

A blatant lie, but it was the best she could come up with so quickly.

'Well, I suppose,' her mother conceded. 'But there is always next year.' Then, with a flash of panic in her eyes, she added, 'Although *you* won't be playing, I'm sure.' When it became obvious she would have to explain, she turned to Mrs. Wetherby and said, 'Each Smythe-Smith daughter must leave the quartet when she marries. It is tradition.'

'Are you engaged to be married, Lady Honoria?' Mrs. Wetherby asked, her brow knit with confusion.

'No,' Honoria replied, 'and I—'

'What she means to say,' her mother interrupted, 'is that we expect her to be engaged by the end of the season.'

Honoria could only stare. Her mother had not shown such determination or strategy during her first two seasons.

'I do hope we're not too late for Madame Brovard,' her mother mused.

Madame Brovard? The most exclusive modiste in London? Honoria was stunned. Just a few days ago her mother had told her to go shopping with her cousin Marigold and 'find something pink.' Now she wanted to get Honoria in to see Madame

195

Brovard?

'She will not use the same fabric twice if it is at all distinctive,' her mother was explaining to Mrs. Wetherby. 'It is why she is considered the best.'

Mrs. Wetherby nodded approvingly, clearly enjoying the conversation.

'But the downside is that if one sees her too late in the season'—Lady Winstead held up her hands in a fatalistic manner—'all the good fabrics are gone.'

'Oh, that is terrible,' Mrs. Wetherby replied.

'I know, I know. And I want to make sure we find the right colors for Honoria this year. To bring out her eyes, you know.'

'She has beautiful eyes,' Mrs. Wetherby agreed. She turned to Honoria. 'You do.'

'Er, thank you,' Honoria said automatically. It was strange, seeing her mother act like . . . well, like Mrs. Royle, to be completely honest. Disconcerting. 'I think I will go to the library now,' she announced. The two older ladies had entered into a spirited discussion about the distinction between lavender and periwinkle.

'Have a good time, dear,' her mother said without even looking her way. 'I tell you, Mrs. Wetherby, if you had a *lighter* shade of periwinkle . . .'

Honoria just shook her head. She needed a book. And maybe another nap. And a slice of pie. And not necessarily in that order.

*　　　*　　　*

Dr. Winters stopped by that afternoon and declared Marcus well on his way to recovery. His fever had

196

cleared entirely, his leg was mending splendidly, and even his sprained ankle—which they'd all quite forgotten about—no longer showed signs of swelling.

With Marcus's life no longer in danger, Lady Winstead announced that she and Honoria would be packing their things and leaving for London immediately. 'It was highly irregular to make the trip in the first place,' she told Marcus privately. 'I doubt there will be talk, given our previous connection and the precariousness of your health, but we both know that society will not be so lenient if we linger.'

'Of course,' Marcus murmured. It was for the best, really. He was beyond bored and would miss having them about, but the season would be starting in earnest soon, and Honoria needed to get back to London. She was an unmarried daughter of an earl and thus in search of a suitable husband; there was no other place for her at this time of year.

He would have to go, too, to keep his vow to Daniel and make sure she didn't marry an idiot, but he was stuck in bed—doctor's orders—and would be for at least another week. After that he would be confined to his home for another week, possibly two, until Dr. Winters was confident that he was free of infection. Lady Winstead had made him promise to follow the doctor's directives.

'We did not save your life to have you squander it,' she told him.

It would be close to a month before he could follow them to town. He found that inexplicably frustrating.

'Is Honoria about?' he asked Lady Winstead, even though he knew better than to inquire about an unmarried young lady to her mother—even with those two. But he was so bored. And he missed her company.

Which was not at all the same thing as missing *her*.

'We had tea just a little while ago,' Lady Winstead said. 'She mentioned she saw you this morning. I believe she plans to find some books for you in the library here. I imagine she'll be by this evening to bring them.'

'That will be much appreciated. I'm almost done with . . .' He looked over at his bedside table. What *had* he been reading? *'Philosophical Inquiries Into the Essence of Human Freedom.'*

Her brows rose. 'Are you enjoying it?'

'Not very much, no.'

'I shall tell Honoria to hurry along with the books, then,' she said with an amused smile.

'I look forward to it,' he said. He started to smile as well, then caught himself and assumed a more serious mien.

'I'm sure she does, too,' Lady Winstead said.

Of this Marcus was not so certain. But still, if Honoria didn't mention the kiss, then neither would he. It was a trifling thing, really. Or if not, then it should be. Easily forgotten. They would be back to their old friendship in no time.

'I think she is still tired,' Lady Winstead said, 'although I can't imagine why. She slept for twenty-four hours, did you know that?'

He did not.

'She did not leave your side until your fever broke. I offered to take her place, but she would not have it.'

'I am very much indebted to her,' Marcus said

198

softly. 'And to you, too, from what I understand.'

For a moment Lady Winstead said nothing. But then her lips parted, as if she was deciding whether to speak. Marcus waited, knowing that silence was often the best encouragement, and a few seconds later, Lady Winstead cleared her throat and said, 'We would not have come to Fensmore if Honoria had not insisted.'

He was not sure what to say to that.

'I told her that we should not come, that it was not proper, since we are not family.'

'I have no family,' he said quietly.

'Yes, that is what Honoria said.'

He felt a strange pang at that. Of course Honoria knew that he had no family; everyone did. But somehow, to hear her say it, or just to hear someone else tell him she'd said it . . .

It hurt. Just a little. And he didn't understand why.

Honoria had seen beyond all that, past his aloneness and into his loneliness. She had seen it—no, seen *him*—in a way even he had not understood.

He had not realized just how solitary his life was until she had stumbled back into it.

'She was most insistent,' Lady Winstead said, breaking into his thoughts. And then, so quietly that he barely heard her: 'I just thought you should know.'

Chapter Fifteen

Several hours later, Marcus was sitting in bed, not even pretending to read *Philosophical Inquiries Into the Essence of Human Freedom*, when Honoria came by for another visit. She held about half a dozen books in her arms and was accompanied by a maid bearing a supper tray.

He was not surprised that she'd waited until someone else had had to come up to his room as well.

'I brought you some books,' she said with a determined smile. She waited until the maid placed the tray on his bed and then set the stack down on the bedside table. 'Mother said you'd likely need entertainment.' She smiled again, but her expression was far too resolute to have been spontaneous. With a little nod, she turned and started to follow the maid out of the room.

'Wait!' he called out. He couldn't let her go. Not yet.

She paused, turned, and gave him a questioning look.

'Sit with me?' he asked, tilting his head toward the chair. She hesitated, so he added, 'I've had only myself for company for the better part of two days.' She still looked uncertain, so he smiled wryly and said, 'I find myself somewhat dull, I'm afraid.'

'Only somewhat?' she replied, probably before she remembered she was trying not to enter into a conversation.

'I'm desperate, Honoria,' he told her.

She sighed, but she had a wistful smile as she did

so, and she walked into the room. She left the door to the hallway open; now that he was not at death's door, there were certain proprieties that must be obeyed. 'I hate that word,' she said.

'"Desperate"?' he guessed. 'You find it overused?'

'No,' she sighed, sitting down in the chair by his bed. 'Too frequently apt. It's a terrible feeling.'

He nodded, although in truth, he didn't think he understood desperation. Loneliness, certainly, but not desperation.

She sat quietly at his side, her hands folded in her lap. There was a long silence, not quite awkward, but not comfortable, either, and then she said rather suddenly, 'The broth is beef.'

He looked down at the small porcelain tureen on his tray, still covered by a lid.

'The cook called it *boeuf consommé*,' she continued, speaking a little faster than she usually did, 'but it's broth, plain and simple. Mrs. Wetherby insists that its curative powers are beyond compare.'

'I don't suppose I have anything other than broth,' he said dolefully, looking down at his sparse tray.

'Dry toast,' Honoria said sympathetically. 'I'm sorry.'

He felt his head hang forward another inch. What he wouldn't give for a slice of Flindle's chocolate cake. Or a creamed apple tart. Or a shortbread biscuit, or a Chelsea bun, or bloody well anything that contained a great deal of sugar.

'It smells quite nice,' Honoria said. 'The broth.'

It did smell quite nice, but not as nice as chocolate would.

He sighed and took a spoonful, blowing on it

201

before taking a taste. 'It's good,' he said.

'Really?' She looked doubtful.

He nodded and ate some more. Or rather, drank some more. Did one eat soup or drink it? And more to the point, could he get some cheese to melt on top of it? 'What did you have for supper?' he asked her.

She shook her head. 'You don't want to know.'

He ate-drank another spoonful. 'Probably not.' Then he couldn't help himself. 'Was there ham?'

She didn't say anything.

'There *was*,' he said accusingly. He looked down at the last dregs of his soup. He supposed he could use the dry toast to soak it up. He hadn't left enough liquid, though, and after two bites, his toast really was dry.

Sawdust dry. Wandering-the-desert dry. He paused for a moment. Hadn't he been wandering the desert thirsty a few days earlier? He took a bite of his entirely unpalatable toast. He'd never seen a desert in his life, and likely never would, but as far as geographical habitats went, it did seem to be offering a multitude of similes lately.

'Why are you smiling?' Honoria asked curiously.

'Am I? It was a sad, sad smile, I assure you.' He regarded his toast. 'Did you truly have ham?' And then, even though he knew he didn't want to know the answer: 'Was there pudding?'

He looked at her. She wore a very guilty expression.

'Chocolate?' he whispered.

She shook her head.

'Berry? Ca—Oh, Lord, did Cook make treacle tart?'

No one made treacle tart like Fensmore's cook.

202

'It was delicious,' she admitted, with one of those amazingly happy sighs reserved for the memories of the very best of desserts. 'It was served with clotted cream and strawberries.'

'Is there any left?' he asked dolefully.

'I should think there must be. It was served in a huge—Wait a moment.' Her eyes narrowed, and she speared him with a suspicious stare. 'You're not asking me to steal you a piece, are you?'

'Would you?' He hoped his face looked as pathetic as his voice. He really needed her to pity him.

'No!' But her lips were pressing together in an obvious attempt not to laugh. 'Treacle tart is not an appropriate food for the sickbed.'

'I don't see why not,' he replied. With utmost honesty.

'Because you're supposed to have broth. And calf's-foot jelly. And cod liver oil. Everyone knows that.'

He forced his stomach not to turn at the mention. 'Have any of those delicacies ever made you feel better?'

'No, but I don't think that's the point.'

'How is it possibly not the point?'

Her lips parted for a quick reply, but then she went quite comically still. Her eyes tipped up and looked off to the left, almost as if she were searching her mind for a suitable retort. Finally, she said, with deliberate slowness, 'I don't know.'

'Then you'll steal me a piece?' He gave her his best smile. His best *I-almost-died-so-how-can-you-deny-me* smile. Or at least that's how he hoped it appeared. The truth was, he wasn't a very accomplished flirt, and it might very well have come

203

across as an *I-am-mildly-deranged-so-it's-in-all-of-our-best--interests-if-you-pretend-to-agree-with-me* smile.

There was really no way to know.

'Do you have any idea how much trouble I could get into?' Honoria asked. She leaned forward in a furtive manner, as if someone might actually be spying on them.

'Not very much,' he replied. 'It's my house.'

'That matters very little when put up against the collective wrath of Mrs. Wetherby, Dr. Winters, and my mother.'

He shrugged.

'Marcus . . .'

But she had no coherent protest beyond that. So he said, 'Please.'

She looked at him. He tried to look pathetic.

'Oh, all right.' She let out a little snort, capitulating with a remarkable lack of grace. 'Do I have to go right now?'

He clasped his hands together piously. 'I would be most appreciative if you would.'

She didn't move her head, but her eyes turned one way, and then the other, and he couldn't quite tell if she was trying to act sneaky. Then she stood, brushing her hands against the pale green fabric of her skirts. 'I will be back,' she said.

'I cannot wait.'

She marched to the door and turned around. 'With tart.'

'You are my savior.'

Her eyes narrowed. 'You owe me.'

'I owe you for a great deal more than treacle tart,' he told her quite seriously.

She exited the room without another word,

204

leaving Marcus with his empty tureen and bread crusts. And books. He looked over at the table, where she'd left the books for him. Carefully, so as not to upset the glass of lukewarm lemon water Mrs. Wetherby had prepared for him, he moved the tray to the other side of the bed. Leaning over, he grabbed the first book and took a look. *Striking and Picturesque Delineations of the Grand, Beautiful, Wonderful, and Interesting Scenery Around Loch-Earn.*

Good Lord, she'd found that in his library?

He looked at the next. *Miss Butterworth and the Mad Baron.* It wasn't something he would normally choose, but compared to the *Striking and Picturesque Delineations of the Grand, Beautiful Et Cetera, Et Cetera Somewhere in the Wilds of Scotland I Shall Bore You to Death*, it looked positively pithy.

He settled in against his pillows, flipped the pages until he was at the opening chapter, and sat down to read.

It was a dark and windy night—

Hadn't he heard that before?

—and Miss Priscilla Butterworth was certain that at any moment the rain would begin, pouring down from the heavens in sheets and streams . . .

By the time Honoria returned, Miss Butterworth had been abandoned on a doorstep, survived the plague, and been chased by a wild boar.

She was quite fleet of foot, Miss Butterworth.

Marcus turned eagerly to Chapter Three, where

he anticipated Miss Butterworth stumbling upon a plague of locusts, and was quite engrossed when Honoria appeared in the doorway, out of breath and clutching a tea towel in her hands.

'You didn't get it, then?' he asked, looking at her over the edge of *Miss Butterworth*.

'Of course I got it,' she replied with disdain. She set the tea towel down and unfolded it to reveal a somewhat crumbly, but nonetheless recognizable, treacle tart. 'I brought an *entire* pie.'

Marcus felt his eyes go wide. He was tingling. Honestly. Tingling with anticipation. Miss Butterworth and her locusts were nothing compared to this. 'You are my hero.'

'To say nothing of having saved your life,' she quipped.

'Well, that, too,' he demurred.

'One of the footmen gave chase.' She looked over her shoulder toward the open door. 'I think he might have thought I was a thief, although really, if I were coming to burgle Fensmore, I'd hardly start with treacle tart.'

'Really?' he asked, his mouth full of heaven. 'It's exactly where I'd start.'

She broke off a piece and popped it in her mouth. 'Oh, it is good,' she sighed. 'Even without the strawberries and cream.'

'I can think of nothing better,' he said with a happy sigh. 'Except, perhaps, chocolate cake.'

She perched on the side of the bed and took another small piece. 'Sorry,' she said, swallowing before she continued, 'I didn't know where to get forks.'

'I don't care,' he said. He didn't. He was just so damned happy to be eating real food, with real flavor. That required real chewing. Why people thought that clear liquids were the key to recovering from a fever he would never know.

He began to fantasize about cottage pie. Dessert was marvelous, but he was going to need some real sustenance. Beef mince. Sliced potatoes, lightly crisped from the oven. He could almost taste it.

He looked over at Honoria. Somehow he did not think she was going to be able to sneak that out of the kitchen in a tea towel.

Honoria reached for another piece of the tart. 'What are you reading?' she asked.

'*Miss Butterworth and the*, er . . .' He looked down at the book, which lay pages down and open on his bed. '*Mad Baron*, apparently.'

'Really?' She looked stunned.

'I couldn't bring myself to crack open *Reflections and Illuminations of a Small Unpopulated Area of Scotland*.'

'What?'

'This one,' he said, handing her the book.

She looked down and he noticed that her eyes had to move quite a distance to take in the entirety of the title. 'It looked quite descriptive,' she said with a little shrug. 'I thought you would enjoy it.'

'Only if I was worried that the fever hadn't done me in,' he said with a snort.

'I think it sounds interesting.'

'You should read it, then,' he said with a gracious wave. 'I shan't miss it.'

Her lips pressed together peevishly. 'Did you look at anything else I brought you?'

'Actually, no.' He held up *Miss Butterworth*. 'This was really quite intriguing.'

'I can't believe you're enjoying it.'

207

'You've read it, then?'

'Yes, but—'

'Did you finish it?'

'Yes, but—'

'Did you enjoy it?'

She did not seem to have a ready reply, so he took advantage of her distraction and pulled the tea towel closer. Another few inches and the treacle tart would be entirely out of her reach.

'I did enjoy it,' she finally said, 'although I found some parts to be implausible.'

He flipped over the book and peered down. 'Really?'

'You're not very far into it,' Honoria said, tugging the tea towel back in her direction. 'Her mother is pecked to death by pigeons.'

Marcus regarded the book with newfound respect. 'Really?'

'It's quite macabre.'

'I cannot wait.'

'Oh, please,' she said, 'you can't possibly want to read this.'

'Why not?'

'It's so . . .' She waved a hand through the air as she searched for the right word. 'Unserious.'

'I can't read something unserious?'

'Well, of course you can. I just find it difficult to imagine that you would choose to.'

'And why is that?'

Her eyebrows rose. 'You're sounding awfully defensive.'

'I'm curious. Why wouldn't I choose to read something unserious?'

'I don't know. You're *you*.'

'Why does that sound like an insult?' Said with

nothing but curiosity.

'It's not.' She took another piece of treacle tart and nibbled at it. And that was when the strangest thing happened. His eyes fell to her lips, and as he watched, her tongue darted from her mouth to lick an errant crumb.

It was the tiniest movement, over in less than a second. But something electric shot through him, and with a gasp he realized it was desire. Hot, gut-clenching desire.

For Honoria.

'Are you all right?' she asked.

No. 'Yes, er, why?'

'I thought I might have hurt your feelings,' she admitted. 'If I did, please accept my apologies. Truly, it wasn't meant to be an insult. You're perfectly nice the way you are.'

'Nice?' Such a bland word.

'It's better than *not* nice.'

It was at this point that a different man might have grabbed her and showed her precisely how 'not nice' he could be, and Marcus was actually 'not nice' enough to imagine the scene in great detail. But he was also still suffering the aftereffects of a near-deadly fever, to say nothing of the open door and her mother, who was likely just down the hall. So instead he said, 'What else did you bring me to read?'

It was a much safer avenue of conversation, especially since he had spent much of the day convincing himself that kissing her had had *nothing* to do with desire. It had been a complete aberration, a momentary burst of madness brought on by extreme emotion.

This argument, unfortunately, was presently

209

being shot to pieces. Honoria had shifted her position so that she could reach the books without standing up, and this meant that she'd moved her bottom quite a bit closer to . . . well, to his bottom, or really, his hip if one wanted to put a fine point on it. There was a sheet and a blanket between them, not to mention his nightshirt and her dress and heaven knew what else she had under it, but dear *God* he had never been as aware of another human being as he was of her right that very moment.

And he still wasn't sure how it had happened.

'*Ivanhoe*,' she said.

What was she talking about?

'Marcus? Are you listening? I brought you *Ivanhoe*. By Sir Walter Scott. Although, look at this, isn't this interesting?'

He blinked, certain he must have missed something. Honoria had opened the book and was flipping through the pages at the beginning.

'His name is not on the book. I don't see it anywhere.' She turned it over and held it up. 'It just says "By the Author of Waverley." Look, even on the spine.'

He nodded, because that was what he thought was expected of him. But at the same time, he couldn't seem to take his eyes off her lips, which were pursed together in that rosebuddish thing she did when she was thinking.

'I haven't read *Waverley,* have you?' She looked up, eyes bright.

'I have not,' he answered.

'Perhaps I should,' she murmured. 'My sister said she enjoyed it. But at any rate, I didn't bring you *Waverley,* I brought you *Ivanhoe*. Or rather, the first volume. I didn't see any point in lugging all three.'

'I have read *Ivanhoe,*' he told her.

'Oh. Well, let's put that one aside, then.' She looked down at the next.

And he looked at her.

Her lashes. How had he never noticed how long they were? It was rather odd, because she hadn't the coloring that usually accompanied long lashes. Maybe that was why he hadn't noticed them; they were long, but not dark.

'Marcus? Marcus!'

'Hmmm?'

'Are you all right?' She leaned forward, regarding him with some concern. 'You look a bit flushed.'

He cleared his throat. 'Perhaps some more lemon water.' He took a sip, and then another, for good measure. 'Do you find it hot in here?'

'No.' Her brow wrinkled. 'I don't.'

'I'm sure it's nothing. I—'

She already had her hand on his forehead. 'You don't feel warm.'

'What else did you bring?' he asked quickly, motioning with his head toward the books.

'Oh, er, here we are . . .' She took hold of another one and read from the cover. '*History of the Crusades for the Recovery and Possession of the Holy Land*. Oh, dear.'

'What is it?'

'I brought only Volume Two. You can't start there. You'll miss the entire siege of Jerusalem and everything about the Norwegians.'

Let it be said, Marcus thought dryly, *that nothing cooled a man's ardor like the Crusades*. Still . . .

He looked at her questioningly. 'Norwegians?'

'A little-known crusade at the beginning,' she

211

said, waving aside what was probably a good decade of history with a flick of her wrist. 'Hardly anyone ever talks about it.' She looked over at him and saw what must have been an expression of complete amazement. 'I like the Crusades,' she said with a shrug.

'That's . . . excellent.'

'How about *The Life and Death of Cardinal Wolsey*?' she asked, holding up another book. 'No? I also have *History of the Rise, Progress, and Termination of the American Revolution*.'

'You really do think I'm dull,' he said to her.

She looked at him accusingly. 'The Crusades are *not* dull.'

'But you brought only Volume Two,' he reminded her.

'I can certainly go back and look for the first volume.'

He decided to interpret that as a threat.

'Oh, here we are. Look at this.' She held up a very slim, pocket-sized book with a triumphant expression. 'I have one by Byron. The least dull man in existence. Or so I'm told. I have never met him myself.' She opened the book to the title page. 'Have you read *The Corsair*?'

'On the day it was published.'

'Oh.' She frowned. 'Here is another by Sir Walter Scott. *Peveril of the Peak*. It's rather lengthy. It should keep you busy for some time.'

'I believe I will stick with *Miss Butterworth*.'

'If you wish.' She gave him a look as if to say, *There is no way you are going to like it*. 'It belongs to my mother. Although she did say you may keep it.'

'If nothing else, I'm sure it will rekindle my love of pigeon pie.'

212

She laughed. 'I'll tell Cook to prepare it for you after we leave tomorrow.' She looked up suddenly. 'You did know that we depart for London tomorrow?'

'Yes, your mother told me.'

'We wouldn't go unless we were certain you were recovering,' she assured him.

'I know. I'm sure you have much to attend to in town.'

She grimaced. 'Rehearsals, actually.'

'Rehearsals?'

'For the—'

Oh, no.

'—musicale.'

The Smythe-Smith musicale. It finished off what the Crusades had begun. There wasn't a man alive who could maintain a romantic thought when faced with the memory—or the threat—of a Smythe-Smith musicale.

'You're still playing the violin?' he asked politely.

She gave him a funny look. 'I've hardly taken up the cello since last year.'

'No, no, of course not.' It had been a silly thing to ask. But quite possibly the only polite question he might have come up with. 'Er, do you know yet when the musicale is scheduled for this year?'

'The fourteenth of April. It's not so very far off. Only a bit more than two weeks.'

Marcus took another piece of treacle tart and chewed, trying to calculate how long he might need to recuperate. Three weeks seemed exactly the right length of time. 'I'm sorry I'll miss it,' he said.

'Really?' She sounded positively disbelieving. He was not sure how to interpret this.

'Well, of course,' he said, stammering slightly.

He'd never been a terrifically good liar. 'I haven't missed it for years.'

'I know,' she said, shaking her head. 'It has been a magnificent effort on your part.'

He looked at her.

She looked at him.

He looked at her more closely. 'What are you saying?' he asked carefully.

Her cheeks turned ever so slightly pink. 'Well,' she said, glancing off toward a perfectly blank wall, 'I realize that we're not the most . . . er . . .' She cleared her throat. 'Is there an antonym for *discordant*?'

He stared at her in disbelief. 'Are you saying you know. . . . ehrm, that is to say—'

'That we're awful?' she finished for him. 'Of course I know. Did you think me an idiot? Or deaf?'

'No,' he said, drawing out the syllable in order to give himself time to think. Although what good that was going to do him, he had no idea. 'I just thought . . .'

He left it at that.

'We're terrible,' Honoria said with a shrug of her shoulders. 'But there is no point in histrionics or sulking. There's nothing we can do about it.'

'Practice?' he suggested, but very carefully.

He wouldn't have thought a person could be both disdainful and amused, but if Honoria's expression was any indication, she had managed it. 'If I thought that practice might actually make us better,' she said, her lip curling ever so slightly even as her eyes danced with laughter, 'believe me, I would be the most diligent violin student the world has ever seen.'

'Perhaps, if—'

'No,' she said, quite firmly. 'We're awful. That's all there is to it. We haven't a musical bone in our bodies, and especially none in our ears.'

He couldn't believe what he was hearing. He'd been to so many Smythe-Smith musicales it was a wonder he could still appreciate music. And last year, when Honoria had made her debut on the violin, she had looked positively radiant, performing her part with a smile so wide one could only assume she'd been lost in a rapture.

'Actually,' she continued, 'I find it all somewhat endearing.'

Marcus was not sure she would be able to locate another living human being who would agree with that assessment, but he saw no reason to say that out loud.

'So I smile,' Honoria went on, 'and I pretend I enjoy it. And in a way I do enjoy it. The Smythe-Smiths have been putting on musicales since 1807. It's quite a family tradition.' And then, in a quieter, more contemplative voice, she added, 'I consider myself quite fortunate to have family traditions.'

Marcus thought of his own family, or rather, the great big gaping hole where a family never had been. 'Yes,' he said quietly, 'you are.'

'For example,' she said, 'I wear lucky shoes.'

He was quite certain he could not have heard her correctly.

'During the musicale,' Honoria explained with a little shrug. 'It is a custom specific to my branch of the family. Henrietta and Margaret are always arguing over who started it, but we always wear red shoes.'

Red shoes. That little curl of desire that had been stamped out by thoughts of crusading amateur musicians sprang back to life. Suddenly nothing in this world could have been more seductive than red shoes. Good Lord.

'Are you sure you're all right?' Honoria asked. 'You're looking somewhat flushed.'

'I'm fine,' he said hoarsely.

'My mother doesn't know,' she said.

What? If he hadn't been flushed before, he was now. 'I beg your pardon?'

'About the red shoes. She has no idea that we wear them.'

He cleared his throat. 'Is there any particular reason you keep it a secret?'

Honoria thought for a moment, then reached out and broke off another piece of treacle tart. 'I don't know. I don't think so.' She popped it in her mouth, chewed, and shrugged. 'Actually, now that I think about it, I don't know why it's red shoes. It could just as easily be green. Or blue. Well, not blue. That wouldn't be the least bit out of the ordinary. But green would work. Or pink.'

Nothing would work as well as red. Of this Marcus was certain.

'I imagine we'll begin rehearsing as soon as I get back to London,' Honoria said.

'I'm sorry,' Marcus said.

'Oh, no,' she told him, 'I *like* the rehearsals. Especially now that all of my siblings are gone, and my house is nothing but ticking clocks and meals on trays. It's *lovely* to gather together and have someone to talk to.' She looked over at him with a sheepish expression. 'We talk at least as much as we rehearse.'

'This does not surprise me,' Marcus murmured.

She gave him a look that said she had not missed his little dig. But she did not take offense; he had known she would not.

And then he realized: he rather liked that he had known she would not take offense. There was something wonderful about knowing another person so well.

'So,' she continued, quite determined to finish the topic, 'Sarah will be at the pianoforte again this year, and she really is my closest friend. We have a grand time together. And Iris will be joining us at the cello. She's almost exactly my age, and I have always meant to spend more time with her. She was at the Royles', too, and I—' She stopped.

'What is it?' he asked. She looked almost concerned.

Honoria blinked. 'I think she might actually be good.'

'At the cello?'

'Yes. Can you imagine?'

He decided to view the question as rhetorical.

'Anyway,' she continued, 'Iris will be playing, as will her sister Daisy, who, I'm afraid to say, *is* dreadful.'

'Ehrm . . .' How to ask this politely? 'Dreadful when compared to most of humanity or dreadful for the Smythe-Smiths?'

Honoria looked like she was trying not to smile. 'Dreadful even for us.'

'That is very grave indeed,' he said, amazingly with a straight face.

'I know. I think poor Sarah is hoping she will be struck by lightning sometime in the next three weeks. She has only just recovered from last year.'

'I take it she didn't smile and put on a brave face?'

'Weren't you there?'

'I wasn't looking at Sarah.'

Her lips parted, but not from surprise, not at first. Her eyes were still lit with anticipation, the kind one feels when one is about to deliver a brilliantly witty remark. But then, before any sound emerged, she seemed to realize what he'd said.

And it was only then that he realized what he'd said.

Slowly, her head tilted to the side, and she was looking at him as if . . . As if . . .

He didn't know. He didn't know what it meant, except that he would have sworn that her eyes grew darker even as she sat there, staring at him. Darker, and deeper, and all he could think was that she could see into him, right down to his heart.

Right down to his soul.

'I was looking at you,' he said, his voice so quiet he barely heard it. 'I was looking only at you.'

But that was before . . .

She put her hand on his. It looked small, and delicate, and pinkishly-pale.

It looked perfect.

'Marcus?' she whispered.

And then he finally knew. That was before he loved her.

Chapter Sixteen

It was extraordinary, Honoria thought, but the world really did stop spinning.

She was sure of it. There could be no other explanation for the headiness, the dizziness, the sheer singularity of the moment, of *that* moment, right there, in his room, with a dinner tray and a stolen treacle tart, and the breathless longing for a single, perfect kiss.

She turned, and she felt her head tilt ever-so-slightly to the side, as if somehow, if she changed her angle, she would see him more clearly. And amazingly, she did. She moved, and he came into focus, which was so very strange, because she would have sworn that her vision had been crystal clear just a moment earlier.

It was as if she'd never really seen him before. She looked into his eyes, and she saw more than color, more than shape. It wasn't that the iris was brown, or the pupil was black. It was that *he* was there, and she could see him, every last bit of him, and she thought—

I love him.

It echoed in her mind.

I love him.

Nothing could have been more stunning, at the same time more simple and true. She felt as if something within her had been dislodged for years, and he had, with five innocent words—*I wasn't looking at Sarah*—bumped it into place.

She loved him. She would always love him. It made such sense. Who could she possibly love but

219

Marcus Holroyd?

'I was looking at you,' he said, so softly she couldn't even be sure she'd heard it. 'I was looking only at you.'

She looked down. Her hand was on his. She didn't remember putting it there. 'Marcus?' she whispered, and she didn't know why it was a question. But she couldn't have made herself say any other word.

'Honoria,' he whispered, and then—

'My lord! My lord!'

Honoria jumped back, nearly falling out of the chair. There was a small commotion in the corridor, the sound of feet hurrying toward them. Hastily, Honoria stood and stepped back behind the chair.

A moment later, Honoria's mother and Mrs. Wetherby came tearing into the room. 'A letter has arrived,' Lady Winstead said breathlessly. 'From Daniel.'

Honoria swayed slightly, then grabbed the back of the chair for support. They had not heard from her brother in over a year. Well, perhaps Marcus had, but she had not, and Daniel had long since stopped trying to write to their mother.

'What does it say?' Lady Winstead asked, even though Marcus was still breaking the seal.

'Let him open it first,' Honoria admonished. It was on the tip of her tongue to say that they ought to leave the room to allow him to read the letter in private, but she could not bring herself to do so. Daniel was her only brother, and she'd missed him so dreadfully. As the months had gone by without even a simple note from him, she'd told herself that he hadn't meant to ignore her. His letter surely

220

had been lost; international post was notoriously unreliable.

But right now she didn't care why she had not heard from him in so long; she just wanted to know what was in his letter to Marcus.

And so they all stood there, staring at Marcus with bated breath. It was beyond rude, but no one was willing to budge.

'Is he well?' her mother finally ventured when Marcus finished the first page.

'Yes,' he murmured, blinking as if he couldn't quite believe what he was reading. 'Yes. He's coming home, actually.'

'What?' Lady Winstead went pale, and Honoria rushed over to her side lest she need support.

Marcus cleared his throat. 'He writes that he has received some sort of correspondence from Hugh Prentice. Ramsgate has finally agreed to let bygones be bygones.'

As bygones went, Honoria could not help but think, this one was rather large. And the last time she'd seen the Marquess of Ramsgate, he'd nearly gone into an apoplectic fit at the sight of her. Granted, that had been over a year earlier, but still.

'Could Lord Hugh be playing a trick?' Honoria asked. 'To lure Daniel back into the country?'

'I don't think so,' Marcus said, looking down at the second page of the letter. 'He's not the sort to do such a thing.'

'Not the sort?' Lady Winstead echoed, disbelief making her voice rise in pitch. 'He ruined my son's life.'

'That's what made it all so very strange,' Marcus said. He was still looking down, reading the words on the paper even as he spoke. 'Hugh Prentice has

221

always been a good man. He is eccentric, but he is not without honor.'

'Does Daniel say when he'll return?' Honoria asked.

Marcus shook his head. 'He is not specific. He mentions that he has a few matters to take care of in Italy, and then he will commence his journey home.'

'Oh, my heavens,' Lady Winstead said, sinking into a nearby chair. 'I never thought I would see the day. I never even allowed myself to think about it. Which of course meant that I thought of nothing but.'

For a moment Honoria could do nothing but stare at her mother. For three years she had not even mentioned Daniel's name. And now she was saying that he was all she had thought about?

Honoria shook her head. There was no point in being angry with her mother. Whatever she had done or been these last few years, she had more than redeemed herself in these last few days. Honoria knew without a doubt that Marcus would not be alive were it not for her mother's nursing skills.

'How long does it take to travel from Italy to England?' Honoria asked, because surely that had to be the most important question.

Marcus looked up. 'I have no idea. I'm not even sure what part of Italy he's in.'

Honoria nodded. Her brother had always had a habit of telling stories and leaving out all the most important details.

'This is very exciting,' Mrs. Wetherby said. 'I know you've all missed him terribly.'

For a moment the room went silent. It was one

222

of those comments that was so obvious that no one quite knew how to agree. Finally, Lady Winstead said, 'Well, it's a good thing we are already planning to leave for London tomorrow. I should hate to be away from home when he arrives.' She looked over at Marcus and said, 'We shall take our leave for the evening. I'm sure you wish to get some rest. Come along, Honoria. We have much to discuss, you and I.'

*   *   *

What Lady Winstead wished to discuss, it turned out, was how they might celebrate Daniel's return. But the discussion did not get very far; Honoria sensibly pointed out that there wasn't much they could do if they did not know the date of his arrival. Her mother managed to ignore this for at least ten minutes, debating small gatherings versus large, and whether Lord Ramsgate and Lord Hugh should be invited, and if they were, could one be certain that they would decline? Any reasonable person would do so, but with Lord Ramsgate, one never could tell.

'Mother,' Honoria said again, 'there is nothing we can do until Daniel arrives. He may not even want a celebration.'

'Nonsense. Of course he will. He—'

'He left the country in disgrace,' Honoria cut in. She hated to be so blunt, but there was nothing else for it.

'Yes, but it wasn't fair.'

'It doesn't matter if it wasn't fair. It is what it is, and he might not wish to remind anyone of it.'

Her mother looked unconvinced, but she let the

223

matter drop, and then there was nothing to do but go to bed.

*   *   *

The following morning, Honoria arose with the sun. They were to depart early; it was the only way to make it to London without having to stop for the night along the route. After a quick breakfast, she made her way to Marcus's room to say good-bye.

And maybe more.

But when she arrived, he was not in his bed. A housemaid was there, however, pulling the sheets from the mattress.

'Do you know where Lord Chatteris is?' Honoria inquired, hoping that nothing was amiss.

'He's just in the next room,' the maid replied. Then her cheeks went a bit pink. 'With his valet.'

Honoria swallowed and probably turned a little pink herself, understanding quite well that this meant that Marcus was taking a bath. The maid departed with her bundle of linens, and Honoria stood alone in his bedchamber for a moment, wondering what to do next. She supposed she would have to say good-bye in writing. She could not wait for him here; it was beyond irregular, beyond even all the other irregularities they had committed in the past week.

There were certain rules of propriety that could be bent when someone was deathly ill, but now Marcus was up and about, and apparently in some degree of undress. There was no way her presence in his room could lead to anything other than complete ruination.

And besides, her mother was most impatient to

be off.

She glanced about the room for paper and pen. There was a small desk by the window, and on his bedside table she saw—

The letter from Daniel.

It lay where Marcus had set it down the night before, two somewhat wrinkled pages filled with the small, tight writing people used when they were trying to save postage. Marcus hadn't told her anything that was in the letter other than the fact that Daniel was coming home. Which was of course the most important thing, but even so, she was ravenous for news. It had been so long since she'd had any information of him. She didn't care if he only mentioned what he'd eaten for breakfast . . . It would be breakfast in Italy and thus terribly exotic. What was he doing? Was he bored? Could he speak Italian?

She stared at the two sheets of paper. Would it be so very terrible if she took a peek?

No. She couldn't. It would be a gross breach of trust, a complete invasion of Marcus's privacy. And of Daniel's.

But then again, what could they possibly have to talk about that would not be of her concern?

She turned, glancing toward the door the maid had motioned to. She couldn't hear anything coming through it. If Marcus was finished with his bath, surely she'd hear him moving about. She looked back at the letter.

She was a very fast reader.

In the end, she didn't really make a decision to read Daniel's letter to Marcus. Rather, she didn't allow herself to decide not to. It was a small distinction, but one that somehow allowed her to ignore her own moral code and do something that would have incensed her if it had been *her* letter lying on the table.

She moved quickly, as if speed might make the sin smaller, and snatched up the two sheets of paper. *Dear Marcus* et cetera et cetera . . . Daniel wrote about the apartment he'd rented, describing all the neighborhood shops in lovely detail but managing to omit the name of the city he was in. He then went on about the food, which he insisted was superior to English fare. After that there was a brief paragraph about his plans to come home.

Smiling, Honoria turned to the second sheet of the letter. Daniel wrote the way he spoke, and she could practically hear his voice coming from the page.

In the next paragraph Daniel asked Marcus to inform his mother of his impending return, which made Honoria smile more broadly. Daniel could never have imagined that they would be standing with Marcus when he read the missive.

And then, at the end, Honoria saw her own name.

I have not heard any news of Honoria marrying, so I assume she is still unwed. I must thank you again for scaring off Fotheringham last year. He's a rotter, and it infuriates me that he even attempted to court her.

What was this? Honoria blinked, as if that might somehow change the words on the page. Marcus had had something to do with Lord Fotheringham not coming up to scratch? She had decided that she did not like Lord Fotheringham and would not accept him, but still . . .

Travers, too, would have been a bad alliance. I hope you did not have to pay him to leave her alone, but if you did, I shall reimburse you.

What? People were being paid to . . . to what? To not court her? That didn't even make sense.

I appreciate your looking out for her. It was a great deal to ask, and I know I did not give you much choice, asking as I did on the eve of my departure. I shall assume the responsibility when I return, and you shall be free to leave London, which I know you detest.

And that was how Daniel ended his letter. Setting Marcus free of the dreadful burden that was, apparently, her.

She set the pages down, then rearranged them so that they would appear as they had been when she had picked them up.

Daniel had asked Marcus to watch over her? Why hadn't Marcus said anything? And how stupid was she, really, that she had not figured it out? It made such perfect sense. All those parties when she'd caught Marcus glowering in her direction—he hadn't been glowering at her because he disapproved of her behavior; he'd been in a bad mood because he was stuck in London until she received a good marriage proposal. No wonder he had seemed so miserable all the time.

And all those suitors who had mysteriously dropped her—he'd *scared* them off. He'd decided they were not what Daniel would want for her, and he'd gone behind her back and scared them off.

She should be furious.

But she wasn't. Not about that.

All she could think about was what he'd said the night before. *'I wasn't looking at Sarah.'*

Of bloody course he hadn't been looking at Sarah. He'd been looking at *her* because he'd been forced to do so. He'd been looking at her because his best friend had made him promise.

He'd been looking at her because she was an obligation.

And now she was in love with him.

A horrified spurt of laughter burst from her throat. She had to get out of his room. The only thing that could make her mortification more complete would be his catching her reading his correspondence.

But she couldn't go without leaving a note. That would be completely out of character; he'd know for sure that something was amiss.

So she found paper, and she found a pen, and she scrawled a perfectly ordinary, perfectly boring farewell.

And then she left.

Chapter Seventeen

The following week
The recently aired-out music room
Winstead House, London

'Mozart this year!' Daisy Smythe-Smith announced. She held her new violin aloft with such vigor that her blond curls nearly bounced out of her coiffure. 'Isn't it gorgeous? It's a Ruggieri. Father bought it for my sixteenth birthday.'

'It's a beautiful instrument,' Honoria agreed, 'but we did Mozart last year.'

'We do Mozart every year,' Sarah drawled from the piano.

'But I didn't play last year,' Daisy said. She shot Sarah a peevish look. 'And this is only your second time in the quartet, so you can hardly complain about what you do *every* year.'

'I believe I may kill you before the season is out,' Sarah remarked in much the same tone she used when saying, *I believe I shall have lemonade instead of tea.*

Daisy stuck out her tongue.

'Iris?' Honoria looked over at her cousin at the cello.

'I don't care,' Iris said morosely.

Honoria sighed. 'We can't do what we did last year.'

'I don't see why not,' Sarah said. 'I can't imagine anyone would recognize it from our interpretation.'

Iris slumped.

'But it will have been printed in the program,'

229

Honoria pointed out.

'Do you really think anyone saves our programs from one year to the next?' Sarah asked.

'My mother does,' Daisy said.

'So does mine,' Sarah answered, 'but it's not as if she pulls them out and compares them side by side.'

'My mother does,' Daisy said again.

'Dear God,' Iris moaned.

'It's not as if Mr. Mozart wrote only one piece,' Daisy said pertly. 'We have loads from which to choose. I think we should play *Eine Kleine Nachtmusik*. It is my absolute favorite. It's so sprightly and gay.'

'It has no piano part,' Honoria reminded her.

'I have no objection,' Sarah said quickly. From behind the piano.

'If I have to do it, you have to do it,' Iris practically hissed.

Sarah actually pulled back in her seat. 'I had no idea you could look so venomous, Iris.'

'It's because she doesn't have eyelashes,' Daisy said.

Iris turned to her with complete calm and said, 'I hate you.'

'That's a terrible thing to say, Daisy,' Honoria said, turning on her with a stern expression. It was true that Iris was extraordinarily pale, with the kind of strawberry blond hair that seemed to render her lashes and brows almost invisible. But she'd always thought Iris was absolutely gorgeous, almost ethereal-looking.

'If she didn't have eyelashes, she'd be dead,' Sarah said.

Honoria turned to her, unable to believe the direction of the conversation. Well, no, that

230

was not completely accurate. She believed it (unfortunately). She just didn't understand it.

'Well, it's *true*,' Sarah said defensively. 'Or at the very least, blind. Lashes keep all the dust from our eyes.'

'Why are we having this conversation?' Honoria wondered aloud.

Daisy immediately answered, 'It's because Sarah said she didn't think Iris could look venomous, and then *I* said—'

'I know,' Honoria cut in, and then, when she realized Daisy still had her mouth open, looking as if she was only waiting for the right moment to complete her sentence, she said it again. 'I *know*. It was a hypothetical question.'

'It still had a perfectly valid answer,' Daisy said with a sniff.

Honoria turned to Iris. At twenty-one, they were the exact same age, but Iris had not had to take part in the quartet until this year. Her sister Marigold had kept the cello part in a death grip until she'd married last autumn. 'Do you have any suggestions, Iris?' Honoria asked brightly.

Iris crossed her arms and hunched over herself in her seat. To Honoria, it looked as if she were trying to fold herself into nothingness. 'Something without the cello,' she muttered.

'If I have to do it, you have to do it,' Sarah said with a smirk.

Iris glared at her with all the fury of a misunderstood artist. 'You don't understand.'

'Oh, believe me, I do,' Sarah said with great feeling. 'I played last year, if you recall. I've had an entire *year* to understand.'

'Why is everyone complaining?' Daisy asked

231

impatiently. 'This is exciting! We get to perform. Do you know how long I have been waiting for this day?'

'Unfortunately, yes,' Sarah said flatly.

'About as long as I have been dreading it,' Iris muttered.

'It is really quite remarkable,' Sarah said, 'that the two of you are sisters.'

'I marvel at it every day,' Iris said flatly.

'It should be a piano quartet,' Honoria said quickly, before Daisy figured out she was being insulted. 'Unfortunately, there aren't many from which to choose.'

No one offered an opinion.

Honoria fought off a groan. It was clear she was going to have to take the reins, lest they fall into musical anarchy. Although she supposed that anarchy might actually be an improvement over the usual Smythe-Smith state of affairs.

It was a sad statement, that.

'Mozart's Piano Quartet no. 1 or Mozart's Piano Quartet no. 2,' she announced, holding up the two different scores. 'Does anyone have an opinion?'

'Whichever one we didn't do last year,' Sarah sighed. She let her head rest against the piano. Then she actually let her head drop to the keys.

'That sounded good,' Daisy said with surprise.

'It sounded like a fish vomiting,' Sarah said into the piano.

'A charming image,' Honoria remarked.

'I don't think fish do vomit,' Daisy remarked, 'and if they did, I don't think it would sound like—'

'Can't we be the first set of cousins to mutiny?' Sarah cut in, lifting her head. 'Can't we simply just say no?'

'No!' Daisy howled.

'No,' Honoria agreed.

'Yes?' Iris said weakly.

'I can't believe you want to do this again,' Sarah said to Honoria.

'It's tradition.'

'It's a wretched tradition, and it will take me six months to recover.'

'I shall never recover,' Iris lamented.

Daisy looked as if she might stomp her foot. She probably would have done if Honoria had not quelled her with a sharp glare.

Honoria thought of Marcus, then forced herself not to think of Marcus. 'It's tradition,' she said again, 'and we are fortunate to belong to a family that prizes tradition.'

'What are you talking about?' Sarah asked, shaking her head.

'Some people have no one,' Honoria said passionately.

Sarah stared at her a moment longer, then said it again. 'I'm sorry, but what are you talking about?'

Honoria looked at all of them, aware that her voice was rising with feeling but completely unable to modulate it. 'I may not like performing in musicales, but I *love* rehearsing with the three of you.'

Her three cousins stared at her, momentarily nonplussed.

'Don't you realize how lucky we are?' Honoria said. And then, when no one leapt to agree, she added, 'To have each other?'

'Couldn't we have each other over a game of cards?' Iris suggested.

'We are Smythe-Smiths,' Honoria ground out,

'and this is what we do.' And then, before Sarah could offer a word of protest, she said, 'You, too, regardless of your last name. Your mother was a Smythe-Smith, and that is what counts.'

Sarah sighed—loud, long, and weary.

'We are going to pick up our instruments and play Mozart,' Honoria announced. 'And we are going to do it with smiles on our faces.'

'I have no idea what any of you are talking about,' Daisy said.

'I will play,' Sarah said, 'but I make no promises about a smile.' She looked at the piano and blinked. 'And I am *not* picking up my instrument.'

Iris actually giggled. Then her eyes lit up. 'I could help you.'

'Pick it up?'

Iris's grin grew positively devilish. 'The window is not far . . .'

'I knew I loved you,' Sarah said with a wide smile.

While Sarah and Iris were making plans to destroy Lady Winstead's brand new pianoforte, Honoria turned back to the music, trying to decide which score to choose. 'We did Quartet no. 2 last year,' she said, even though only Daisy was listening, 'but I'm hesitant to choose Quartet no. 1.'

'Why?' Daisy asked.

'It's rather famous for being difficult.'

'Why is that?'

'I don't know,' Honoria admitted. 'I've just heard that it is, and often enough to make me wary.'

'Is there a Quartet no. 3?'

'I'm afraid not.'

'Then I think we should do no. 1,' Daisy said boldly. 'Nothing ventured, nothing gained.'

'Yes, but it is a wise man who understands his limits.'

'Who said that?' Daisy asked.

'I did,' Honoria answered impatiently. She held up the score to Quartet no. 1. 'I don't think we could possibly learn this, even if we had three times as long to practice.'

'We don't have to learn it. We'll have the music in front of us.'

This was going to be much worse than Honoria had feared.

'I think we should do no. 1,' Daisy said emphatically. 'It will be embarrassing if we perform the same piece as last year.'

It was going to be embarrassing regardless of what music they chose, but Honoria didn't have the heart to say it to her face.

On the other hand, whichever piece they performed, they would surely butcher it past recognition. Could a difficult piece played badly be that much worse than a slightly less difficult piece played badly?

'Oh, why not?' Honoria acquiesced. 'We'll do no. 1.' She shook her head. Sarah was going to be furious. The piano part was especially difficult.

On the other hand, it wasn't as if Sarah had deigned to take part in the selection process.

'A wise choice,' Daisy said with great conviction. 'We're doing Quartet no. 1!' she called out over her shoulder.

Honoria looked past her to Sarah and Iris, who had actually pushed the pianoforte several feet across the room.

'What are you doing?' she nearly shrieked.

'Oh, don't worry,' Sarah said with a laugh. 'We're

235

not *really* going to push it out the window.'

Iris positively collapsed on the piano stool, her entire body shaking with laughter.

'This isn't funny,' Honoria said, even though it was. She'd love nothing more than to join her cousin in silliness, but someone had to take charge, and if she didn't do it, Daisy would.

Good heavens.

'We've chosen Mozart's Piano Quartet no. 1,' Daisy said again.

Iris went utterly pale, which for her meant almost ghostlike. 'You're joking.'

'No,' Honoria replied, in all honesty a bit fed up. 'If you had a strong opinion, you should have joined the conversation.'

'But do you know how difficult it is?'

'That's why we want to do it!' Daisy proclaimed.

Iris looked at her sister for one moment and then turned back to Honoria, who she clearly judged to be the more sensible of the two. 'Honoria,' she said, 'we cannot do Quartet no. 1. It's impossible. Have you ever heard it played?'

'Only once,' Honoria admitted, 'but I don't remember it very well.'

'It's impossible,' Iris cried. 'It's not meant for amateurs.'

Honoria was not so pure of heart that she was not enjoying her cousin's distress just a little bit. Iris had been complaining all afternoon.

'Listen to me,' Iris said again. 'If we attempt this piece, we will be massacred.'

'By whom?' Daisy asked.

Iris just looked at her, completely unable to articulate a reply.

'By the music,' Sarah put in.

236

'Oh, you've decided to join the discussion, then,' Honoria said.

'Don't be sarcastic,' Sarah snipped.

'Where were the two of you when I was trying to pick something out?'

'They were moving the piano.'

'Daisy!' all three of them yelled.

'What did I say?' Daisy demanded.

'Try not to be so literal,' Iris snapped.

Daisy hmmphed and started leafing through the music score.

'I have been trying to keep everyone's spirits up,' Honoria said, planting her hands on her hips as she faced Sarah and Iris. 'We have a performance to practice for, and no matter how much either of you complains, there is no getting out of it. So stop trying to make my life so difficult and do what you're told.'

Sarah and Iris could only stare.

'Er, please,' Honoria added.

'Perhaps this would be a good time for a short break,' Sarah suggested.

Honoria groaned. 'We haven't even started.'

'I know. But we need a break.'

Honoria stood still for a moment, feeling her body deflate. This was exhausting. And Sarah was right. They did need a break. A break from doing absolutely nothing, but a break nevertheless.

'Besides,' Sarah said, giving her a sly look, 'I'm parched.'

Honoria raised an eyebrow. 'All this complaining has made you thirsty?'

'Precisely,' Sarah returned with a grin. 'Have you any lemonade, darling cousin?'

'I don't know,' Honoria said through a sigh, 'but

I suppose I could inquire.' Lemonade did sound nice. And to be perfectly honest, not practicing also sounded nice. She got up to ring for a maid and had barely sat down again when Poole, Winstead House's longtime butler, appeared in the doorway.

'That was fast,' Sarah remarked.

'A caller for you, Lady Honoria,' Poole intoned.

Marcus?

Honoria's heart thumped wildly in her chest until she realized it couldn't possibly be Marcus. He was still confined to Fensmore. Dr. Winters had insisted.

Poole came over with his tray and held it forward so that Honoria could take the calling card.

THE EARL OF CHATTERIS

Good heavens, it *was* Marcus. What the devil was he doing in London? Honoria completely forgot to be mortified or angry or whatever it was she was feeling (she had not quite decided) and went straight to out-and-out fury. How dare he risk his health? She had not slaved at his bedside, braving heat, blood, and delirium, only to have him collapse in London because he was too foolish to stay home where he belonged.

'Admit him at once,' she snapped, and she must have sounded rather fierce, because all three of her cousins turned to stare at her with identical expressions of shock.

She scowled at them all. Daisy actually took a step back.

'He should not be out and about,' Honoria growled.

'Lord Chatteris,' Sarah said, with complete

238

confidence.

'Stay here,' Honoria said to the others. 'I shall return shortly.'

'Need we practice in your absence?' Iris inquired.

Honoria rolled her eyes, refusing to dignify that with a response.

'His lordship is already waiting in the drawing room,' Poole informed her.

Of course. No butler would insult an earl by forcing him to leave his calling card on the silver tray and depart.

'I'll be right back,' Honoria said to her cousins.

'You said that,' Sarah said.

'Don't follow me.'

'You said that, too,' Sarah said. 'Or something quite synonymous.'

Honoria gave her one last glare before leaving the room. She had not told Sarah much about her time at Fensmore, just that Marcus had taken ill, and she and her mother had aided in his convalescence. But Sarah knew her better than anyone; she was going to be curious, especially now that Honoria had nearly lost her temper at the mere sight of Marcus's calling card.

Honoria marched through the house, her anger growing with every step. What on earth was he thinking? Dr. Winters could not have been more clear. Marcus was to stay in bed for a week and then remain at home for another week after that, possibly two. In no mathematical universe could that equate to his being here in London at that moment.

'What on earth were you—' She thundered into the drawing room but stopped short when she saw him standing by the fireplace, a veritable picture of health. 'Marcus?'

He smiled, and her heart—wretched, traitorous organ—melted. 'Honoria,' he said. 'It's lovely to see you, too.'

'You look . . .' She blinked, still not quite believing her eyes. His color was good, his eyes had lost that sunken look, and he appeared to have regained whatever weight he'd lost. ' . . . well,' she finally finished, unable to keep the surprise from her voice.

'Dr. Winters declared me fit to travel,' he explained. 'He said he had never seen anyone recuperate from a fever with such speed.'

'It must have been the treacle tart.'

His eyes grew warm. 'Indeed.'

'What brings you to town?' she asked. She *wanted* to add, 'Since you've been recently released from your obligation to ensure that I don't marry an idiot.'

She was, perhaps, just a little bit bitter.

But not angry. There was no point, and indeed no reason, to be angry with him. He had only been doing what Daniel had asked of him. And it wasn't as if he had thwarted any real romances. Honoria had not been terribly enamored of any of her suitors, and the truth was, had any of them proposed, she probably would not have accepted.

But it was embarrassing. Why couldn't someone have told her that Marcus had been meddling in her affairs? She might have made a fuss—oh, very well, she would definitely have made a fuss—but not a big one. And if she had known, she would not have misinterpreted his actions at Fensmore. She wouldn't have thought that maybe he might be falling a little bit in love with her.

240

And she wouldn't have allowed herself to fall in love with him.

But if there was one thing she was sure of, it was that she was not going to let him know that anything was out of the ordinary. As far as he knew, she was still oblivious to his machinations.

So she put her best smile on her face and was quite sure she looked terribly interested in everything he had to say as he answered, 'I didn't want to miss the musicale.'

'Oh, now I know you're lying.'

'No, really,' he insisted. 'The knowledge of your true feelings will bring an entirely new dimension to the endeavor.'

She rolled her eyes. 'Please. No matter how much you think you are laughing with me, and not at me, you cannot escape the cacophony.'

'I am pondering discreet balls of cotton for my ears.'

'If my mother catches you, she shall be mortally wounded. And she, who saved *you* from a mortal wound.'

He looked at her with some surprise. 'She still thinks you're talented?'

'Every one of us,' Honoria confirmed. 'I think she is a little sad that I am the last of her daughters to perform. But I suppose the torch will soon pass to a new generation. I have many nieces who are practicing their little fingers off on their tiny little violins.'

'Really? Tiny ones?'

'No. It just sounds better to describe them that way.'

He chuckled at that, then fell silent. They were both silent, just standing there in the drawing room, uncharacteristically awkward and, well, silent.

It was odd. It was not like them at all.

'Would you care to take a stroll?' he asked suddenly. 'The weather is fine.'

'No,' she said, a little more brusquely than she would have liked. 'Thank you.'

A shadow passed over his eyes and then was gone so quickly she thought she might have imagined it. 'Very well,' he said stiffly.

'I can't,' she added, because she hadn't really meant to hurt his feelings. Or maybe she had, and now she felt guilty. 'My cousins are all here. We're practicing.'

A faint look of alarm crossed his face.

'You will probably want to find some sort of business that removes you from Mayfair entirely,' she told him. 'Daisy has not yet managed *pianissimo*.' At his blank stare, she added, 'She's loud.'

'And the rest of you aren't?'

'Touché, but no, not like that.'

'So what you are saying is that when I do attend the musicale, I should endeavor to secure a seat at the back?'

'In the next room, if you can manage it.'

'Really?' He looked remarkably—no, make that comically—hopeful. '*Will* there be seats in the next room?'

'No,' she replied, rolling her eyes yet again. 'But I don't think the back row is going to save you. Not from Daisy.'

He sighed.

'You should have considered this before you rushed your convalescence.'

'So I am coming to realize.'

'Well,' she said, trying to sound as if she was a very busy young lady with many appointments and quite a few things to do who also happened not to be pining over him in the least, 'I really must be going.'

'Of course,' he said, giving her a polite nod of farewell.

'Good-bye.' But she didn't quite move.

'Good-bye.'

'It was very good seeing you.'

'And you,' he said. 'Please give my regards to your mother.'

'Of course. She will be delighted to hear that you are so well.'

He nodded. And stood there. And finally said, 'Well, then.'

'Yes,' she said hastily. 'I must go. Good-bye,' she said again. This time she did leave the room. And she didn't even look over her shoulder.

Which was more of an achievement than she would ever have dreamed.

Chapter Eighteen

The truth was, Marcus thought as he sat in his study in his London home, he knew very little about courting young ladies. He knew a great deal about avoiding them, and perhaps even more about avoiding their mothers. He also knew quite a lot about discreetly investigating other men who were courting young ladies (more specifically, Honoria), and most of all he knew how to be quietly menacing while he convinced them to abandon their pursuit.

But as for himself, he had not a clue.

Flowers? He'd seen other men with flowers. Women liked flowers. Hell, he liked flowers, too. Who didn't like flowers?

He thought he might like to find some of the grape hyacinths that reminded him of Honoria's eyes, but they were small blooms, and he didn't think they would work well in a bouquet. And furthermore, was he supposed to hand them to her and tell her that they reminded him of her eyes? Because then he would have to explain that he was talking about a very specific part of the flower, at the bottom of the petal, right near the stem.

He could not imagine anything that might make him feel more foolish.

And the final problem with flowers was that he had never given them to her before. She would be immediately curious, and then suspicious, and if she did not return his feelings (and he had no particular reason to suppose that she did), then he'd be stuck there in her drawing room, looking like a complete ass.

All things considered, this was a scenario he'd rather avoid.

Safer to court her in public, he decided. Lady Bridgerton was hosting a birthday ball the next day, and he knew that Honoria would attend. Even if she didn't want to, she would still go. There would be far too many eligible bachelors in attendance for her to decline. This included Gregory Bridgerton, about whom Marcus had revised his opinion— he was far too wet behind the ears to take a wife. If Honoria decided that she was interested in the young Mr. Bridgerton after all, Marcus was going to have to intercede.

244

In his usual quiet and behind-the-scenes manner, of course. But still, it was another reason why he needed to be in attendance.

He looked down at his desk. On the left was an engraved invitation to Bridgerton House. On the right was the note Honoria had left for him at Fensmore when she'd departed the week before. It was a stunningly nondescript missive. A salutation, a signature, two ordinary sentences in between. There was nothing that might indicate that a life had been saved, a kiss had occurred, a treacle tart had been stolen. . . .

It was the sort of note one wrote when one wished to thank a hostess for a perfectly correct and polite garden party. It was not the sort one wrote to someone one might consider marrying.

Because that was what he intended. As soon as Daniel got his bloody arse back to England, he was going to ask him for her hand. But until then, he had to court her himself.

Hence his dilemma.

He sighed. Some men knew instinctively how to talk to women. It would have been very convenient to have been one of those men.

But he wasn't. Instead, he was a man who knew only how to talk to Honoria. And lately even that wasn't working out so well for him.

Thus, the next night, he found himself in one of his least favorite places on earth: A London ballroom.

He assumed his usual position, off to the side, his back to the wall, where he could watch the proceedings and pretend he didn't care. Not for the first time, it occurred to him that he was inordinately fortunate not to have been born female. The young lady to his left was a wallflower; he got to be dark, standoffish, and brooding.

The party was a mad crush—Lady Bridgerton was immensely popular—and Marcus couldn't tell if Honoria was there or not. He didn't see her, but then again he also couldn't see the door through which he himself had entered. How anyone expected to have a fine time amidst so much heat and sweat and crowding he would never know.

He stole another glance at the young lady next to him. She looked familiar, but he couldn't quite place her. She was perhaps not quite in the first blush of youth, but he doubted she was much older than he was. She sighed, the sound long and weary, and he could not help but think that he was standing next to a kindred spirit. She, too, was glancing over the crowd, trying to pretend that she was not searching for someone in particular.

He thought about saying good evening, or perhaps asking if she knew Honoria and, if so, had she seen her. But just before he turned to greet her, she turned in the opposite direction, and he could have sworn he heard her mutter, 'Blast it all, I'm getting an éclair.'

She drifted off, weaving her way through the crowds. Marcus watched her with interest; she seemed to know exactly where she was going. Which meant that if he'd heard her correctly . . .

She knew where one could get an éclair.

He immediately took off after her. If he was going to be stuck here in this ballroom without even seeing Honoria, who was the only reason he'd subjected himself to this crush, he was damned well going to get dessert.

He'd long since perfected the art of moving

with purpose, even when he had no particular aim or goal, and he managed to avoid unnecessary conversations simply by keeping his chin high and his gaze sharp and above the crowd.

Until something struck him in the leg.

Ouch.

'And what's that face for, Chatteris?' came an imperious female voice. 'I barely touched you.'

He held himself still, because he knew that voice, and he knew there was no escaping it. With a small smile, he looked down into the wrinkled face of Lady Danbury, who had been terrifying the British Isles since the time of the Restoration.

Or so it seemed. She was his mother's great-aunt, and he would swear she was a hundred years old.

'An injury to my leg, my lady,' he said, giving her his most respectful bow.

She thumped her weapon (others might call it a cane, but he knew better) against the floor. 'Fell off your horse?'

'No, I—'

'Tripped down the stairs? Dropped a bottle on your foot?' Her expression grew sly. 'Or does it involve a woman?'

He fought the urge to cross his arms. She was looking up at him with a bit of a smirk. She liked poking fun at her companions; she'd once told him that the best part of growing old was that she could say anything she wanted with impunity.

He leaned down and said with great gravity, 'Actually, I was stabbed by my valet.'

It was, perhaps, the only time in his life he'd managed to stun her into silence.

Her mouth fell open, her eyes grew wide, and he would have liked to have thought that she even went pale, but her skin had such an odd tone to begin with that it was hard to say. Then, after a moment of shock, she let out a bark of laughter and said, 'No, really. What happened?'

'Exactly as I said. I was stabbed.' He waited a moment, then added, 'If we weren't in the middle of a ballroom, I'd show you.'

'You don't say?' Now she was *really* interested. She leaned in, eyes alight with macabre curiosity. 'Is it gruesome?'

'It *was,*' he confirmed.

She pressed her lips together, and her eyes narrowed as she asked, 'And where is your valet now?'

'At Chatteris House, likely nicking a glass of my best brandy.'

She let out another one of her staccato barks of laughter. 'You have always amused me,' she pronounced. 'I do believe you are my second favorite nephew.'

He could think of no reply other than 'Really?'

'You know that most people find you humorless, don't you?'

'You do like to be blunt,' he murmured.

She shrugged. 'You're my great-great-nephew. I can be as blunt as I wish.'

'Consanguinity has never seemed to be one of your prerequisites for plain speaking.'

'Touché,' she returned, giving him a single nod of approval. 'I was merely pointing out that you are quite stealthy in your good humor. This I applaud wholeheartedly.'

'I am aquiver with glee.'

She wagged a finger at him. 'This is precisely what I am talking about. You're really quite amusing, not that you let anyone see it.'

He thought about Honoria. He could make her laugh. It was the loveliest sound he knew.

'Well,' Lady Danbury declared, thumping her cane, 'enough of that. Why are you here?'

'I believe I was invited.'

'Oh, pish. You hate these things.'

He gave her a little shrug.

'Watching out for that Smythe-Smith girl, I imagine,' she said.

He'd been looking over her shoulder, trying to locate the éclairs, but at that, he turned sharply back.

'Oh, don't worry,' she said with a dismissive roll of her eyes. 'I'm not going to set it about that you're interested in her. She's one of the ones with a violin, isn't she? Good heavens, you'd go deaf in a week.'

He opened his mouth to defend Honoria, to say that she was very much in on the joke, except it occurred to him that it wasn't a joke to her. She knew perfectly well that the quartet was awful, but she carried on because it was important to her family. That she could take her place on the stage and pretend that she thought she was a virtuoso violinist—it took tremendous courage.

And love.

She loved so deeply, and all he could think was—*I want that*.

'You've always been close with that family,' Lady Danbury said, breaking into his thoughts.

He blinked, needing a moment to return to the present conversation. 'Yes,' he finally said. 'I went to school with her brother.'

'Oh, yes,' she said, sighing. 'What a farce that

was. That boy should never have been chased out of the country. I've always said Ramsgate was an ass.'

He stared at her in shock.

'As you said,' she said pertly, 'consanguinity has never been a prerequisite for blunt speaking.'

'Apparently not.'

'Oh, look, there she is,' Lady Danbury commented. She tipped her head to the right, and Marcus followed her gaze to Honoria, who was chatting with two other young ladies he could not identify from a distance. She didn't see him yet, and he took advantage of the moment to drink in the sight of her. Her hair looked different; he could not pinpoint what she'd done to it—he never had understood the finer points of female coiffure—but he thought it was lovely. Everything about her was lovely. Maybe he should have thought of some other, more poetic way to describe her, but sometimes the most simple words were the most heartfelt.

She was lovely. And he ached for her.

'You *do* love her,' Lady Danbury breathed.

He whipped around. 'What are you talking about?'

'It's written all over your face, trite as the expression may be. Oh, go ahead and ask her to dance,' she said, lifting her cane and motioning with it toward Honoria. 'You could do a great deal worse.'

He paused. With Lady Danbury it was difficult to know how to interpret even the most simple of sentences. Not to mention that she still had her cane elevated. One could never be too careful when that cane was in motion.

'Go, go,' she urged. 'Don't worry about me. I'll

find some other poor unsuspecting fool to torture. And yes, before you feel the need to protest, I did just call you a fool.'

'That, I think, may be the one privilege that consanguinity does allow.'

She cackled with delight. 'You are a prince among nephews,' she proclaimed.

'Your second favorite,' he murmured.

'You'll rise to the top of the list if you find a way to destroy her violin.'

Marcus shouldn't have laughed, but he did.

'It's a curse, really,' Lady Danbury said. 'I'm the only person I know my age who has perfect hearing.'

'Most would call that a blessing.'

She snorted. 'Not with that musicale looming over the horizon.'

'Why do you attend?' he asked. 'You're not particularly close with the family. You could easily decline.'

She sighed, and for a moment her eyes grew soft. 'I don't know,' she admitted. 'Someone needs to clap for those poor things.'

He watched as her face changed back to its normal, unsentimental visage. 'You're a nicer person than you let on,' he said, smiling.

'Don't tell anyone. Hmmph.' She thumped her cane. 'I'm through with you.'

He bowed with all the respect due a terrifying great-great-aunt and made his way toward Honoria. She was dressed in the palest of blue, her gown a frothy confection that he couldn't possibly describe except that it left her shoulders bare, which he decided he approved of, very much.

'Lady Honoria,' he said once he reached her

side. She turned, and he bowed politely.

A flash of happiness lit her eyes and then she gave a polite bob, murmuring, 'Lord Chatteris, how lovely to see you.'

This was why he hated these things. Her entire life she'd called him by his given name, but put her in a London ballroom and suddenly he was Lord Chatteris.

'You remember Miss Royle, of course,' Honoria said, motioning to the young lady on her right, who was dressed in a darker shade of blue. 'And my cousin, Lady Sarah.'

'Miss Royle, Lady Sarah.' He bowed to each in turn.

'What a surprise to see you here,' Honoria said.

'A surprise?'

'I had not thought—' She cut herself off, and her cheeks turned curiously pink. 'It's nothing,' she said, quite obviously lying. But he could not press her on it in so public a venue, so instead he said the staggeringly insightful and interesting, 'It's quite a crush this evening, wouldn't you say?'

'Oh, yes,' the three ladies murmured, with varying degrees of volume. One of them might have even said, 'Indeed.'

There was a little lull, and then Honoria blurted, 'Have you heard anything more from Daniel?'

'I have not,' he replied. 'I hope this means that he has already begun his return journey.'

'So then you don't know when he will be back,' she said.

'No,' he replied. Curious. He would have thought that was clear from his previous statement.

'I see,' she said, and then she put on one of those *I'm--smiling-because-I-have-nothing-to-say*   smiles.

Which was even more curious.

'I'm sure you cannot wait for him to return,' she said, once several seconds had passed without anyone contributing to the conversation.

It was obvious there was a subtext to her statements, but he had no clue what it was. Certainly not *his* subtext, which was that he was waiting for her brother to return so that he might ask for his permission to marry her.

'I'm looking forward to seeing him, yes,' he murmured.

'As are we all,' Miss Royle said.

'Oh, yes,' chimed in Honoria's heretofore silent cousin.

There was another long pause, then Marcus turned to Honoria and said, 'I hope you will save me a dance.'

'Of course,' she said, and he thought she looked pleased, but he was finding it uncommonly difficult to read her this evening.

The other two ladies stood there, utterly still, eyes large and unblinking. It brought to mind a pair of ostriches, actually, and then Marcus realized what was expected of him. 'I hope you will all three save dances for me,' he said politely.

Dance cards were immediately brought forth. A minuet was assigned to Miss Royle, a country dance for Lady Sarah, and for Honoria he claimed a waltz. Let gossipmongers do with it what they would. It wasn't as if he'd never waltzed with her before.

Once the dances had been sorted out, they stood there again, a silent little quartet (all quartets should be so silent, Marcus thought), until Honoria's cousin cleared her throat and said, 'Actually, I think the dancing is beginning right now.'

Which meant that it was time for the minuet.

Miss Royle looked over at him and beamed. Belatedly he remembered that her mother had a mind to pair the two of them up.

Honoria looked over at him as if to say—*Be very afraid*.

And all he could think was—*Damn it, I never got one of those éclairs*.

*   *   *

'He likes you,' Sarah said, the moment Marcus and Cecily headed off for their minuet.

'What?' Honoria asked. She had to blink. Her eyes had become unfocused from staring at Marcus's back as he'd walked away.

'He likes you,' Sarah said.

'What are you talking about, of course he does. We have been friends forever.' Well, that was not quite true. They had known each other forever. They had become friends—true friends—quite recently.

'No, he *likes* you,' Sarah said, with great exaggeration.

'What?' Honoria said again, because clearly she'd been reduced to idiocy. 'Oh. No. No, of course not.'

But still, her heart leapt.

Sarah shook her head slowly, as if coming to a realization even as she spoke. 'Cecily told me she suspected it, back when the two of you went to check on him at Fensmore after he was caught out in the rain, but I thought she was imagining things.'

'You should pay attention to your first

254

inclinations,' Honoria said briskly.

Sarah scoffed at that. 'Didn't you see the way he was staring at you?'

Honoria, practically begging to be contradicted, said, 'He wasn't staring at me.'

'Oh, yes he was,' Sarah countered. 'Oh, and by the way, in case you were worried, I am not interested in him myself.'

Honoria could only blink.

'Back at the Royles',' Sarah reminded her, 'when I was pondering the possibility that he might fall rather quickly in love with me?'

'Oh, right,' Honoria recalled, trying not to notice how her stomach turned to acid at the thought of Marcus falling in love with someone else. She cleared her throat. 'I'd forgotten.'

Sarah shrugged. 'It was a desperate hope.' She looked out over the crowd, murmuring, 'I wonder if there are any gentlemen here who might be willing to marry me before Wednesday.'

'Sarah!'

'I'm joking. Good heavens, you should know that.' And then she said, 'He's looking at you again.'

'What?' Honoria actually jumped in surprise. 'No, he can't be. He's dancing with Cecily.'

'He's dancing with Cecily and looking at *you*,' Sarah replied, sounding rather satisfied with her assessment.

Honoria would have liked to have thought that that meant he cared, but after having read Daniel's letter, she knew better. 'It's not because he cares for me,' she said, shaking her head.

'Really?' Sarah looked as if she might cross her arms. 'Then what, pray tell, is it?'

255

Honoria swallowed, then looked furtively about. 'Can you keep a secret?'

'Of course.'

'Daniel asked him to "watch over me" while he is gone.'

Sarah was unimpressed. 'Why is that a secret?'

'It's not, I suppose. Well, yes, it is. Because no one told me about it.'

'Then how do you know?'

Honoria felt her cheeks grow warm. 'I might have read something I wasn't meant to,' she muttered.

Sarah's eyes grew wide. 'Really?' she said, leaning in. 'That is so unlike you.'

'It was a moment of weakness.'

'One you now regret?'

Honoria thought about that for a moment. 'No,' she admitted.

'Honoria Smythe-Smith,' Sarah said, positively grinning, 'I am so proud of you.'

'I would ask why,' Honoria replied warily, 'but I'm not sure I want to know the answer.'

'This is probably the most improper thing you've ever done.'

'That's not true.'

'Oh, perhaps you forgot to tell me about the time you ran naked through Hyde Park?'

'Sarah!'

Sarah chuckled. 'Everybody has read something they weren't meant to at some point in their lives. I'm just glad you have finally chosen to join the rest of humanity.'

'I'm not so stiff and proper,' Honoria protested.

'Of course not. But I wouldn't call you adventurous.'

'I wouldn't call you adventurous either.'

'No.' Sarah's shoulders drooped. 'I'm not.'

They stood there for a moment, a little bit sad, a little bit reflective. 'Well,' Honoria said, trying to inject a note of levity back into the air, 'you're not going to run naked through Hyde Park, are you?'

'Not without you,' Sarah said slyly.

Honoria laughed at that, then impulsively put her arm around her cousin's shoulders and gave her a little squeeze. 'I love you, you know that.'

'Of course I do,' Sarah replied.

Honoria waited.

'Oh, yes, and I love you, too,' Sarah said.

Honoria smiled, and for a moment all felt right with the world. Or if not right, then at least normal. She was in London, at a ball, standing next to her favorite cousin. Nothing could have been more ordinary. She tilted her head a bit to the side, gazing out over the crowd. The minuet really was a lovely dance to watch, so stately and graceful. And maybe it was Honoria's imagination, but it seemed as if the ladies were dressed in similar colors— shimmering across the dance floor in blues, greens, and silvers.

'It almost looks like a music box,' she murmured.

'It does,' Sarah agreed, then spoiled the moment by saying, 'I hate the minuet.'

'You do?'

'Yes,' she said. 'I don't know why.'

Honoria kept looking out at the dancers. How many times had they stood this way together, she and Sarah? Side by side, both staring off at the crowd as they carried on a conversation without ever once looking at each other. They didn't really need to; they knew each other so well that facial expressions were not necessary to know what the other was feeling.

Marcus and Cecily finally came into view, and Honoria watched as they stepped forward and back. 'Do you think Cecily Royle is setting her cap for Marcus?' she asked.

'Do you?' Sarah countered.

Honoria kept her eyes on Marcus's feet. He was really quite graceful for such a large man. 'I don't know,' she murmured.

'Do you care?'

Honoria thought for a moment about how much of her feelings she was willing to share. 'I believe I do,' she finally said.

'It won't matter if she does,' Sarah replied. 'He's not interested in her.'

'I know,' Honoria said softly, 'but I don't think he's interested in me, either.'

'Just you wait,' Sarah said, finally turning to look her in the eye. 'Just you wait.'

*   *   *

An hour or so later, Honoria was standing by an empty platter at the dessert table, congratulating herself for having captured the last éclair, when Marcus came to claim his waltz.

'Did you get one?' she asked him.

'Get what?'

'An éclair. They were heavenly. Oh.' She tried not to smile. 'I'm sorry. From your expression I can see that you did not.'

'I have been trying to get over here all evening,' he admitted.

'There might be more,' she said, in her best

imitation of optimism.

He looked at her with a single raised brow.

'But probably not,' she said. 'I'm terribly sorry. Perhaps we can ask Lady Bridgerton where she got them. Or'—she tried to look devious—'if her own chef made them, perhaps we can hire him away.'

He smiled. 'Or we could dance.'

'Or we could dance,' she agreed happily. She placed her hand on his arm and allowed him to lead her toward the center of the ballroom. They had danced before, even the waltz once or twice, but this felt different. Even before the music began, she felt as if she were gliding, moving effortlessly across the polished wooden floor. And when his hand came to rest at the small of her back, and she looked up into his eyes, something hot and liquid began to unravel within her.

She was weightless. She was breathless. She felt hungry, needy. She wanted something she could not define, and she wanted it with an intensity that should have scared her.

But it didn't. Not with Marcus's hand at her back. In his arms she felt safe, even as her own body whipped itself up into a frenzy. The heat from his skin seeped through her clothing like nourishment, a heady brew that made her want to rise to her tiptoes and then take off in flight.

She wanted him. It came to her in an instant. This was desire.

No wonder girls ruined themselves. She had heard of girls who'd 'made mistakes.' People whispered that they were wanton, that they had been led astray. Honoria had never quite understood it. Why would someone throw away a lifetime of security for a single night of passion?

Now she knew. And she wanted to do the same thing.

'Honoria?' Marcus's voice drifted down to her ears like falling stars.

She looked up and saw him gazing at her curiously. The music had begun but she had not moved her feet.

He cocked his head to the side, as if to ask her a question. But he didn't need to speak, and she didn't need to answer. Instead, she squeezed his hand, and they began to dance.

The music dipped and swelled, and Honoria followed Marcus's lead, never taking her eyes off his face. The music lifted her, carried her, and for the first time in her life, she felt as if she understood what it meant to dance. Her feet moved in perfect time to the waltz—*one-two-three one-two-three*—and her heart soared.

She felt the violins through her skin. The woodwinds tickled her nose. She became one with the music, and when it was done, when they pulled apart, and she curtsied to his bow, she felt bereft.

'Honoria?' Marcus asked softly. He looked concerned. And not *whatever-can-I-do-to-make-her-adore-me* concerned. No, it was definitely more along the lines of *Dear-God-she's-going-to-be-ill*.

He did not look like a man in love. He looked like a man who was concerned that he was standing next to someone with a nasty stomach ailment.

She had danced with him and felt utterly transformed. She, who could not carry a tune or tap her feet to a rhythm, had become magic in his arms. The dance had been just like heaven, and it killed her that he had not felt the same way.

He couldn't have done. She could barely stand,

260

and he just looked . . .

Like himself.

The same old Marcus, who saw her as a burden. A not wholly unpleasant burden, but a burden nonetheless. She knew why he could not wait for Daniel to return to England. It meant he could depart London and go back to the country, where he was happier.

It meant he would be free.

He said her name again, and she somehow managed to pull herself from her daze. 'Marcus,' she said abruptly, 'why are you here?'

For a moment he stared at her as if she'd sprouted a second head. 'I was invited,' he replied, a little indignantly.

'No.' Her head hurt, and she wanted to rub her eyes, and most of all, she wanted to cry. 'Not here at this ball, here in London.'

His eyes narrowed suspiciously. 'Why do you ask?'

'Because you hate London.'

He adjusted his cravat. 'Well, I don't *hate*—'

'You hate the season,' she cut in. 'You told me so.'

He started to say something, then stopped after half a syllable. That was when Honoria remembered—he was a terrible liar. He always had been. When they were children, he and Daniel had once pulled an entire chandelier from the ceiling. To this day, Honoria still wondered how they'd done it. When Lady Winstead had demanded that they confess, Daniel had lied right to her face, and so charmingly that Honoria could see that their mother had not been sure if he was telling the truth.

Marcus, on the other hand, had gone a bit red

261

in his cheeks, and he'd tugged at his collar as if his neck was itchy.

Just as he was doing right now.

'I have . . . responsibilities here,' he said awkwardly.

Responsibilities.

'I see,' she said, almost choking on the words.

'Honoria, are you all right?'

'I'm fine,' she snapped, and she hated herself for being so short of temper. It wasn't his fault that Daniel had burdened him with, well, *her*. It wasn't even his fault for accepting. Any gentleman would have done so.

Marcus held still, but his eyes flitted to either side, almost as if he was looking for some explanation as to why she was behaving so strangely. 'You're angry . . .' he said, a little bit placatingly, maybe even condescendingly.

'I'm not angry,' she bit off.

Most people would have retorted that she sounded angry, but Marcus just looked at her in that annoyingly self-composed manner of his.

'I'm not angry,' she muttered, because his silence practically demanded that she say something.

'Of course not.'

Her head snapped up. That *had* been patronizing. The rest she might have been imagining, but not this.

He said nothing. He wouldn't. Marcus would never make a scene.

'I don't feel well,' she blurted out. That, at least, was true. Her head hurt and she was overheated and off-balance and all she wanted was to just go home and crawl into bed and pull her covers over her face.

262

'I will take you to get some air,' he said stiffly, and he put his hand at her back to lead her to the French doors that opened onto the garden.

'No,' she said, and the word burst forth overly loud and dissonant. 'I mean, no, thank you.' She swallowed. 'I believe I will go home.'

He gave a nod. 'I will find your mother.'

'I'll do it.'

'I'm happy to—'

'I can do things for myself,' she burst out. Dear God, she hated the sound of her own voice. She knew it was time to shut up. She couldn't seem to say the right words. And she couldn't seem to stop. 'I don't need to be your responsibility.'

'What are you talking about?'

She couldn't possibly answer that question, so instead she said, 'I want to go home.'

He stared at her for what felt like an eternity, then gave her a stiff bow. 'As you wish,' he said, and he walked away.

So she went home. As she wished. She'd got exactly what she'd asked for.

And it was awful.

Chapter Nineteen

The day of the musicale
Six hours before the performance

'Where is Sarah?'

Honoria looked up from her music. She had been scribbling notes in the margin. Nothing she wrote made any sense, but it gave her the illusion that she knew a little something about what she was doing, so she made sure to have some sort of notation on every page.

Iris was standing in the middle of the music room. 'Where's Sarah?' she said again.

'I don't know,' Honoria said. She looked one way, and then the other. 'Where's Daisy?'

Iris waved an impatient arm toward the door. 'She stopped to attend to herself after we arrived. Don't worry about *her*. She wouldn't miss this for the world.'

'Sarah's not here?'

Iris looked about ready to explode. 'Do *you* see her?'

'Iris!'

'I'm sorry. I don't mean to be rude, but where the devil is she?'

Honoria let out an irritated exhale. Didn't Iris have something more important to worry about? *She* hadn't made a complete fool of herself in front of the man she'd only recently realized she loved.

Three days had passed, and she felt ill just thinking about it.

Honoria couldn't remember exactly what she'd

said. Instead, she recalled the terrible sound of her voice, all jerky and choked. She remembered her brain begging her mouth to *just stop talking,* and she remembered her mouth having none of it. She'd been completely irrational, and if he had considered her a responsibility before, now he must think her a chore.

And even before that, before she had started spouting nonsense and acting so emotional that the men of the world must surely think themselves justified in considering women the flightier sex, she'd still been a fool. She'd danced with him as if he'd been her salvation, she'd looked up at him with her heart in her eyes, and he'd said—

Nothing. He hadn't said anything. Just her name. And then he'd looked at her as if she'd gone green. He'd probably thought she was going to cast up her accounts and ruin another perfectly good pair of his boots.

That had been three days earlier. Three days. Without a word.

'She should have been here at least twenty minutes ago,' Iris grumbled.

To which Honoria muttered, '*He* should have been here two days ago.'

Iris turned sharply. 'What did you say?'

'Perhaps there was traffic?' Honoria asked, making a quick recovery.

'She lives only half a mile away.'

Honoria gave her a distracted nod. She looked down at the notes she'd made on page two of her score and realized she'd written Marcus's name. Twice. No, three times. There was a little M.H. in curlicue script hiding next to a dotted half note. Good Lord. She was pathetic.

'Honoria! Honoria! Are you even listening to me?'

Iris again. Honoria tried not to groan. 'I'm sure she'll be here soon,' she said placatingly.

'Are you?' Iris demanded. 'Because I'm not. I knew she was going to do this to me.'

'Do what?'

'Don't you understand? She's not coming.'

Honoria finally looked up. 'Oh, don't be silly. Sarah would never do that.'

'Really?' Iris gave her a look of utter disbelief. And panic. '*Really*?'

Honoria stared at her for a long moment, and then: 'Oh, dear God.'

'I told you you shouldn't have chosen Quartet no. 1. Sarah's actually not that bad on the pianoforte, but the piece is far too difficult.'

'It's difficult for us, as well,' Honoria said weakly. She was beginning to feel sick.

'Not as difficult as on the piano. And besides, it really doesn't matter how difficult the violin parts are, because—' Iris cut herself off. She swallowed, and her cheeks turned pink.

'You won't hurt my feelings,' Honoria told her. 'I know I'm dreadful. And I know Daisy is even worse. We'd do an equally bad job with any piece of music.'

'I can't believe her,' Iris said, starting to pace frantically about the room. 'I can't believe she would do this.'

'We don't *know* that she isn't going to play,' Honoria said.

Iris spun around. 'Don't we?'

Honoria swallowed uncomfortably. Iris was right. Sarah had never been twenty—no, now it was

266

twenty-five—minutes late for a rehearsal.

'This wouldn't have happened if you hadn't chosen such a difficult piece,' Iris accused.

Honoria stomped to her feet. 'Do not try to lay the blame on me! I'm not the one who spent the last week complaining about— Oh, never mind. I'm here, and she's not, and I don't see how that is my fault.'

'No, no, of course,' Iris said, shaking her head. 'It's just— Oh!' She let out a loud cry of angry frustration. 'I can't believe she would do this to me.'

'To us,' Honoria reminded her quietly.

'Yes, but I'm the one who didn't want to perform. You and Daisy didn't care.'

'I don't see what that has to do with it,' Honoria said.

'I don't *know*,' Iris wailed. 'It's just that we were all supposed to be in this together. That's what you said. Every single day you said it. And if I was going to swallow my pride and humiliate myself in front of every single person I know, then Sarah was going to have to do it, too.'

Just then Daisy arrived. 'What's going on?' she asked. 'Why is Iris so upset?'

'Sarah isn't here,' Honoria explained.

Daisy looked over at the clock on the mantel. 'That's rude of her. She's almost a half an hour late.'

'She's not coming,' Iris said flatly.

'We don't know that for sure,' Honoria said.

'What do you mean she's not coming?' Daisy echoed. 'She can't not come. How are we meant to perform a piano quartet without a piano?'

A long silence fell over the room, and then Iris gasped. 'Daisy, you're brilliant.'

267

Daisy looked pleased, but nonetheless said, 'I am?'

'We can cancel the performance!'

'No,' Daisy said, shaking her head quickly. She turned to Honoria. 'I don't want to do that.'

'We'll have no choice,' Iris went on, her eyes lighting with glee. 'It's just as you said. We can't have a piano quartet without a piano. Oh, Sarah is *brilliant.*'

Honoria, however, was not convinced. She adored Sarah, but it was difficult to think of her planning something quite so unselfish, especially under these circumstances. 'Do you really think she did this in an attempt to cancel the entire performance?'

'I don't care why she did it,' Iris said frankly. 'I'm just so happy I could—' For a moment she literally could not speak. 'I'm free! We're free! We're—'

'Girls! Girls!'

Iris broke off midcheer as they all turned to the door. Sarah's mother, their aunt Charlotte—known to the rest of the world as Lady Pleinsworth—was hurrying into the room, followed by a young, dark-haired woman who was dressed in well-made yet terribly plain clothing that marked her instantly as a governess.

Honoria had a very bad feeling about this.

Not about the woman. She looked perfectly pleasant, if perhaps a little uncomfortable at having been dragged into a family squabble. But Aunt Charlotte had a frightening gleam in her eye. 'Sarah has taken ill,' she announced.

'Oh, no,' Daisy cried, sinking dramatically into a chair. 'Whatever will we do?'

'I'm going to kill her,' Iris muttered to Honoria.

268

'Naturally, I could not allow the performance to be cancelled,' Aunt Charlotte went on. 'I could never live with myself if such a tragedy came to pass.'

'Her, too,' Iris said under her breath.

'My first thought was that we could break with tradition and have one of our former musicians play with the group, but we have not had a pianist in the quartet since Philippa played in 1816.'

Honoria stared at her aunt in awe. Did she actually remember such details, or had she written them down?

'Philippa is in confinement,' Iris said.

'I know,' Aunt Charlotte replied. 'She has less than a month left, poor thing, and she's enormous. She might have managed with a violin, but there is no way she could fit at the piano.'

'Who played before Philippa?' Daisy asked.

'No one.'

'Well, that can't be true,' Honoria said. Eighteen years of musicales, and the Smythe-Smiths had produced only two pianists?

'It is,' Aunt Charlotte confirmed. 'I was just as surprised as you. I went through all of our programs, just to be certain. Most years we are two violins, a viola, and a cello.'

'A string quartet,' Daisy said needlessly. 'The classic set of four instruments.'

'Do we cancel, then?' Iris asked, and Honoria had to shoot her a look of warning. Iris was sounding a bit too excited at the possibility.

'Absolutely not,' Aunt Charlotte said, and she motioned to the woman next to her. 'This is Miss Wynter. She will substitute for Sarah.'

They all turned to the dark-haired woman

standing quietly to the side and slightly behind Aunt Charlotte. She was, in a word, gorgeous. Everything about her was perfection, from her shiny hair to her milky-white skin. Her face was heart-shaped, her lips full and pink, and her eyelashes were so long that Honoria thought they must touch her brows if she opened her eyes too wide.

'Well,' Honoria murmured to Iris, 'at least no one will be looking at *us*.'

'She is our governess,' Aunt Charlotte explained.

'And she plays?' Daisy asked.

'I wouldn't have brought her over if she did not,' Aunt Charlotte said impatiently.

'It's a difficult piece,' Iris said, her tone bordering on truculence. 'A very difficult piece. A very *very*—'

Honoria elbowed her in the ribs.

'She already knows it,' Aunt Charlotte said.

'She does?' Iris asked. She turned to Miss Wynter in disbelief and, to be completely honest, despair. 'You do?'

'Not very well,' Miss Wynter answered in a soft voice, 'but I have played parts of it before.'

'The programs have already been printed,' Iris tried. 'They have Sarah listed for the piano.'

'Hang the program,' Aunt Charlotte said irritably. 'We will make an announcement at the beginning. They do it all the time at the theater.' She waved her hand toward Miss Wynter, accidentally batting her in the shoulder. 'Consider her Sarah's understudy.'

There was a slightly impolite moment of silence, and then Honoria stepped forward. 'Welcome,' she said, firmly enough so that Iris and Daisy would

270

understand that they were to follow her lead or else. 'I am delighted to meet you.'

Miss Wynter dipped into a tiny curtsy. 'And I you, er . . .'

'Oh, I'm terribly sorry,' Honoria said. 'I am Lady Honoria Smythe-Smith, but please, if you are to play with us, you must use our given names.' She motioned to her cousins. 'This is Iris, and this is Daisy. Also Smythe-Smiths.'

'As I once was,' Aunt Charlotte put in.

'I am Anne,' Miss Wynter said.

'Iris plays cello,' Honoria continued, 'and Daisy and I are both violinists.'

'I shall leave the four of you to your rehearsals,' Aunt Charlotte said, making toward the door. 'You have a very busy afternoon ahead of you, I'm sure.'

The four musicians waited until she was gone, and then Iris pounced. 'She's not really sick, is she?'

Anne started, clearly surprised by the fervor in Iris's voice. 'I beg your pardon?'

'Sarah,' Iris said, and not kindly. 'She's faking. I know it.'

'I really couldn't say,' Anne said with great diplomacy. 'I didn't even see her.'

'Maybe she has a rash,' Daisy said. 'She wouldn't want anyone to see her if she had spots.'

'Nothing less than permanent disfigurement would satisfy me,' Iris growled.

'Iris!' Honoria scolded.

'I don't know Lady Sarah very well,' Anne said. 'I was hired only this year, and she doesn't need a governess.'

'She wouldn't listen to you, anyway,' Daisy said. 'Are you even older than she is?'

'Daisy!' Honoria scolded. Dear heavens, she was

271

doing a lot of scolding.

Daisy shrugged. 'If she is using our Christian names I think I can ask her how old she is.'

'Older than *you* are,' Honoria said, 'which means that no, you cannot ask.'

'It's of no concern,' Anne said, giving Daisy a small smile. 'I am twenty-four. I have charge of Harriet, Elizabeth, and Frances.'

'God help you,' Iris murmured.

Honoria could not bring herself to contradict. Sarah's three younger sisters were, when taken one by one, perfectly lovely. Together, however . . . There was a reason the Pleinsworth household never lacked for drama.

Honoria sighed. 'I suppose we should rehearse.'

'I must warn you,' Anne said, 'I'm not very good.'

'That's all right. Neither are we.'

'That's not true!' Daisy protested.

Honoria leaned over so that the others couldn't hear and whispered to Miss Wynter, 'Iris is actually quite talented, and Sarah was adequate, but Daisy and I are dreadful. My advice to you is to put on a brave face and muddle through.'

Anne looked slightly alarmed. Honoria responded with a shrug. She would learn soon enough what it meant to perform at a Smythe-Smith musicale.

And if not, she'd go insane trying.

*   *   *

Marcus arrived early that night, although he wasn't quite sure whether it was to secure a seat in the front, or one at the back. He'd brought flowers— not grape hyacinths, no one had those, anyway—

272

but rather two dozen cheerful-looking tulips from Holland.

He'd never brought a woman flowers before. It did make him wonder what the devil he'd done with his life up to now.

He'd thought about skipping the performance. Honoria had been acting so strangely at Lady Bridgerton's birthday ball. She had clearly been angry with him about something. He had no idea what, but he wasn't even sure that mattered. And she had seemed uncharacteristically distant when he had first come upon her after his return to London.

But then, when they'd danced . . .

It had been magic. He would have sworn she'd felt it, too. The rest of the world had simply fallen away. It had been just the two of them amidst a blur of color and sound, and she hadn't stepped on his feet even once.

Which was truly a feat in and of itself.

But maybe he'd been imagining it. Or maybe it had simply been a one-sided emotion. Because when the music had stopped, she had been short, and curt, and even though she had said she did not feel well, she'd refused all his offers of assistance.

He would never understand women. He'd thought she might be the exception, but apparently not. And he'd spent the last three days trying to figure out why.

In the end, however, he'd realized he could not miss the musicale. It was, as Honoria had explained so eloquently, tradition. He had attended every one since he'd been of an age to be in London on his own, and if he did not attend after claiming it was the very reason he'd come back to London so

273

quickly after his illness, Honoria would see it as a slap in the face.

He could not do that. It did not matter that she had been angry with him. It did not matter that he was angry with *her,* and he thought he had every right to be. She'd behaved in a most strange and hostile manner and had not given him any indication why.

She was his friend. Even if she never loved him, she would always be his friend. And he could no more hurt her deliberately than he could slice off his right hand.

He might have fallen in love with her only recently, but he had known her for fifteen years. Fifteen years to know what sort of heart beat within her. He was not going to revise his opinion of her because of a single, odd night.

He made his way to the music room, which was a hive of activity as the servants readied for the upcoming performance. He really just wanted to catch a glimpse of Honoria, perhaps offer a few words of encouragement before the concert.

Hell, he thought *he* needed encouragement. It was going to be painful to sit there and watch her put on the performance of her life just to please her family.

He stood stiffly at the side of the room, wishing that he hadn't arrived so early. It had seemed a good idea at the time, but now he had no idea what he'd been thinking. Honoria wasn't anywhere to be found. He should have realized she wouldn't be; she and her cousins were surely warming up their instruments elsewhere in the house. And the servants were all giving him queer looks, as if to say, *What are you doing here?*

He lifted his chin and regarded the room in much the same way he did at most formal events. He probably looked bored, he certainly looked proud, and neither one was strictly true.

He suspected that none of the other guests were going to arrive for at least thirty minutes, and he was wondering if he might wait in the drawing room, which would surely be empty. That was when he caught a flash of something pink, and he realized it was Lady Winstead, dashing about the room with uncharacteristic frenzy. She spied him, and then rushed over. 'Oh, thank heavens you're here,' she said.

He took in the frantic expression on her face. 'Is something wrong?'

'Sarah has taken ill.'

'I'm sorry to hear that,' he said politely. 'Will she be all right?'

'I have no idea,' Lady Winstead replied somewhat sharply, considering that she was talking about the health of her niece. 'I haven't seen her. All I know is, she's not here.'

He tried to tamp down the giddy feeling in his chest. 'Then you'll have to cancel the musicale?'

'Why does everyone keep asking that? Oh, never mind. Of course we cannot cancel. The Pleinsworth governess apparently can play, and she is taking Sarah's part.'

'Then all is well,' he said. He cleared his throat. 'Isn't it?'

She looked at him as if he were a slow-learning child. 'We don't know if this governess is any good.'

He did not see how the governess's skills at the piano would make any difference in the overall quality of the performance, but he declined to make this statement aloud. Instead he said something like: 'Oh, well.' Or perhaps, 'Quite so.' Either way, it served the purpose of making a noise without saying anything at all.

Which was really the best he could hope for under the circumstances.

'This is our eighteenth musicale, did you know that?' Lady Winstead asked.

He did not.

'Every one of them has been a success, and now this.'

'Perhaps the governess will be very talented,' he said, trying to comfort her.

Lady Winstead gave him an impatient look. 'Talent matters little when one has had only six hours to practice.'

Marcus could see that there was no way this conversation was going to go anywhere but in a circle, so he asked politely if there was anything he could do to facilitate the performance, fully expecting her to say no, which would then leave him free to enjoy a solitary glass of brandy in the drawing room.

But to his complete surprise and—one must be honest—horror, she took his hand in a fervent grip and said, 'Yes!'

He froze. 'I beg your pardon?'

'Could you bring some lemonade to the girls?'

She wanted him to— '*What*?'

'Everyone is busy. Everyone.' She waved her arms as if to demonstrate. 'The footmen have already rearranged the chairs three times.'

Marcus glanced out at the room, wondering what could possibly be so complicated about twelve even rows.

'You want me to bring them lemonade,' he repeated.

'They will be thirsty,' she explained.

'They're not *singing*?' Good God, the horror.

She pressed her lips together in irritation. 'Of course not. But they have been rehearsing all day. It's strenuous work. Do you play?'

'An instrument? No.' It was one of the few skills his father had not deemed it necessary that he learn.

'Then you will not understand,' she said with great drama. 'Those poor girls will be parched.'

'Lemonade,' he said again, wondering if she wished him to bring it in on a tray. 'Very well.'

Her brows rose, and she looked a little annoyed at his slowness. 'I assume you're strong enough to carry the pitcher?'

As insults went, it was just preposterous enough not to bother him. 'I believe I can manage, yes,' he said dryly.

'Good. It's over there,' she said, waving her hand toward a table at the side of the room. 'And Honoria is just through that door.' She pointed toward the back.

'Just Honoria?'

Her eyes narrowed. 'Of course not. It's a quartet.' And with that, she was off, directing the footmen, interrogating the maids, and generally attempting to supervise what appeared to be, in Marcus's opinion, a rather smoothly run affair.

He walked over to one of the refreshment tables and picked up a pitcher of lemonade. There didn't seem to be any glasses set out yet, which did make him wonder if Lady Winstead meant for him to pour the lemonade down the girls' throats.

277

He smiled. It was an entertaining image.

Pitcher in hand, he made his way through the door Lady Winstead had indicated, moving quietly so as not to disturb whatever rehearsal might be underway.

There was no rehearsal.

Instead, he saw four women arguing as if the fate of Great Britain depended on it. Well, no, actually, only three of the women were arguing. The one at the piano, whom he assumed was the governess, was wisely staying out of it.

What was remarkable was that the three Smythe-Smiths managed to do it all without raising their voices, a tacit agreement, he assumed, in light of the guests they knew must be arriving soon in the next room.

'If you would just smile, Iris,' Honoria snapped, 'it would make it all so much easier.'

'For whom? For you? Because I assure you, it won't make it easier for me.'

'I don't care if she smiles,' the other one said. 'I don't care if she ever smiles. She's evil.'

'Daisy!' Honoria exclaimed.

Daisy narrowed her eyes and glared at Iris. 'You're evil.'

'And you're an idiot.'

Marcus glanced over at the governess. She was resting her head against the pianoforte, which led him to wonder how long the three Smythe-Smiths had been at it.

'Can you *try* to smile?' Honoria asked wearily.

Iris stretched her lips into an expression so frightening that Marcus almost left the room.

'Good God, never mind,' Honoria muttered. 'Don't do that.'

'It is difficult to feign good humor when all I wish is to throw myself through the window.'

'The window is closed,' Daisy said officiously.

Iris's stare was pure venom. 'Precisely.'

'Please,' Honoria begged. 'Can't we all just get along?'

'I think we sound wonderful,' Daisy said with a sniff. 'No one would know we'd only had six hours to practice with Anne.'

The governess looked up at the sound of her name, then back down when it became clear she need not reply.

Iris turned on her sister with something bordering malevolence. 'You wouldn't know good— Euf! Honoria!'

'Sorry. Was that my elbow?'

'In my ribs.'

Honoria hissed something at Iris that Marcus supposed only she was meant to hear, but it was clearly about Daisy, because Iris gave her younger sister a disparaging glance, then rolled her eyes and said, 'Fine.'

He looked back over at the governess. She appeared to be counting spots on the ceiling.

'Shall we try it one last time?' Honoria said with weary determination.

'I can't imagine what good it might do.' This came from Iris, naturally.

Daisy gave her a withering stare and snipped, 'Practice makes perfect.'

Marcus thought he saw the governess try to stifle a laugh. She finally looked up and saw him standing there with his pitcher of lemonade. He put his finger to his lips, and she gave a little nod and smile and turned back to the piano.

'Are we ready?' Honoria asked.

The violinists lifted their instruments.

The governess's hands hovered over the keys of her pianoforte.

Iris let out a miserable groan but nonetheless put her bow to her cello.

And then the horror began.

Chapter Twenty

Marcus could not possibly have described the sound that came forth from the four instruments in the Smythe-Smith rehearsal room. He was not sure there were words that would be accurate, at least not in polite company. He was loath to call it music; in all honesty, it was more of a weapon than anything else.

In turn, he looked at each of the women. The governess seemed a little frantic, her head bobbing back and forth between the keys and her music. Daisy had her eyes closed and was weaving and bobbing, as if she were caught up in the glory of the—well, he supposed he had to call it music. Iris looked as if she wanted to cry. Or possibly murder Daisy.

And Honoria . . .

She looked so lovely that *he* wanted to cry. Or possibly murder her violin.

She did not look as she had in last year's musicale, when her smile had been beatific and her eyes aglow with passion. Instead she attacked her violin with grim determination, her eyes narrowed, her teeth gritted, as if she were leading her troops

280

into battle.

She was the glue holding this ridiculous quartet together, and he could not have loved her more.

He wasn't sure if they had intended to do the entire piece, but thankfully Iris looked up, saw him, and let out a loud enough 'Oh!' to halt the proceedings.

'Marcus!' Honoria exclaimed, and he would have sworn she looked happy to see him, except that he wasn't so sure he trusted his judgment on the matter any longer. 'Why are you here?' she asked.

He held up the pitcher. 'Your mother sent me in with lemonade.'

For a moment she stared, and then she burst out laughing. Iris followed suit, and the governess even cracked a smile. Daisy just stood there, looking baffled. 'What is so funny?' she demanded.

'Nothing,' Honoria sputtered. 'It's simply—good heavens, the entire day—and now my mother has sent an earl in to serve us lemonade.'

'I don't find that funny,' Daisy said. 'I find it inappropriate in the extreme.'

'Pay no attention to her,' Iris said. 'She has no sense of humor.'

'That is not true!'

Marcus held himself extremely still, allowing only his eyes to glance over at Honoria for guidance. She gave a tiny nod, confirming Iris's assessment.

'Tell us, my lord,' Iris said with great exaggeration, 'what did you think of our performance?'

Under no circumstance was he going to answer that. 'I'm just here to serve lemonade,' he said.

'Well done,' Honoria murmured, standing up to join him.

'I hope you have glasses,' he said to her, 'because there were none for me to bring in.'

'We do,' she said. 'Please, won't you pour for Miss Wynter first? She has been working the hardest, having joined the quartet only this afternoon.'

Marcus murmured his assent and walked over to the piano. 'Er, here you are,' he said a bit stiffly, but then again, he was not used to proffering drinks.

'Thank you, my lord,' she said, holding forth a glass.

He poured, then gave her a polite bow. 'Have we met?' he asked. She looked deuced familiar.

'I don't believe so,' she replied, and she quickly took a drink.

He gave a mental shrug and moved on to Daisy. He would have supposed that the governess simply had one of those faces that always looked familiar, except that she didn't. She was staggeringly beautiful, but in a quiet, serene way. Not at all the sort of person a mother usually wished to hire as a governess. He supposed that Lady Pleinsworth had felt safe in doing so; she had no sons, and if her husband ever left Dorset, Marcus had never seen him.

'Thank you, my lord,' Daisy said when he poured for her. 'It is most democratic of you to take on such a task.'

He had no idea what to say to that, so he just gave her an awkward nod and turned to Iris, who was rolling her eyes in open mockery of her sister. She smiled her thanks when he served her, and he finally was able to turn back to Honoria.

'Thank you,' she said, taking a sip.

'What are you going to do?'

She looked at him questioningly. 'About what?'

'The musicale,' he said, thinking that should be obvious.

'What do you mean? I shall play. What else can I do?'

He indicated the governess with a subtle motion of his head. 'You have a perfect excuse for canceling.'

'I can't do that,' Honoria replied, but there was more than a twinge of regret in her voice.

'You don't need to sacrifice yourself for your family,' he said quietly.

'It isn't a sacrifice. It's—' She smiled sheepishly, maybe a little wistfully. 'I don't know what it is, but it isn't a sacrifice.' She looked up, her eyes huge and warm in her face. 'It's what I do.'

'I—'

She waited for a moment, then said, 'What is it?'

He wanted to tell her he thought she was quite possibly the bravest, most unselfish person he knew. He wanted to tell her that he would sit through a thousand Smythe-Smith musicales if that was what it took to be with her.

He wanted to tell her he loved her. But he couldn't say it here. 'It's nothing,' he said. 'Just that I admire you.'

She let out a little laugh. 'You may take that back by the end of the evening.'

'I could not do what you do,' he said quietly.

She turned and looked at him, startled by the gravity in his voice. 'What do you mean?'

He was not quite sure how to phrase it, so he finally went with, haltingly, 'I don't enjoy being at the center of attention.'

Her head tilted to the side, she regarded him for

283

a long moment before saying, 'No. You don't.' And then: 'You were always a tree.'

'I beg your pardon?'

Her eyes grew sentimental. 'When we performed our awful pantomimes as children. You were always a tree.'

'I never had to say anything.'

'And you always got to stand at the back.'

He felt himself smile, lopsided and true. 'I rather liked being a tree.'

'You were a very good tree.' She smiled then, too—a radiant, wondrous thing. 'The world needs more trees.'

*   *   *

By the end of the musicale, Honoria's face ached from smiling. She grinned through the first movement, beamed through the second, and by the time they got through the third, she might as well have been at the dentist, she'd shown so much of her teeth.

The performance had been every bit as awful as she had feared. In fact, it had quite possibly been the worst in the history of Smythe-Smith musicales, and that was no shabby feat. Anne was reasonably accomplished on the piano, and had she been given more than six hours to figure out what she was doing, she might have done a decent job of it, but as it was, she'd been consistently one and one-half bars behind the rest of the quartet.

Which was complicated by the fact that Daisy had always been one and one-half bars *ahead*.

Iris had played brilliantly, or rather, she could have played brilliantly. Honoria had heard her practicing on her own and had been so stunned by her level of skill she would not have been surprised if Iris had suddenly stood up and announced that she was adopted.

But Iris had been so miserable at having been forced onto the makeshift stage that she'd moved her bow with no vigor at all. Her shoulders had slumped, her expression had been pained, and every time Honoria cast a glance at her, she'd appeared on the verge of running herself through with the neck of her cello.

As for Honoria herself . . . Well, she'd been dreadful. But she'd known she would be. Actually, she thought she might have been even worse than usual. She'd been so focused on keeping her mouth stretched into that rapturous smile that she'd frequently lost her place in the score.

But it had been worth it. Much of the first row of the audience was filled with her family. Her mother was there, and all of her aunts. Several sisters, scads of cousins . . . They were all beaming back at her, so proud and so happy to be a part of the tradition.

And if the other members of the audience looked mildly ill, well, they had to have known what they were getting into. After eighteen years, no one attended a Smythe-Smith musicale without some inkling of the horrors that lay ahead.

There was quite a round of applause, almost certainly to celebrate the end of the concert, and when they were done, Honoria kept on smiling and greeted the guests with courage enough to approach the stage.

She suspected most doubted their ability to maintain a straight face while congratulating the musicians.

And then, just when she thought she was done having to pretend that she believed all the people who were pretending they had enjoyed the concert, the final well-wisher arrived.

It wasn't Marcus, blast it. He appeared to be deep in conversation with Felicity Featherington, who everyone knew was the prettiest of the four Featherington sisters.

Honoria tried to stretch her now clenched jaw into a smile as she greeted—

Lady Danbury. Oh, dear God.

Honoria tried not to be terrified, but dash it all, the lady *scared* her.

Thump thump (went the cane), followed by: 'You're not one of the new ones, are you?'

'I beg your pardon, ma'am?' Honoria replied, because truly, she had no idea what that meant.

Lady Danbury leaned in, her face twisted into such a squint that her eyes nearly disappeared. 'You played last year. I'd check my program, but I don't save programs. Too much paper.'

'Oh, I see,' Honoria answered. 'No, ma'am, I mean, yes, I'm not one of the new ones.' She tried to keep track of all of the double negatives and finally decided that it didn't matter if she'd said it correctly, Lady Danbury appeared to understand what she'd meant.

Not to mention that at least half her brain was focused on Marcus, and the fact that he was *still* talking to Felicity Featherington. Who, Honoria could not help but note, looked exceptionally pretty that evening in a gown the exact shade of primrose *she* had intended to purchase before she'd had to leave London to care for Marcus when he had a fever.

286

There was a time and a place for everything, Honoria decided, even pettiness.

Lady Danbury leaned over and peered down at the violin in her hands. 'Violin?'

Honoria wrenched her gaze back to Lady Danbury. 'Ehrm, yes, ma'am.'

The elderly countess looked up with a shrewd look in her eye. 'I can see that you wanted to make a comment about it not being a pianoforte.'

'No, ma'am.' And then, because it had been that sort of evening, Honoria said, 'I was going to make a comment about it not being a cello.'

Lady Danbury's wrinkled face erupted into a smile, and she chuckled loudly enough to make Honoria's mother look over in alarm.

'I find it difficult to distinguish between a violin and a viola,' Lady Danbury said. 'Don't you?'

'No,' Honoria replied, feeling a bit braver now that she was getting warmed up, 'but that might be because I actually play the violin.'

Well, she thought as an addendum, *'play' might be too ambitious a verb.* But this she kept to herself.

Lady Danbury gave her cane a thump. 'I didn't recognize the gel at the piano.'

'That is Miss Wynter, the governess for the younger Pleinsworth girls. My cousin Sarah took ill and needed a replacement.' Honoria frowned. 'I thought there was to be an announcement.'

'There may have been. I'm sure I wasn't lis-tening.'

It was on the tip of Honoria's tongue to say that she hoped Lady Danbury hadn't been listening to anything that night, but she swallowed the retort. She had a cheerful façade to maintain, and she fully blamed Marcus—and, to a lesser extent, Felicity

287

Featherington—for making her so irritable.

'Who are you looking at?' Lady Danbury asked slyly.

Honoria was *very* quick to answer, 'No one.'

'Then who are you looking *for*?'

Good heavens, the woman was like a barnacle. 'Again, no one, ma'am,' Honoria said, she hoped sweetly.

'Hmmmph. He's my nephew, you know.'

Honoria tried not to be alarmed. 'I beg your pardon?'

'Chatteris. My great-great-nephew, if one must put a fine point on it, but all those greats do make one feel ancient.'

Honoria looked at Marcus, then back at Lady Danbury. 'Mar—I mean, Lord Chatteris is your nephew?'

'Not that he visits as often as he should.'

'Well, he doesn't like London,' Honoria murmured without thinking.

Lady Danbury let out a sly chuckle. 'You know that, do you?'

Honoria *hated* that her cheeks were growing warm. 'I have known him nearly all my life.'

'Yes, yes,' Lady Danbury said, rather dismissively, 'so I've heard. I—' Something seemed to catch her attention, and then she leaned in with a terrifying look in her eye. 'I'm going to do you a *very* big favor.'

'I really wish you wouldn't,' Honoria said weakly, because surely nothing good could come of that expression on Lady Danbury's face.

'Pfft. Leave it all to me. I have an excellent record with this sort of thing.' She paused. 'Well, one for one, anyway, but I'm optimistic for the

288

future.'

'What?' Honoria asked desperately.

Lady Danbury ignored her. 'Mr. Bridgerton! Mr. Bridgerton!' she called enthusiastically. She waved her hand, but unfortunately that particular appendage was attached to her cane, and Honoria had to weave and bob to the right to avoid getting her ear lopped off.

By the time Honoria got herself straightened out, they had been joined by a handsome man with a devilish gleam in his green eyes. It took her a moment, but just before he was introduced, she recognized him as Colin Bridgerton, one of Gregory Bridgerton's older brothers. Honoria did not know him personally, but she had heard her older sisters sigh about him incessantly when they were out and unmarried. His charm was almost as legendary as his smile.

And his smile was presently directed at her. Honoria felt her stomach flip and quickly set it back to rights. If she weren't desperately in love with Marcus (whose smile was far more subtle, and thus far more meaningful), this would be a dangerous man indeed.

'I have been out of the country,' Mr. Bridgerton said smoothly, just after he kissed her hand, 'so I am not sure that we have been introduced.'

Honoria nodded and was about to say something utterly forgettable when she saw that his hand had been bandaged.

'I hope your injury is not severe,' she said politely.

'Oh, this?' he held up his hand. His fingers were free to waggle, but the rest of it looked rather like a mitt. 'It's nothing. An altercation with a letter

289

opener.'

'Well, please do be careful of infection,' Honoria said, somewhat more forcefully than was *de rigueur*. 'If it grows red, or swollen, or even worse, yellow, then you must see a doctor at once.'

'Green?' he quipped.

'I beg your pardon?'

'You listed so many colors about which I must be wary.'

For a moment Honoria could only stare. Wound infection was not a laughing matter.

'Lady Honoria?' he murmured.

She decided to proceed as if he'd said nothing. 'Most importantly, you must watch for reddish streaks spreading from the wound. Those are the worst.'

He blinked, but if he was startled by the turn of the conversation, he did not show it. Instead he looked down at his hand with a curious eye and said, 'How red?'

'I beg your pardon?'

'How red do the streaks have to be before I must worry?'

'How do you know so much about medicine?' Lady Danbury cut in.

'Do you know, I'm not sure how red,' Honoria told Mr. Bridgerton. 'I would think anything stripey ought to be a cause for alarm.' Then she turned to Lady Danbury and said, 'I helped someone recently who had a terribly infected wound.'

'Hand?' Lady Danbury barked.

Honoria could not begin to imagine what she was talking about.

'Was it her hand? Arm? Leg? It's all in the details, gel.' She gave her cane a thump, narrowly

290

missing Mr. Bridgerton's foot. 'Otherwise the story is dull.'

'Sorry, ehrm . . . Leg.' Honoria did not see any reason to mention that it had been a *he,* not a *she.*

Lady Danbury was silent for a moment, and then she positively cackled. Honoria had no idea why. Then she said something about needing to talk with the other violinist, and she wandered off, leaving Honoria alone—or as alone as two people could be in a crowded room—with Mr. Bridgerton.

Honoria couldn't help but watch her make her way over to Daisy, and Mr. Bridgerton said, 'Don't worry, she's mostly harmless.'

'My cousin Daisy?' she asked dubiously.

'No,' he replied, momentarily nonplussed. 'Lady Danbury.'

Honoria looked past him to Daisy and Lady Danbury. 'Is she deaf?'

'Your cousin Daisy?'

'No, Lady Danbury.'

'I don't believe so.'

'Oh.' Honoria winced. 'That's too bad. She might be by the time Daisy is through with her.'

At that Mr. Bridgerton could not resist looking over his shoulder. He was rewarded with the sight—or, more correctly, the sound—of Daisy making all her sentences loud and slow for Lady Danbury. He winced, too.

'That's not going to end well,' he murmured.

Honoria could do nothing but shake her head and murmur, 'No.'

'Is your cousin fond of her toes?'

Honoria blinked in confusion. 'I believe so, yes.'

'She'll want to watch that cane, then.'

Honoria looked back just in time to see Daisy

let out a small shriek as she tried to jump back. She was not successful with the latter; Lady Danbury's cane had her pinned rather firmly.

They stood there for a moment, both trying not to smile, then Mr. Bridgerton said, 'I understand you were in Cambridge last month.'

'I was,' Honoria replied. 'I had the pleasure of dining with your brother.'

'Gregory? Really? You'd classify it as a pleasure?' But he was grinning as he said it, and Honoria could instantly picture what life must be like in the Bridgerton household: a great deal of teasing and a great deal of love.

'He was most gracious to me,' she said with a smile.

'Shall I tell you a secret?' Mr. Bridgerton murmured, and Honoria decided that in his case, it was right and proper to listen to gossip—he was an incredible flirt.

'Must I keep the secret?' she asked, leaning forward ever-so-slightly.

'Definitely not.'

She gave him a sunny smile. 'Then yes, please.'

Mr. Bridgerton leaned in, just about as far as she had done. 'He has been known to catapult peas across the supper table.'

Honoria gave him a very somber nod. 'Has he done this recently?'

'Not too recently, no.'

She pressed her lips together, trying not to smile. It was lovely to witness this type of sibling teasing. There used to be so much of it in her home, although most of the time she'd been but a witness. She was so much younger than the rest of her siblings; in all honesty, most of the time they'd probably just forgotten to tease her.

'I have but one question, Mr. Bridgerton.'

He cocked his head.

'How was this catapult constructed?'

He grinned. 'Simple spoon, Lady Honoria. But in Gregory's devious hands, there was nothing simple about it.'

She laughed at that, and then quite suddenly felt a hand at her elbow.

It was Marcus, and he looked furious.

Chapter Twenty-one

Marcus could not remember the last time he had been moved to violence, but as he stood there, staring into Colin Bridgerton's smirky face, he was sorely tempted.

'Lord Chatteris,' Bridgerton murmured, greeting him with a polite nod. A polite nod and a *look*. If Marcus had been in a better mood, he might have been able to articulate just what it was about that look that so irritated him, but Marcus wasn't in a good mood. He *had* been in a good mood. He'd been in a *very* good mood, as a matter of fact, despite having just endured what was possibly the worst rendition of Mozart ever known to man.

It did not matter that some tragic portion of his ears had died tonight; the rest of him had been awash with happiness. He'd sat in his seat and watched Honoria. If she'd been a grim warrior during her final rehearsal, then she was a happy member of the corps for the concert. She'd smiled all the way through, and he'd known that she hadn't

293

been smiling for the audience, or even for the music. She'd been smiling for the people she loved. And he could, for however brief a moment, imagine that he was one of those people.

In his heart, she'd been smiling for him.

But now she was smiling at Colin Bridgerton, he of the famous charm and sparkling green eyes. That had been almost tolerable, but when Colin Bridgerton had started smiling at *her* . . .

Some things could not be borne.

But before he could intercede, he had to extricate himself from his conversation with Felicity Featherington—or, rather, Felicity Featherington's mother, who had him in the verbal equivalent of a vise. He had probably been impolite; no, he had certainly been impolite, but escape from the Featheringtons was not something one accomplished with tact or subtlety.

Finally, after literally wrenching his arm from Mrs. Featherington's grasp, he made his way over to Honoria, who was all aglow, laughing merrily with Mr. Bridgerton.

He had every intention of being polite. He really did. But just as he approached, Honoria took a little step to the side, and he saw, peeking out from the hem of her skirt, a flash of red satin.

Her lucky red shoes.

And suddenly he was on fire.

He didn't want another man seeing those shoes. He didn't want another man even *knowing* about them.

He watched as she stepped into place, the seductive little scrap of red hiding itself back beneath her skirt. He stepped forward and said, in perhaps a frostier voice than he'd intended, 'Lady

Honoria.'

'Lord Chatteris,' she replied.

He hated when she called him Lord Chatteris.

'How lovely to see you.' Her tone was that of a polite acquaintance, or perhaps a very distant cousin. 'Are you acquainted with Mr. Bridgerton?'

'I am,' was Marcus's succinct reply.

Bridgerton nodded, then Marcus nodded, and that, it seemed, was the extent of the conversation the two men wished to share.

Marcus waited for Bridgerton to make up some excuse to leave, because surely he would understand that that was what was expected of him. But the annoying sod just stood there grinning, as if he hadn't a care in the world.

'Mr. Bridgerton was just saying—' Honoria began, at the precise time that Marcus said, 'If you will excuse us. I require a private word with Lady Honoria.'

But Marcus was louder, and more to the point, he actually finished his sentence. Honoria clamped her mouth shut and retreated into stony silence.

Mr. Bridgerton gave him an assessing stare, holding his ground for just long enough to make Marcus's jaw clench, and then, as if the moment had never occurred, he turned charming in the space of a second, executed a jaunty bow, and said, 'But of course. I was just thinking that I should like a glass of lemonade above all things.'

He bowed, he smiled, and he was gone.

Honoria waited until he was out of earshot, then she turned to Marcus with an angry scowl. 'That was incredibly rude of you.'

He gave her a stern look. 'Unlike the younger Mr. Bridgerton, this one is not wet behind the ears.'

'What are you talking about?'

'You should not be flirting with him.'

Honoria's mouth fell open. 'I wasn't!'

'Of course you were,' he retorted. 'I was watching you.'

'No, you weren't,' she shot back. 'You were talking with Felicity Featherington!'

'Who stands a full head shorter than I am. I could see right over her.'

'If you must know,' Honoria ground out, quite unable to believe that he was acting like the aggrieved party, 'your *aunt* called him over. Do you expect me to be rude and cut him here in my own home? At an event to which, I might add, he possesses an invitation?'

The last she was not strictly positive about, but she couldn't imagine that her mother *wouldn't* have invited one of the Bridgertons.

'My aunt?' he asked.

'Lady Danbury. Your great-great-great-great . . .'

He glared at her.

'Great-great-great-great . . .' she continued, just to be annoying.

Marcus said something under his breath, then said, in only a slightly more appropriate tone, 'She is a menace.'

'I like her,' Honoria said defiantly.

He didn't say anything, but he *looked* furious. And all Honoria could think was, *Why*? What on earth did he have to be so angry about? She was the one who was in love with a man who clearly thought of her as a burden. A burden with whom he had a pleasant friendship, but still, a burden. Even now he was still guided by his stupid promise to Daniel, scaring away gentlemen whom he deemed inappropriate.

If he wasn't going to love her, then at least he could stop ruining her chances with everyone else.

'I'm leaving,' she declared, because she simply could not take it any longer. She didn't want to see him, and she didn't want to see Daisy, or Iris, or her mother, or even Mr. Bridgerton, who was off in the corner with his lemonade, being charming to Felicity Featherington's older sister.

'Where are you going?' he demanded.

She didn't answer. She didn't see that it was any of his business.

She left the room without a backward glance.

*   *   *

Bloody hell.

Marcus would have liked to have chased Honoria right out of the room, but nothing would have caused a bigger scene. He would also like to have thought that no one had noticed their argument, but Colin Bridgerton was smirking in the corner over his glass of lemonade, and Lady Danbury had that *I-am-all-knowing-and-all-powerful* look on her face that Marcus normally disregarded.

This time, however, he had a sinking suspicion that she had somehow orchestrated his downfall.

Finally, when the annoying Mr. Bridgerton raised his bandaged paw in mock salute, Marcus decided he had had enough, and he strode out the same door through which Honoria had exited. To hell with the gossips. If anyone noticed that they had both left and wanted to make a fuss over it, they could bloody well demand that Marcus propose marriage.

He had no problem with that.

After searching the garden, the drawing room, the music room, the library, and even the kitchens, he finally found Honoria in her bedroom, a location he forced his mind to disregard. But he'd spent enough time at Winstead House to know where the private apartments were, and after he'd gone through every other bloody room in the house, well, did she really expect that he wouldn't find her there?

'Marcus!' she nearly shrieked. 'What are you doing here?'

Apparently, she had expected that he wouldn't find her here.

The first words out of his mouth were the absolutely ill-advised 'What is wrong with you?'

'What is wrong with me?' She sat up quickly on her bed, scooching her body toward the headboard rather like a crab. 'What is wrong with you?'

'I'm not the one who stormed out of the party to go sulk in a corner.'

'It's not a party. It's a musicale.'

'It's *your* musicale.'

'And I'll sulk if I want to,' she muttered.

'What?'

'Nothing.' She glared at him, crossing her arms tightly across her chest. 'You shouldn't be here.'

He flicked his hand palm up through the air as if to say (with great sarcasm), *Oh, really?*

She looked at his hand, and then at his face. 'What is that supposed to mean?'

'You just spent the better part of a week in *my* bedroom.'

'You were almost dead!'

She had a rather good point, but he was not

prepared to admit it. 'Now see here,' he said, getting back to the point that actually mattered, 'I was doing you a favor when I asked Bridgerton to leave.'

Her mouth fell open in outrage. 'You—'

'He is not the sort of person with whom you should be associating,' he said, cutting her off.

'*What?*'

'Will you keep your voice down?' he hissed.

'I wasn't making noise until you came in,' she hissed right back.

He took a step forward, unable to keep his body entirely in check. 'He is not the right man for you.'

'I never said he was! Lady Danbury brought him over.'

'She is a menace.'

'You said that already.'

'It bears repeating.'

She scrambled—finally!—off the bed. 'What on earth is so "menacing" about introducing me to Colin Bridgerton?'

'Because she was trying to make me jealous!' he fairly yelled.

They both went absolutely silent, and then, after a quick look toward the open door, he hastily went over and shut it.

When he turned back to Honoria, she was standing so still he could see her swallow. Her eyes were huge in her face—that owlish stare of hers that had always unnerved him. In the flickering candlelight, they glowed nearly silver, and he felt himself almost mesmerized.

She was beautiful. He knew that already, but it hit him again, with a force that nearly knocked him to his knees.

'Why would she want to do that?' she asked softly.

He clamped his teeth together in an attempt not to answer, but finally he said, 'I don't know.'

'Why would she think she *could* do it?' Honoria pressed.

'Because she thinks she can do anything,' Marcus said desperately. Anything to avoid telling the truth. It wasn't that he didn't want to tell her he loved her, but this wasn't the time. This wasn't the *way* he wanted to do it.

She swallowed again, the movement painfully exaggerated by the stillness of the rest of her. 'And why do you think it's your job to select which men I do and do not associate with?'

He didn't say anything.

'*Why*, Marcus?'

'Daniel asked me to,' he said in a tight, even voice. He wasn't ashamed of it. He wasn't even ashamed of not having told her. But he did not appreciate being backed into a corner.

Honoria took a long, shaky breath, then let it back out. She brought one hand to her mouth, capturing the last puff of air, and then squeezed her eyes shut. For a moment, he thought she might cry, but then he realized she was just doing what she needed to contain her emotions. Sorrow? Fury? He couldn't tell, and for some reason this struck a stake in his heart.

He wanted to know her. He wanted to know her completely.

'Well,' she finally said, 'he's coming back shortly, so you are absolved of your responsibilities.'

'No.' The word came from him like an oath, emerging from the very core of his being.

300

She looked at him in impatient confusion. 'What do you mean?'

He stepped forward. He wasn't sure what he was doing. He knew only that he couldn't stop. 'I mean no. I don't want to be absolved.'

Her lips parted.

He took another step. His heart was pounding, and something within him had gone hot, and greedy, and if there was anything in the world besides her, besides him—he did not know it.

'I want you,' he said, the words blunt, and almost harsh, but absolutely, indelibly true.

'I want you,' he said again, and he reached out and took her hand. '*I* want you.'

'Marcus, I—'

'I want to kiss you,' he said, and he touched one finger to her lips. 'I want to hold you.' And then, because he couldn't have kept it inside for one second longer, he said, 'I burn for you.'

He took her face in his hands and he kissed her. He kissed her with everything that had been building within him, every last aching, hungry burst of desire. Since the moment he had realized he loved her, this passion had been growing within him. It had probably been there all along, just waiting for him to realize it.

He loved her.

He wanted her.

He needed her.

And he needed her now.

He'd spent his life being a perfect gentleman. He'd never been a flirt. He'd never been a rogue. He hated being the center of attention, but by God, he wanted to be the center of *her* attention. He wanted to do the wrong thing, the bad thing.

301

He wanted to pull her into his arms and carry her to her bed. He wanted to peel every last inch of her clothing from her body, and then he wanted to worship her. He wanted to show her all the things he wasn't sure he knew how to say.

'Honoria,' he said, because he could at least say her name. And maybe she'd hear what he felt in his voice.

'I . . . I . . .' She touched his cheek, her eyes moving searchingly across his face. Her lips were parted, just enough so that he could see the pink tip of her tongue darting out to moisten them.

And then he couldn't bear it. He had to kiss her again. He needed to hold her, to feel her body pressed against his. If she'd said no, if she'd shaken her head or made any indication that she didn't want this, he would have turned and walked out of the room.

But she didn't. She just stared at him, her eyes wide and full of wonder, and so he pulled her forward, wrapped his arms around her, and kissed her again, this time allowing himself to let go of the last thread of restraint he'd been holding so tightly.

He pulled her against him, reveling in the curves and hollows of her body. She let out a little moan— of pleasure? of desire?—and it set the flame within him ablaze.

'Honoria,' he moaned, his hands moving frantically along her back, down to the delicious curve of her bottom. He squeezed, and then he pressed, forcing the gentle softness of her belly against his arousal. She let out a little gasp of surprise at the contact, but he didn't have it in him to pull away and explain. She was an innocent, he knew that, and she probably had no idea what it meant when his body reacted like this.

He should go more slowly, guide her through this, but he couldn't. There were limits to a man's control, and he had passed his the moment she'd reached out and touched his cheek.

She was soft and pliant in his embrace, her untutored mouth eagerly returning his kisses, and he swept her up into his arms, carrying her swiftly to the bed. He laid her down with as much tenderness as he could manage, and then, still fully clothed, he came down atop her, nearly exploding at the sensation of her body beneath his.

Her gown had those little puffed sleeves that ladies seemed to prefer, and Marcus soon found that they settled against her skin rather loosely when she was lying down. His fingers found the edge and slid underneath, baring one of her milky shoulders.

With a ragged breath he drew back and looked down at her. 'Honoria,' he said, and if he hadn't been wound so tightly, he might have laughed. Her name was the only sound he seemed to be able to make.

Maybe it was the only word that mattered.

She looked up at him, her lips full and swollen with intimacy. She was the most beautiful thing he'd ever seen, her eyes glowing with desire, her chest rising and falling with each quickening breath.

'Honoria,' he said again, and this time it was a question, or maybe a plea. He sat up to pull off his coat and shirt. He needed the feel of the air on his skin; he needed the feel of *her* on his skin. When his clothing hit the floor, she reached up and touched him, laying one soft hand on his chest. She whispered his name, and he was undone.

Honoria wasn't sure when she'd made her decision to give herself to him. Maybe it was when he had said her name, and she'd reached out and touched his cheek. Or maybe it was when he'd looked at her, his eyes hot and hungry, and said, 'I burn for you.'

But she had a feeling it was the moment he'd burst into the room. Right then, something within her had known that this would happen, that if he did anything to indicate that he loved her, or even just that he wanted her, she would be lost. She'd been sitting on her bed, trying to figure out how the evening had gone so inexplicably awry, and then all of a sudden he was there, as if she'd conjured him.

They had argued, and if anyone had been there to ask, she would have insisted that her only aim had been to boot him from the room and bar the door, but deep within, something inside of her was beginning to kindle and glow. They were in her room. She was on her bed. And the intimacy of the moment was overwhelming.

And so when he closed the distance between them and said, 'I burn for you,' she could no more deny her desire than she could her own breath. When he laid her back upon the bed, she could only think that this was where she belonged, and he belonged there with her.

He was hers. It was as simple as that.

He pulled off his shirt, baring his firmly muscled chest. She'd seen it before, of course, but not like this. Not with him looming over her, his eyes full of a primitive need to claim her.

And she wanted that. Oh, how she wanted it. If

he was hers, then she would gladly be his. Forever.

She reached out and touched him, marveling in the heat of his body. She could feel his heart leap within him, and she heard herself whisper his name. He was so handsome, so serious, and so . . . *good.*

He was good. He was a good man, with a good heart. And dear God, whatever it was he was doing with his lips at the base of her neck . . . he was very good at that, too.

She'd kicked off her slippers before he'd even arrived in her room, and with her stockinged feet, she ran her toes along his—

She burst out laughing.

Marcus drew back. His eyes were questioning but also very, very amused.

'Your boots,' she sputtered.

He went still, then turned his head slowly toward his feet. And then: 'Damn it.'

She started laughing even harder.

'It's not funny,' he muttered. 'It's . . .'

She somehow held her breath.

'. . . funny,' he admitted.

She started laughing so hard the entire bed was shaking. 'Can you get them off?' she gasped.

He gave her a supercilious look and pushed himself to a sitting position at the edge of the bed.

After taking a few breaths, she managed to say, 'Under no circumstances am I taking a knife to you to remove them.'

His reply was a loud thunk as his right boot hit the floor. And then: 'No knife will be necessary.'

She tried for a serious expression. 'I am very pleased to hear it.'

He dropped his other boot and turned back to her with a heavy-lidded stare that made her insides melt. 'So am I,' he murmured, stretching out alongside her. 'So am I.'

His fingers found the small row of buttons at the back of her gown, and the blush-colored silk seemed to melt away, falling from her body like a whisper. Honoria's hands came instinctively to cover her breasts. He didn't argue, he didn't try to pull them away. Instead he just kissed her again, his mouth hot and passionate against hers. And with every deepening moment, she grew more relaxed in his arms until suddenly she realized it wasn't her hand at her breast, it was his.

And she loved it.

She hadn't realized that her body—any part of her body—could feel so sensitive, so needy. 'Marcus!' she gasped, her back arching in shock as his fingers found the rosy tip.

'You are so beautiful,' he breathed, and she *felt* beautiful. When he looked at her, when he touched her, she felt like the most beautiful woman ever created.

His mouth replaced his fingers, and she let out a quiet moan of surprise, her legs stretching straight and hard as she dug her fingers into his hair. She had to grab something. She had to. Otherwise she would quite simply fall off the face of the earth. Or float away. Or just disappear, exploding from the heat and energy coursing within her.

Her body felt so foreign, so completely unlike anything she'd ever imagined. And at the same time, it all felt so natural. Her hands seemed to know exactly where to go, and her hips knew how to move, and when his lips moved down her belly, trailing along after the edge of her dress that he was so assiduously peeling from her skin, she knew

306

that it was right, and it was good, and she didn't just want it, she wanted more. And straightaway, please.

His hands grasped her thighs and gently prodded them open, and she melted into position, moaning, 'Yes,' and, 'Please,' and, 'Marcus!'

And then he kissed her. This she had not expected, and she thought she might die from the pleasure. When he parted her, she had held her breath, preparing herself for his intimate invasion. But instead he worshipped her with his mouth, his tongue, his lips, until she was a writhing, panting, incoherent bundle of need.

'Please, Marcus,' she begged, and she wished she knew exactly what she was begging for. But whatever it was, she knew he could give it to her. He would know how to quench the exquisite ache within her. He could send her to heaven, and he could bring her back down to earth so she could spend a lifetime in his arms.

He pulled away from her for a moment, and she nearly cried from the loss of his touch. He was practically tearing off his breeches, and when he returned, they were matched up lengthwise, his face near hers, his hand in hers, and his hips settling urgently between her legs.

Her lips parted as she tried to breathe evenly. When she looked at him, his eyes were on her face, and all he said was, 'Take me.'

The tip of him pressed against her, then opened her, and she understood. It was so difficult, because all she wanted was to clench every muscle in her body, but somehow she made herself relax enough so that with each stroke, he entered her more deeply, until with a gasp of surprise she realized that he was fully sheathed within her.

He shuddered with pleasure, and he began to move in a new rhythm, sliding back and forth within her. She started saying things, she didn't know what. Maybe she was begging him, or pleading, or trying to make some sort of deal so that he would see this through, and bring her with him, and make it end, and make it never stop, and—

Something happened.

Every speck of her being pulled together into a tight little ball and then shot apart, like one of those firecrackers she'd seen set off over Vauxhall. Marcus, too, cried out and surged forward one last time, spilling himself within her, before collapsing completely.

For several minutes, Honoria could do nothing but lie there, marveling in the warmth of his body next to hers. Marcus had pulled a soft blanket over them, and together they had made their own little heaven. His hand was on hers, their fingers entwined, and she could not imagine a more peaceful, lovely moment.

It would be hers. This. For the rest of her life. He had not mentioned marriage, but this didn't concern her. This was Marcus. He would never abandon a woman after a moment like this. And he was probably just waiting for the right way to propose. He liked to do things properly, her Marcus.

Her Marcus.

She liked the way that sounded.

Of course, she thought with a gleam in her eye, he had not been the least bit proper this evening. So maybe . . .

'What are you thinking about?' he asked.

'Nothing,' she lied. 'Why do you ask?'

He shifted position so that he could lean on his elbow and look down upon her. 'You have a terrifying look on your face.'

'Terrifying?'

'Devious,' he amended.

'I'm not sure which I prefer.'

He chuckled, a low, hearty rumble that echoed from his body to hers. Then his face sobered. 'We will have to be getting back.'

'I know,' she said with a sigh. 'We will be missed.'

'I won't, but you will.'

'I can always tell my mother that I took ill. I'll say I caught whatever it was that afflicted Sarah. Which is to say, nothing, but nobody knows that but Sarah.' She pressed her mouth together in a peevish line. 'And me. And Iris. And probably Miss Wynter, too. Still.'

He laughed again, then leaned down and kissed her lightly on the nose. 'If I could, I would stay here forever.'

She smiled as the warmth of his words slid through her like a kiss. 'I was just thinking that this is just like heaven.'

He was silent for a moment, and then, so softly she wasn't sure she heard him correctly, he whispered, 'Heaven couldn't possibly compare.'

Chapter Twenty-two

Luckily for Honoria, her hair had not been dressed in an elaborate style. What with the extra rehearsals that afternoon, there hadn't been time for it. So it was not difficult for her to replicate the coiffure.

Marcus's cravat was another story. No matter what they did, they could not restore its crisp, intricate knot.

'You will never be able to let your valet go,' Honoria told him after her third attempt at it. 'In fact, you might need to increase his wages.'

'I already told Lady Danbury he stabbed me,' Marcus murmured.

Honoria covered her mouth. 'I am trying not to smile,' she said, 'because it's not funny.'

'And yet it is.'

She held out as long as she could. 'It is.'

He grinned down at her, and he looked so happy, so carefree. It made Honoria's heart sing. How strange and yet how splendid that her happiness could be so dependent on the happiness of another.

'Let me try,' he said, and he took the ends and positioned himself in front of her mirror.

She watched him for about two seconds before declaring, 'You're going to have to go home.'

His eyes did not leave the reflection of his neckcloth in the mirror. 'I haven't even got past the first knot.'

'And you're not going to.'

He gave her a supercilious look, brow quirked and all.

'You're never going to get it right,' she pronounced. 'I must say, between this and your boots, I am revising my opinion on the impracticalities of couture, male versus female.'

'Really?'

Her gaze dropped to his boots, polished to a perfect shine. 'No one has ever had to take a knife to *my* footwear.'

'I wear nothing that buttons up the back,' he

310

countered.

'True, but I may choose a dress that buttons in the front, whereas you cannot go out and about without a neckcloth.'

'I can at Fensmore,' he muttered, his fingers still trying to work with the increasingly wrinkled cloth.

'But we're not at Fensmore,' she reminded him with a grin.

'I surrender,' he said, yanking the cravat off entirely. He stuffed it into his pocket, shaking his head as he said, 'It's for the best, really. Even if I did get this blasted thing tied right, it would make no sense for me to return to the musicale. I'm sure everyone thinks I've gone home.' He paused, then added, 'If they've thought of me at all.'

As there were several unmarried young ladies in attendance, and perhaps more to the point, several mothers of unmarried young ladies, Honoria was fairly certain that his absence had been noted.

But still, his plan was a good one, and together they sneaked down the back stairs. Honoria's plan was to cut through several rooms to the rehearsal space near the musicale, while Marcus was going to slip outside through the servants' entrance. At the spot where they needed to part ways, Marcus looked down at her, gently touching her cheek with his hand.

She smiled. She had far too much happiness bursting within her to keep it inside.

'I will call upon you tomorrow,' he said.

She nodded. And then, because she could not stop herself, she whispered, 'Kiss me good-bye?'

He needed no further urging, and he leaned down, taking her face in his hands as he captured her mouth in a passionate kiss. Honoria felt herself burning, then melting, then quite positively evaporating. She almost laughed with joy, and she rose to her tiptoes, trying to get closer and then—

He was gone.

There was a terrible cry, and Marcus went flying across the small space of the hallway, slamming against the opposite wall.

Honoria let out a shriek and ran forward. An intruder had got into the house, and he had Marcus by the throat. She didn't even have time to be terrified. Without thinking, she hurled herself at the intruder, jumping onto his back. 'Let go,' she ground out, trying to grab his arm to stop him from punching Marcus again.

'For the love of God,' the man snapped. 'Get off me, Bug.'

Bug?

She went slack. 'Daniel?'

'Who the bloody hell else would it be?'

Honoria could think of quite a few answers to that, considering that he'd been out of the country for over three years. Never mind that he'd written that he planned to return; he hadn't seen fit to tell anyone *when*.

'Daniel,' she said again, and she jumped off his back. She took a step away and just stared at him. He looked older, which of course he was, but he looked older in more than just years. Maybe more tired, maybe more world-weary. Or maybe it was just his recent travels. He was still dusty and windblown; anyone would look tired and world-weary after the long journey from Italy to London.

'You're back,' she said stupidly.

'Indeed,' he said sharply, 'and what the devil is

312

going on?'

'I—'

Daniel put up a hand. 'Stay out of it, Honoria.'

Hadn't he just asked her a question?

'Dear God, Daniel,' Marcus said, coming to his feet. He was wobbling a bit, rubbing the back of his head where it had connected with the wall. 'Next time, consider telling us—'

'You bastard,' Daniel hissed, and he slammed his fist into Marcus's cheek.

'Daniel!' Honoria shrieked. She jumped again onto his back, or rather she tried to; he shook her off like—

Well, like a bug, annoying as that was.

She tried to scramble back to her feet in time to stop him again, but Daniel had always been agile, and right now he was furious. Before she could even get herself upright, he'd punched Marcus again.

'I don't want to fight you, Daniel,' Marcus said, wiping blood from his chin with his sleeve.

'What the hell were you doing with my sister?'

'You're—'

Euf!

'—insane,' Marcus grunted, his voice seemingly swallowed up by the force of Daniel's fist in his belly.

'I asked you to watch over her,' Daniel ground out, punctuating each word with a vicious blow to Marcus's midsection. 'To watch. Over. Her.'

'Daniel, stop!' Honoria pleaded.

'She's my sister,' Daniel spat.

'I know,' Marcus growled back. He appeared to be regaining his equilibrium, and he drew back his arm and slammed his fist into Daniel's jaw. 'And

313

you—'

But Daniel wasn't interested in talking, at least not unless Marcus was answering his very specific questions. Before Marcus could finish his sentence, Daniel got him by the neck and pinned him to the wall. 'What,' he hissed again, 'were you doing to my sister?'

'You're going to kill him,' Honoria shrieked. She rushed forward again, trying to pull Daniel back, but Marcus must have been able to fend for himself, because his knee shot up, catching Daniel squarely in the groin. Daniel let out a sound that was positively inhuman, and he went down, taking Honoria with him.

'The two of you are mad,' she gasped, trying to untangle her legs from her brother's. But they weren't listening; she might as well have been speaking to the floorboards.

Marcus touched his hands to his throat, wincing as he rubbed where Daniel had choked him. 'For the love of God, Daniel,' he said. 'You nearly killed me.'

Daniel glared up at him from the floor even as he panted through his pain. 'What were you doing to Honoria?'

'It doesn't—' She tried to intercede, tried to say it didn't matter, but Marcus cut her off with 'What did you see?'

'It doesn't matter what I saw,' Daniel snapped. 'I asked you to watch over her, not to take advan—'

'You *asked* me,' Marcus cut in angrily. 'Yes, let's think about that. You asked me to watch over your young, unmarried sister. Me! What the hell do I know about bringing out a young lady?'

'Apparently more than you should,' Daniel spat.

314

'You had your tongue down her—'

Honoria's mouth fell open, and she smacked her brother on the side of his head. She would have hit him again, if only because Daniel had given her a shove in return, but before she could make a move, Marcus came hurtling through the air.

'Hhhhhrrrrrrccccchhhh!' A sound emerged from his mouth that was completely unintelligible. It was the sound of rage, pure and simple, and Honoria just managed to scoot out of the way before Marcus threw himself on the man he'd always considered his one true friend.

'For God's sake, Marcus,' Daniel gasped between blows. 'What the hell is wrong with you?'

'Don't you ever talk about her like that,' Marcus seethed.

Daniel slid out from under him and staggered to his feet. 'Like what? I was insulting *you*.'

'Really?' Marcus drawled, also rising. 'Well, then this'—his fist connected with the side of Daniel's face—'is for the insult. And *that*'—other fist, other side of the face—'is for abandoning her.'

It was very sweet of him, but Honoria wasn't sure that was quite accurate. 'Well, he didn't really—'

Daniel clutched at his mouth, which was now dripping blood. 'I was going to hang!'

Marcus shoved Daniel's shoulder, then shoved him again. 'You could have come back long ago.'

Honoria gasped. Was that true?

'No,' Daniel responded, shoving Marcus right back. 'I couldn't. Or did you not realize that Ramsgate is absolutely insane?'

Marcus crossed his arms. 'You did not write to her for over a year.'

'That's not true.'

315

'It's true,' Honoria said, not that anyone was listening to her. And that was when she realized it. They weren't going to listen to her. Not in this fight, at least.

'Your mother was wrecked,' Marcus said.

'There was nothing I could do about that,' Daniel returned.

'I'm leaving,' Honoria said.

'You could have written to her.'

'My mother? I did! She never wrote back.'

'I'm leaving,' Honoria repeated, but they were now almost nose to nose, hissing epithets and heaven knew what else. She shrugged. At least they weren't trying to kill each other any longer. All would be well. They had brawled before and likely would again, and she had to admit that a little piece—oh, very well, a bigger than little piece—of her had been thrilled that they had come to blows over her. Not so much her brother, but Marcus . . .

She sighed, remembering the fierce expression on his face when he had defended her. He loved her. He hadn't said it yet, but he did, and he would. He and Daniel would sort out whatever they needed to sort out, and this love story—*her* love story, she thought dreamily—would have a blissfully happy ending. They would marry, and have scads of babies who would grow up to become the happy, teasing family she'd once had. The happy, teasing family Marcus had always deserved. And there would be treacle tart at least once a week.

It would be grand.

She shot one last glance at the men, who were shoving each other's shoulders, although thankfully without quite so much force as before. She might as well get back to the musicale. Someone had to tell

316

their mother that Daniel was back.

* * *

'Where'd Honoria go?' Daniel asked a few minutes later.

They were sitting side by side on the floor, leaning against the wall. Marcus's legs were bent; Daniel's stretched out long. At some point their poking and shoving had petered out, and in silent agreement they'd slumped down the wall, wincing with pain as their minds finally caught up with their bodies and realized what they'd done to each other.

Marcus lifted his head and looked around. 'Back to the party, I imagine.' He really hoped that Daniel wasn't planning to turn belligerent again, because he just wasn't sure he had the energy to launch himself at him again.

'You look like hell,' Daniel said.

Marcus shrugged. 'You look worse.' At least he hoped so.

'You were kissing her,' Daniel said.

Marcus shot him an annoyed glare. 'And?'

'And what are you going to do about it?'

'I *was* going to ask you for her hand before you punched me in the gut.'

Daniel blinked. 'Oh.'

'What the hell did you think I was going to do? Seduce her and toss her to the wolves?'

Daniel went instantly tense, and his eyes flashed with fury. 'Did you sedu—'

'Don't,' Marcus bit off, holding up a hand. 'Do not ask that question.'

Daniel held his tongue, but he eyed Marcus with suspicion.

317

'Don't,' Marcus said again, just to make it clear. He reached up and touched his jaw. Damn, it hurt. He looked over at Daniel, who was wincing as he flexed his fingers and inspected the bruises on his knuckles. 'Welcome home, by the way.'

Daniel looked up, quirking a brow.

'Next time, tell us when you plan to arrive.'

Daniel looked as if he might reply but then just rolled his eyes.

'Your mother did not mention your name for three years,' Marcus said quietly.

'Why are you telling me this?'

'Because you left. You left, and—'

'I didn't have a choice.'

'You could have come back,' Marcus said dismissively. 'You know you—'

'No,' Daniel interrupted. 'I couldn't. Ramsgate had someone following me on the Continent.'

Marcus was silent for a moment. 'I'm sorry. I didn't know.'

'It's all right.' Daniel sighed, then let the back of his head rest against the wall. 'She never answered my letters.'

Marcus looked up.

'My mother,' Daniel clarified. 'I'm not surprised she never mentioned my name.'

'It was very difficult for Honoria,' Marcus said softly.

Daniel swallowed. 'How long have you, er . . .'

'Just this spring.'

'What happened?'

Marcus felt himself smile. Well, with one side of his mouth. The other was beginning to swell up. 'I'm not sure,' he admitted. It didn't seem right to tell him about the mole hole, or the sprained ankle,

318

or the infection on his leg, or the treacle tart. Those were just events. They weren't what had happened in his heart.

'Do you love her?'

Marcus looked up. He nodded.

'Well, then.' Daniel gave a one-shouldered shrug.

It was all they needed to say. It was all they ever *would* say, Marcus realized. They were men, and that was what they did. But it was enough. He started to reach out, to pat Daniel on the leg or maybe the shoulder. But instead he gave him a friendly poke in the ribs with his elbow. 'I'm glad you're home,' he said.

Daniel was quiet for several seconds. 'Me, too, Marcus. Me, too.'

Chapter Twenty-three

After leaving Marcus and Daniel in the hall, Honoria slipped quietly into the rehearsal room. It was empty, as she'd expected, and she could see a strip of light spilling onto the floor where the door to the main room was ajar. Honoria checked her reflection one last time in a mirror. It was dark, so she couldn't be sure, but she thought she looked presentable.

There were still quite a few guests milling about, enough so that Honoria was hopeful that she had not been missed, at least not by anyone outside her family. Daisy was holding court near the center of the room, explaining to anyone who would listen how her Ruggieri violin had been constructed.

Lady Winstead was standing off to the side, looking terribly happy and content, and Iris was—

'Where have you been?' Iris hissed.

Right next to her, apparently.

'I wasn't feeling well,' Honoria said.

Iris snorted with disgust. 'Oh, next you're going to tell me you've caught whatever it is Sarah has.'

'Er, maybe.'

This was met with a sigh. 'All I want to do is leave, but Mother won't hear of it.'

'I'm sorry,' Honoria said. It was difficult to sound truly sympathetic when she herself was so brimming with joy, but she tried.

'The worst is Daisy,' Iris said malevolently. 'She's been prancing around like— I say, is that blood on your sleeve?'

'What?' Honoria twisted her neck to take a look. There was a penny-sized splotch on the puffy part of her sleeve. Heaven only knew which man it belonged to; they'd both been bleeding by the time she'd left. 'Oh. Er, no, I don't know what that is.'

Iris frowned and looked closer. 'I think it's blood.'

'I can tell you for a fact that it's not,' Honoria lied.

'Well, then what is—'

'What did Daisy do?' Honoria cut in quickly. And when Iris just blinked at her, she said, 'You said she was the worst.'

'Well, she *is*,' Iris declared fervently. 'She needn't do anything specific. She just—'

She was cut off by a loud trill of laughter. Coming from Daisy.

'I may cry,' Iris announced.

'No, Iris, you—'

'Allow me my misery,' Iris cut in.

'Sorry,' Honoria murmured contritely.

'This was the single most humiliating day of my life.' Iris shook her head, her expression almost dazed. 'I cannot do this again, Honoria. I tell you, I cannot. I don't care if there's no other cellist waiting to take my spot. I cannot do it.'

'If you marry . . .'

'Yes, I'm aware of that,' Iris nearly snapped. 'Don't think it did not cross my mind last year. I almost accepted Lord Venable just to get out of having to join the quartet.'

Honoria winced. Lord Venable was old enough to be their grandfather. And then some.

'Just please don't disappear again,' Iris said, the choke in her voice almost breaking through into a sob. 'I can't manage when people come up to compliment me on the performance. I don't know what to say.'

'Of course,' Honoria said, taking her cousin's hand.

'Honoria, there you are!' It was her mother, hurrying over. 'Where have you been?'

Honoria cleared her throat. 'I went upstairs to lie down for a few minutes. I was suddenly exhausted.'

'Yes, well, it was a long day,' her mother said with a nod.

'I don't know where the time went. I must have fallen asleep,' Honoria said apologetically. Who knew she was such a good liar? First the blood and now this.

'It is of no consequence,' her mother said before turning to Iris. 'Have you seen Miss Wynter?'

Iris shook her head.

'Charlotte is ready to go home and can't find her

anywhere.'

'Perhaps she went to the retiring room?' Iris suggested.

Lady Winstead looked dubious. 'She's been gone quite a long time for *that*.'

'Er, Mother,' Honoria said, thinking of Daniel back in the corridor, 'if I might have a word with you.'

'It will have to wait,' Lady Winstead said, shaking her head. 'I'm beginning to grow worried about Miss Wynter.'

'Perhaps she needed a lie down as well,' Honoria suggested.

'I suppose. I do hope Charlotte thinks to give her an extra day off this week.' Lady Winstead gave a little nod, as if agreeing with herself. 'I believe I will go find her right now and make that suggestion. It is the least we can do. Miss Wynter truly saved the day.'

Honoria and Iris watched her leave, then Iris said, 'I suppose it depends upon your definition of the word *"saved."'*

Honoria let out a little giggle and looped her arm through her cousin's. 'Come with me,' she said. 'We shall take a turn about the room and look happy and proud while we're doing it.'

'Happy and proud is beyond my capabilities, but—'

Iris was interrupted by a resounding crash. Or not exactly a crash. More like a splintering sound. With a few pops. And twangs.

'What was that?' Iris asked.

'I don't know.' Honoria craned her neck. 'It sounded like—'

'Oh, Honoria!' they heard Daisy shriek. 'Your

322

violin!'

'What?' Honoria walked slowly toward the commotion, not quite able to put two and two together.

'Oh, my heavens,' Iris said abruptly, her hand coming to her mouth. She lay a restraining hand on Honoria, as if to say—*It's better if you don't look.*

'What is going on? I—' Honoria's jaw went slack.

'Lady Honoria!' Lady Danbury barked. 'So sorry about your violin.'

Honoria only blinked, staring down at the mangled remains of her instrument. 'What? How . . .?'

Lady Danbury shook her head with what Honoria suspected was exaggerated regret. 'I have no idea. The cane, you know. I must have knocked it off the table.'

Honoria felt her mouth opening and closing, but no sound was emerging. Her violin didn't look as if it had been knocked off a table. Honestly, Honoria was at a loss as to how it could have got into such a state. It was absolutely wrecked. Every string had snapped, pieces of wood were completely detached, and the chin rest was nowhere to be seen.

Clearly, it had been trampled by an elephant.

'I insist upon buying you a new one,' Lady Danbury announced.

'Oh. No,' Honoria said, with a strange lack of inflection. 'It's not necessary.'

'And furthermore,' Lady Danbury said, ignoring her completely, 'it will be a Ruggieri.'

Daisy gasped.

'No, really,' Honoria said. She couldn't take her eyes off the violin. There was something about it that was absolutely riveting.

323

'I caused this damage,' Lady Danbury said grandly. She waved her arm through the air, the gesture directed more toward the crowd than toward Honoria. 'I must make it right.'

'But a Ruggieri!' Daisy cried.

'I know,' Lady Danbury said, placing a hand on her heart. 'They are terribly dear, but in such a case, only the best will do.'

'There's quite a waiting list,' Daisy said with a sniff.

'Indeed. You mentioned that earlier.'

'Six months. Maybe even a year.'

'Or longer?' Lady Danbury asked, with perhaps a touch of glee.

'I don't need another violin,' Honoria said. And she didn't. She was going to marry Marcus. She would never have to play in another musicale for the rest of her life.

Of course she could not say this to anyone.

And he had to propose.

But that seemed a trifling matter. She was confident that he would.

'She can use my old violin,' Daisy said. 'I don't mind.'

And while Lady Danbury was arguing with her about that, Honoria leaned toward Iris and, still staring at the mess on the floor, said, 'It's really remarkable. How do you suppose she did it?'

'I don't know,' Iris said, equally baffled. 'You'd need more than a cane. I think you'd need an elephant.'

Honoria gasped with delight and finally ripped her eyes from the carnage. 'That's exactly what I was thinking!'

They caught each other's eyes and then burst out

laughing, both with such fervor that Lady Danbury and Daisy stopped arguing to stare.

'I think she's overset,' Daisy said.

'Well, of course, you nitwit,' Lady Danbury barked. 'She's just lost her violin.'

'Thank *God*,' someone said. With great feeling.

Honoria looked over. She wasn't even sure who it was. A fashionable gentleman of middling age with an equally fashionable lady at his side. He reminded her of the drawings she'd seen of Beau Brummell, who had been the most fashionable man alive when her older sisters had made their debuts.

'The girl doesn't need a violin,' he added. 'She needs to have her hands bound so she can never touch an instrument again.'

A few people tittered. Others looked very uncomfortable.

Honoria had no idea what to do. It was an unwritten rule in London that while one could mock the Smythe-Smith musicale, one must never *ever* do so within earshot of an actual Smythe-Smith. Even the gossip columnists never mentioned how dreadful they were.

Where was her mother? Or Aunt Charlotte? Had they heard? It would kill them.

'Oh, come now,' he said, directing his words to the small crowd that had gathered around him. 'Are we all so unwilling to state the truth? They're dreadful. An abomination against nature.'

A few more people laughed. Behind their hands, but still.

Honoria tried to open her mouth, tried to make a sound, any sound that might be construed as a defense of her family. Iris was clutching onto her arm as if she wanted to die on the spot, and Daisy

325

looked simply stunned.

'I beg of you,' the gentleman said, turning to face Honoria directly. 'Do not accept a new violin from the countess. Do not ever even touch one.' And then, after a little titter directed toward his companion, as if to say—*Just wait until you hear what I have to say next,* he said to Honoria, 'You are abysmal. You make songbirds cry. You almost made me cry.'

'I may still do so,' his companion said. Her eyes flared and she shot a gleeful look toward the crowd. She was proud of her insult, pleased that her cruelty held such a witty edge.

Honoria swallowed, blinking back tears of fury. She'd always thought that if someone attacked her publicly she'd respond with cutting wit. Her timing would be impeccable; she'd deliver a set-down with such style and panache that her opponent would have no choice but to slink away, proverbial tail between his legs.

But now that it was happening, she was paralyzed. She could only stare, her hands shaking as she fought to maintain her composure. Later tonight she'd realize what she should have said, but right now her mind was a swirling, inchoate cloud. She couldn't have put together a decent sentence if someone had placed the complete works of Shakespeare in her hands.

She heard another person laugh, and then another. He was winning. This awful man, whose name she did not even know, had come to her house, insulted her in front of everyone she knew, and he was winning. It was wrong for so many reasons except the most basic. She *was* dreadful at the violin. But surely—*surely*—-people knew better than to act in such a manner. Surely someone would come forward to defend her.

And then, over the muted laughs and hissing whispers came the unmistakable sound of boots clicking across a wooden floor. Slowly, as if in a wave, the crowd lifted their heads toward the door. And what they saw . . .

Honoria fell in love all over again.

Marcus, the man who had always wanted to be the tree in the pantomimes; Marcus, the man who preferred to conduct his business quietly, behind the scenes; Marcus, the man who *loathed* being the center of attention . . .

He was about to make a very big scene.

'What did you say to her?' he demanded, crossing the room like a furious god. A bruised and bloody furious god who happened to be lacking a cravat, but still, most definitely furious. And in her opinion, most definitely a god.

The gentleman standing across from her recoiled. Actually, quite a few people recoiled; Marcus did look a bit wild.

'What did you say to her, Grimston?' Marcus repeated, not stopping until he was directly in front of her tormentor.

A flash of memory lit through Honoria. It was Basil Grimston. He'd been away from town for several years, but during his heyday he had been known for his brutal wit. Her sisters had hated him.

Mr. Grimston lifted his chin and said, 'I said only the truth.'

One of Marcus's hands made a fist; his other hand cradled it. 'You would not be the first person I struck this evening,' he said calmly.

That was when Honoria finally got a good look

at him. He looked positively untamed—his hair was sticking every which way, his eye was ringed with shades of black and blue, and his mouth looked as if it was beginning to swell on the left side. His shirt was ripped, stained with blood and dust, and if she wasn't mistaken there was a tiny feather stuck to the shoulder of his coat.

She thought he might be the most handsome man she'd ever seen.

'Honoria?' Iris whispered, her fingers digging hard into her arm.

Honoria just shook her head. She didn't want to talk to Iris. She didn't want to turn her head away from Marcus for even a second.

'What did you say to her?' Marcus asked yet again.

Mr. Grimston turned toward the crowd. 'Surely he must be removed. Where is our hostess?'

'Right here,' Honoria said, stepping forward. It wasn't strictly true, but her mother wasn't anywhere to be found, and she figured she was the next best thing.

But when she looked at Marcus, he gave her a little shake of his head, and she quietly stepped back into place next to Iris.

'If you do not apologize to Lady Honoria,' Marcus said, his voice so mild as to be terrifying, 'I will kill you.'

There was a collective gasp, and Daisy faked a swoon, sliding elegantly into Iris, who promptly stepped aside and let her hit the floor.

'Oh, come now,' Mr. Grimston said. 'Surely it won't come to pistols at dawn.'

'I'm not talking about a duel,' Marcus said. 'I mean I will kill you right here.'

'You're mad,' Mr. Grimston gasped.

Marcus shrugged. 'Perhaps.'

Mr. Grimston looked from Marcus to his friend, to the crowd, and then back to his friend again. No one seemed to be offering him any advice, silent or otherwise, and so, as any dandy about to get his face smashed in would do, he cleared his throat, turned to Honoria, and said to her forehead, 'I beg your pardon, Lady Honoria.'

'Do it properly,' Marcus bit off.

'I apologize,' Mr. Grimston said through clenched teeth.

'Grimston . . .' Marcus warned.

Finally, Mr. Grimston lowered his gaze until he was looking Honoria in the eye. 'Please accept my apologies,' he said to her. He looked miserable and sounded furious, but he said it.

'Thank you,' she said quickly, before Marcus could decide the apology did not pass muster.

'Now leave,' Marcus ordered.

'As if I would dream of staying,' Mr. Grimston said with a sniff.

'I'm going to have to hit you,' Marcus said, shaking his head in disbelief.

'That won't be necessary,' Mr. Grimston's friend said quickly, casting a wary eye at Marcus. She stepped forward, grabbed his arm, and yanked him back a step. 'Thank you,' she said to Honoria, 'for a lovely evening. You can be sure that if anyone asks, I shall say it passed without incident.'

Honoria still didn't know who she was, but she nodded anyway.

'Thank God they're gone,' Marcus muttered as they departed. He was rubbing his knuckles. 'I really didn't want to have to hit someone again.

Your brother has a hard head.'

Honoria felt herself smile. It was a ridiculous thing to smile about, and an even more ridiculous time to smile. Daisy was still lying on the floor, moaning in her faux swoon, Lady Danbury was barking at anyone who would listen that there was 'nothing to see, nothing to see,' and Iris would not stop asking her questions about heaven knew what.

But Honoria wasn't listening to Iris. 'I love you,' she said, as soon as Marcus's eyes fell on her face. She hadn't meant to say it right then, but there was no keeping it in. 'I love you. Always.'

Someone must have heard her, and that someone must have told another someone, who told another someone, because within seconds, the room fell into a hush. And once again, Marcus found himself at the absolute center of attention.

'I love you, too,' he said, his voice firm and clear. And then, with the eyes of half the *ton* on him, he took her hands, dropped to one knee, and said, 'Lady Honoria Smythe-Smith, will you do me the very great honor of becoming my wife?'

Honoria tried to say yes, but her throat was choked with emotion. So she nodded. She nodded through her tears. She nodded with such speed and vigor that she almost lost her balance and had no choice but to sway into his arms when he stood back up.

'Yes,' she finally whispered. 'Yes.'

Iris told her later that the entire room was cheering, but Honoria didn't hear a thing. In that perfect moment, there was only Marcus, and her, and the way he was smiling as he rested his nose against hers.

'I was going to tell you,' he said, 'but you beat me

to it.'

'I didn't mean to,' she admitted.

'I was waiting for the right time.'

She stood on her toes and kissed him, and this time she did hear the cheer that erupted around her. 'I think this *is* the right time,' she whispered.

He must have agreed, because he kissed her again. In front of everyone.

Epilogue

'I'm not sure the front row is the best vantage point,' Marcus said, casting a look of longing over the rest of the empty chairs. He and Honoria had arrived early at this year's Smythe-Smith musicale; she had been most insistent that they do so in order to secure the 'best' seats.

'It's not about vantage points,' she said, looking up and down the front row with a discerning eye. 'It's about listening.'

'I know,' he said morosely.

'And anyway, it's not even really about listening, it's about showing our support.' She gave him a bright smile and lowered herself into her chosen seat—front row, dead center. With a sigh, Marcus took the seat on her right.

'Are you comfortable?' he asked. Honoria was with child, and far enough along that she really shouldn't be making public appearances, but she had insisted that the musicale was an exception.

'It's a family tradition,' she replied. And for her, that was explanation enough.

For him, it was why he loved her.

It was so strange, being a part of a family of his own. Not just the hordes of Smythe-Smiths, who were so legion in number that he still couldn't keep track. Every night as he lay down next to his wife, he couldn't quite believe that she belonged to him. And he to her. A family.

And soon they would be three.

Amazing.

'Sarah and Iris are still very disgruntled about performing,' Honoria whispered, even though there was no one else around.

'Who is taking your place?'

'Harriet,' she said, then added, 'Sarah's younger sister. She's only fifteen, but there was no one else before her.'

Marcus thought about asking if Harriet was any good, then decided he didn't want to know the answer.

'It is two sets of sisters in the quartet this year,' Honoria said, apparently only just then realizing it. 'I wonder if that has ever happened before.'

'Your mother will know,' he said absently.

'Or Aunt Charlotte. She has become quite the family historian.'

Someone passed by them on their way to a seat in the corner, and Marcus glanced around, noticing that the room was slowly filling up.

'I'm so nervous,' Honoria said, giving him an excited grin. 'This is my first time in the audience, you know.'

He blinked in confusion. 'What about the years before you played?'

'It's different,' she said, giving him a *you-couldn't-possibly-understand* look. 'Oh, here we are, here we are. It's about to start.'

Marcus patted her on the hand, then settled into his seat to watch Iris, Sarah, Daisy, and Harriet take their positions. He thought he might have heard Sarah groan.

And then they started to play.

It was awful.

He'd known it would be awful, of course; it was

always awful. But somehow his ears managed to forget just *how* awful it was. Or maybe they were even worse than usual this year. Harriet dropped her bow twice. That couldn't be good.

He glanced over at Honoria, certain he'd see an expression of empathy on her face. She'd been there, after all. She knew exactly how it felt to be on that stage, creating that noise.

But Honoria didn't look the least bit upset for her cousins. Instead, she gazed upon them with a radiant smile, almost like a proud mama basking in the glow of her magnificent charges.

He had to look twice to make sure he wasn't seeing things.

'Aren't they wonderful?' she murmured, tilting her head toward his.

His lips parted with shock. He had no idea how to answer.

'They've improved so much,' she whispered.

That might very well have been true. If so, he was ferociously glad that he had not sat in on any of their rehearsals.

He spent the rest of the concert watching Honoria. She beamed, she sighed; once she put a hand over her heart. And when her cousins set down their instruments (or in the case of Sarah, rolled her eyes as she lifted her fingers from the keys), Honoria was the first on her feet, clapping wildly.

'Won't it be wonderful when we have daughters who can play in the quartet?' she said to him, giving him an impulsive kiss on the cheek.

He opened his mouth to speak, and in all honesty, he had no idea what he planned to say. But it certainly wasn't what he *did* say, which was, 'I

335

cannot wait.'

But as he stood there, his hand resting gently at the small of his wife's back, listening to her chatter with her cousins, his eyes drifted down to her belly, where a new life was taking shape. And he realized it was true. He couldn't wait. For any of it.

He leaned down and whispered, 'I love you,' in Honoria's ear. Just because he wanted to.

She didn't look up, but she smiled.

And he smiled, too.